I0760274

# CLEVELAND CURSE

**Volume 1**

*A Novel*

DAVE EIFERT

**Copyright © 2025 by Dave Eifert**

All rights reserved. No part of this book may be used or reproduced in any manner whatsoever without written permission except in the case of brief quotations embodied in critical articles or reviews.

Produced by GMK Writing and Editing, Inc.
Managing Editor: Katie Benoit
Copyedited by Amy Paradysz
Proofread by Elizabeth Crooks
Text design and composition by Libby Kingsbury
Cover design by Libby Kingsbury
Layout Artist: Joanna Beyer
Printed by IngramSpark

Print ISBN: 978-1-966981-07-7
Ebook EISN:978-1-966981-08-4

Visit the author at theclevelandcursebook.com

Disclaimer:
This is a work of fiction. While the novel draws upon real aspects of Cleveland football history, it blends those elements with an imaginative, Faustian storyline. Dialogue, character portrayals, and scenes have been invented or altered and should not be taken as accurate representations of real events or individuals. The use of real names, organizations, and events is solely for purposes of storytelling and not intended to suggest sponsorship or commercial endorsement. This novel is intended as a playful mash-up of fact and folklore—crafted with deep respect for the real people and events that inspired it and with gratitude for the protections afforded by the First Amendment and Ohio's right-of-publicity laws.

*I dedicate this book to my father, David Eifert Sr.,*
*who got me into this mess in the first place.*

# ACKNOWLEDGMENTS

To my wife, Mary, who often questioned if Browns fans were even the kind of people who would buy a book in the first place, yet allowed me to hide away in my office, researching and writing off and (mostly) on for a decade; to my daughter, Caroline, who expertly and gently edited (and re-edited due to my stupidity) this book, and offered sage advice and encouraging words; and my son, Christopher, who read this book in all the free time (between 2 a.m. and 3 a.m.) afforded a young investment banker and paid the highest compliment: "I keep thinking I'm reading a real book, by an actual author."

Deepest thanks to you all from the bottom of my heart.

Thanks also to the dean of Cleveland sports authors, Terry Pluto, who answered an email I sent him and put me on the path to eventually finding my way to getting this thing published. Thanks to Jay Crawford for agreeing to read my book long before it was published and offering to interview me on his Emmy Award-winning *Ultimate Cleveland Sports Show*. Thanks to author Seth Wickersham who graciously answered my question in the only Twitter/X direct message I have ever sent, providing me insight into one of the events covered in this book.

Sincere appreciation is due Melissa Stickney, who offered encouragement and the suggestion to get involved with Literary Cleveland and and seek legal advice regarding the mingling of fact and fiction in this book. Early encouragement and light editing of the first chapters was graciously bestowed by Jackie Czarnota who stole some time away from teaching AP English and raising her young kids to help a stranger.

A big thank-you to the Cleveland Public Library! Their excellent archives, all available online, were a treasure trove that I was able to benefit from right from my office desk chair. Wikipedia, Pro Football

Reference, and Pro Football Database provided background, statistics, and links to other sites.

Thanks to Comrade Dobler whose YouTube channel provided so many Cleveland Browns game videos that I naturally assumed that he specialized only on our favorite footballers. Turns out he's got over 2,400 videos, from all teams. Wow!

Thanks to the *Cleveland Plain Dealer* and their excellent roster of sportswriters, spanning the decades, including Chuck Heaton, Bill Livingston, Tony Grossi, Bud Shaw, Mary Kay Cabot, and Terry Pluto. And more to be named in the acknowledgments of Book Two.

Thank you to the Reverend Doctor Mark Giuliano, former pastor of Old Stone Church (First Presbyterian Church in Cleveland). He walked his book-writing path alongside me on mine (though he finished much faster!). His result is the excellent book *Making It Home: I Set Out to See the World and Made It All the Way to Cleveland.*

Thanks and gratitude to Mark Kurtz—a Cincinnati Bengals fan, no less—for diving into the manuscript and offering constructive feedback and encouragement.

Finally, this book would not have ever made its way to you, the reader, without the expertise, patience, and competence of Gray Krebs and his team at GMK Writing and Editing, Inc. Gary—thanks for playing Dr. Frankenstein and bringing this monster to life!

Amy Paradysz provided skillful copyediting, sanding off rough edges and polishing dull sentences until they shined. Libby Kingsbury is responsible for the way the book looks, inside and out. It's a lot easier on the eyes now. Joanna Beyer figured out how to make the voluminous contents all fit into a neat 6- by 9-inch package. Elizabeth Crooks prevented you from tripping over a rough road of misspelled words. Katie Benoit pulled the whole tapestry together from a collection of loose strings. Without her coordination, scheduling, fixing, and patience, this book would not have made it to print. Thank you all.

# CONTENTS

# AUTHOR'S NOTE

Curses, football, and Faustian bargains—welcome to Cleveland! As a lifelong (and long-suffering) Browns fan, *The Cleveland Curse* is my love letter to the city's football lore, told with a heavy dose of imagination. Real games, legendary players, and unforgettable heartbreaks form the foundation of this story, but I've layered in fantasy to explore an age-old question: How is it possible that the Browns have been so bad for so long?

Think of this novel as a playful mash-up of fact and folklore, crafted with deep respect for the real people and events that inspired it—and with gratitude for the First Amendment and Ohio's right-of-publicity laws. I hope it entertains and maybe even redeems a little sports heartbreak along the way.

I was compelled to write this book as a form of emotional therapy. There was a deep need to redirect nearly a lifetime of frustration—that all Browns fans feel deep in their bones—into something productive for myself and hopefully for the 2.3 million fellow tortured souls who (whether they want to be or not) are Cleveland Browns fans.

With only five winning seasons since the 1980s, despite hundreds of efforts including, but not limited to, building (so far) one new stadium, hiring new coaches with alarming frequency, replacing front office personnel regularly, infusing the team with what would seem to be an unfair number of high draft picks, securing veteran All-Pro players in free agency, embracing analytics, and even bringing back Brownie the Elf, the Browns have never made it to the Super Bowl.

Worse yet, they've rarely fielded a winning team. Meanwhile, the original Cleveland Browns, who were moved to Baltimore and became the Ravens, are consistently a top team. The Pittsburgh Steelers never have a losing season. Remaining division-mate Cincinnati has been to the big game more than once and currently has a team that could win it soon.

It seems that the Browns' default condition is disarray, that their one core competency is losing. That for them to have a decent year, everything—every single thing—has to go just right . . . just to not finish last in the American Football Conference (AFC) North, let alone win a playoff game. It's inexplicable.

That is why I resorted to fiction to tell this tale. To explain the inexplicable. To make sense of the senseless. And maybe, just maybe, if enough fans know about the Curse, it will finally be broken.

## 1

# I CAN'T TAKE IT ANYMORE

NOVEMBER 30, 2015 – *MONDAY NIGHT FOOTBALL* IN CLEVELAND

*"Grandpa, why do the Browns always lose?"*

Bobby, with the combination of inquisitiveness and innocence only found in a six-year-old, had heard enough commentary from his elders over the last few days to know two things: They were obsessed with the Cleveland Browns, and the Cleveland Browns apparently did not win very often. Bobby's question was swallowed up in the electric din of *Monday Night Football* by the shores of an icy Lake Erie and went unanswered.

Back in Cleveland for Thanksgiving, Rob, Bobby, Grandpa, everybody had had a great time. Grandma had made sure the family made the short trek to Tremont to take Bobby on a tour of the *A Christmas Story* house. Bobby didn't understand what was so great about the leg lamp. Grandpa thought the Browns game would be the "capper to the whole week." The introduction of the fourth generation to a bona fide family tradition: going to watch the Browns.

Rob wasn't sure he wanted to expose Bobby to the losingest team in the NFL, dating back to when the Old Browns of his youth bolted town to become the team that they were tied with right now with three seconds left. Plus, there were all the drunks, the language ... not to mention the fact that the game wouldn't end until midnight. Rob looked over at Bobby, swaddled in his brand-new wardrobe of Cleveland Browns merchandise, pulled snugly over three other layers of sweatshirts and coats. He looked about as pleased to be wearing it all as Ralphie from *A Christmas Story* was to wear the bunny suit. Should a six-year-old be exposed to all this? Should anyone be exposed to all this?

"Alright, Bobby, this is for the win! Our field goal kicker is a rookie, but he hasn't missed all year." Grandpa Joe had affected an optimistic tone of voice as he offered these observations to his grandson. Bobby and his family lived out of town, and he was attending his first Browns game with his dad, grandpa, and uncle. Bobby's dad, Rob, had moved out West after college, an example of what they call "brain drain" around here. Rob was hesitant to bring Bobby to the game, but Joe was insistent. "It's a family tradition," he had said. "We took you to games before you could walk!"

The clock showed three seconds left in the fourth quarter. The Browns, at 2-8, were in the midst of yet another disastrous season. But hey, they'd already beaten the Ravens earlier this year—in Baltimore! Plus, the Ravens, at 3-7, were having a very rare bad year of their own. The NFL had unwittingly set up a *Monday Night Football* clunker. Still, the score was tied, and the Browns had a chance to win . . . against these bastards who stole our team!

Even Rob had begun to feel those embers inside him start to glow a brighter orange. Maybe it was the $10 beers? Maybe the tribal peer pressure? Rob had bled orange and brown as a kid. These last couple of decades he had ascribed that fact to the immaturity of youth. *Maybe there is more to it,* he began thinking. Bringing Bobby and keeping him up way too late was beginning to feel right.

With a win tonight, not only would they get a measure of revenge against Baltimore, but they would also stave off a losing season record . . . at least for another week. Who knows? Maybe this introduction of the fourth generation would be the beginning of the Browns turning things around. Maybe the family would be able to reminisce that, ever since Bobby went to his first game, the Browns made a return to respectability.

"Let's go Brownies!! WOOF! WOOF! WOOF!" Rob echoed the chants coming from over in the Dawg Pound. Yes, this actually felt good! The Browns would either win it now or, even with a missed field goal, at least go to overtime.

Grandpa pressed the ancient transistor radio to his ear.

"The Browns line up for a chance to win it with a field goal. Travis Coons is a rookie this year, but what a year he is having. Eighteen for

18, including the two he's made already tonight. His season long is 44 yards. This will be a 50-yard attempt to win it. The snap, the hold, the kick. . . . It's up! It's . . . blocked! Baltimore has blocked the kick! Whoa, Baltimore has recovered! That's Will Hill . . . he is running it back! He's past midfield! Gets past some would-be tacklers! He is to the 30, the 20, the 10 . . . he takes it in for the touchdown! Will Hill, on the blocked field goal attempt, with no time left, runs it back 68 yards, for the Baltimore touchdown! The Browns lose on an unbelievable play! Wow, now I've seen everything!"

Grandpa switched off the radio in numb disbelief.

At first . . . stunned silence. From Grandpa, Rob, Bobby. From 73,000 other tortured souls. There would be no victory cheers tonight. There wouldn't even be any jeers. Rather than a chorus of satisfying, lusty boos, or shouted epithets pouring forth from the crowd, it was something else: a collective deflation. It was as if everyone had been punched in the gut.

Grandpa was the first to act. He picked up his seat cushion, made sure he had the transistor radio, and bolted, grumbling, "Let's go!" His eighty-year-old legs hadn't moved this fast since the days of Bernie Kosar . . . maybe even since the days of Brian Sipe!

As his sons and grandson caught up with him in the line to get the hell out, he announced in a voice more resolute than frustrated, "That's it. I'm done. I'm done with my seats. I've had season tickets for fifty years. No more. They have not won a championship since I have had these seats. No Super Bowls . . . unbelievable!" Rob covered Bobby's ears as Grandpa swore like Ralphie's dad in *A Christmas Story*.

Nobody was going to try to talk him out of it. Even if they had wanted to keep going to the games themselves, they knew that Joe, like most of the crowd, had had enough. There was no sense trying to speak on any kind of rational level.

"Why do they always lose, Grandpa?" It's an innocent question. One that Grandpa and his sons had stopped asking. It was just the way it was . . . the way it had been for *soooooo* long. Yet it could still sting when the loss was delivered in a way that exposed you as a sucker, as someone who had dared to hope in a team that is beyond all hope, as someone from a city that has been languishing in decline since the Lyndon B. Johnson administration.

Weren't these types of losses God's way of rapping on the glass to get your attention, trying to tell you, "Hey dummy, what's keeping you here? The weather sucks. The Rust Belt is way past its prime. It's pathetic that you and everybody else in town care so much about a football team. They don't care about you. Their players don't lose sleep over what happens in your life. Furthermore, your loyalty is misplaced and won't ever be rewarded. Hello?! The Browns haven't won a championship in most people's lifetimes. And they are the best of the bunch, of this sorry Cleveland professional sports landscape! Pay attention! This is yet another hint to move on . . . from this team . . . from this town . . . from your pathetic life!"

In more lucid moments, these musings fade into background noise . . . it's just nagging self-doubt, not a message from God. And so, squelching these thoughts, and championing the rational concept of something called "the law of averages," we fall back into the rhythms pumped out by the big hearts that circulate anemic orange and brown blood through our collective body. We keep going back for more. We earnestly proclaim, "Wait 'til next year!" We treat the draft day like it's the Super Bowl. We don't move down South or out West. We remain loyal. Loyal to exactly what? We've never stopped to consider the question.

Bobby repeated, "Grandpa, why do they always lose?" Before Grandpa could answer, a tall man in a long, dark-gray cashmere overcoat looked down at the boy and stated flatly: "It's the Curse."

Rob said, "Yeah, I think this team has been cursed with bad management."

"Ah, if only that was all it was," the stranger replied, his lips curled into a menacing smirk. Grandpa didn't appreciate the interloper's smug attitude. "Oh yeah, what makes you such an expert?" he spat, his tone embarrassing his sons.

The stranger's eyes locked on Grandpa's for a full second, and though he didn't speak further, he didn't need to. He vanished in the crowded hallway as quickly as he had appeared.

Funny how a crowd can be either an irritating obstacle to getting home or a joyous gathering of believers, reveling in the afterglow, all depending on the last-second outcome of a game that stood at a stalemate after 59 minutes and 57 seconds of play. Grandpa decided to walk down the ramps rather than wait for the escalators. He just wanted out!

Out of FirstEnergy Stadium, out of his season tickets, out of a relationship with this team that felt like a bad marriage to an unfaithful partner. Or a life sentence for a crime he didn't commit.

As they shuffled their way down the ramps, Bobby pointed toward the escalator and exclaimed, "Look, there's that man again!" The stranger, who seemed to have been too far away to hear Bobby, nevertheless turned and said, "I've just been going to and fro on the earth and walking up and down on the escalators," simpered, then descended out of sight.

Grandpa mumbled under his breath, "Maybe it is a curse."

Just imagine how cursed Grandpa would have felt if he had known then that the Browns would only win one more game that year, that they would only win one game the entire 2016 season, that the 2017 season would end at 0-16, and that their ironic "perfect season" would be punctuated with a mordant parade around the frigid "Factory of Sadness" that they were attempting to escape right now?

2

# THE BROWNS' LAST NFL CHAMPIONSHIP

December 26, 1964 – Cleveland Municipal Stadium

*At the northern edge of the nation's eighth-largest city, hard against the* shores of a frigid Lake Erie, Cleveland Municipal Stadium stood like a bulwark against the gales that would blow in from the Great Lakes. Its pale-ochre brick façade was several shades lighter than the steel mills' sulfur-laden smoke set against the low gray clouds that blocked out the sun for most of each winter. Outside, it was quiet. Boxing Day, the day after Christmas, 1964. Besides being the holiday season, it was Saturday. A lull. An incidental Sabbath, the kind that today's world cannot even fathom. For football fans, this was the calm before the storm. Tomorrow, the Baltimore Colts would play the Cleveland Browns for the NFL Championship.

Inside the venerable stadium, it was darker and gloomier than it was outside. Built during the Depression, the former "Lakefront Stadium" was now starting to show its age, not that the offices or locker rooms were ever posh to begin with. Lakefront Stadium was the first major stadium to be financed with public money. Back then, officials must have felt a sense of stewardship; they definitely opted for spartan over sumptuous. The mood was somewhat dark, too. The Browns were big underdogs for tomorrow's NFL Championship Game.

Baltimore was coached by former Browns player, Northeast Ohio native, and future Hall of Famer Don Shula, and quarterbacked by one of the stars of the league, future Hall of Famer Johnny Unitas. In 1964, the Colts had scored more points and had allowed fewer points than any other team in the NFL's Western Conference during the regular season. The Browns had managed the same feat in the Eastern Conference, though their 10-3-1 record wasn't as impressive as Baltimore's 12-2 mark. The odds-makers and sportswriters were nearly unanimous that Baltimore would win the game.

Arthur Bertram Modell had bought the Browns in 1961. He had fired the legendary coach—the guy the team was named after—following the 1962 season. Paul Brown and his Cleveland Browns had won all four championships in the short-lived All-America Football Conference. When the league folded after the 1949 season, the Browns joined the National Football League. Against the established big boys of the NFL, the Browns were expected to struggle.

Instead, they won the NFL Championship in 1950, their first year in the league. Paul Brown would lead his team to six more championship games over the next seven years, winning the NFL Championship two more times. All told, in seventeen years, spanning two leagues, Paul Brown got his team to the big game eleven times. His Browns were crowned champions seven times. Then, after not making the playoffs for two years, Art Modell brought Brown into his office and told him the team was going in another direction. In other words, he was being fired.

Between the three-year playoff drought, the Colts being heavily favored, and the previous coach getting canned despite establishing himself as a legend, it's no wonder the mood inside Cleveland Municipal Stadium was as overcast as the gray December sky. The darkest clouds descended over the offices of Art Modell and second-year head coach Blanton Collier.

Art Modell sat at his office desk expecting visitors. Although only in his thirties, he was the owner of an NFL team. Art's father had died young, an indirect victim of the Depression, when Art was just fourteen. Art dropped out of high school to help the family make ends meet. After Art served in the U.S. Army Air Corp during World War II, the GI Bill enabled him to enroll in television school in New York.

In the late 1940s, Art co-founded a television production company and produced a successful daytime television show. He parlayed this success into positions as partner with various New York advertising agencies. During the 1950s, he forged a career so successful that he was in position to become majority owner of the Cleveland Browns in 1961.

Today's scheduled meeting was with television and marketing people, a continuation of what had gotten him here in the first place. It could be argued that the multibillion-dollar colossus that the NFL would one day become can trace its genesis to these early meetings set up by Modell.

Before his expected guests arrived, however, there was a knock on his open office door.

"Mr. Modell, there is a man here to see you," his secretary informed him.

"Just one? Where are the rest of them?" Art asked her, thinking that this was one member of the party he was expecting to arrive soon. "Ah, just send him in."

The man, smartly dressed in a suit and long, dark-gray cashmere overcoat, didn't waste time with pleasantries. "Mr. Modell, the Cleveland Browns haven't won a championship since 1955. Tomorrow is your chance to show the world that Art Modell can put this team back on top."

Puzzled, Art furrowed his brow, cocked his head, and stammered in his Brooklyn accent, "Uh, I'm sorry, are you here for the 10 o'clock meeting?"

The man didn't answer his question. He just carried on: "You got rid of Paul Brown. The Browns haven't been to a championship since you've owned the team. . . ."

"Did Paul Brown send you? Who are you?"

"I am not here on behalf of Paul Brown."

The man set his briefcase on the table and clicked open its clasps. As he reached inside, Art's secretary knocked and informed Art that his scheduled visitors had arrived.

"Mr. Modell, all your best laid plans with the TV men, with the advertising people, will come to nothing, if your team cannot deliver on the field. I am here to offer. . . ."

Art began to experience something like vertigo. The stranger's voice and the din of the guests outside his office began to reverberate, echoing through Art's brain. He could no longer hear this stranger who had barged into his office, into his life. A thousand thoughts raced through his mind: *Who is this man? Why is he here? How did he get into my office? How does he know about my meeting with the TV and advertising people?*

Art interrupted, blurting out the question, like a sinking swimmer shouting desperately for help before being pulled back under: "Who the hell are you?"

"Oh my, Art. It's been so long, and your life is fleeting. You can have all you want, and it all starts with a win tomorrow. I can make that happen for you."

Art was used to swimming with some big fish, both in Cleveland and back in New York; still, he was taken aback by the magnetism and certitude emanating from his uninvited visitor. It was as though he held all the cards.

Art's secretary poked her head in the office and asked, "Mr. Modell, how long do you expect it to be before you can meet with your guests?" She hated to interrupt, but she had begun to sense the impatience of the powerful New Yorkers crowding her office.

"It'll just be another minute," Art said, mindful that he needed to show respect for the time of those who had come from New York to meet with him. He didn't want to screw up some potentially lucrative arrangements because of this guy whose name he still didn't even know. Art's response was more than just an acknowledgment of the importance of his guests' time; it was a plea to break the incantation he felt he was falling under. It was *his* office, after all. *His* team, dammit.

The man removed a stack of stapled legal-size papers from the briefcase and began to slide them across Art's desk. Art wondered, *What is this? The Colts' playbook? Their game plan for tomorrow's game? Is this man going to offer this in exchange for a small fortune?*

"I will not do anything illegal," Art stated defiantly.

The man laughed, making sport of Art's defensiveness. "There is nothing illegal, nor against league rules, I can assure you. I'm not offering you Baltimore's game plan. There are no Cuban Missile Crisis spy photos," he said, raising his hands and wiggling his fingers, like some childhood bogeyman, making light of Art's conspiratorial worries. Then he leaned in and looked Art dead in the eye. "Art, you're an ambitious man. I have ambitions in this world, too. You win tomorrow and you are on your way. It's as simple as that."

"When are you going to tell me how much all this will cost me?"

"Money? Oh, no, I don't want your money, Arthur."

"Look, I've got an important meeting. . . ."

"Art, hypothetically speaking, if a win tomorrow costs you a win here and there in the future . . . not championship games like this one . . . and you magically had the power to make that trade, would you? Winning the championship tomorrow could put you over the moon."

"I can't afford any trouble, I. . . ."

"Don't worry, you won't get in any trouble. You'll just need to sign at the bottom of the last page, and I can leave you to your other guests."

"I am not signing anything until I've had a chance to read it, and I haven't got time now. There are important people waiting for me." Art mopped his brow with his handkerchief. He was sweating profusely despite the chilly air in this drafty old stadium's office suite. Art's trademark resourcefulness resurfaced with an inspired thought.

"Take those papers down the hall to my coach. We have a working partnership on the football operation. If there's nothing in there to get me in trouble, have him sign the papers. My secretary can point you to his office." As the man departed, Art felt an immense relief, like he could breathe again. After mouthing a few pleasantries to his invited guests, he excused himself to wash his hands and splash some cold water on his face.

The transistor radio on Blanton Collier's desk squawked through its tinny speaker: ". . . and it's their sixth number-one song this year! These lads from Liverpool aren't just a one-hit wonder, that's for sure. I hope you got a chance to see them at Public Hall a few weeks back. This is WJW radio—Cleveland. The time is 10:25, currently 32 degrees and cloudy. In sports news, tomorrow the Cleveland Browns take on the Baltimore Colts in the National Football League Championship Game, here in Cleveland. The Browns are 7-point underdogs, which, at home, is a lot!"

Collier reached over in disgust and switched the radio off. He hadn't really been listening to it anyway, so absorbed was he in preparing to beat the Colts. But just hearing the radio announcer say "Cleveland Browns" roused him in time to glean the prevailing sentiment surrounding the game.

The deep, soul-crushing pessimism that afflicts modern Browns fans wouldn't be felt for decades, but Coach shuddered at even a hint of naysaying as he desperately searched for any last-minute edge that he could use in the battle tomorrow.

Needing some background noise to fill the void, Collier cued up an old Christmas record that was in the office. Yes, Christmas Day had passed. No, he was not feeling at all jolly. He just needed something in the background as he went about the eleventh-hour desperation planning. Still not settled after a minute of looking at the game plan, with anguish in his heart, he decided to pray.

"Dear God, I know this game is probably not at the top of your list of concerns, but please . . . we've got a bunch of good guys. Our fans haven't seen us win a championship in nine years . . . I don't know what else to do . . . show me what to do. . . ."

Maybe it was the week of almost no sleep. Coach Collier was not normally given to such dramatic, heartfelt prayers. God, being God, knew Coach wasn't expressing his underlying concern: saving his own skin! Collier had worked under Paul Brown for just a year before Brown had gotten the ax. Collier didn't want to suffer the same fate by failing to bring home a championship in his second year at the helm.

God also knew that Coach would probably broach that subject around the edges by expressing concern for his family . . . God was right.

"God, please—I need this job, my family depends on me. A win tomorrow, and I'm safe . . . please give me some direction. Show me the—"

*Knock, knock, knock* came the rapid rapping on Coach's office door. Jarred from an emotional or spiritual plane back to the here and now, Coach hollered, "C'mon in." Before the visitor entered, Coach looked up, arching his eyebrows, as if to say to God, "Wow, that was fast!"

Seeing a dapper stranger enter his office, Coach was fully restored to his normal mode of interrelating with the world. He chided himself for being lost in a flight of fancy over these last few moments, when there was so much to attend to, and such high stakes. And now, someone he doesn't know deigns to further intrude on his time? Yet, Coach was polite; rising to his feet, he offered, "Yes, how can I help you?"

"Mr. Modell sent me to you. He said you wouldn't have much time, getting ready for the game and all. But see, that's why I'm here. I want to help you win the championship."

Coach sat back in his chair. He allowed a wide grin to spread across his face and brighten his eyes behind horn-rimmed glasses. "Oh yeah? Can ya play defense?" Coach laughed. "That Baltimore offense is really something, even the radio was saying they're gonna cream us." His guest was tall and fit. But too polished, too worldly to be a football player, Coach thought. After his little joke, Coach sat erect in his chair, and asked, "Now, how exactly is it that you can help us win the championship?"

The visitor produced the papers that he had gotten out for Modell. "It's all spelled out in here ... don't worry, it's nothing illegal, it's not Baltimore's game plan or playbook. Mr. Modell was about to sign this himself but was late for an important meeting, so he sent me down here to you. I know you are busy. It's just a simple signature, and I will be out of your way."

Blanton Long Collier's mother didn't raise any dummies down in Paris, Kentucky. Coach's soft-spoken manner and Southern drawl led many to underestimate his keen intelligence. He wasn't about to just sign something without at least getting a sense of what he was signing. But the timing! He didn't have the time to wade through what looked to be dozens of papers. Worse yet, the eight-and-a-half by fourteen-inch dimensions telegraphed that this packet would be littered with dreaded legalese.

Coach pulled the packet to the spot in front of him on the desk. He flipped open to the first page. Scanning the first sentence, he read, "In consideration of the circumstances in which the Cleveland Browns (hereby referred to in this document as "Team"), being a member team of the National Football League. . . ."

Coach was right. This document was going to be lousy with legal-speak. After a week of nearly no sleep, and the biggest game of his life looming the next day, this was just too much. "Now, who did you say you are, and why again are you here?"

"Coach Collier, you followed Paul 'Bear' Bryant at Kentucky. Now you are following Paul Brown here in the NFL. Glory need not be reserved for your predecessors. Tomorrow's championship is being televised by CBS. Besides the 70,000 fans in the stadium, untold millions will be watching. Tomorrow, one team will win. The other will lose. One will be remembered as the National Football League champion. I know you want that team to be your team, the Browns. That's what Mr. Modell wants, too. If he hadn't needed to run off to the meeting with the businesspeople, he'd have signed this by now, and I would not be bothering you."

"Mr. Modell said it was okay?"

"He sent me down here to you, didn't he? If he didn't want this done, don't you think he'd have sent me packing?"

"What is the gist of this? I won't stand for cheating."

"Mr. Modell said something along the same lines. He said he would not sign anything that would get him into legal trouble. Signing this will not."

"I want to read this. I just haven't got the time. In a nutshell, what is this all about?"

"I asked Mr. Modell this question, and I'll ask you: If you had to give up something in the future, to guarantee a victory tomorrow . . . a game here and a game there . . . would you do it?"

"Well, now . . . I don't know, I mean it really would depend on—"

"Nonsense, man!" The dapper man impatiently interrupted. "Are you prepared to go against the team's owner by not signing what he has already given his approval to?" The coach's hesitancy, mixed with the Christmas carols playing in the background, were grating on this man's nerves.

Coach, exhausted, not knowing what to believe but losing his will to fight, grabbed a pen from his drawer. He flipped to the last page. He set pen to paper. Before he scrawled his signature, he stopped.

"Now, wait. This is not a trade agreement, is it? You talked about winning tomorrow, and maybe losing some future games . . . this isn't a trade contract, is it? Jim Brown! You are trying to get us to trade Jim Brown!"

Coach put the pen down and started leafing through the papers, squinting through those thick glasses, scanning page after page, expecting telltale words to jump out at him. "Trade," "Jim Brown," or anything along those lines. Coach had, again, lost his composure. The way the papers were flying, he appeared to have lost his marbles, too.

The man, cigarette burning, blew a smoke ring that wafted up then disappeared, like some tawdry dissipating halo. He steadily put his hand down on the dwindling packet.

"Coach, you have my word: that is not what this is all about. Jim Brown will retire as a Cleveland Brown. And, no, he won't be traded away and come back only at the tail end of his career to play a last pathetic game in a Browns uniform. He will play only for the Cleveland Browns and will retire as a Cleveland Brown. Coach, with all due respect, you are exhausted. You are not thinking straight. I guarantee you the Cleveland Browns will win tomorrow's game. You only need to sign the last page."

Coach, from the depths of exhaustion and confusion, emerged in a rare moment of clarity. He was again aware of his surroundings. He noticed a few flakes of snow being blown around outside his window and could hear the music from the record he had put on. "Joy to the world!" rang the refrain, and Coach thought, *how about that!*

The music was still making the visitor chafe, but Coach was now becoming too buoyant to notice the visitor's discomfort. He thought how nice it would be to just go home and enjoy the rest of the day. Coach had lost track of his pen. The visitor produced a much more elegant one from his suit's breast pocket. It was made of gold, and it was warm, almost hot.

In anticipation of the signing, and to expedite his departure, the visitor picked his briefcase up off the floor, jarring the record player in the process. Just as Coach scrawled out his signature, the record skipped, tauntingly blaring, "Far as the curse is found, far as the curse is found, far as, far as . . . far as the curse is found! Far as the curse is found, far as, far as . . . far as the curse is found! Far as the curse is found, far as, far as. . . ."

The record spun for at least sixty revolutions before Coach was able to lift the needle.

3

# CHAMPIONSHIP EVE

EVENING OF DECEMBER 26, 1964, CLEVELAND

*The Browns were staying at the Pick-Carter Hotel on Prospect Avenue,* about a half mile from Cleveland Municipal Stadium, just as they did the night before all their home games. After the team meal, the players decided to take in a movie, all together for a change, rather than fanning out in smaller groups to as many as all six of the still-vibrant downtown theaters.

Whether this united front was to promote team bonding before the most important game of their lives, or because the movie appealed to all the teammates universally, can be debated. The movie title, *Sex and the Single Girl*, and its two female leads, Natalie Wood and Lauren Bacall, may have had some impact. Nor were all the Browns the only ones there. Reportedly, the entire Colts team was in the same theater at the same time!

After the movie, the Browns decamped to their hotel, two by two, as they each were paired up with a roommate. These were professional athletes, some of them future Hall of Famers, who each had a comfortable home within easy driving distance, and here they were bunking up, each with a roommate!

Jim Brown and his roommate, offensive guard John Wooten, made their way up to the tenth floor. Jim wanted to get back to the room to watch "The Browns Spectacular" on TV. Unbelievably, a large contingent of Colts fans were staying at the same hotel. At least one of them kept calling the phone in Jim and John's room, taunting, "We're going to kick your ass."

Jim Brown and John Wooten tried to escape the harassment by going across the street to a snack bar. The plan backfired as Colts fans, armed with musical instruments, serenaded the duo with a rendition of "Taps." Jim Brown paid and quietly left the establishment without saying a word to the Baltimore brass section. Jim snarled to John as they walked back across the street, "We are going to kick the crap outta them."

# 4

# CHAMPIONSHIP VIEWED FROM SANDUSKY

December 27, 1964 – En route from
Cleveland to Sandusky, Ohio

*Lakewood High School seniors Ted, Jackson, John, and Bill were all* headed west. Counterintuitively they were driving farther away from Cleveland to watch the big game. Art Modell, the team owner and a former ad agency executive, had seen to it that the NFL Championship Game featuring his Cleveland Browns would not be broadcast in their hometown! While this justifiably enraged the fans, it made sense to Modell. Would fans fork over $10 per ticket if they could stay home and watch for free on television?

More importantly, how would it look to millions of television viewers from across the country to see Modell's stadium half empty? Despite drawing an average of 80,000 fans per game during the regular season, Modell wasn't taking any chances. As it would turn out, demand for tickets was so high that they sold out early, and if new seats could have magically been built fast enough, another 50,000 would have crammed into the old stadium to be there. But Modell didn't relent. So the four young men, and thousands of others, drove to somewhere outside the blackout zone to watch the game on TV.

Ted had somehow convinced his dad to let him drive his 1958 Buick Century that day. John yelled from the backseat, twenty minutes into the one-hour trip, "Hey, pull over and let's get some beer." That sounded like a good idea. Five minutes and $1.10 later, the boys had procured and begun enjoying a six-pack of Pabst to hold them until they got to the Holiday Inn. It took all forty of the remaining minutes of the trip to agree that Ted, who had outlaid the cash for the six-pack, would get $0.20 for each beer consumed by the other drinkers, to make everything "fair and square."

This quartet were not the only fans with the bright idea of heading for the Sandusky Holiday Inn for the big game. The parking lot was packed with cars, the hotel bar crammed. A singular TV hung on the wall in the corner, a Christmas ornament dangling from one of its rabbit ears. It was almost impossible to make out anything from the only place left to stand.

But at least they were there . . . and there was beer. The boys had left Lakewood early, in case they encountered any lake effect snow along the way. Since they didn't, and since game time was pushed back from 1:30 to 2:00, they were able to each consume a few more beers before kickoff. With each successive round, they wormed their ways closer to the TV and could now actually see and hear the broadcast.

"Good afternoon, everybody, and welcome to CBS's broadcast of the NFL Championship Game between the Baltimore Colts and the Cleveland Browns, live from Cleveland Municipal Stadium." The CBS Television broadcast crew of Cleveland's Ken Coleman, Baltimore's Chuck Thompson, and future NFL Hall of Famer and Emmy Award winner Frank Gifford would call today's game.

"It's the second-largest crowd ever on hand to see an NFL Championship Game with 77,544 fans on hand, plus millions more in TV Land." Someone in the bar shouted, "Yeah, even though we had to drive an hour to get to TV Land," and those who weren't too nervous about the game had a chuckle. "The temperature is around the freezing mark, but there is a fifteen-mile-per-hour wind with gusts of twenty to twenty-five whipping in off Lake Erie," Gifford continued.

"That's right, Frank," Coleman added. "It'll be interesting to see how that affects these two high-powered passing attacks and quarterbacks Johnny Unitas and Frank Ryan."

The four seniors had a mix of emotions now, amplified by the alcohol. Primarily, it was excitement that coursed through their veins. Their Browns were playing for the championship! In almost equal measure was nervous fear . . . fear that the Browns would lose to the heavily favored Colts . . . fear that the Browns would be embarrassed on national TV. But there was also something else. Something they wouldn't have felt if the Browns had been contending for a championship at this time last year. Something bittersweet.

Each of the boys had played football for Lakewood High, and flag and Pop Warner for years as youth growing up in Northeast Ohio—the cradle of tackle football. Only now, with none of them expecting to play in college, football was behind them. Ted would no longer be handing off to John on a fullback dive up the middle. Jackson would no longer be trying to sack the other team's quarterback. Bill would never again line up for a 30-yard field goal with the game on the line. In some ways, the boys could relate more to announcer Frank Gifford, who had retired from playing football a few weeks earlier, than to Browns rookies Sid Williams and Leroy Kelly, who were much closer to their own age. If there was a moment's introspection, it didn't last long as the game got underway.

Ted, a former high school team captain and two-year starting quarterback, felt compelled to lead this team of revelers into battle: "Let's go, Browns! Let's go, Browns! Let's go, Browns!" he shouted as his classmates, then the whole bar, joined in. If Ted couldn't be in the stadium, he wanted to bring some of the fervor of the stadium to Sandusky. The cheers went on as the kickoff sailed toward the Browns' returner, rookie Walter "The Flea" Roberts, who returned the ball to the Browns' 21-yard line.

Coach Collier had elected to take the ball after winning the coin toss. That meant the Browns got the ball first. But they would start out the game battling two foes: the imposing Colts defense and the formidable, gusting wind. As the Browns' offense broke from the huddle, John yelled what everyone was thinking: "Give it to Jim Brown!"

Coleman announced, "First and 10 from the 21-yard line. Handoff to Jim Brown, no, fake to Brown. Ernie Green runs the ball and is tackled after a 2-yard gain by Gino Marchetti."

Gifford added, "Good idea by the Browns, but the trickery did not fool the Colts' defense."

Chuck Thompson jumped in: "Okay, second and 8 from the Browns' 23, Ryan hands off to Jim Brown. He breaks off left tackle, finds a crease, and makes it out past the 30. It'll be close to a first down."

Back in the bar, John shouted, "That's what I said before—give the ball to Jimmy Brown!"

The TV informed: "Jimmy Brown with a nice run there. He was swarmed with tacklers at about the 31 . . . the officials are bringing out the chains to measure for the first down." Big Jim made the first down. The Browns would then lose some yardage setting up a third and 13. A delay of game penalty would make it third and 18.

Coleman: "Frank Ryan back to pass, he throws over the middle for Jim Brown. Brown CATCHES IT with one hand and picks up 18 yards and a first down!"

Gifford: "Wow, you can tell the superstar has come to play today. He led the league in rushing again this year, and that was a fine, one-handed catch."

After a few more plays, the drive would stall around midfield, causing Cleveland's Gary Collins to punt on fourth down.

The Colt's star running back, Lenny Moore, would gain 21 yards on Baltimore's first offensive play, to their 43-yard line. Johnny Unitas dropped back, then pulled the ball down and ran on the Colt's second play—for a gain of 7 yards.

"They're kicking our ass!" Ted pointed out to his friends and anyone else in earshot.

"Second and 3, Colts on the move," Thompson announced. "Unitas hands to Jerry Hill who plows into the Browns' line . . . fumble, it looks like Hill has fumbled!"

Coleman chimed in: "Modzelewski's got it, Dick Modzelewski has recovered the fumble on the Cleveland 49!" The stadium roared. The Sandusky Holiday Inn bar roared. The boys gave each other bear hugs, lifting each other off the ground.

But the jubilation was short-lived. The Browns put together a modest drive, but it ended in a Frank Ryan interception on an underthrown ball to Paul Warfield, almost certainly a result of the stiff wind, still in the Browns' face. The vaunted Baltimore duo of Johnny Unitas and Raymond Berry would connect on a big pass play to position the Colts in Browns territory for the first time of the game. Unitas would extend the drive to the Browns' 25 with a scramble on the next play. The boys felt a sense of impending doom. That year, the Colts had scored more points than any other team in the NFL. The Colts still had the wind at their backs and were beginning to find their rhythm.

Star tight end John Mackey would receive a Unitas pass to start the second quarter, showing the Colts could throw into the wind. The gain brought them to the 19-yard line. The Browns' defense would stiffen, and the Colts faced fourth and 2. Baltimore opted to attempt the short field goal.

Chuck Thompson: "Lou Michaels in to kick, Bobby Boyd in to hold ... the snap, the ... FUMBLE! Bobby Boyd has fumbled the snap! He picks it up and runs, and is tackled by Costello, the Browns' middle linebacker, at the 25-yard line."

The refs would rule that Boyd was down by contact at the 28-yard line. A replay would show that the snap was true, and on line, until it was pushed down, and to the right, as if by an invisible finger, the instant before Boyd could gather it in. The wind was looming as an almost supernatural force. Like the crowd in Cleveland Municipal Stadium, the fans in Sandusky heaved a heavy sigh of relief. Given this reprieve, the Browns would not do much on their possession and punted.

The Colts made a foray just into Browns territory, and Unitas decided to throw to his talented tight end John Mackey. The pass was wobbly and just a little short, but Mackey was wide open. Whether it was the wind again or just a last-instant lapse in his concentration, Mackey batted the ball straight up in the air. Cleveland's Ross Fichtner knocked Mackey to the ground. Linebackers Vince Costello and Galen Fiss converged on the airborne ball. Costello prevailed, making the interception at their 29-yard line.

For a scoreless game, the Browns fans sure felt like they'd been riding the brand-new Blue Streak roller coaster at nearby Cedar Point.

The Browns ran a few plays. With time running down in the first half, Frank Ryan dropped back as speedy rookie Paul Warfield streaked down the left side and angled toward the post, deep into Colts territory. He and Colts safety Jim Welch got tangled up around the 23-yard line and fell down. Pass interference was called on the Browns' rookie receiver. The first half of the NFL World Championship Game ended in a scoreless tie.

"Two of the highest-scoring teams in history, and not a single point scored in the first half," Gifford observed.

"Yeah, that pansy Johnny Unitas is no match for the Browns' defense!" Bobby shouted at the TV.

"Let's just hope we can score on the Colts' defense," John replied. "We'll never win if we can't score."

## 5

# DOUBLING DOWN ON THE DEAL

CLEVELAND MUNICIPAL STADIUM – OWNER'S BOX AT HALFTIME

*Art Modell: "Why does the band look so flat? I brought them up here* from Florida. They're supposed to put on a show!" Art had signed the Florida A&M Marching Band as his halftime act, after having been impressed with their high stepping, fancy dancing, energetic moves during a halftime show at the Orange Bowl.

NFL Commissioner Pete Rozelle: "Maybe they aren't used to marching on frozen fields, Art."

This halftime was a letdown. Art wanted the world to see his operation was the best. The halftime show was supposed to blow people away. Instead, the band just stood there playing their instruments.

Modell mumbled under his breath, "And what about this guaranteed victory? Who was that charlatan?" Just then, Modell saw the mysterious man in the section right below his box. The man turned and locked eyes with Modell, who sent someone from his suite down to escort the stranger up to Modell's owner's suite.

As soon as the escort delivered the man to his suite, Modell held him up at the door. Modell stepped out into the hallway with the man and closed the door behind them.

"What is this nonsense about a guaranteed victory?" Modell yelled. "You said you could 'promise' we would win . . . that it wouldn't even be close . . . and we haven't even scored a point! It's halftime and there is no score! It's a boring game! My team is on TV, and nobody's scoring!"

He couldn't control his anger. He felt everything was reflecting poorly on him, personally.

The stranger smiled, his cool demeanor the opposite of Modell's. He reached into his cashmere overcoat and produced the contract that he had put in front of Modell and Coach Collier yesterday. "Mr. Modell, your coach did sign off on this contract, but I really wanted your full weight and authority behind it. I'd like you to sign . . . but before you do, do you want your team to squeak by the Colts today, or really outclass them?"

"Oh, who are you anyway? I don't even know who you are, or what you are peddling here!"

The man opened the contract to a new page, one that hadn't been initialed by Blanton Collier. "Now, Art, this page goes beyond X's and O's; if you want to win big today, just sign at the bottom of the page."

Art saw this page was titled "Expansion of the Agreement beyond the Cleveland Browns to Cleveland's other professional teams and the Cleveland Community." He quickly scanned the document for any telltale clauses involving trading Jim Brown or another key player. "What is this, a bunch of riddles?" Art had seen some verbiage that looked more like poetry than typical prose. He was half-convinced that this debonair gentleman was a crackpot, but only half-convinced. "What is this mumbo-jumbo?"

"Arthur, do you want to really crush Baltimore today, or merely win? You know, they are favored by a touchdown."

"I know that!" Modell shot back. "The Cleveland Browns ruled football when they came into the league; I want to show the world that Art Modell has made them dominant again, and I'll do it with or without you, *whoever you are*, whatever it takes!"

"Whatever it takes? Would you mortgage the future to briefly regain the glory of the past?"

"I want to win this game! I want to prove the pundits wrong—show them that Art Modell's Browns are back on top!"

"Mr. Modell, the game is already halfway over. It won't be easy to blow the Colts out with only one half to go."

"Look, I will sign these papers. I want to win. I don't want to get in any personal trouble . . . you said the other day I won't get in trouble."

"Well, Art, there will be hell to pay." The man paused for dramatic effect. "Among many other things, Baltimore will get its revenge, eventually. Now, do you want that to affect Art Modell, or to affect the Browns fans?"

"What do you mean? My interests are the same as the fans'."

"Oh, is that why you blacked out TV coverage within a one-hour drive?"

"That was different. That's just business."

"Well, Art, I have written this agreement such that it will be like you made it today: as favorable as possible for Arthur Modell ... in other words, Baltimore will get its revenge on Cleveland, not on Art Modell."

"What in hell are you talking about?"

"Interesting choice of words, Art. Arthur, if you had the ability to win today, by a landslide, but it came at the cost of Cleveland having to pay the price later, and for a long time, would you do it? What if the Indians would have to hit a rough patch in order for you to win this game? What if other teams would be denied championships? What if the city itself had to suffer? Would it all be worth it, just to win this game?"

"You said 'win this game by a landslide.' Listen, I don't care about any of that. I just want to win this game, whatever it takes." Modell almost couldn't believe he was arguing with this stranger, who he now thought *had* to be nuts. *Who talks like this? Who was he to make offers?* Modell's rational mind just wanted to get this man out of here, but part of Art felt a strange aura of magnetism radiating from this character. Part of Modell felt like this guy did have control over the outcome, and that he'd *better* sign.

"I need to get back to watch the second half and mingle with my guests."

The man produced a gold pen, one of those old-fashioned fountain pens. It was heavy in Modell's hand, substantial. And it was very warm. Modell supposed the heat was from being in the man's breast pocket. He placed the papers against the closed suite door and signed on the proverbial dotted line.

It was chilly out here in the hallway, yet Modell was sweating, just like the last time he dealt with this mysterious man. The man smiled as he took the papers from Modell and was off in a flash. As Modell opened the door to this suite, he noticed he still had the man's pen and started to call down the hall, then decided he would keep it as part of the deal.

Meanwhile, back in Sandusky. . . .

"Forty-year-old Lou Groza is set to kick it off with the wind at his back," informed Ken Coleman as the second half got underway. "Wow, that ball is going to land beyond the end zone, out past the pitcher's mound."

Baltimore would gain 3 yards in two plays and were set up for third and 7 at their 23-yard line.

Chuck Thompson: "Unitas back to pass; they are setting up a screen. Unitas passes right into Jerry Hill's hands. He's got blockers in front of him! Wait, he dropped the ball. He gets it back and gets to the line of scrimmage . . . but they are blowing the play dead. It's an incomplete pass."

Gifford: "Unitas couldn't have thrown it any better than that. Hill must have taken his eye off the ball. That would have been a first down and maybe a lot more."

Thompson: "Tom Gilburg in to punt. Good snap . . . the kick is away. Oh, the wind! Gilburg's punt only goes about 25 yards. It bounces and trickles out of bounds at the Baltimore 38."

The boys in Sandusky jumped and hollered. Jackson teased Bill, "Even you coulda punted farther than that." Bill shot back, "Yeah, so could your mother."

Frank Gifford: "Oh my, that wind that helped Groza's kickoff sail 80 yards, really worked against Gilburg's punt there. The Browns will have first and 10 in Baltimore territory."

Coleman: "On first and 10, Ryan back, screen pass to Jim Brown. Jim takes it . . . [Dick] Schafrath lays a nice block on the defender. Jim Brown carries three, four Colts defenders for a 15-yard gain to the Baltimore 23-yard line!"

Gifford: "That looked like the same play Baltimore ran right before they had to punt, but with a much different result! Jim Brown has already made some nice catches today."

The Browns would not be able to sustain the drive, and on the fourth down, Lou Groza came in to attempt a 43-yard field goal.

Coleman: "Snap to the holder Bobby Franklin, the kick . . . is GOOD! Lou Groza's field goal finally breaks the scoreless tie, and the Browns lead 3-0!"

Gifford: "With that field goal, Lou Groza has now scored in his twelfth championship game—that has got to be some kind of record!"

The Colts could do nothing in their next possession against the Browns' inspired defense. The Browns got the ball back with good field position at around their own 35-yard line.

Coleman: "Ryan pitches to Jim Brown. Brown gets through the line. Some nice blocks, this is a big gain! Jim Brown still rumbling. [Gene] Hickerson comes *way* down field and takes out Guy Reese. Finally, Brown is caught and taken down by Jerry Logan at the Colts' 18-yard line!"

You'd have sworn the Lakewood High boys had just run the play themselves, so jubilant . . . and *sweaty* had they become! The joy and the sweat would immediately increase in intensity.

Coleman: "Ryan back to pass. Steps up in the pocket . . . Fred Miller gets a hand on him, but Ryan gets the ball away . . . to Collins in the back of the end zone! Touchdown! Gary Collins with the juggling catch!"

The boys embraced in a four-way bear hug. With two quick scores, they could sense momentum building against the heavily favored Colts.

Gifford: "The Browns have really come to life here in the third quarter. These teams had the top two offenses in the league this year. The Browns are starting to show how good theirs is. We'll see if the Colts can get theirs into gear."

The Colts' offense would have its work cut out for it. Their next possession started at their 6-yard line after a return to the 12, but with a clipping penalty knocking it back. The Colts' horrors continued as the tough Browns defense prevented a first down, forcing another Gilburg punt, this time from the 12-yard line. The wind thwarted the punt again, as this one went a measly 27 yards. The Browns would be taking over at the Baltimore 39-yard line . . . practically in Groza's field goal range.

Coleman: "First and 10 for the Browns at the Baltimore 39. Ryan gives to Brown, Brown to Warfield on the reverse. Fumble! They fumbled the exchange! But the ball bounces right back to Warfield. He runs right . . . and is tackled at the 42. Whoa—that was lucky, only a 3-yard loss."

Gifford: "Yes, the Browns seem to be getting the benefit of the bouncing ball today . . . and Baltimore seems to be snake bitten. That could have been a turnover, or easily a 10-yard loss."

Coleman: "Second and 13. Ryan back to pass. Good protection. Gary Collins is streaking down the field. Boyd slips down! Collins hauls it in at the 5 and goes in for the touchdown! Oh my! These Browns have come alive here in the third quarter!"

Gifford: "That's the third score in 8 minutes for Cleveland. It's like someone flipped a switch! With Groza's extra point, it is now Cleveland 17, Baltimore 0."

On the next Colts possession, the Browns' LB Galen Fiss tackled the Colts' Jerry Hill so hard that the ref had to pluck the ball out of Hill's hands. He was in a daze. A few plays later, Johnny Unitas and Lenny Moore would not execute a clean handoff and would fumble the ball back to the Browns at midfield.

"This is the best quarter of football in the history of football," yelled Jackson, as John shook up his fresh bottle of beer and sprayed it champagne-style on his buddies (and several other fans so caught up in the game that they didn't mind).

Would the tide turn now that the Browns had to face the wind at the start of the fourth quarter?

Coleman: "Ryan back to pass. Over the middle, to Paul Warfield. Warfield is tackled at the 1-yard line! It'll be first and goal at the 1!"

The boys wore beer, sweat, and big smiles on their faces in equal measure. "Give it to Jimmy Brown! Give it to Jim Brown!" they all yelled at the TV.

Indeed, the next play was a dive over the middle by Jim Brown. Modern instant replay would probably confirm this as a touchdown, but despite spirited protests by the Browns, the ruling was that the Colts had stopped him. On second down, Ryan slipped and couldn't make the handoff to Brown, losing 2 yards. Ultimately, Lou "The Toe" Groza, who had gotten the scoring started, came on for a short field goal attempt from a sharp angle. Geometry, schmeometry! He solved the angle and extended the Browns' lead to 20-0.

"I can't believe we couldn't get a touchdown there," lamented Jackson.

"Points are points, Jackson, don't get greedy," warned Ted. Still, Ted was secretly disappointed Jim Brown, his favorite player, wasn't able to get into the end zone. Amidst the merrymaking there was an undercurrent of concern. The Colts were a near unanimous favorite. They still had the best quarterback in the league, Johnny Unitas, and his dangerous targets, split end Raymond Berry and flanker Jimmy Orr. Talented running back Lenny Moore still loomed in the backfield, even though the time for running the ball was running out.

A 20-point lead was great! But that 20 might as well have been lit up in flashing neon. Twenty points was not just one point less than 21. It was an open invitation to end up getting beat by the slimmest of margins. All Baltimore would need to do was score three touchdowns, each followed by an extra point. Even so, the good people of the Sandusky Holiday Inn lobby bar were happy, albeit a little unsettled.

On the Colts' next drive, Jim Kanicki drove up the middle and sacked Unitas for a 3-yard loss. Then things would get interesting for Baltimore, and the Cleveland fans would get nervous.

Thompson: "Unitas back to pass. He throws downfield. Complete to Jimmy Orr. A beautiful pass and catch gets the ball out to the Baltimore 42-yard line."

Gifford: "You knew it was only a matter of time before Johnny got going. Let's see if this is the start of something."

Thompson: "Ball at the 42. Unitas drops back to pass. The blocking is solid, he's got plenty of time. He throws deep, down the sideline for Jimmy Orr, who's beat his man! Orr makes a beautiful catch at the 14-yard line. That was a dandy catch, and a perfect pass from Unitas! Now wait a minute, the official is signaling no catch."

Gifford: "They are saying he didn't have control of the ball before he fell out of bounds. The ruling is an incomplete pass."

The television showed a replay that confirmed what the refs had called.

The Lakewood boys, like the rest of the joint, the fans at Cleveland Municipal Stadium, and all-around Northern Ohio, let out a deep sigh. A stay of execution. The Colts would have to punt yet again. At least this time it wouldn't be into the jaws of that miserable wind.

Thompson: "Gilburg in to punt. Gilburg from the 30-yard line, gets it away, a much better punt now, with the wind at his back. It is taken by Walter Roberts at the 22, out to the 25, the 30, to the 35. He's taken down at the 36-yard line by Tom Matte."

The announcer's narration was drowned out by the boisterous wave of cheers. This excellent field position, this late in the game, with Jim Brown in your backfield . . . well, the game wasn't won yet, but it was looking now like there was no way to lose.

During the commercial break, the boys finally realized how desperately they had to pee! As there were "no vacancies" in the bathrooms off the lobby, they took the path of least resistance to the parking lot. "Come on, Bill, run! Behind the building!" Finding a dumpster behind the hotel, the boys opened the floodgates. "Hurry up, boys, the Browns are liable to score before you're finished whizzing," Ted advised. They hustled back inside, enjoying the refreshing air before ducking back into the dank, dark den that the lobby bar had become.

The crowd was going crazy when the four boys got back to the bar. Frank Ryan had just hit Johnny Brewer on a 15-yard pass on third and 7 for a first down just over midfield. After a 4-yard run by Jim Brown, Ryan threw an incomplete to Collins. But on this bizarrely magical day, the Browns could do no wrong—and a lot of that had to do with the fact that the Colts could do no right. On this play, the Colts' Jerry Logan was flagged for pass interference. First and 10 for the Browns on the Colts' 45.

"Did the announcer just say 'Colt 45'? I believe he's telling us to have another drink," John opined to his fellow fans. (It is doubtful that John realized that "Colt 45" was named after one of the guys playing against the Browns today: number 45 on the Colts, fullback Jerry Hill. This most famous of malt liquors was introduced the previous year by Baltimore-based National Brewing.)

After a nice gain by Jim Brown that was wiped out by a holding penalty, the Browns faced second down and long yardage.

Coleman: "Second down and 26 yards. Ball at the Browns' 49-yard line. Ryan back to pass. He's got time. Going long for Collins! Good coverage by Bobby Boyd, but Collins makes the catch and runs in for the touchdown!"

"Yes! Yes! I can't believe this! Game over!" Ted yelled. He and his buddies practically knocked each other over, jumping and bumping into each other. Technically over six minutes were left on the game clock, but Ted was right; the game was out of reach now for the Colts. With Groza's extra point, the score now stood at 27-0.

The boys would get to see the Browns' Modzelewski intercept Unitas, but then have to eventually punt. But even this didn't result in the Colts getting possession, as a Colts defensive holding penalty gave the Browns the ball back at the Baltimore 26.

"I almost feel bad for the Colts," Billy said. "This is kinda strange, almost like they got a hex on 'em or something."

"Shut up, Billy, kick 'em when they're down, I say," was John's retort. "Those Colts fans were pretty cocky, playing "Taps" downtown last night, it said so in the paper!"

But Billy did have a point. This was kind of strange—the mighty Colts offense scoreless. Nobody could remember seeing Don Shula's Colts make so many mistakes. True, the wind hurt them. But, somehow, it didn't seem to bother the Browns.

"Call it strange, call it what you want," exclaimed Ted. "I call it wonderful."

Finally, it was first and 10 on the Baltimore 16-yard line, with the game clock at around 30 seconds and running down. A few fans ran out on the field, stopping the clock. Then more poured out of the stands, and one of the goal posts was torn down. The refs tried to restore order, and the Browns tried to run a play. It was no use.

With the game decided, and for the safety of the players and all involved, the refs called the game. Torrents of fans flooded the field. The Browns players were swallowed up in delirious masses of fans. About thirty Cleveland cops engulfed Frank Ryan like an ocean of deep blue and escorted him to the locker room—possibly the only time in history a Ph.D. in mathematics has had to be protected from throngs of jubilant, adoring fans.

Like nearly 80,000 fans at Cleveland Municipal Stadium, and millions more in TV Land holed up in bars, hotels, relatives' houses, Ted, John, Jackson, and Bill were ecstatic with the thrill of victory. Resounding victory! They were also three sheets to the wind and in no shape to drive back home. The reception desk informed the four that there was no room in the (Holiday) Inn. Although only a little after 5 p.m., it was getting dark. Ted used the pay phone to inform his dad that he would not be coming immediately home, and to pass the word to the other parents. Like everyone in Cleveland, Ted's dad was too happy to be mad.

When, after a leisurely meal, the boys were still not sober, they decided to pull a wad of blankets out of the Century's trunk and catch a few winks in the car. At around 10 or 11 p.m., they woke up. Feeling somewhat sober, and still incredibly happy, they drove back toward Cleveland—home of the NFL Champion Browns.

6

# CELEBRATION TIME!

Tuesday, December 29, 1964

*"C'mon, have a cigar!" Modell commanded, his voice garbled, as he* chomped on a big Dominican of his own.

"Art, I don't smoke those things! I'm a lady!" Margie, Modell's secretary objected, in the overly dramatic manner of one who is tipsy, bordering on plastered.

The champagne had been uncorked first thing this morning, as the only orders of business were to clean out desks, retrieve potted plants, slap each other on the back, and let the boss take everyone out to lunch. (And smoke a cigar.)

"Margie, if you want a job here next year, you'd better take one," Modell teased.

He offered a stogie to the college kid who'd come in to tabulate some year-end statistics. Statistics and champagne typically don't pair very well, so Modell insisted the kid prioritize the champagne. Today was a day for celebration. The season was over. There would be plenty of time for the kid to come back after the spring semester to tabulate.

Just then, head coach Blanton Collier entered the room, cardboard box in his arms, having just finished cleaning out his own office.

"There he is! The winning coach! Here, Coach, have a cigar!" Modell grabbed a bottle of bubbly from a tub of ice and handed it to Collier.

Collier graciously accepted the fruits of his labors, but before he partook, he reached into his cardboard box and produced the contract. "Art, the day before the game this man I'd never seen before came into my office and had me sign this. I just received this by mail today. He said you had authorized it. That you just didn't have time to sign it."

Collier handed the legal-size packet to Modell, who started to laugh. Before Modell could speak, Collier said, "It slipped my mind to mention it before now."

"Well, you *have* been a little busy," Modell said. "Winning us a championship!" He removed his cigar, took a swig from the bottle he held, then popped the cigar back in his mouth.

"Who *was* that guy? Do you know him?"

"Like you, I had never met him before in my life until he burst into my office the day before the game. I had a meeting, so I sent him down to you."

"Well, I was a little busy just about then myself, boss!" Collier announced to the laughter of the office revelers, including Modell. "Say, that man was a little . . . *unusual.* What was he talking about—guaranteeing we'd beat Baltimore?"

"Hell if I know," Modell said. "I have no idea who he is, or where he came from. I have no earthly idea how he planned to help us win that game. Believe me, I am as baffled as you are!"

Modell had started thumbing through the contract as he was talking with Collier. But he wasn't really looking at it. This was not the time for that. The Browns had won. Who cared how. Now was the time to revel in a well-deserved celebration.

"Art, I signed it. I saw no harm. He said that you would have done it yourself, but that you'd run out of time." Collier was starting to freak himself out a little bit, now that he was recalling the legalese and the cryptic clauses he'd only briefly and distractedly glanced at in the documents.

"Relax," Modell said. "I don't know who that crackpot was. I'm not worried about anything coming back to bite us. You know that lunatic visited me again at halftime of the game! He asked me to sign some more papers. I signed those, too!"

"I've never heard anything like it."

"I know! The guy's off his rocker!" Modell punctuated his remark, using the cigar like a conductor flicks his baton. But then, his brow furrowed. He cocked his head, pondering.

Collier sensed something change in his boss. "What is it, Art?"

"Well, we were tied at halftime, 0-0," Modell said. "We couldn't get anything going. I signed the papers to get the kook out of my hair. And then in the second half . . . well, you know . . . you were there! We dominated!"

Modell hustled back behind his desk, to his briefcase, and produced the addendum to the contract that he'd received by mail today.

"Hmmm," Collier said. "Well, we made some halftime adjustments, Art."

Modell stared straight ahead, toward Collier but not really at him. He was deep in thought. He chose to rationalize the startling second half awakening as having everything to do with his coach's adjustments and his team's execution. Collier could read Modell's face immediately. A huge weight had been lifted.

"Blanton, let's not sell your coaching short. Let's not sell the play of the Cleveland Browns short. We won that game fair and square! That's all there is to it!"

Modell took both contracts and considered using his cigar to light them ablaze, right there in the office. But he hadn't quaffed enough champagne to be so foolish.

"Hey, kid," Modell addressed the college statistician. "Hey, do me a favor. Will you file these for me?"

"Uh, yes sir. Where should I file them?"

"Heck, I don't care," Modell bellowed. "You can roll 'em up and stash them in that bottle, once you finish drinking from it!" He was lighthearted now and wanted to get back to celebrating.

The college kid started to ask Modell if he was kidding, but Modell was heading down the hallway, looking for any other employees who hadn't yet been congratulated and given a cigar. The kid did as he was told. He drank the bottle dry and shook whatever liquid that remained in it onto the floor.

He then rolled up the papers as tightly as he could and inserted them into the bottle. He found a discarded cork. He had to file it down, and it was tight, but he eventually got it to fit. He grabbed one of the uninflated balloons that was lying around and slid it over the cork prophylactic-style. It was something he'd never have done if he wasn't feeling the effects of former contents of the bottle.

He noticed a hole in the office's cinder block wall.

The college kid figured it was the closest thing to a wine cellar, and thus an appropriate place to "file" the champagne bottle and its contents. As he inserted the bottle into the hole in the wall, he realized the hole was deeper than the opening in the wall. When he inserted the bottle, only the top of the orange balloon was visible, but just barely as it was partially shrouded in shadow. He figured Modell or someone would find it soon enough, crack it open, have a little laugh and put these crazy contracts in the appropriate filing cabinet.

Modell returned to the room. "Everyone . . . finish up what's in your glass. It's time for the NFL champions to go to lunch!"

**7**

# ON SET

EARLY JULY 1966 BOREHAMWOOD, ENGLAND . . .
OR 1944 OCCUPIED FRANCE

***The pungent scent of gunpowder was omnipresent. Fires blazed in*** *every direction. The wail of sirens and the hum of idling diesel engines stirred a constant pulse of adrenaline through their overstressed bodies. Sniper fire had them pinned down. It was coming from the rooftop or an upper-floor window. Having already killed his supposed brother-in-arms with a spray of friendly fire from his machine gun, R.T. Jefferson was now back outside the chateau.*

*The real enemy was still inside: dozens of Hitler's officers, many with female companions. Just an hour or so beforehand, the scene inside the chateau had been the picture of tranquility and civilized repose. A string quartet performed from a mezzanine. Fine paintings and tapestries adorned the walls. The Nazi officers looked resplendent in their uniforms. The women on their arms radiated elegance in colorful dresses. None of it attested to the hardship imposed on Europe by the man whose painted portrait was hung in nearly every room. Twelve scruffy American GIs and their leader had arrived and spoiled the party.*

*The psychopath and racist among them, aptly named Maggot, stabbed a female guest, and then threatened his American comrades with a hail of machine gun fire. This is when R.T. dispatched his fellow American GI. The ruckus alarmed the Germans, and a Nazi general directed all officers to take cover in the basement-level shelter. In the panicked confusion, American GIs Reisman and Wladislaw, disguised as Nazi officers, accompanied them downstairs, then stopped short of the safe chamber and locked the Nazis in from the outside.*

*Outside the chateau, Jefferson and the other GIs were now desperately prying the vents off the airshafts that led down to the bunker below.*

*"Gimme the gasoline!" shouted their leader, Major Reisman. Fiendishly the major poured the gas down one of the shafts. "Jefferson, Wladislaw, come on, let's go!" barked Reisman. They too, feverishly tilted their cans, spilling their flammable contents down the shafts.*

*"How many grenades we got?" Reisman asked.*

*"Enough to blow up the world, sir!" Wladislaw responded.*

*"Alright, drop a mess of 'em down each tube—now!" Reisman ordered Jefferson and Wladislaw. "But don't pull the pins! Oh—and make sure you save six or seven for Jefferson!"*

*Jefferson, Wladislaw, and Major Reisman dropped the grenades down each shaft by the dozen. They remembered not to pull the pins. The grenades gathered atop the air shaft grates in the ceiling of the Nazis' underground chamber. The GIs found more gas to pour down the tubes. Dozens of panicked Nazi officers and their guests tried in vain to reach through the grates to somehow throw the grenades back up the shaft. It wasn't working. All the while, more gas was dousing them from above.*

*Rat-a-tat-a-tat! Machine gun fire burst from an upper window of the chateau. Some of the GIs were hit, killed on the spot. Wladislaw, Reisman, and Jefferson took cover behind a hulking German armored vehicle.*

*"Okay, Jefferson—your turn: one grenade per shaft!" Reisman ordered. "Remember, pull the pin, throw it in, and run to the next shaft until you've hit all six. But you gotta move FAST, 'cause this whole thing's gonna blow!"*

*Wladislaw and Reisman strafed the chateau, their bullets seeking Nazi snipers. All the men's adrenaline had been flowing full throttle for hours, ever since they parachuted out of the plane under cover of darkness. Jefferson needed his adrenaline to get him through this last phase.*

*"We'll see you at the bridge!" Reisman shouted. He and Wladislaw fired up the German vehicle. Jefferson began running toward the closest air shaft, his heart in his throat. He pulled the pin and threw the grenade down the first vent, and sprinted to the second, then the third. He had seven seconds to get through the whole task and get far enough away to not be blown to bits. The sixth grenade was sent down its shaft, and Jefferson sprinted away, toward the bridge.*

*"C'mon! Run!" Reisman and Wladislaw implored, looking back from the slowly moving truck.*

*The blast lit the sky and sent Jefferson flying forward. When he landed, he was sprawled face down in a puddle.*

*"Jefferson! Jefferson!" Major Reisman screamed. His voice had the tone of a barked order, but there was a deep concern underneath it.*

*Now Wladislaw implored, "Jefferson, c'mon!"*

*Jefferson didn't move. Under heavy fire again, both from the chateau and from Nazi reinforcements in various vehicles coming to the aid of those in the chateau, the GIs in the German armored vehicle didn't have the luxury of waiting for Jefferson to magically revive.*

*As they drove on, themselves injured, Wladislaw took one last look back. Jefferson was face down in the puddle, dead.*

"Cut! Excellent!" exclaimed Mr. Aldrich.

"Man, this is worse than football," said Jim Brown, the actor playing Jefferson. He was sure that when he got back to wardrobe and took off his military fatigues, he was going to see a case of severe road rash on both knees.

The director, Robert Aldrich, had worked the cast and crew hard this week. Filming on *The Dirty Dozen*, although over schedule, was now nearing completion.

"Alright everyone, nice work tonight; we'll see you back up here tomorrow."

## Tuesday, July 5, 1966 – London, England

Jim Brown was still at the top of his game. And the top of Jim Brown's game is synonymous with the pinnacle of performance in NFL history. In 1965 Jim Brown was the league's best running back by every measure, having run for the most yardage, just as he had in all but one of his years in the NFL. He was a proud man, and his pride still drove him to be the best.

The Browns reached the 1965 NFL Championship Game . . . but lost to the Green Bay Packers. As in the championship victory in 1964, Jim Brown was held without a touchdown in the 1965 championship game. This gnawed at Jim all off-season; he was eager to get back to another NFL season and another championship. He yearned to finally put an exclamation mark on his nearly decade-long career.

But football wasn't the only high-profile outlet for Jim Brown's ambitions and considerable talents. He was becoming an accomplished Hollywood movie actor. His first film came out during the Browns' 1964 championship season. Jim played Sergeant Franklyn in *Rio Conchos*, which debuted on October 28. There were dozens of fans who caught his performance on the silver screen on Friday night, then watched him run for 149 yards in the Sunday matinee at the stadium in a victory over Pittsburgh!

In the summer of 1966, Jim was in England filming a movie that would go on to become a cinematic classic: *The Dirty Dozen*. Though Jim was not yet thirty, and nowhere near the point of slowing down on the gridiron, he was already becoming firmly established in what could be the next phase of his professional life. His character, Robert Jefferson, was a meaty supporting role. Robert Jefferson was in a military prison, and thus a candidate for the Dirty Dozen mission, because he was convicted of a killing a White officer, even though it was in self-defense.

Jim paced in his hotel room during his one day off per week of the arduous filming. The pressure had been building. Jim still loved football and wanted badly to play at least another year, but he had other irons in the fire. He had been involved in starting the Negro Industrial Economic Union, and in recruiting teammates and other players to join the fight. This organization sought to help Black people enter into and succeed in business. Jim was also getting involved in racial justice issues by this time.

And, of course, most pressing at this particular moment was his pursuit of an acting career. Filming was supposed to have wrapped on *The Dirty Dozen* by early June. It hadn't. On June 16, Art Modell issued a press release informing,

> No veteran Browns' player has been granted or will be given permission to report late to our training camp at Hiram College—and this includes Jim Brown. Should Jim fail to report to Hiram at check-in time deadline, which is Sunday, July 17, then I will have no alternative to suspend him without pay.

"Why couldn't the coward have just called me on the phone?" Jim was as hurt as he was angry. Jim would directly ask this question in the letter he was now writing to Mr. Arthur Modell, although he would have the forbearance to affect a courteous and friendly but firm tone. He couldn't have stated the central theme of the letter any more candidly:

> I am writing to inform you that in the next few days I will be announcing my retirement from Football. This decision is final and is made only because of the future that I desire for myself, my family, and if not to sound corney [sic] my race."
>
> Your friend,
> Jim Brown

Neither Art Modell nor anyone else in the world knew it yet, but the Cleveland Browns had just lost the best player in the league at the height of his powers. With one unforeseen, almost inexplicable move, Modell's team had just taken a lurching step backward, farther from the goal line of another NFL Championship and just as the "Super Bowl era" was about to dawn.

Jim Brown smiled slightly in his room in the heart of London. He felt lighter now. He picked up the script and read some lines. He was Robert Jefferson now, moving on toward new goals of his own.

On Thursday, July 14, 1966, the news hit the papers. "Jim Brown Quits Football" blared the headline of the *Plain Dealer.* The news eclipsed the surprise death of a prominent Cleveland Democratic chairman and the news of a Navy jet downing a Soviet MIG near Hanoi.

8

# ONSET OF HOUGH RIOTS

July 18–23, 1966, Cleveland

*The pungent scent of gunpowder was omnipresent. Fires blazed in* every direction. The wail of sirens and the hum of idling diesel engines stirred a constant pulse of adrenaline through their overstressed bodies. Sniper fire had them pinned down. It was coming from the rooftop or an upper-floor window. Lieutenant Higginbotham and his crew were responding to a fire call—one of hundreds that had been telephoned in over the last few days. He and his men wanted to do what they were trained to do—what they were born to do: put out the fires and save lives.

Instead, they were afraid they might lose their own lives. "We were not hired to fight a guerilla war, but that's what this is! What the hell is this world coming to?" He was shouting at nobody in particular. Sure, his men heard him, but it was more like a plea to a higher power to help make sense out of this bedlam. Presently the citizens he was sworn to help protect were shooting at him!

Days later he could only curse and shake his head when he saw that the building they were trying to protect had burned to the ground. The irony! The seven-story apartment building had recently been purchased by Housing Our People Economically (HOPE) to be renovated into low-income housing for residents of the Hough neighborhood. Had it not burned down, it would have been a step in the right direction at defusing an increasingly combustible situation.

The sparks that set this week aflame came a few days earlier when the match was struck on July 18. The kindling had been piling up and drying for much longer.

In 1799, Oliver and Eliza Hough settled the land that would bear their name. On it they built a farm. Eventually the land was subdivided and other farmers settled there throughout the early and mid-1800s. In a spirit of civic generosity, upon their deaths, the Houghs left the land to the occupants who dwelled within. As the city of Cleveland grew, Hough was annexed by the thriving metropolis in 1873. The Houghs' property that had been subdivided into large farmsteads was now further subdivided; a gridwork of streets was laid out, and houses were built.

Between 1880 and 1920, prominent citizens built lavish homes in Hough. Prestigious private schools like Laurel and University School educated the prosperous families' children. Worcester R. Warner and Ambrose Swasey built identical mansions side by side, then built their industrial machine tool company right down the street.

An area along Euclid Avenue that formed the southern border of Hough and extended west to E. 17th was dubbed Millionaire's Row. Among the hundreds of mansions, one—not even the largest—belonged to John D. Rockefeller, the richest man in the world. The famous nineteenth-century American traveler and author Bayard Taylor exclaimed, "Euclid Street [is] the most beautiful in the world, it's only rival being the Prospekt Nevsky in St. Petersburg, Russia."

After World War I, more European immigrants began moving into Hough. Some of the mansions were configured to accommodate multiple families. After World War II, many of these families moved out in what would become known as White Flight as working-class African Americans moved in to take their places.

By the mid-1960s, Hough's population had swollen to its high-water mark of 66,000, making it one of the most densely populated areas of the city. Though accounting for only 7 percent of Cleveland's people, it was home to 19 percent of welfare cases and 20 percent of major crimes. Ninety percent of Hough's population was Black. With the hemorrhaging tax base, city services dwindled. Uncollected trash sullied the sidewalks, the stench intensifying with the heat of the summer. Absentee landlords failed to maintain the housing stock, 20 percent of which was dilapidated. The kindling was piling up.

Over a nine-month period from 1963 to 1964, a coalition of African American civil rights groups called the United Freedom Movement protested inferior quality segregated schools. Cleveland's mayor and other power brokers left the complaints unaddressed.

In early 1966, restless youth roved through Hough throwing rocks and causing mischief. In April, the United States Commission on Civil Rights held hearings in Cleveland on racial inequality issues. Local television broadcasted the hearings. The seething unrest and severity of the underlying issues was on full display. Hough had become a tinderbox. Then came the heat of July.

On July 16, Margaret Sullivan, a twenty-six-year-old prostitute who frequented a local watering hole at the corner of Hough and East 79th, died of a heart attack, leaving behind three children aged ten and younger. The Seventy Niner's Café and Bar, like most businesses in Hough, was owned by Whites, in this case by Abe and Dave Feigenbaum. On July 17, an African American prostitute named Louise attempted to leave a cigar box to collect cash at Seventy-Niner's to benefit the children of her recently deceased colleague. Reportedly, the Feigenbaums refused to allow this.

On July 18, Louise returned to Seventy-Niner's, and the owners or employees immediately kicked her out, reportedly using racial epithets to get their point across. Accounts vary as to details, but apparently a Black patron was refused his requested glass of water and a sign stating "No Water for Ni***rs" may have been posted on the door of the establishment. Every provocation raised the sweltering temperature a few degrees, and it was nearing fever pitch.

An hour later, at around 8 p.m., Seventy-Niner's Café and Bar was robbed.

An agitated crowd of about 300 surrounded the establishment by the time the Feigenbaums arrived at 8:20 p.m. The crowd was hurling rocks at the windows, smashing glass, and making a mess of the place. Dave Feigenbaum pulled out a pistol, and Abe Feigenbaum brandished a shotgun. But rather than use these weapons, they ducked inside their business and dialed the police. Repeatedly. The police did not respond.

After a half hour, they called the Cleveland Fire Department. Ten minutes later firefighters pulled up in a ladder truck with the siren blaring. With no fire blazing at Seventy-Niner's, the firefighters called the police, who took *their* call and arrived on the scene just as the last gasp of twilight yielded to darkness around 9:30 p.m. The crowd-turned-mob moved west along Hough Avenue, looting, setting fires, and throwing rocks.

Four blocks west of Seventy-Niner's is where the sniper, who was firing at Lieutenant Higgenbotham and his firefighting comrades, was set up, at the corner of Hough and East 75th. The sniper was not alone in fighting the firefighters; a mob of 100 commandeered a nearby pumper truck that was trying to put out the blaze that engulfed the HOPE building. Deprived of their truck, and with bullets whizzing past them, more than a few firefighters jumped in the backs of cop cars.

"Get me the hell out of here!" shouted a firefighter with a wife and six kids. "Go! Go! Go!"

"Where ya wanna go?" asked the cop, as he sped west down Euclid.

"Just take me back to the station. I can't do anything out here without a truck! I can't believe these people. We are trying to keep their neighborhood from burning down, and they're shooting at us!"

"It's bedlam. I can't understand it."

"Where the hell do these people think they are gonna live, if all these buildings, all these houses burn down? They're idiots! And they're trying to kill us!"

"Do you think they are militants from the outside? Black Panthers or something?"

"I don't know, man. There had to be 100 people take that pumper truck. And there's like thousands of people causing havoc in the streets. They can't all be outsiders or Commies or whatever. Some of 'em have got to *live* here."

"I don't understand it. I just know if they're coming after firemen, imagine what they'll do to us cops. I mean, before this everybody loved the firemen, but people around here already hated us."

That first night a dozen police were injured. Eight civilians were shot—not necessarily by police. Joyce Arnett, a twenty-six-year-old mother of three, was fatally shot while standing at her window on East 81st Street. Police attributed the killing to sniper fire, while many Hough residents blamed a stray bullet from a policeman's gun. Ten buildings were destroyed by fire.

Police arrested fifty-three Hough rioters. The next day, Mayor Ralph Locher toured the area. Initially he resisted the pleas of the city council to call in the Ohio National Guard. Later that day, he relented. At 3:30 p.m., Governor Jim Rhodes declared a state of emergency and sent in 1,500 National Guard troops. This marked the first time in U.S. history the National Guard had been called in for a racial incident.

Despite the National Guard presence, violence began right around sunset. By the time the night was over, sixty-seven more fires had been started, extensive looting had occurred, sixty more people had been arrested, and thirty-six-year-old African American Perry Giles had been shot in the back of the head and killed by a sniper.

On July 20, Mayor Locher phoned U.S. Vice President Hubert Humphrey asking for federal assistance in rebuilding Hough after the riots. A group of Cleveland clergy petitioned the president of the United States of America, Lyndon Johnson, to declare Hough a federal disaster area, thereby authorizing federal disaster relief funds.

There were now 1,700 National Guard troops in Cleveland, with 1,000 on duty at a time. Some, toting machine guns, followed firefighters on their runs to cover them as they attempted to fight the blazes. Military vehicles were stationed at every other intersection along the twenty-four-block length of Hough Avenue. Despite this, looting continued, not just under cover of darkness, but throughout the day. Police helicopters took fire as the police identified mob formations and the hotspots of heavy looting.

By the riot's fourth day, July 21, several people in the Cleveland political establishment, including Mayor Locher, blamed Black nationalists and outsiders for initiating and continuing the riots. Cleveland's West Side U.S. Congressional representative, Michael Feighan, claimed he had evidence that the rioters "have had training in firearms and Molotov cocktails." He pledged to have the House Judiciary Committee hold hearings into the cause of the riots.

All was quiet on the Western Reserve front during daylight hours, and firefighters had the luxury of lounging in the station for the first time in nearly a week. Lieutenant Higginbotham savored a spoonful of some chili one of his men had made and grabbed a newspaper off the kitchen table. He hadn't had time to read one since the riots broke out. It was a week old, from July 14.

The front-page headline shrieked, "Jim Brown Quits Football." Higginbotham had been devastated when he'd read that just seven days prior. Now he ironically laughed under his breath. "Shit, that seems like a million years ago. I was worried about Jim Brown quitting. Now I'm worried all my men are gonna quit . . . and I can't blame 'em."

The day had been peaceful, but action lit up (literally) after dark. A staggering 115 fires burned, along with twenty false alarms. Higginbotham's men hadn't quit, and they were busy!

Police shot a mother, her three children, and her teenaged nephew at East 107th and Cedar. So far, the National Guard presence had not seemed to be much of a deterrent to the rioters.

By July 22, a counter-reaction to the rioting had developed and was mobilizing in small bands and assembling into growing vigilante groups. Last night's police shooting of the mother, her three children, and her nephew had further enraged the Black residents. Cleveland council member Morris Jackson, who represented Hough, pressed for martial law. The Cleveland *Plain Dealer* also called for this extreme measure from its front page. Mayor Locher refused, insisting that with the National Guard's presence the situation had been improving.

Major General Erwin C. Hostetler, adjutant general of the Ohio Army National Guard, issued an order to his troops to shoot rioters and arsonists. A chorus of voices from City Hall and the local media claimed the uprising was orchestrated by Black nationalists operating out of the JFK House, a local, privately run African American community center.

Friday evening started off peacefully. It was the calm before the storm. Around 3 a.m., twenty-nine-year-old Benoris Toney, father of five, left his home on Lamont Avenue to pick up a friend from work on the West Side, according to his wife, Eareace. As he drove his 1963 Buick down Euclid Avenue a car pulled up alongside his. The car carried six men and youths, all of them White.

Panicked, Toney pulled into the parking lot of Dougherty Lumber at 12100 Euclid and did a quick U-turn. He was coincidentally headed toward a score of police officers, still stationed there after earlier disturbances in the area. The other car followed his into the parking lot, pulled up along the passenger side, and shot through the rolled-up front passenger window with a shotgun, hitting Toney in the face. His car hadn't even come to a stop, and a cop had to tear open the door, jump onto the injured man's lap and apply the brakes before his car rolled into the assembled officers.

An ambulance took Toney to the hospital, but he died the next day. The shooter, Warren LaRiche, was apprehended by the police and tried for the murder. The trial ended in a deadlocked all-White jury. He was tried a second time in February 1967, again by an all-White jury, which acquitted him. His claim was self-defense—that Toney had pointed a gun at him.

Earlier that night, police had disbanded a group of 125 White men who had gathered in the Little Italy neighborhood just west of Hough. At around 4 a.m., Black Hough resident Sam Winchester lay dying in an ambulance on its way to the hospital. He'd been shot at the corner of E 116th and Regalia Avenue. He claimed the shooter was a White man.

After the early Saturday morning shootings, which were a result of the continuing violence from Friday evening, the riots died down. There was minimal disturbance or destruction Saturday evening or Saturday night into Sunday morning. Thunderstorms rolled in Sunday afternoon and kept people indoors. The rains extinguished the smoldering rage. After five harrowing days, the Hough riots were over. By Tuesday, the first 500 National Guard troops left Cleveland. By the end of the week, the balance of 1,200 had departed.

Besides the hundreds of torched buildings and houses, the dozens of looted and damaged stores and business, there was a human toll. Four people had been killed and more than fifty had been injured. Clevelanders pined for the time—less than two weeks earlier—when Jim Brown's retirement seemed their most vexing problem.

9

# BALTIMORE'S REVENGE—WHAT REVENGE?

*The Browns didn't play Baltimore during the 1965 season. But the* Browns did get back to the NFL Championship Game that year. After the 1965 regular season, and an earlier playoff round, the NFL Championship Game wasn't played until 1966, on January 2. This season the Browns played against a budding dynasty: the Green Bay Packers of the Vince Lombardi era. The Browns would lose 23-12 in the last non–Super Bowl era NFL Championship Game. History would prove that the Browns had lost to a colossus, as Green Bay would dominate the early Super Bowl epoch.

Even though winning isn't everything (wink, wink), it always hurts to lose. At least Art Modell's team had *gotten* to the championship. Baltimore had a good season in 1965 but had lost to Green Bay in the previous playoff round. Modell relished the fact that the Browns made it further than the Colts did. It was a small solace in the aftermath of a painful loss. Even so, Modell was happy that that the strange character's dire talk about Baltimore's revenge didn't seem to be worth the paper the cockamamie "contract" was written on.

The Colts and Browns didn't play each other in the 1966 regular season either. Neither team made the playoffs, as both finished with 9-5 records. This was the first year in a decade that Jim Brown wasn't playing football in the NFL. (Modell didn't seem to think about the stranger's prediction that Jim Brown would retire as a Cleveland Brown; when he had originally heard that, he naturally assumed it wouldn't happen until years later.)

The talk of calamity and of Baltimore's revenge against Cleveland receded further and further from Modell's mind. He wondered with a laugh how he could have ever entertained for a moment that some cashmere-coated charlatan could alter the course of his fortunes. The Browns had won the 1964 championship. It had been all about the Browns, and of course Modell's brilliant leadership. The victory had been earned. It had nothing to do with that mystery man.

In 1967, for the third consecutive year after the Browns dealt the Colts a decisive blow in the 1964 NFL Championship Game, the teams did not face each other. It was not often that Modell thought about the crazy man and his crazy contract. But on this Christmas night, the day after the Browns' loss to the Cowboys in the divisional playoff round, he had a chance to reflect once more upon that odd period in late 1964.

"I really outfoxed that crackpot." Modell said this aloud to nobody but himself. The Colts had gone 11-1-2 in 1967. The Browns had only managed a 9-5 record. Yet it was the Browns, not the Colts, who made the playoffs! "So, we lost in the first round, big deal! Baltimore never even got in." And with that, Art took another sip of his Manhattan, snuffed out his cigar, and headed upstairs to bed.

The next year, 1968, finally brought these two teams together during the regular season. That season, 1968, also brought back a ghost from the Cleveland Browns' past: Paul Brown. His new team, the Cincinnati Bengals, made their debut in the American Football League (AFL). It had already been announced that the AFL and NFL would merge in 1970. The Bengals didn't fare well in their inaugural season, and Modell didn't need to worry about the new competition at the southern end of the state.

Jim Brown was no longer with the Browns, having retired after the 1965 season. Another key piece of that 1964 championship team, six-foot-three, 200-pound Frank Ryan, was not playing by the end of the 1968 season either. He'd been one of the gutsiest quarterbacks to ever play the position and was revered by his teammates for standing in the pocket until the last possible millisecond, ignoring the impending carnage, so his receivers could get open. His fearless style was now catching up with him as injuries mounted. Bill Nelson was now the Browns' starting quarterback.

Johnny Unitas had won the NFL's Most Valuable Player Award in 1967, but he sustained a nasty arm injury in the 1968 preseason and hadn't played much to this point in the 1968 season, although he'd start this game. Baltimore's runner Lenny Moore retired after the 1967 season.

None of these major personnel changes mattered. The Browns once again dominated the juggernaut Colts. The Colts were undefeated at 5-0 coming into this game, which was played on Baltimore's home turf. Unitas completed only eight passes in this rematch—four to his receivers and four to Cleveland defenders! So much for Baltimore's retribution.

Modell visited the visitors' locker room at Memorial Stadium and basked in sweet victory with his team. True, the stakes were not nearly as high as the last time these two teams had played each other. But Modell's subconscious mind must have still harbored some paranoia about the impending payback predicted by that odd fellow. Alas, with this resounding victory, Modell extinguished the last faint cinder of foreboding that had smoldered since he signed those silly papers nearly four years ago.

## 10

# BALTIMORE'S REVENGE— A MEASURE OF REVENGE IS SERVED

DECEMBER 29, 1968 – CLEVELAND MUNICIPAL STADIUM

***The regular season matchup would not be the only time the Colts played*** the Browns during the 1968 campaign. The Colts had won five straight games to start the season. Then the Browns dealt them their first loss. Baltimore would then reel off nine straight victories to close out the season, including a first-round playoff victory over the Vikings.

The Browns had won their division at 10-4 and then had beaten the Cowboys in the first round of the playoffs. Thus, the stage was set. The Colts and Browns were again on a collision course to decide the championship of the NFL. (Unlike the last time they played, there would still be another game for the winner to play—the Super Bowl, which would pit the champion of the NFL against the champion of the AFL.)

Like four years ago, this NFL Championship Game was being played in Cleveland. This was the sixth NFL Championship Game to be played at Cleveland Municipal Stadium. A sellout crowd of 78,410 braved the cold and wind to witness what they hoped would be Cleveland's fifth NFL Championship. As was the case four years ago, the Colts were favored by roughly a touchdown.

Art Modell told those with him in his suite: "I feel good about this game. We were supposed to lose to them in '64, and we creamed 'em. We were supposed to lose to them this season, and we creamed 'em." He held up his small glass of Old Panther Juice, prompting his suite guests to follow suit. "To victory, and a trip to the Super Bowl! Let's cream 'em!" Everyone clanked their glasses to consummate the toast.

There would not be much more to celebrate for Browns fans on this Sunday.

The Colts were driving in the first quarter. It seemed they would strike pay dirt. Then Cleveland defensive back Ben Davis intercepted Earl Morrall's pass at the Browns' 14-yard line to end the threat. The Browns efficiently drove past midfield to the Colts' 35-yard line, Bill Nelson completing a pair of long passes to Paul Warfield and Milt Morin. Art was not alone in feeling this game was shaping up like the '64 championship tilt. Maybe the old magic that led to the Browns shutting out the favored Colts in 1964 was still in force.

Alas, the drive stalled. The Browns' storied kicker, Lou Groza, who had broken the scoreless tie the last time these teams tangled in an NFL Championship match, had retired after a twenty-one-year career after the 1967 season. Rookie Don Cockroft came in to attempt a 42-yard field goal.

Not far away from Modell and his guests in the owner's suite, the CBS television crew was busy calling today's game. The CBS crew may have been even more impressive than the teams on the field that day. Tom Brookshire would go on to be the lead NFL broadcast analyst for CBS in the mid-seventies. To express the cachet of that role, consider that Pat Summerall preceded him, and John Madden succeeded him. That is some elite company! His partners for this NFL Championship telecast were Pat Summerall and Jack Buck—both Hall of Fame broadcasters.

Summerall: "Don Cockroft will come out to try a 42-yarder."

Brookshire: "The rookie kicker has made 75 percent of his attempts this year, but he's only 2 of 6 from beyond 40 yards."

Buck: "The snap, hold, the kick is up. Blocked! The kick was blocked by—"

Brookshire: "I believe that was Bubba Smith."

Summerall: "Ah, big Bubba Smith; he used that 6-foot 7-inch body and long wingspan to bat down that field goal attempt. He's the number-one draft pick a year ago, out of Michigan State."

All the pregame confidence that had been borne aloft since the interception had just run into some turbulence. The first quarter ended in a scoreless tie, just as it had four years earlier. Like the '64 game, it was a field goal that started the scoring, but this time it was by Baltimore, as kicker Lou Michaels nailed a 28-yarder. In 1964, Lou Groza's field goal in the third quarter opened the floodgates. Michaels' opening salvo in the second quarter would have a similar effect on this game.

Tom Matte had about 100 friends and family in the Cleveland Municipal Stadium stands that day. Matte had grown up in East Cleveland and, like his friends and family, had been a rabid Browns fan. After starring at Shaw High, he played well enough at Ohio State to be in the running for the Heisman trophy. Baltimore selected him as their first-round draft pick in 1961. Despite being drafted by Baltimore, he almost ended up fulfilling a lifetime dream of playing for his hometown Browns.

Matte was injured during his rookie year with the Colts and put on "injury waiver." This designation opened the door to Art Modell, who invited him to Cleveland and had him checked out at the Cleveland Clinic. When the results came back favorable, Modell offered Matte a contract—at a 30 percent increase over what he had been making for Baltimore. It was a chance to play for his favorite team and in the same backfield as Jim Brown!

The deal sounded too good to be true, and maybe even a little shady. Upon returning to Baltimore, Matte divulged to the Colts' owner, Carroll Rosenbloom, that he would like to go play for his hometown team and that the Browns had given him an offer. Rosenbloom asked if it was for more money. When Matte affirmed this to be true, Rosenbloom said he'd match it and kept him a Colt.

As a runner, Matte was overshadowed by star Lenny Moore, until Moore's retirement after the '67 season. Matte was Baltimore's leading rusher in 1968 and made the Pro Bowl. He was most famous, so far, for playing quarterback for the Colts for three games in 1965 after starter Johnny Unitas and backup Gary Cuozzo went down with injuries. But today, Matte's boyhood fantasy would come true. He would have the game of his life in Cleveland Municipal Stadium, like he had always dreamed of. The only difference: He was playing against the Browns rather than for them.

Buck: "Matte goes in for the score from 1 yard out! Colts are up 9-0, pending the extra point attempt. Michaels makes the extra point, and Baltimore extends its lead to 10-0, here in second-quarter action."

The Browns couldn't muster any offense, and once again the Colts had possession.

Summerall: "The Colts are driving once again. Second down and 3. Morrall back to pass. He has Mackey, who's down inside the Cleveland 15-yard—"

Buck: "Now wait a minute, Mackey's fumbled the ball!"

Summerall: "It looks like the Browns have it!"

Brookshire: "It looks like the ball has been recovered by number 40, defensive back Erich Barnes."

On the sidelines, coach Blanton Collier raised his arms, then implored the offense: "Let's turn this into some points!"

Shivering Cleveland fans finally had something to cheer. In the owner's box, the mood brightened from the gloom that had slowly set in. Modell exclaimed, "Maybe this will turn it around!"

Summerall: "Well, the Browns really dodged a bullet there. That was a key takeaway. Baltimore looked like they were about to extend their lead. Let's see if this is the spark the Browns need."

Buck: "Browns from their own 23-yard line, first and 10, with a few minutes left in the first half. Nelson takes the snap. He's going back to pass. Throws downfield . . . intercepted!"

Brookshire: "That's linebacker Mike Curtis who stepped in front of that pass and intercepted it. He's down at the Browns' 33-yard line."

Summerall: "Well, it looks like the Browns just can't get going today; they give the ball right back to Baltimore."

Browns fans were not accustomed to this. A feeling of disbelief washed over the stadium. Something strange was going on. This was the twenty-third year the Cleveland Browns football team had been in existence, and they had won the league championship eight times. They had competed in the NFL Championship Game another five times but lost. So, they had won a lot. Certainly, they had lost too, but this felt different. Instead of capitalizing on a turnover, they gave it right back. The pendulum seemed to swing in only the wrong direction. The Browns' owner started to feel a pit in his stomach.

Baltimore had moved from the 33-yard line to the Browns' 12, with about a minute left until halftime.

Buck: "Morrall is under center, the snap, he hands to Matte . . . Matte gets through the line, and he's free! Matte takes it in for the touchdown!"

Modell pounded the railing in his suite. His heart sank, and the walls seemed to close in on him. The pit in his stomach grew.

Brookshire: "The Browns missed a couple of tackles on that play that allowed Matte to score easily."

Summerall: "Michaels splits the uprights, and it's the Colts 17 to nothing over the Browns, and we are out of time in the first half. I'd say Tom Matte is having the game of his life here today. He's got about 100 friends and family out in the stands today that he must be making very happy."

Brookshire: "Yes, Cleveland's Leroy Kelly led the league in rushing this year, but Baltimore has really held him in check so far today."

Modell was not happy but not completely despondent either. "Last time we played them here, we scored 27 in the second half, and held them scoreless," he said. "If we do that again, we'll win by 10."

He was trying to convince himself, as much as anyone else within earshot. He remembered that meeting four years ago, right outside his box. He had become convinced since then that the mystery man was nothing more than a deranged pretender. But now a seed of doubt had begun to germinate in his mind. Modell pushed away these thoughts, preferring to think instead about Coach Collier's halftime adjustments and how they hopefully would affect the same result as in the 1964 game.

Maybe Collier had gotten a message through to his team. The Browns forced Baltimore to punt on the first possession of the third quarter, and the Browns advanced into Baltimore territory for only the second time in the game. After the drive bogged down, Cockroft was called upon to attempt a 50-yarder.

Summerall: "Don Cockroft is on to attempt the field goal and try to get Cleveland on the board. The snap, good hold, the kick is up . . . wide, no good."

The fans deflated.

Buck: "Wait, there is a flag on the play. If it's against Baltimore, Cleveland will get another chance. The referee signals that it is against Baltimore, the Browns will get another shot."

The fans puffed back up.

Summerall: "Okay, let's try this again. Cockroft will get another chance to pick up the Browns and give the fans something to cheer about. This one will be from 45 yards."

Modell watched from his box. Maybe this gift penalty would turn this game around. "The snap, the kick is up, he . . . missed it again, he missed from 50 and now he missed again from 45!"

Matte's cheering contingent was delirious but was drowned out by Browns fans, who were starting to boo. Modell was angry and embarrassed. How could this happen? The Colts were great—they'd only lost once all year, but it was Art's team that had beaten them. The Browns had always seemed to have the Colts' number. But now the Browns weren't simply being beaten by a great team. Cleveland was uncharacteristically turning the ball over. And how could you explain back-to-back missed field goals?

"Why am I paying this Cockroft?" Modell yelled. "He's got one job to do, and he hasn't made a single kick today! Lou Groza is older than I am, but he would have made these kicks!"

Modell was hot. Like the fans, he was looking for a sign that the Browns could claw their way back into the game. But with every opportunity they were given—even when they were given a do-over—they could not capitalize. Modell was beginning to realize that this game was the exact opposite of the 1964 championship game.

Baltimore took possession but couldn't keep the chains moving and had to punt. The Browns' offense was stonewalled yet again, and they punted right back to the Colts. Baltimore got the ball with decent field position.

Buck: "Cleveland drops Mackey for a 6-yard loss to the Cleveland 44. Maybe the Browns' defense can start turning things around here for Cleveland. Second and 16. Richardson has gotten behind the Browns' secondary! Morrall sees him—"

Summerall: "Oh, but the pass is underthrown, this could be an interception—"

Buck: "Richardson adjusts and makes the catch at the 5!"

Summerall: "Erich Barnes, the Browns cornerback had position on it. But it seems like he never saw the ball! I thought for sure the Browns would have made the interception there, but instead it's first and goal for Baltimore at the 5."

Brookshire: "Baltimore now will have an excellent chance to pull further away if they can score again here."

Buck: "Matte on first and goal, got halfway to goal. He's tackled inside the 3-yard line."

Summerall: "If Cleveland can hold Baltimore to a field goal here, they may have a chance to get back in this game. That is, if they can bring their offense to life."

Buck: "Second and goal, just outside the 2-yard line. The give to Matte. He breaks through! Touchdown!"

Brookshire: "The local boy who played at Shaw High and Ohio State has gone in for his second touchdown of the game. He's got scores of friends and family in the stands—who are probably all Browns fans normally—but he is putting on a show for them today."

Summerall: "The extra point is good. With 2:17 left in the third quarter, the Colts lead 24 to 0."

After the Colts' kickoff resulted in a touchback, Coach Collier sent eleven-year veteran quarterback Frank Ryan into the game in relief of Bill Nelson. Nelson had played pretty darned well ever since he relieved Ryan in the third game of the season, but today he had completed only 10 of 26 passes and hadn't moved the team all game.

Buck: "Ryan is a fellow whom the Cleveland crowd really got on during the year, but now they'll be rooting for him to try to do something about the 24 to nothing deficit with 2:08 remaining in the third quarter. First and 10 Cleveland from their own 20."

With Ryan at the helm in 1964, the Browns scored points in a hurry, piling up 27 in the championship game's second half.

"Maybe Ryan can work his old magic," Modell muttered.

The fans in the stands shivered, holding their breath in anticipation. Hope danced tenuously through the frigid stadium, like the isolated flurries of snow. It was eerily quiet in TV Land (again, miles from Cleveland as the game was blacked out in town). If the Browns were to have a chance, it would have to start *now*.

Buck: "Ryan breaks the huddle. The snap. Ryan fumbles the ball! And Shinnick recovers! Frank Ryan fumbled the ball and Baltimore's Don Shinnick has recovered. Baltimore will go from the Browns' 20."

The fragile snowflake of hope melted away. By this stage of the game, when *everything* had to go right, things continued to go wrong . . . very, very wrong.

Those who had entered Modell's owner's suite about three hours ago, thrilled to be a part of the big event and buoyed with a reasonable hope of victory, now felt a supreme discomfort. *What do you say to a proud owner without sounding trite?* Modell, sensing their unease, tried, unconvincingly, to mask the pain and embarrassment he felt.

"You win some, you lose some . . . isn't that what they say?" Modell said. "Hey, we got 'em last time, when it was for all the marbles. This game is not as big as the '64 championship. That was a *real* championship." The anger Modell had felt earlier had given way to something closer to panic or paranoia. He even went out into the hallway behind his suite. Of course, the mystery man from four years ago was nowhere to be found.

Baltimore closed out the third quarter with three running plays for 17 yards, giving them a second and goal from the 3 to start the fourth. Some fans threw whatever projectiles they had onto the field in disgust. Others started filing silently for the exits. A broken running play and an incomplete pass prevented another Colts touchdown, but they got the field goal and now led 27-0. Art's wife Pat said, "This is exactly opposite from last time." It was eerie. The perfect symmetry in these two championship matchups between the Colts and the Browns seemed like an impossible coincidence.

The Browns would try again to change their fortunes. Frank Ryan stayed in the game and made pass after pass. After one first down, a few incompletions, and suffering Ordell Braase's third sack of the game, Don Cockroft had to come in to punt on fourth and 16. The Colts would take over on their 33-yard line and put together one of those run-heavy drives that takes time off the clock. Eventually they were stopped, and the Colts' Lou Michaels came on to attempt his third field goal. He wouldn't make it, as the ball hit the upright. But (of course) the Browns were offsides. Baltimore got the ball back, first and goal from the eight.

"It's like they are trying to lose . . . they can't do anything right!" one of the disgruntled remaining fans fumed as he got up to leave. With about 4:30 minutes left, reserve running back Timmy Brown ran it in from the 4-yard line for the touchdown. The extra point made it 34-0. The Colts had managed to avenge the loss from four years ago—and earned a berth to Super Bowl III against Joe Namath and the New York Jets.

With the stadium now mostly empty, and only his wife Pat still with him in the suite, Art Modell sat quietly in a shadowy corner. Pat saw he was trembling and knew not to talk to him just now. The prediction had come true. That crazy mystery man with his mumbo-jumbo contract had told him Baltimore would get even.

Amid her husband's rambling ruminations, Pat could make out this comment: "We beat them 27-0. Today they were beating us 27-0... and went on to score one more time, just to one-up us!"

That couldn't just be a coincidence. He continued his nervous musings, though they were inaudible now:

*Now, where was that contract? Did I even keep a copy of it? What else was in that contract? It was so many pages. Is this the extent of the damage? We shut them out in the championship game. They shut us out in the playoffs. Quid pro quo . . . this for that? Now is everything even?* Art's mind raced. *Where is that man? I don't know his name, or address. I don't have a phone number. With the contract being so many pages, there must have been more to it. . . .*

Agitated, feeling like he was backed into a corner, Modell snapped, "Come on, let's go home!"

The next morning Art added an extra spoonful of sugar to his morning coffee as he read the front-page article from Chuck Heaton in the *Plain Dealer*. He needed that extra sweetener to try to get the bad taste out of his mouth. Beneath the headline "Browns' Title Bid Ends 34-0," the article began:

It had been 1964 all over again yesterday—but in reverse—as midnight struck for the Cinderella Browns on a cold, gray day at the stadium. They saw their National Football League title dreams snuffed out 34-0, by the Baltimore Colts who were shutout victims of the Cleveland team just four years ago in the championship game on the lakefront.

Before Modell could read about local boy Tom Matte whom he almost had under contract a few years ago until Baltimore's rival owner matched Modell's contract offer, and before he got down to the part about winning coach Don Shula who'd played locally at John Carroll University and started his NFL playing career in 1951 playing for the Cleveland Browns, he was interrupted by a phone call.

"Congratulations, Arthur, on making the playoffs this year." It was that worldly, taunting voice that seemed to always haunt him at times like this. Modell, recognizing the caller's voice, immediately knew the apparent congratulations were meant as an ironic dig at the lopsided loss his team had just endured. He didn't reply. He strongly considered hanging up the phone.

The caller spoke again: "Mr. Modell, you may be wondering whether we are 'all square,' as I think you might phrase it. After all, you knew that 1964 championship came at a cost, and that Baltimore would have its revenge. I feel it's my duty to inform you that yesterday's defeat is best thought of as a down payment only. Rest assured there will be years of installments yet to be paid."

The caller once again had unleashed the emotions of anger, then fear, in the beleaguered owner. Modell turned bright red, and sweat beads formed on his brow. "I really don't appreciate you calling me to rub in it in! The papers have already got that covered!"

"Arthur, Arthur, how do you think the people in Baltimore felt four years ago? This too shall pass. It won't pass for a while . . . a long while, but it will pass."

"Why do you talk in riddles? Why can't you just tell me what I signed? And when this thing will be behind me. If this thing is even true. If you aren't a figment of my imagination. I should put someone else on the line."

Modell then started calling for his wife as he paced the living room, the curly phone cord stretching to its limits every time he neared the kitchen. "Pat! Pat! Can you come to the phone?" It was no use. She was out of earshot.

"Mr. Modell, you were so eager to put your stamp on history and to win the big game. Perhaps a little patience could have spared you from the aftermath. Arthur, think of the irony. You cashed in all your chips too early. You worked hard to get the NFL involved with television, and now that marriage is really taking hold. And the Super Bowl has ratcheted football's popularity up a notch . . . or ten. But it'll be the Colts going to Super Bowl III this year. And it's now the NFL's Broadway moment."

Modell couldn't take it anymore. "I need to go. Goodbye!" He got the phone's receiver out of his hand and onto the cradle like it had just come out of a hot oven. He seethed with anger at this intrusion. Over the course of the morning, the anger gave way to anxiety as he wondered what the stranger meant by this was the down payment, and there would be plenty of installments yet to pay, or whatever he'd said.

It irked Modell that the Super Bowl, pitting the NFL champions against the AFL champions, had boosted professional football's stature to the next level. And now the Colts were going while his team fell one game short. So, Modell's emotions shifted again, and anxiety was elbowed aside by anguish. He vowed to himself right then: *Come hell or high water, Art Modell will get to the Super Bowl!*

He wasn't wrong.

## 11

# BURNING RIVER

### June 22, 1969 – Cuyahoga River Fire

*As they crossed the bridge, the steel wheels threw off a fusillade of sparks.* This is not all that unusual on a train like theirs. But today most of these glowing-hot metal shavings landed on some oil-soaked debris that had floated downstream and collected below, where the river's current pinned the refuse to the bridge supports.

Almost to the other side of the Cuyahoga, they looked back and saw flames rising up from the water and starting to engulf the bridge. "Wow, look at that, a burning river!" exclaimed Virgil, the engineer. Dontay, the brakeman, put down his book, and said, "Ha, the River Acheron!" Virgil burst out laughing, "Ack-er-on? Man, you people talk funny. It's pronounced 'Ack rin.' And this here's Cleveland. Akron's about 50 miles away, dummy. And the river's called the Cuyahoga. It goes down to Akron, though. But you can't get there by boat, because it's dammed."

"I'll say it's damned, looks like this whole place is damned," Dontay retorted.

And thusly history's most famous river fire began. This would be the twelfth or thirteenth time the Cuyahoga had ignited in flames. This was hardly the worst fire . . . far from it. Nobody died, unlike in the fire in the early 1900s. Damage was only around $50,000 compared to the millions of dollars of damage in the 1952 Cuyahoga River fire. This fire was small and so unremarkable that nobody took a photo, and it escaped local reporting at the time. However, the times, they were a-changin', as Bob Dylan had pointed out in 1964.

A movement that would become known as environmentalism was taking root. In 1968, the citizens of Cleveland had already overwhelmingly approved a $100 million bond issue to clean up the river. That was the good news. The bad news for Cleveland's national reputation was that this same newfound consciousness would cause *TIME* magazine to make a poster child of the Cuyahoga River fire in its August issue on the environment. (The photo on *TIME*'s cover was from the far more destructive 1952 fire.)

This event then precipitated the national environmental movement, resulting in federal involvement in reducing pollution and cleaning up the nation's water and air. The federal legislature passed the National Environment Policy Act in 1970. From this legislation, the Environmental Protection Agency (EPA) was born. By 1972, the EPA had promulgated the Clean Water Act to reduce pollution and return rivers to a state that would be conducive to mass swimming, be habitable by fish, and support other wildlife.

This little river fire became the symbol for wanton destruction of the environment. The environmental movement that it helped galvanize would improve the air and water quality of the nation and indeed the world. But Cleveland's reputation went up in proverbial flames. What was only years before the sixth largest city in the United States, and a mighty industrial center, was now reduced to being the "Mistake on the Lake."

Fortunately, the Browns' 1969 season wouldn't be so dire. They made the playoffs, beating Dallas 38-14 in the first round, before losing in the NFL Championship Game to the Vikings.

12

# SUPER BOWL III

January 12, 1969 – The Orange Bowl, Miami

*Art Modell seethed. He tried to hide his rage in this group of NFL owners* and coaches in a suite at the Orange Bowl. (Orange Bowl, as in the venue, not the college bowl game.) He'd just watched this cocky kid they called Broadway Joe lead the underdog New York Jets to a Super Bowl victory over the powerhouse Baltimore Colts. The Colts—the team Modell had beaten in the NFL Championship Game when the NFL Championship Game was the ultimate test.

Modell reflected back to the Browns' crowning achievement under his ownership. Looking back, it seemed the old NFL Championship Game—when that contest crowned the professional football champion—was almost minor league compared with the spectacle of the Super Bowl. The Super Bowl was the big leagues. Tonight strengthened Modell's resolve. He *had* to get his team to the Super Bowl. He *deserved* it!

And these Colts . . . the Browns hadn't played them again after beating them in the 1964 NFL Championship, until this season. The Browns were the only team to beat them this season until the Jets did in the Super Bowl. But the Browns' win was in the regular season. They had met again, just two weeks ago, in the 1968 NFL Championship. The teams were in a scoreless tie after the first quarter, and Art remembered back to 1964, when the teams were tied at halftime, before the Browns lowered the boom, winning 27-0. This year, Baltimore began earlier, scoring 17 in the second quarter, and piling on from there to win 34-0.

But tonight the heavily favored Baltimore Colts of the supposedly superior NFL lost to the upstart New York Jets of the supposedly lowly AFL. Modell's good friend Wellington Mara, owner of the New York Giants, may as well have been his mortal enemy with his comment, "How 'bout that, Arthur? It kind of reminds me of your Browns, how they came out of the All-America Football Conference in 1950 and won the NFL Championship their first year in the league—of course, that was before you were in the picture."

Modell feigned a smile, and mumbled something unintelligible but with enough of an attempt at a friendly tone so as to not betray his fury.

Modell's inner monologue started playing. *I brought advertising and TV to the game and just when it gets big, we keep falling short. I'm about sick of hearing about the glory days of Paul Brown. If I'd never bought the Browns and brought my televison and advertising contacts to the NFL, we all would be in frigid New York or Baltimore to play this game, not sunny Miami. And the networks wouldn't be paying top dollar for the privilege of showing the game. And advertisers wouldn't be spending $75,000 for a 30-second spot. . . .* His musings were interrupted again by Mara.

"Arthur, I tell you what. I've got a problem on my hands in New York. This Namath kid is a sensation. The papers love him. He's bringing the casual fan over to the Jets. I will tell you this: This is becoming a quarterback's game, more than ever. And if you can find one who's good-looking and brash, and can back it up on the field, that's tough to beat, tough to beat."

Modell tried a half-hearted joke. "You don't suppose I could convince Otto Graham to come out of retirement, do you?"

"Arthur, he's an old man by now. He retired fifteen years ago . . . no, I think we need to go young, like this long-haired Namath fellow."

The only problem was there weren't any Joe Namaths in the 1969 draft. Not even close. The two quarterbacks taken in the first round would go on to be NFL starters for only a combined three years. University of Southern California running back O.J. Simpson was taken number one that year by the AFL's Buffalo Bills. (Can you imagine playing your home games in Los Angeles as a senior in college and playing them in Buffalo the next season as a pro?)

In 1969 the Browns managed to get a Pro Bowl performance out of their veteran quarterback, Bill Nelson, who'd been acquired from Pittsburgh the year before. It was his first and last Pro Bowl season. He was joined by halfback Leroy Kelly and receiver Paul Warfield at the Pro Bowl that year. Last year's first-round draft pick, Ron Johnson, a record breaker at halfback at Michigan, didn't take well to the conversion to fullback, rushing for only 472 yards. But the Browns made it to the NFL Championship for the second year in a row.

One of the original Cleveland Browns, the great Dante Lavelli, sent a telegram to the team on the eve of the 1969 NFL Championship Game urging them to "Go out the way we came in!" Lavelli was urging the Browns to win the last-ever NFL Championship Game, just as they'd won the NFL Championship their very first year in the league, in 1950. After this season, the NFL and AFL would merge. There would henceforth be only one league: the NFL. Despite Lavelli's well-wishes, the Browns lost the last NFL Championship ever played, to the Minnesota Vikings, 7-27.

One week later Art Modell was in New Orleans to watch the NFL's Vikings take on the AFL's Kansas City Chiefs in Super Bowl IV. Like the previous year, the NFL team was heavily favored; they'd dominated the NFL all year, while the AFL's Chiefs had "backed into the playoffs" by finishing second in their own division. But like last year, the AFL team played David and slew the NFL Goliath. Quarterback Len Dawson became the fourth quarterback to win the MVP Award in the four Super Bowls played.

As the MVP Award was being handed to the Chiefs quarterback, Modell and the other owners with whom he'd been watching the game started to decamp from their box seating.

"Arthur, what did I tell you last year?" Mara said. "These quarterbacks are the key to the modern game."

"Well, I'll have you know that my quarterback will be playing next week in the NFL Pro Bowl."

Art's boast was just bluster. He knew his quarterback was literally on his last legs. He'd had several knee operations and would likely need to go under the blade this off-season. Nor was there anyone decent on the bench behind him.

Worse than that, Modell was beginning to feel like he'd felt in early 1964. At that point he'd owned the team for three years and hadn't made the playoffs yet. They'd broken through that season and beat the Colts to win it all in 1964. But in the five years since then, though they'd reached the NFL Championship three times, they'd lost them all.

Worse still, the Super Bowl was now the big game and, in never again winning the NFL Championship Game, the Browns hadn't earned the right to play in one yet. The AFL and NFL were merging next season, money was coming into the game. TV, advertising, fame and fortune. Modell felt in his bones he needed to do something, and with the draft just over two weeks away, he needed to do something fast.

Modell, and others, including Mara, boarded a streetcar for the ride from Tulane back to the hotel. Mara was seated a row behind Modell. Midway through the short trip, Mara seemed to repeat himself: "Arthur, you really ought to get yourself a quarterback and sooner rather than later." Modell just stared ahead thinking, *Okay, give it a rest, Mara, we've already been over that territory.*

The streetcar's brakes screeched as it slowed for its next stop.

"You know, sometimes you need to part with something of value to get something of value in return, just like in 1964."

Modell turned around, wondering what Mara was talking about. Only it wasn't Mara who was speaking! It was someone a row farther back. Modell's eyes bulged from behind the silver-rimmed glasses. It was that cashmere-coated man. Modell fumbled for words. He began to speak, but it was too late. The man was getting off at this stop. The leather soles of his shoes clicked step by step into the night, and he was gone.

13

# PHIPPS / WARFIELD

SPRING 1970

***The 1969 draft class had been historically weak at quarterback. 1970's*** crop contained at least two blue chippers: Terry Bradshaw, whom it seemed certain would go to Pittsburgh at number one, and Purdue's Mike Phipps, who probably would follow not far behind. The problem for Art Modell and the Browns: They were a victim of their own success, and thus not scheduled to pick until position 21. There was no way Phipps would be around that long. If the Browns were going to try to land their quarterback of the future, one to take them into the 1970s, one to kick off this new merged AFL-NFL era, one to get them to the elusive and all-important Super Bowl, they would need to do some horse trading.

Mike Phipps followed Bob Griese as the starting quarterback at Purdue University. Griese had set all kinds of school records at Purdue. And his college success translated to sustained success in the NFL. Nobody could know for sure, just prior to the 1970 NFL draft, but Griese's early career hinted at what would be. By the time Griese retired he'd made eight Pro Bowls, was a two-time First Team All-Pro, and a two-time Super Bowl champion. Griese was ultimately enshrined in the NFL Hall of Fame.

Meanwhile, Phipps, two inches taller and physically bigger than his predecessor, was rewriting the records Griese had set at Purdue before the ink was even dry. It seemed Phipps was Griese 2.0: bigger, stronger, faster. Better.

So, when the 1970 draft was approaching, Modell knew he had to do whatever it took to get Phipps. On the eve of the first day of the draft, the Browns pulled off a pair of franchise-altering trades: They sent the man many considered the most dangerous wide receiver in football to Miami for the number three pick. Then they shipped starting defensive end Jim Kanicki, plus last year's first-round pick, fullback Ron Johnson, and a backup linebacker, Wayne Meylan, to the New York Giants for wide receiver Homer Jones.

Fan reaction was soundly tilted against the trades. In the *Plain Dealer* article "Sizzling Browns' Fans Scorch Phone Lines," transcripts of calls like this one from Bonnie O'Neill of Cleveland outnumbered positive reactions about ten to one: "It's the most ridiculous trade ever made. Warfield was experienced and good. Who is Phipps?"

Warfield's teammates had the gridiron pulled out from beneath their cleats by the trade. Fellow wide receiver Gary Collins was quoted in the Cleveland *Plain Dealer:* "Shocked. I can't believe it. I can't believe it. If anyone was secure on any team in pro football, I thought Paul Warfield was. I thought I might [be traded]. Paul Warfield is the best receiver in pro football. You've got to miss him. I never watched Homer Jones that closely because he's not my style. He's fast as the devil, but he doesn't have as many moves as Paul."

Well, we already saw that Phipps was a better version of Griese while at Purdue. And by the time of this trade Griese had picked up in the NFL where he'd left off in college. Phipps was bigger and stronger than Griese. Besides, the Browns would be getting Homer Jones to take Warfield's position at wide receiver. Before we admit with 20-20 hindsight that history would prove Bonnie O'Neill was absolutely right, let's take a look at the receiver that Art's friend, Giants owner Wellington Mara, was willing to trade:

### HOMER JONES 6'2", 215 POUNDS

He was drafted in 1963 by the Houston Oilers of the AFL in the fifth round at number thirty-three overall. The New York Giants also drafted him, in the 1963 NFL draft's twentieth round, number 278. He hurt his knee in Oilers training camp and was cut. The Giants paid his bus fare to New York and paid for knee surgery. He started playing for the Giants in 1964, the same year that Paul Warfield was drafted by the Browns.

He had three 1,000-yard seasons for the Giants and made the Pro Bowl in 1967 and 1968. In 1967 he led the league in touchdown receptions with 13. In 1965 he invented the "spike" of the ball in the end zone after scoring a touchdown. He started all 14 games for Giants in 1969, but although he caught 42 passes (he'd never caught more than 49 in a season), he averaged only 17.7 yards per catch—his lowest season average by far. He'd gone from catching 13 touchdowns in '67 to 7 in 1968, to just 1 in 1969.

If you look at the NFL all-time record for career yards per catch, Paul Warfield is number four on that list, with an incredible 20.1 yards per catch. Who is number one? None other than Homer Jones! His yards per catch figure is an insane 22.3!

Jones' Cleveland Browns debut was an auspicious one: the first-ever *Monday Night Football* game. He returned the second half opening kickoff for a touchdown against Joe Namath's New York Jets, and the Browns won 31-21. But knee injuries would plague him that year. He'd end up starting only four games and make just ten catches all year for 141 yards and one touchdown. After one season with the Browns, Jones was traded to St. Louis in 1971 but had to retire before playing a single game for them. It looks bleak when you consider Warfield's and Jones's production after the big trade.

### Before the trade:

**Paul Warfield** '64–'69 with Browns: 215 rec., 44 touchdowns, 1-time NFL Championship, 3-time Pro Bowler.
**Homer Jones** '64–'69 with Giants: 214 rec., 35 TDs, 2x Pro Bowler.

### After the trade:

**Paul Warfield** '70–'74 with Dolphins: 156 rec., 33 TDs, 2x Super Bowl Champion, 5x Pro Bowler, 2x All-Pro.
**Homer Jones** '70 Browns, '71 traded to Cardinals: 10 rec., 1 TD with Browns in '70, retired due to injury before playing for St. Louis in '71.

Then Warfield played two more years for the Browns after playing the 1975 season for the Memphis Southmen in the short-lived World Football League. Warfield scored a total of six more touchdowns over the final two seasons in Cleveland, totaling 52 overall while in a Browns uniform. He made the Hall of Fame in his first year of eligibility. As recently as 2019, NFL.com writer Elliot Harrison rated Paul Warfield number one on his "Top 20 Traded Players" list. Trading away Warfield was the Browns equivalent of the Indians trading Rocky Colavito.

In reality, Warfield was *not* traded for Jones. Warfield was traded to Miami for their number three pick, which became Mike Phipps. Had Phipps followed the same trajectory that his predecessor at Purdue, NFL Hall of Famer Bob Griese, traced through his NFL career, the Browns would have made a solid or perhaps brilliant trade. Phipps was bigger than Griese, stronger than Griese, and had erased all Griese's Purdue passing records. So, how did Phipps do for the Cleveland Browns?

He didn't start until his third year in the NFL. He was the primary starter for the Browns for most of four seasons and was traded to Chicago after seven years in the league. Too bad he wasn't a defensive end, because he led the NFL in sacks and sack yardage in 1973. Over his career, he threw almost exactly twice as many interceptions as touchdowns. Phipps probably could have used an elite receiver; too bad they had to trade one to bring Phipps aboard.

Whatever way you look at it (from a Cleveland perspective), the whole thing was an unmitigated disaster:

**Warfield** goes to Miami, continues to excel, wins two Super Bowls, is named All-Pro twice more, and is named to the Hall of Fame.

**Phipps** comes to Cleveland, never establishes himself, mix of cheers and apathy when he leaves after seven years. In Chicago he salvages his career record, bolstering his Browns-era record of 24-25-2 to a career record of 38-31-2 after going 14-6 for the Bears.

**Jones** comes to Cleveland, makes ten catches, retires after one injury-riddled season.

**Johnson** goes to Gotham to play for the Giants, lives up to his first-round status with two 1,000-yard seasons. His quarterback Fran Tarkenton exclaims, "Johnson is the best halfback in football today . . . period! He's just a devastating football player."

**Kanicki** goes to the Giants, starts all fourteen games in year one and nine in year two, then retires.

The Indians have the "Curse of Rocky Colavito." The Browns one-upped them with the "Curse of Paul Warfield."

14

# BIRTH OF THE MODERN NFL

1970

*Professional football reconfigured into NFL-only with two conferences:* the National Football Conference and the American Football Conference. Rather than keep the original NFL's sixteen teams together as the new NFC and lump the ten AFL teams into the AFC, as some owners wished, the Browns, Steelers, and Colts agreed to "come over" from the NFL to the AFC.

This was the year the Browns took quarterback Mike Phipps out of Purdue with the number three pick overall. They'd select solid defensive tackle Jerry Sherk in the second round. But Steelers got Hall of Famers Terry Bradshaw number one overall and, with the first pick in round three, cornerback Mel Blount, who was inducted in 1989.

The first *Monday Night Football* game ever was played in week one of the 1970 season and featured "Broadway Joe" Namath and the New York Jets, who were one year removed from their Super Bowl victory after the 1968 season, against Art Modell's team in Cleveland Municipal Stadium. The Browns shone under the bright lights and won 31-21, despite New York rolling up twice as many yards. It was a great start to the decade, but the glory wouldn't persist through the season and certainly not through the seventies.

The Browns finished second in the AFC Central at 7-7 and failed to make the playoffs. In a blow to Modell, Paul Brown's Cincinnati Bengals won the division, earning a spot in the postseason. Cincinnati would not last long in the playoffs, but that wasn't much consolation to

Modell. The Bengals lost to Colts in the first round. Modell's nemesis since after the 1964 season, the Colts, ended up beating Dallas to win the Super Bowl. The Super Bowl!

The Browns would win the division (for the first and last time in the 1970s) at 9-5 in 1971. They lost in the playoffs first round. To the *Colts*!

In 1972, Cleveland would improve its record to 10-4. But it was only good for second place as the historically inept Pittsburgh Steelers were starting their ascendancy to 1970s domination. The Browns made the playoffs as a wild-card and, in the fourth quarter, led the heavily favored Miami Dolphins.

With their historic lossless season on the line, the Dolphins drove 80 yards to pull ahead with a little over four minutes left. The Browns had two chances to reclaim the lead and win the game. Their first series ended in a punt, the second in an interception. It was Mike Phipps's fifth (FIFTH!) interception of the game! Miami's quarterback, Earl Morrall (remember him from the Baltimore Colts?), completed passes to former Brown Paul Warfield twice on the game-winning drive.

Miami, in large part because of the contribution of Paul Warfield, would win their next playoff game and then the Super Bowl to finish 17-0 for the NFL's first and only perfect season. While it wasn't the Colts who victimized the Browns this year, it was former Colts coach Don Shula, with the Dolphins since 1970, who led Miami to glory.

The Browns would not taste the playoffs again in the 1970s. The Rolling Stones named an album for them, *Sucking in the Seventies*. Okay, maybe the Stones had other reasons for naming their album . . . but it fits. Former doormat Pittsburgh won four Super Bowls in the decade. The Browns who had gone 16-4 against Pittsburgh in the 1950s and 15-5 against them in the 1960s, won only 5 of 20 contests against their rivals in the 1970s.

## October 3, 1970 – Cleveland Municipal Stadium

Nobody knew it at the time. Probably nobody knows it now. But the October 3, 1970, game against the Steelers would be historically significant, marking the official end of an era. The Browns would play a Pittsburgh team that had not won its division since the Steelers were formed in 1933. The Steelers had never won a playoff game in their history. Conversely, the Browns had won the division thirteen times, had won seven playoff games, including four NFL Championships, all since 1950. (These figures don't even include their dominant AAFC stint.)

On this early October day in 1970, Browns rookie Mike Phipps came on in relief of starter Don Gault and threw for one touchdown. It was enough to outduel fellow rookie Terry Bradshaw, who gift-wrapped three interceptions.

The historic significance: With that day's win, Cleveland would reach its high-water mark in games above .500 against the Pittsburgh Steelers at 23. Since the Browns entered the NFL in 1950, they'd played the Steelers twice each season. After that October 3 game, the Browns' all-time record against the sad sacks from Western Pennsylvania stood at 32-9. By the end of the 1970 season, Pittsburgh would get revenge and cut Cleveland's edge to 22 games. The delta would bounce between 21 and 22 until 1974 when the Steelers began to steadily to chip away.

Nobody could imagine it in 1970, but one day in the next millennium, the Steelers would balance the scale. Slowly, agonizingly, the Browns' massive advantage ebbed away to nothing. Then Pittsburgh methodically added coin after golden coin to their side of the scale in a quest to tip it in their favor in equal magnitude to the Browns' massive advantage of October 3, 1970.

15

# BOMB CITY, USA

## Mid-1970s in Cleveland

*While Cleveland was not famous for football in this decade of disco and* the gas shortage, there were two things that put the city in the national spotlight. Like the Cuyahoga River fire in the late 1960s, these were things that further damaged whatever prestige the city had left. They inculcated the idea that this metropolis on the shores of Lake Erie was more "Mistake on the Lake" than "Best Location in the Nation."

Like in most big American cities, there was organized crime in Cleveland throughout the twentieth century. The various factions had their criminal specialties and territories. There were plenty of innocent victims, but largely these gangs operated in the shadows. Rival gangs were usually the target of their killings.

In the seventies, the Cleveland criminal underground exploded (literally) onto the front pages of papers throughout the nation. Danny Greene lit the fuse. Greene was an intelligent, athletic kid who lost his mother three days after she gave birth to him. His dad took to drinking and sent him to live at Parmadale, a Catholic orphanage a few miles away.

When his father remarried, he took the six-year-old Danny back in. But his father's new wife and Danny fought, and Danny repeatedly ran away, eventually moving in for good with his paternal grandfather. The grandfather worked the night shift. Danny roamed the streets and caused mischief. He'd have failed out of school, but the nuns valued his athletic prowess, and he could lay on the charm.

He was kicked out of St. Ignatius High School for tardiness and for fighting with the Italian kids, whom he hated. He attended public Collinwood High School for a while but was expelled due to truancy. He joined the Marine Corps and excelled at boxing and marksmanship. After two years he was honorably discharged.

Danny Greene returned to Cleveland and became a longshoreman. In the early sixties when the International Longshoreman's Association removed the local union president, they appointed Greene to that role. He easily won reelection at the end of the term. He didn't shy away from using violence and intimidation to help both workers and management to see the wisdom of his ways. Greene unlawfully enriched himself along the way. He was soon expelled from the union and convicted of embezzlement, a charge that was later appealed and overturned.

By the time the seventies rolled around, Greene had worked as muscle for the Mafia and for Shondor Birns, the leader of Cleveland's Jewish mob. When the long-serving head of the Cleveland Mafia, John Scalish, died, Shondor Birns backed James Licavoli to become boss. Danny Greene was connected to Licavoli's rival, mobbed-up union leader John Nardi. This put Greene and the powerful and popular Birns at odds.

The relative peace and nonviolence that marked Scalish's reign were replaced by bloodshed. Besides the run-of-the-mill shootings, something new sent shockwaves of terror through the community. The weapon of choice was car bombs. Between 1975 and 1977, thirty-seven car bombs exploded in Cleveland and its suburbs, earning Cleveland the nickname Bomb City, USA. Greene was a suspect in the lion's share of the bombings.

Greene ordered the bombing that killed Shondor Birns on the day between Good Friday and Easter Sunday in 1975. The blast was so strong that it blew its victim through the roof of his Lincoln, several feet into the air. When his body landed beside his suddenly convertible car in the parking lot near St. Malachi's church on West 25th, it was not in one piece. It was as if he'd been sawed in half at the waist.

On October 6, 1977, as Greene walked to his car in a parking lot after visiting a dentist in an eastern suburb, the hunter became the hunted. The bomber was bombed. The car next to his had been planted with explosives. When Greene got close, the charge was detonated, and Greene was killed immediately.

The bombings ended along with Danny Greene's earthly life. But the aftershocks would haunt Clevelanders for years and further sully whatever was left of Cleveland's reputation.

16

# BANKRUPT!

December 15, 1978

*Barely a month after Danny Greene was blown up, the thirty-one-*year-old "Boy Mayor" Dennis Kucinich was elected mayor of Cleveland. He may not have used bombs, but he was incendiary, and he made enemies. Kucinich practiced "confrontational politics" and was unyielding in fighting for what he thought was right, consequences be damned.

Cleveland was already in a cash crunch, and the previous mayor, Republican Ralph Perk, had made the controversial decision to sell the city-owned Municipal (Muny) Light electrical utility to the investor-owned Cleveland Electric Illuminating (CEI) company.

Part of the reason the city was in dire financial straits was the history of foul play where CEI lobbied Cleveland City Council for restrictive policies preventing Muny Light from issuing bonds to repair its generators. Without working generators, Muny Light was forced to buy power from CEI. CEI price gouged, and Muny lost money with every electron they sold, racking up $14 million in debt. In 1975 the city filed a $328 million anti-trust suit against CEI.

Kucinich's predecessor, Perk, eventually relented and agreed to sell Muny Power to CEI. The plan was that CEI would then forgive the city's debt, and the city would drop the lawsuit against CEI.

Once in power, Kucinich stopped the sale and revived the anti-trust lawsuit. This left the city $14 million in debt. Through court actions, CEI moved to attach city-owned property. The banks, the business community, George Forbes, and the city council all were all in favor of selling Muny Light to CEI. The brash young mayor wouldn't buckle and proposed to lay off 600 city workers, including 400 police and firefighters, to make up for the mountain of debt. He also proposed a hike in the city's income tax.

In mid-December 1978, three of the banks that held notes on the city's debt showed up at City Hall. They presented the notes to the City of Cleveland's treasurer and demanded that the city redeem them. They explained they were open to "a financial plan satisfactory to all parties involved."

It was a showdown. The banks were there to force the city's hand. This was the stuff of front-page news, and not just in Cleveland. Reporters from across the country came to document the standoff.

On December 14, an hour before midnight, the city council gave Kucinich a choice to sell Muny Light or claim default on the loan. An hour later, at City Hall, in a closed-door meeting with city council members, bankers, and executives from CEI, Kucinich refused to sell.

That meant that Cleveland became the first major city since the Great Depression to enter bankruptcy.

In August 1978, Kucinich squeaked through a recall election, which would have removed him from office. But his tenure was not to last much longer. In 1979, George Voinovich, who had been serving as lieutenant governor of Ohio, beat Kucinich by 20,000 votes to unseat the Boy Mayor.

When Melvin G. Holli of the University of Illinois at Chicago surveyed historians, political scientists, and urban experts in 1993, they determined Kucinich to be the seventh worst out of 730 mayors who served U.S. cities between 1820 and 1993. He ranked second worst since 1960. From Holli's 1999 book *The American Mayor: The Best & The Worst Big-City Leaders*:

> Cleveland's "boy" mayor had failings that were not the sins of venality or graft for personal gain, but rather matters of style, temperament, and bad judgment in office. Kucinich earned seventh place the hard way: by his abrasive, intemperate, and confrontational populist political style, which led to a disorderly and chaotic administration.

In the 1970s, football in Cleveland was not good. But there were a lot of worse things to take your mind off the Browns.

## 17

# CARDIAC ARREST—RED RIGHT 88

JANUARY 4, 1981 – CLEVELAND MUNICIPAL STADIUM, DIVISIONAL ROUND AFC PLAYOFFS

*"Damn, this is some cold-ass weather!" Tyrone stammered out the words* from beneath his fur hat, with its ear flaps battened down in a vain effort to keep his head from freezing off. "Browns better win this game. I'm not standin' out here for four hours for a loss." The trickle from his nose had frozen solid in his mustache.

"You kiddin' me?" Willie said. "These the Kardiac Kids, man. They ain't gonna lose. They might go down by three touchdowns, but they'll find a way to come back." Though he must have been frozen, Willie didn't seem quite as affected by the cold. Well, at least his *mouth* didn't seem to be affected by the cold.

"Yeah, and besides, this is our weather," Tyrone said. "This California team ain't used to this shit. Man, they got palm trees and shit out there, they ain't got ice and snow and nasty wind."

Willie's massive boom box told him and everyone else in section 42 what they already knew: "Game time weather today: zero degrees, and with the wind-chill at 36 below, this is the coldest game since the 1967 Ice Bowl between the Cowboys and Packers."

Tyrone handed Willie the silver flask he'd smuggled in. "Have a sip a' this. It'll warm you up. Well, it won't, but you won't care as much."

The Browns were in the playoffs for the first time in seven years. They came close last year, with the emergence of quarterback Brian Sipe and what were dubbed the Kardiac Kids because of their habit of winning (and sometimes losing) games in the final seconds. The '79 Browns were the most exciting team in football with twelve games decided in the last minute, most of them wins. The most notable loss was to the Steelers at Three Rivers. The defending Super Bowl champions beat the Browns 33-30 in overtime to plunge a dagger into Cleveland's 1979 playoff hopes.

The 1980 season was when the Browns finally broke through. They beat out the four-time Super Bowl Champion Steelers and the formidable Houston Oilers to win the toughest division in the NFL—the AFC Central. And, as in 1979, this year's Kardiac Kids won (and lost) with a flair for the dramatic.

*. . . We interrupt this frigid playoff game to flash back to some highlights of the magical 1980 season:*

Week 7 – Initially up by a score of 13-0, the Browns gave up three successive touchdowns to the Packers and trailed 21-13 with just over 7 minutes left in the game. Cleveland's Dino Hall returned the kickoff to the Browns' 31. Two plays, 69 yards, and just 28 seconds later, Sipe had connected with Ozzie Newsome in the end zone. After Cockroft's point after touchdown (PAT), the Browns were down 21-20.

Green Bay put together a drive, taking more than 4 minutes off the clock. They were finally stopped on a third and 7 and had to punt. The Browns would start their drive at their own 13-yard line with just 1:53 on the clock. Sipe passed and scrambled his way down the field. A holding penalty and two missed pass attempts had the Browns facing third down and 20 at the Packers' 46 with just 25 seconds left. We now join Browns radio broadcasters Gib Shanley and Jim Mueller.

Shanley: "Oh, what a ballgame. The Kardiac Kids are at it again."

Mueller: "Are we gonna go down to the wire or are we gonna go down to the wire?!"

Shanley: "Why not, we've done it all year."

Mueller: "Clock down to 24 seconds."

Shanley: "Time to get nervous! Sipe throwing to Logan! He got it over the 20, 10, 5, touchdown! Dave Logan!"

Mueller: "Touchdown by Dave Logan, 46 yards, I don't believe it!"

Shanley: "Sixteen seconds remaining, what a play!"

The Browns prevailed, 26-21 to improve to 4-3 on the season.

One week later: The Browns had not beaten the Steelers in over four years. Cleveland trailed Pittsburgh by scores of 10-0, 20-7, and

26-14 during this game at Cleveland Stadium. Cleveland began the fourth quarter down 12 points against the defending World Champions. Sipe hit Greg Pruitt on a short pass for a touchdown with about 5:30 minutes left, his third touchdown pass of the game—all to halfbacks. Pittsburgh was unable to score, and Cleveland got the ball back. The Browns navigated down to the Pittsburgh 18 with time running out in the fourth quarter. Again, Gib Shanley and Jim Mueller pick up the action:

Mueller: "...and the Kardiac Kids are at work today. Another pressure play for Brian Sipe."

Shanley: "Sipe to throw ... to Newsome, and ... HE GOT IT! In the corner of the end zone! Brian Sipe has now thrown for four."

Mueller: "And another Kardiac finish."

Cockroft would make the extra point, breaking the 26-26 tie, giving the Browns their first lead. But could they hold it? The defense held Pittsburgh to a three and out. Pittsburgh returned the favor.

Pittsburgh's reserve quarterback, who'd played well in place of the injured Terry Bradshaw all game, got the ball back with 3:53 on the clock, at the Steeler's 20. Cliff Stoudt completed three passes for 20 yards. On second and 5, he threw toward the sideline to Jim Smith. Browns cornerback Ron Bolton cut in front of Smith and made the interception! The Browns ended up punting, but Pittsburgh ran out of time. The next morning the Cleveland *Plain Dealer* ran a story called "Comeback by Browns Ends Steelers' Spell." Could this little quarterback and his Kardiac Kids reverse the Curse? Could this really be the year?

The rematch was three weeks later at Three Rivers Stadium, which had opened in 1970 and in which the Cleveland Browns had never won. This time, Pittsburgh—after trailing all game—would come from behind with a 16-13 defeat of the Browns. Terry Bradshaw hit Lynn Swann for a touchdown with eleven seconds left in the game. Even in defeat, these Kardiac Kids could stop your heart!

In the next-to-last game of the 1980 season, against the Vikings, the Browns were still in the hunt for the AFC Central Division championship. At 10-4 the Browns had a one-game edge on the Houston Oilers. A win at Minnesota would ensure a playoff berth for the Browns. The Vikings, with a win, or a loss by the Detroit Lions, would win the NFC Central. A lot was riding on this game.

Halfway through the fourth quarter, the Browns held a 23-9 lead. Things were looking good. But these Kardiac Kids had a knack for drama. As it was often said in this era, tickets to Cleveland games should carry the disclaimer: "The Surgeon General has determined that watching the Browns could be hazardous to your health." That would certainly ring true today.

Minnesota scored a touchdown but missed the extra point. The score stood at 23-15. The Vikings kicked off, and Cleveland started out at their 25. Cleveland ran three times for a first down, then ran some more. They were milking the clock. Uncharacteristically boring for the Kardiac Kids but, so far, effective.

Time was down to 2:18. On second and 8, the Browns went against convention, and Sipe dropped back to pass. A screen to Cleo Miller was the call, but he was well covered. Sipe checked down to Reggie Rucker who was at about the first down marker at the 50. The pass went instead directly to the Minnesota defensive back Bobby Bryant. Interception.

Five plays, 47 yards, and just 37 seconds later, Tommy Kramer hit Ahmad Rashad in the end zone. It was Rashad's first touchdown catch in ten games, despite having amassed about 1,000 receiving yards. This time the PAT was good, and the Vikings trailed by only a single point. One minute 35 seconds remained.

The Vikings lined up for an onside kick. Rick Danmeier's kick traveled only 9 yards, instead of the required 10. The Browns automatically got the ball, at the Minnesota 44, with 1:35 left to play. Things were still looking good. After a few runs, a penalty on the Browns, and after the Vikings had burned their last two timeouts, the Browns called a timeout. Twenty-three seconds stood between them and victory. It was fourth down and about 2 yards to go. The Browns opted to punt.

Fourteen seconds left, no timeouts, 80 yards from the end zone. Probably 50 or so yards to field goal range. It was not looking good for the Vikings. The first-down play was a pass but surprisingly to the middle of the field. It was a perfectly executed lateral from Joe Senser to Ted Brown that made the play work. Brown received the lateral at the Minnesota 30 and hustled down to the Browns' 46, making it out of bounds to stop the clock at 0:05.

Minnesota had time for only one more play. Too far for a field goal. Not enough time to complete a pass in field goal range and get out of bounds to stop the clock. The Browns had led the game for 59 minutes and 55 seconds. Could these Kardiac Kids hold on and win the game, and with it, the divisional championship?

Minnesota lined up three receivers on the right side. Kramer dropped back behind midfield and heaved it high and long. A gaggle of Browns defenders and Vikings receivers were clustered together in a moving mob between the 10- and 5-yard lines as the ball was dropping from the apex of its arc.

Time ticked down from 0:01 to 0:00. The first hand to touch the football was Cleveland's Thom Darden's. He deflected it at the 5, upward, and it came down into the waiting hands of Ahmad Rashad, who gathered it in at the 1. The players' momentum carried them all into the end zone. Touchdown Minnesota! Victory Minnesota! Instant NFC Central Champions: Minnesota!

The Kardiac Kids had struck again. But this time it was a heart attack, not just palpitations. All Browns fans could do was watch their TVs in disbelief. Winning all game, it all evaporated in an instant. A literal instant. AFC Central rival Houston won big that day. Houston and Cleveland both now stood at 10-5. Still, the Browns could win the division and make the playoffs with a victory in the season's final week, against division foe Cincinnati. Cue the dramatic NFL Films score! *Dah—da-dah—da-da-dah. . . .*

18

# PAUL BROWN'S BENGALS BID FOR REVENGE

DECEMBER 21, 1980 – CINCINNATI RIVERFRONT STADIUM

*Final week of the regular season: Even if they could manage a win today* against the Browns, the Bengals would finish with a losing record at 7-9. Win or lose, they were assured of missing the playoffs. However, they could play spoilers and prevent the Browns from winning the division by knocking them off. In fact, by beating Cleveland the Bengals could knock Cleveland completely out of the playoffs . . . just like they did last year! The Kardiac Kids' magical dreams could end in a nightmare. The Curse would be extended.

Were the Bengals motivated to win? Consider this: Their owner, Paul Brown, the very namesake of the Cleveland Browns, had been fired as head coach by the current owner of today's opponent, Art Modell. Cincinnati's head coach, Forrest Gregg, had been Cleveland's head coach until he was fired by Art Modell in 1977—one year after winning the Associated Press Coach of the Year Award. These Bengals were desperate to make the Browns lose. It was as though these Bengals were crouched in the jungle, eying their prey, muscles tensed, teeth clenched, raring to pounce, and thirsty for brown and orange blood!

These Kardiac Kids who'd come out of nowhere last year and just missed the playoffs would not be denied this year. Would they? What was the point of all the drama and magic, if it would all end here today on the frozen artificial turf of Riverfront Stadium? True, the entertainment value had been very high; even casual fans caught "Kardiac disease"... and were happy for having the ailment. But the playoffs and championships were what Arthur Modell wanted, and so did the fans.

Art had fired Paul Brown and Forrest Gregg to try to get back to prominence. Had he not fired Paul Brown, would there even be a Cincinnati Bengals football team? Ironically, it was now Paul Brown and his team who would actively engage in preventing the Browns from reaching their dream—to arrest these Kardiac Kids.

"In the season finale the Bengals and Browns traded blow for blow; touchdown for touchdown, in one of 1980's most spectacular games," narrated John Facenda in the NFL Films recap of the game. The blows were fierce. Brian Sipe, who was sacked only seventeen times in the previous fifteen games, was taken down four times by the Bengals in the first half alone, and six times in the game. Bengals wide receiver (and punter) Pat McInally was popped hard by Thom Darden (who received a roughing penalty) and was removed from the field on a stretcher after lying on the frosty field for ten minutes. It didn't take a doctor to see it was unlikely he would return to action in today's game—or possibly ever.

The Bengals would draw first blood soon after, with a 42-yard field goal. The Browns' offense was stymied for most of the first half by the rabid Bengals defense. Finally, Sipe hooked up on a 65-yard completion to Dave Logan. Soon thereafter, Cincinnati strip-sacked the Browns' quarterback and recovered to stop the threat. Moments later, with about 10 minutes left in the half, Bengals quarterback Jack Thompson scrambled in from 13 yards to put Cincinnati up 10-0. Art Modell's brow started beading with sweat, despite the arctic conditions.

Finally, with good pass protection from the offensive line, Sipe struck. He lofted a beautiful pass to a wide-open Reggie Rucker along the right sideline for a 42-yard touchdown. Don Cockroft added the PAT, and the Bengals' lead was cut to 3. This inspired the Browns' defense, and they forced a punt. After Cleveland made some headway, the Bengals bagged Sipe once again and forced a Browns punt.

The short punt skittered along, hitting a retreating Cincinnati player along the way. Live ball! Hall recovered it at the Cincinnati 9. A few plays later, with mere seconds left in the half, Cockroft tied the score with a field goal.

Shortly after halftime, Cincinnati's Ray Griffin intercepted a Sipe pass and returned 52 yards for a touchdown. Cincy reclaimed the lead, 17-10. An afternoon "double feature" was about to ensue. Within a few minutes, Browns' reserve wide receiver Ricky Feacher would score on a pair of touchdown passes from the league leader in touchdown passes: a 35 yarder, then a 34 yarder.

Sandwiched between these scores, which came only two minutes apart, were a Jack Thompson interception, a three and out by the Browns, a Browns punt that again was muffed by the Cincinnati returner, and another fumble recovery by Dino Hall. Phew, what a game! With these scores, the Browns took back the lead, 24-17.

Swift revenge.

When Thom Darden laid out Pat McInally early in the game, it was reasonable to wonder if he would *ever* play football again. For him to return to this game was beyond imagination. But that is what he did! He would catch three passes in the second half for 83 yards. None was bigger than the one he caught with 15 seconds left in the third quarter: a 59-yard bomb down the left sideline. He was caught and tackled at about the 2, but landed on top of Cleveland's would-be tackler, never hitting the ground, and he bounced into the end zone for the touchdown. The score was 24-24 heading to the fourth quarter.

Sipe threw another interception and the Bengals put together a combination of runs and pass plays. Another pass to McInally gave Cincinnati a first down at the Cleveland 22-yard line. On second down, Thompson passed over the middle and was intercepted by Thom Darden at the 8. He returned it to the 27 to squelch the present threat and give the Kardiac Kids some hope of their own.

Sipe started the drive with a short completion to Calvin Hill. From here, though, the high-flying aerial offense would shift to a running attack. The Browns astonishingly ran seven straight times, with Mike Pruitt carrying the load, smashing through the 1,000-yard mark in the process.

Finally, the Pruitt express was halted, and Cockroft was sent in with around a minute and a half left to try the field goal. He made it, and the Browns took back the lead, 27-24. Could they hold it, win the division, and head to the playoffs for the first time in seven years? Or would these kooky Kardiac Kids take it down to the wire?

Venerable Ken Anderson came into the game as quarterback for the home team. After a handoff for a short run and an incomplete pass, he hooked up with Steve Kreider for 32 yards, to the Browns' 43-yard line—still outside of field goal range. Well less than a minute remained. These Browns wouldn't be the Kardiac Kids if it was easy. Anderson connected with Dan Ross for 9 yards, to the 34, but he stayed in bounds. With time ticking down, Anderson fired the ball out of bounds to stop the clock with 0:04 remaining.

Everyone's hearts were in their throats! Modell was panicking. To be knocked out of the playoffs after such a year would be a crime. To have it happen at the hands of Paul Brown and Forrest Gregg would be like going to the electric chair! For that to happen two years in a row would be like catching fire in the electric chair and being slowly roasted in agony!

Still too far for a field goal, Cincinnati would try to win it the way Minnesota did the previous week . . . with a last-second pass for a touchdown. To lose back-to-back like that and miss the playoffs, that would be too much to bear! Cleveland fans watching from home had to change the channel. Or take a bathroom break. Or head to the fridge for another beer. Only a true masochist could bear to watch the action play out live.

The television announcers narrated the action:

"Four seconds left in the ballgame, what a way to end the season!"

"I'll say. The Bengals will either score a touchdown here and possibly knock the Browns out of the playoffs for the second straight year, or, if they can't, the Browns will win the division and play on in two weeks."

"The snap to Anderson, back to pass. He hits Kreider toward the right sideline, but well in bounds! He's taken down at the 14 by Ron Bolton! That's it, ballgame! Browns win! The Cleveland Browns are AFC Central Champions and going to the playoffs for the first time since '72!"

"What a way to get in! These Kardiac Kids have got to be the most exciting team I have ever seen!"

Sam Rutigliano, United Press International's coach of the year, was ecstatic and appreciative of his players after the game. In just his second year as a head coach, they had gotten him to the playoffs. The team would be able to enjoy Christmas and have a weekend off from football as the wild-card round was played.

19

# RED RIGHT 88 CONTINUED

BACK TO JANUARY 4, 1981 – CLEVELAND MUNICIPAL STADIUM

... *We now rejoin the 77,655 frigid fans in Cleveland where the Raiders* were set to take on the Browns. Before kickoff, Willie pressed the button on the boom box to play the cassette tape. He cranked it up loud. It was a song everyone knew by heart. Though it had only been released a few weeks ago, you couldn't escape it in Cleveland. The record had sold something like 150,000 copies.

Like the Christmas carol it was based on, the song goes on, and on, but the end of it went like this:

*On the twelfth day of Christmas, Art Modell gave to me:*
*The Browns in the playoffs*
*Dave Logan leapin'*
*Doug Dieken blockin'*
*DeLeone a-hikin'*
*Kardiac Kids a-winnin'*
*Darden interceptin'*
*Newsome a-catchin'*
*B o t h P r u i t t s Moooves*
*Alzado attackin'*
*Brian Sipe a-passin'*
*Don Cockroft a-kickin'*
*On a Rutigliano Super Bowl team*

Willie held up the boom box in one hand and a flask in the other as the fans of section 42 howled in approval. "Sipe-Er-Bowl! Sipe-Er-Bowl!" The chant spread around the cavernous stadium, until the old steel, aluminum, and concrete structure seemed to convulse. Or maybe it was just everyone shivering!

"Man, it sure is damn cold, let's start this game!" Tyrone exclaimed to no one, to everyone.

The fans' perseverance was not rewarded with offensive highlights, as neither team could score in the first quarter. How could they? Not only were their offenses lined up against the opponent's eleven defenders, they also had to contend with something even more formidable: the weather. It was like trying to summit Mount Everest.

Walking 100 feet, even uphill, is simple enough—at sea level. But on Everest, in the oxygen-depleted, frigid atmosphere at 29,000 feet above sea level, taking even a few steps requires immense will, intense concentration, and is still extremely difficult.

And so it was on the shores of Lake Erie at just 580 feet above sea level, in the equally inhospitable conditions at Cleveland Municipal Stadium. Nothing but pure misery for the wide receivers trying to make a catch, the running backs trying to make a cut, the kickers trying to make a field goal, the numb-handed quarterbacks trying to accept the snap from the centers. And if the quarterback could get the snap, good luck trying to steer the ball through the snarling wind toward a target who may or may not get to where he intends to be to try to catch the ball.

Some first quarter "highlights":

On Oakland's first possession: three and out, punt.

On Cleveland's first possession: three and out, punt.

Oakland's second possession: no first downs, long pass by Jim Plunkett intercepted by Ron Bolton.

Cleveland ran three times and achieved the game's first first-down. Then a dropped pass, and Mike Pruitt slipping before taking the hand-off, and the Browns had to punt again.

On third and 7, Plunkett made a nice pass, good enough for a first down . . . but it was dropped. Punt.

Sipe passed, and missed, passed and the receiver couldn't hold on, passed for Reggie Rucker, but was picked off by Oakland's Lester Hayes. The Molester's sixteenth interception of the season!

Oakland then went three and out, punt.

Cleveland tried a long pass to Rucker again on third down. Incomplete. Punt.

On third and 3, Plunkett put a long pass right into Raymond Chester's hands. He couldn't hold on. Incomplete. Punt.

Keith Wright received the punt for the Browns and almost broke free, returning it to the Browns' 40. His head hit the frozen turf during the tackle, knocking him out cold; he couldn't return to action.

The Browns mounted a drive. A 20-yard pass to Rucker (that he caught!) to the Oakland 40. A few more positive plays and it was first and 10 from around the 28-yard line. The first quarter had dwindled down to just 7 seconds remaining. Reggie Rucker ran a fly pattern. The league's best passer lofted a ball that came down right into the basket, right over the shoulder into Rucker's waiting hands.

On the NBC telecast, both Don Criqui and John Brodie exclaimed, "Touchdown!"—and a half beat later, "He dropped the ball!" Rucker's momentum would take him through the end zone, and unable to slow himself on the ice and snow, he fell into the third base dugout. Fortunately, he was unhurt . . . but probably not happy.

The first quarter ended with a score of 0-0.

The teams changed ends to start the second quarter, and now the Browns would be heading into the wind, toward the open end of the stadium, toward Tyrone and Willie's end. The Browns now had the ball, second and 10 at the Raiders' 29.

"Man, Reggie coulda caught that ball! But he wanted to score in front of us," Willie told Tyrone, and anyone else in earshot.

"That would be nice, but I just wish we got the touchdown," Tyrone replied flatly. If the wind and cold hadn't already taken their breath away, the action they saw developing now would have had that effect. Ozzie Newsome was streaking toward the left-side goal line pylon. Sipe's pass was up. It was headed to Newsome, and he was running right toward section 42!

As the ball came down, it sailed just past Newsome's outstretched hands. His momentum carried him through the end zone and almost up the embankment.

"Aw man, shit! I wish he caught that!" Willie yelled.

"Yeah, he woulda probably handed the ball to us, too," Tyrone added.

"Aw man, don't tell me that!"

"Third down, we still got a shot."

"C'mon Browns, let's go!"

On third down, Sipe took a deep drop.

"He's goin' for it," Tyrone said.

Dave Logan was well covered, so Sipe checked down to a running back, but the pass was broken up.

Don Cockroft came on for the field goal attempt.

"Well, three's better than nothin'," Tyrone said.

"He ain't made nothin' yet," shot back Willie.

Now a hush descended on the crowd. The snap and hold were good. The kick . . . it barely went anywhere! It was probably never more than 12 feet off the ground and barely made it past the goal line.

"Aww shit," was all Willie could muster.

The Raiders finally got their first first-down of the game on their first play of the second quarter—a Plunkett pass to Raymond Chester for about 11 yards. Before Tyrone could express how nervous he was feeling, Plunkett was strip-sacked on the very next play. Number 91, defensive tackle Henry Bradley, forced the fumble, and number 90, defensive end Marshall Harris, recovered on the Raiders' 23-yard line!

"We got it now!" Willie yelled. "We got it now!"

Sipe dropped back to pass. Seeing nobody open, he did see a seam and ran for 10 yards to the 13-yard line.

"Way to go Sipe!" Willie liked what he saw. "Man, for such a scrawny dude, Sipe's tough!"

No gain on a Cleo Miller run set up second and 10. Then it happened again. Dave Logan streaked down the left sideline, again toward Willie and Tyrone. Sipe lofted the ball toward him, as he had toward Ozzie. This time it was not overthrown. But Raider's cornerback Dwayne O'Steen got inside position on Logan and knocked the ball away. Third and 10.

"Not again!" Willie yelled. "C'mon, we need a touchdown, Browns!"

Moving the ball was like scaling the Himalayas. Scoring was like trying to do it without using bottled oxygen. Again, Sipe dropped back. Reggie Rucker ran left to right through the end zone. Sipe threw the perfect pass. It came down in Rucker's hands.

NBC announcer Don Criqui: "He got it! No, they ruled he got it out of bounds."

Brodie: "Yeah, that's one of those plays, that if the field hadn't been frozen, he'd have been able to slow his momentum and get his other foot in bounds."

"Rucker should have two touchdowns now!" Willie complained. "We should be up 14-nothin'." Tyrone just nodded and pulled his hat down over his ears.

"Aw, man," Willie said. "Here comes Cockroff again."

"Well, this is a short one . . . like 30 yards," Tyrone said. "We'll take 3."

Again, a good snap, and a good hold. But again, the ball looked like a frozen, waterlogged pillow coming off Cockroft's foot. It was a better kick than last time. But only slightly better, and not good enough. Though a short attempt, it barely had the distance, but it missed wide left. It was like trying to climb an icy mountain wearing hockey skates. Still no score.

Oakland had to punt after three plays on fourth and 12. The Browns' Dino Hall returned it 4 yards to midfield.

"Man, our D got 'em locked down!" Willie said. "We just need to score!"

He was right. But he wasn't prophetic. At least not yet. The Browns gained around 20 yards, then gave most of it back when Ted Hendricks sacked Sipe on a third and 10. Again the Browns punted. Johnny Evans managed to send it only 26 yards, and the announcers, now calibrated to these artic conditions called it a good punt!

The Raiders ran a couple plays and found themselves at third and 3. Plunkett dropped back and threw toward the right sideline. He connected, but not with his receiver. Ron Bolton jumped the route, intercepted, and ran in untouched, from 42 yards out for the touchdown!

"Yeah! That's right! That's it, R.B., way to go!" Willie was pumped! He held his hands up to signal touchdown, and turned to face the fans behind him, his silver flask in one gloved hand, the other formed in a fist. "Yeah!" and he fist-bumped the high school kid behind him.

An extra point should be a gimme in the NFL. But when Cockroft came out, the crowd wasn't taking it for granted. Willie and Tyrone had had front row seats this quarter for his two botched field goal attempts. Tyrone was even quieter than usual, and eying the venerable kicker with suspicion. The snap and hold were good. But the kick? This time it looked like a bag of potatoes coming off the frozen field. This time it was dead straight. But it didn't make it to the crossbar. It was another low, short kick. It may have been partially blocked. It was not pretty, and it was no good. Still, the Browns held the lead, 6-0.

The Raiders would get a good return off the subsequent kickoff to their 36. Then, the team that had so far eked out just one first down, would methodically march down the field over the next 4 minutes. Plunkett would hook up with tight end Raymond Chester on a 26-yard pass to the Browns' 2-yard line with a minute left in the half.

On first and goal from the 2, Mark Van Eeghen would slip as he took the handoff and then fumble. It bounced right back to him, and he fell on it for a 1-yard gain. A Browns blitz would cause Plunkett to throw the ball away. His receiver was wide open. On third and 1, Van Eeghen scored the touchdown. The score was 6-6 pending the PAT. Whether it was Chris Bahr, or the fact that he was kicking on the opposite side of the field, his result was better than any of Cockroft's. Raiders 7. Cleveland 6.

Dino Hall returned the short kickoff to the Cleveland 35. With just 14 seconds left, Sipe wasn't just going to take a knee and head into the locker room. He took a deep drop and competed a long pass to Rucker, who got out of bounds at the Oakland 47 with 8 seconds. It wasn't the end of the game, but could the Kardiac Kids be up to something just before halftime? Sipe went for it all! He threw long for Logan, but Lester Hayes matched Ron Bolton with his second interception of the half. Browns down by 1 point going into halftime.

As the players and coaches headed to the locker rooms, Willie moaned, "Man, this ain't no fair. They get to go inside now, but we the ones payin' and we gotta stay outside and freeze!" At this particular moment, he wasn't the only one wishing the Browns played in a dome.

"Willie, next week they play in San Diego. Can you imagine sittin' there watching the game in shorts and a tank top, and sweatin' in the sun?"

"Yeah, that's where Sipe come from, man, he grew up out there. I don't even know how he can stand it out here in this cold, he's one tough dude. He is one tough and scrawny dude!"

"Well, I just hope we beat the Raiders and he can go back home and play in front of his mother and his cousins."

"Yeah, and after they beat the Chargers, you know what you got? The Sipe-er-Bowl!"

Willie and Tyrone started chanting. "Sipe-er-Bowl! Sipe-er-Bowl! and all of section 42 joined them, "SIPE-ER-BOWL! SIPE-ER-BOWL!!"

Before there could be a Sipe-er-Bowl, Brian Sipe would need to engineer a comeback—something that, fortunately, he had made a habit of the last two years. However, he had never had a half like this before: eighteen pass attempts and only six completions, but two of those were to Lester Hayes of the Oakland Raiders. The weather had taken a toll on the Browns' vaunted passing attack. It had hurt the Raiders' offense too, as evidenced by these halftime statistics:

First downs: Raiders, 6; Browns, 6
Yards rushing: Raiders, 27; Browns, 44
Yards passing: Raiders, 62; Browns, 38
Total yards: Raiders, 89; Browns, 82
Passing: Raiders, 7/18; Browns, 4/18
Turnovers: Raiders, 3; Browns, 2
Time of possession: Raiders, 15:59, Browns, 14:01

As can be seen from these underwhelming totals, the weather was the big winner of the first half. A cruel phenomenon was at play. The cold weather was responsible for the incompletions. The incompletions were responsible for stopping the game clock. The stopped game clock was responsible for forcing the players to play in the cold longer. And the longer they played in the cold, the less likely they were to complete passes. Worse yet for the players and especially for the fans, the second half promised more of the same.

Art Modell paced in the owner's suite. It was cold and drafty. He and his guests were shivering. While his guests chatted, ate, and drank, he reflected. It was almost exactly fifteen years ago that he'd won his first NFL championship in this very stadium. So far it had been his last. Was there really something to that crackpot and the mumbo-jumbo contract he'd signed?

Modell wished he could see that character now. Get him backed up against a wall and ask him flat out: "What did that contract say? Was there anything to it? How long were its terms? When will my Browns win again? When will we be on top again?"

Fifteen years was too long.

A guest broke Art's reverie, commenting, "We get the ball first in the second half, Art. I think we'll start taking charge."

The Browns would start at their own 39-yard line after Charles White returned the second half opening kickoff 25 yards from the 14. The weather would take a toll on a Calvin Hill run that went for 18 yards, out to the Oakland 28. The Browns' guards pulled right and formed a wall that took out would-be tacklers. Hill was free, though his momentum was carrying him gradually toward the sideline. The blockers had prevailed, and he had daylight, maybe all the way to the end zone. On any other day, he'd have made the gentle cut inside, effortlessly, unconsciously. But today, the frozen field made a mockery of any notion of cutting up the field, and Hill coasted, against his will, to the sideline and out of bounds.

A few plays later, on third and 3 from the 12, Sipe threw into the end zone but over the head of Dave Logan, whose momentum carried him into a snowbank, where he sank right down to his knees. They'd have to settle for a field goal—or an attempted field goal. The Browns were now heading toward the closed end of the stadium, where Cockroft had not yet made any attempts. This one would be about the same distance as an extra point. (But Cockroft had missed one of those already, too.) This time, his kick actually looked like an NFL field goal attempt. It was high, it was straight, it was GOOD! The Browns took the lead 9-7.

Oakland couldn't get a first down and punted after three plays. Dino Hall made a nice return to the Browns' 36-yard line. On second and 10, Sipe tossed it downfield to Greg Pruitt for a big gain to the Oakland 39.

"Pruitt can do it!" Willie yelled. "That's my man, that's my man!"

On a third and long, Sipe connected with Logan to the 24-yard line.

"Let's go Browns! Let's go Browns! Let's go Browns!"

The whole stadium was cheering as one. The Browns missed on a third and 5 from the 19. Cockroft came on to try a 36-yarder. Could he score again on this side of the field?

This time Cockroft didn't miss. He didn't make it either. Paul McDonald, the backup quarterback and holder, couldn't field the snap and never got the ball set. He picked it up and tried to run, but to no avail. The Raiders dodged a bullet and took over at their own 24-yard line.

They would make one first down but then miss a pass on third and 15 and need to punt. Little Dino Hall returned it to the Oakland 44, finally taken down on a solid tackle by the punter, Ray Guy.

"Yeah baby! That's the way, Dino!" Willie yelled, fired up over the excellent field position. "That's the way!"

The very next play Sipe hit Logan for a 22-yard gain to the Oakland 22.

"Whew, we are movin' now, we movin', T, we are movin'!" Willie—and more than 78,000 other freezing fans—were excited!

After a penalty on Oakland's defensive back, Dwane O'Steen, the Browns had a first down on the Oakland 9. On second and goal Oakland poked the ball out of Sipe's hand for a fumble, but the Browns recovered. Third and goal from around the 10. Sipe would pass into double coverage at the goal line to Dave Logan. Logan seemed to have it for a moment, but the ball popped loose, and like Logan and O'Steen, it just lay there in the icy end zone for several agonizing seconds.

Once more Cockroft came in to attempt another field goal, this time from what would normally be a very makeable 30 yards.

"Come on Cockroff, c'mon, man, ya gotta make this one."

It's doubtful "Cockroff" could hear Willie imploring him to make the kick. But he did it! And the Browns extended their lead 12-7, with 2:40 left in the third quarter.

The Raiders went three and out and punted. Dino Hall fumbled the return but recovered it himself and the Browns would start one more drive with the wind at their backs, and the sound kicking surface up ahead of them, should they need it, and be able to get that far in under two minutes. It was not to be. First a penalty on the Browns (their first of the game), then a bad center to quarterback exchange and a fumble that the Browns recovered, but all they could do was retreat and punt.

Johnny Evans's kick was not long, but Oakland misplayed it and the ball rolled all the way to the Raiders' 20. The Browns were lucky to make the best of a bad situation. After one uneventful play, the teams switched ends to begin the fourth quarter. The Raiders would have the wind at their backs the rest of the way. On a third down, under heavy pressure, Plunkett threw the ball under duress, underhand, to Mark Van Eeghen for a big first down. The next play was a long completion to Cliff Branch. The Raiders were moving.

"I don't like this. I do NOT like this!" Willie had seen the Raiders struggle all game long except when they pulled ahead after a long drive. This was starting to feel the same way.

On second down, Plunkett threw to Chester, all the way to the Browns' 16-yard line, a 27-yard gain!

"Oh shit . . . oh, man, this ain't good, T, this is NOT good." After a no-gain run, Plunkett hit Chester's outstretched hands at the goal line, but he couldn't haul it in. Third and 9, Plunkett dropped back again, and the Browns' Clarence Scott blitzed from the secondary and sacked the Oakland quarterback. But the Browns had jumped offsides, nullifying the play that would have forced the Raiders to try a field goal.

Replay third down, but now from just inside the 10-yard line, with 3 yards to go to make it first and goal. Plunkett dropped back to pass, looking into the end zone. Everyone was covered. He checked down to Kenny King who caught it at around the 5 and made his way to the 2 before being tackled. First and goal, Raiders.

"No! No! No!" Willie narrated the play. "Okay, hold 'em now! Stop 'em three times, make 'em kick a field goal!" The teams were way down at the other end of the field, and Tyrone and Willie wouldn't be able to tell if Oakland scored until they heard the crowd and watched the replay.

As the game clock ticked down to ten minutes, Oakland ran up the middle.

"Damn, did he get in?" Willie listened, looked around. He must not have. "Okay, stop 'em two more times. DEE-FENSE! DEE-FENSE! DEE-FENSE!" Willie shouted, trying to fire up the twelfth man.

From where Willie and Tyrone were sitting, it looked like the same play on second down. Indeed, it was, Van Eeghen off right guard, making it about half the distance to the goal line. Again, the Browns had held them out of the end zone.

"C'mon, one more time, D! Hey, we stopped 'em twice, we can stop 'em again, T!"

"I hope you right, Willie, I sure do."

For Oakland, the third try was the charm. Van Eeghen made it into the end zone to put the Raiders up 13-12, pending the extra point. Chris Bahr added the PAT and Oakland had a 2-point lead with around nine minutes left in the game.

"We got 'em right where we want 'em now, Willie," offered Tyrone.

"Man, what the *hell* are you talkin' about, T?"

"Willie, we the Kardiac Kids, remember?"

With that, Willie smiled. Tyrone was right. The Browns had made coming back to win a habit. Why stop now?

Dino Hall made a great kickoff return to the Browns' 41. Sipe tried to hit Greg Pruitt on a long pass on the first-down play, but overthrew him, overcompensating for the stiff wind. On second down, Sipe threw for Pruitt again, this time in the right flat. Again, the pass was incomplete. Third down and 10.

"Come on, Sipe! We need this! Right now, right now!" Willie was nervous now. The crowd was getting quiet.

The Raiders sent a blitz, but the O-line protected Sipe. He threw long, over the middle for Rucker. The frozen projectile hit his outstretched hand but glanced off and fell to the ground. The Browns would have to punt.

"Damn, this ain't good!" Willie's dreams were beginning to crumble.

"Willie, there's still a lot of time if we can stop 'em." Tyrone was right. But *could* they stop them? Both teams had enjoyed better success going the way Oakland would be going in this fourth quarter.

Johnny Evans got off a decent punt, considering the ball looked like a frozen rib roast coming off his foot. Oakland fair caught the ball at their own 27. Kenny King got almost 5 yards on the first play from scrimmage.

"Aw, T, this ain't good." Willie's spirit was flagging.

On second down, linebacker R.L. Jackson emphatically knocked Whittington back after no gain. The linebacker was fired up, and this helped buoy the crowd. On third and 5, Plunkett calmly checked down to Whittington over the middle for a 9-yard gain and a first down. The clock was running, and down to around 7 minutes.

"Come on, Browns! We gotta stop 'em!" Willie was almost delirious. The season was slipping away on this frozen field.

After a half-yard loss on first down, Plunkett took a deep drop. The Browns' pass rushing specialist Elvis Franks beat his man and sacked the QB for a big loss, back to the 33. Third and 19.

"Come on, sack 'em again! Elvis is in the building!" Willie was getting his trademark swagger back. He high-fived Tyrone through their heavy gloves.

Plunkett dropped back, but then Van Eeghen had the ball and was gaining ground. It was a draw play. Panic set in, but the Browns dropped the running back before he could gain the first down. When that fact set in, Willie whooped and high-fived people two rows behind him, knocking over a couple of people who were between.

The Kardiac Kids were down to what might be their last shot. They started from their 25-yard line with about 4:30 minutes left. Sipe dropped back to pass. With nobody open, he took off running and gained 10 or 12 yards. When the tackler hit him, the football went flying backward and landed near the line of scrimmage.

The cheers that had been building with every yard Sipe gained turned to shrieks of terror. Everything went slow motion, as the fans willed the Browns to fall on the fumble. But it was the Raiders who recovered. Everyone was silent in the stands. Even Willie was silent. Dumbfounded. This is not how the Kardiac Kids' season should end!

Van Eeghen ran for 1 yard. Then for 7 yards! Third down and just 2 to go, on the Browns' 16-yard line. The Raiders were already in field goal range, and the clock kept running. Down below 4 minutes now.

"I can't believe this." Willie summed up what every fan must be feeling. The Kardiac Kids had not even scored an offensive touchdown. Willie offered up a desperate, "C'mon D!"

Van Eeghen over the middle. The refs stopped the clock at 2:50 to measure for the first down.

"Oh, man, don't make it." Willie was pleading. It was six inches short! "Woo! Yeah!" Willie was happy.

"You think they'll kick a field goal, or go for it?" Tyrone asked.

"I hope they go for it and don't make it." Willie's choice would be the best possible outcome. They—and 78,243 others—waited to see what Oakland would do. Oakland's offense stayed on the field. No wide receivers. They were going to run it. If they gained six inches, they could run out the clock and end the Browns' season.

Van Eeghen ran off left tackle. He was met by linebackers R.L. Jackson and Bam Bam Ambrose.

"He didn't get it! He didn't get it! We stopped 'im!" Willie was voicing his desired result more so than informing the fans of section 42. The players were about 100 yards away. But Willie could see R.L. Jackson jump and celebrate, so he felt pretty good.

"They stopped 'im, T. We got 'im." The chain gang came onto the field and the crowd got awfully quiet. Willie was right! The Kardiac Kids were getting the ball back. The crowd erupted! All the Browns had to do was drive from inside their own 15-yard line with just 2:22 left and try to make a kick from a spot on the field that Cockroft had been 0-3 from. Or score their first touchdown of the game. In other words, standard fare for these Kardiac Kids.

As the Browns got ready for their final drive, Don Criqui in the NBC booth put it best: "Fasten all seat belts! The Kardiac Kids, they call them. They will give you those heart palpitations. Fasten all seat belts, here we go!"

Sipe took a deep drop and fired the ball toward the right sideline to Reggie Rucker, but the pass was low and got to Rucker on a bounce. On second and 10, Sipe slipped on some ice as he backpedaled but somehow kept his balance. He fired down the left sideline, short for Ozzie Newsome. Sipe got crushed just after releasing the pass. Ozzie adjusted and made the catch. His defender, Otis McKinney, lost his footing and Ozzie headed up field, but McKinney lunged from his prone position to get Ozzie's ankles and prevent a huge gain, and possibly a touchdown. The clock ticked down to 2:00.

First and 10 from the Browns' 43, and Sipe came out slinging, but way too long for Greg Pruitt. On second and 10 it looked like a broken play, and Sipe scrambled for a yard or two.

"Man, they just can't move this direction!" Willie was right. The only score of the day at the open end of the stadium was the pick-six by Ron Bolton. It was ridiculously hard for either offense to advance the ball in the *opposite* direction. But this way was next to *impossible*! Third down and about nine, and the Browns got the play off with 1:24 left. The pass fell incomplete. Willie buried his head in his big gloves.

Then he heard the call: "Illegal contact on the defense, 5 yards and a first down." Hope, almost snuffed out, flickered again. Instead of fourth and 10, it was now first down! Only 1:19 remained.

"Kardiac magic, my man," Willie beamed to Tyrone.

Sipe dropped back and heaved up a pass that came down in Greg Pruitt's hands, in stride. Pruitt made some more yards and got out of bound at the Oakland 28-yard line.

"They're driving, T! They are drivin'! Go Browns! Come on, Sipe, c'mon!"

Sipe narrowly avoided the pass rush and lofted the ball toward the right sideline to Ozzie. Ozzie caught it but was out of bounds. Second and 10, with just over a minute remaining.

John Brodie would offer prophetic words at this point: "It's almost expected, when you see the Browns with the ball at home with two minutes to play, this game is just getting underway. Two points down, a field goal is not a certainty if you get it within the 10-yard line. You recall they missed an extra point. They missed two field goals from close range going the exact same way they're going now. If they get a chance, they're going to try to get it in the end zone."

On second and 10, the Browns caught the Raiders off guard. Sipe handed the ball to Mike Pruitt on a draw play that picked up 14 yards, down to the 14! He stayed in bounds, but the Browns had timeouts to burn. The sky had partially cleared. The sun gave light and cast shadows, but any heat it had was lost in the arctic atmosphere and didn't make it down to the frozen field or frigid fans. No one would mind the hypothermia if the Browns could just pull this one out. The fans would be able to watch the AFC Championship Game from the climate-conditioned comfort of their homes, and the players would play in 100-degree warmer (that is to say, temperate) conditions in San Diego.

On first and 10 from the 14 with 54 seconds left, the Browns opted for another Mike Pruitt run. This one was stopped after a 1-yard gain. Timeout. Brian Sipe and Coach Sam Rutigliano, that magical duo, conversed on the sidelines. What would these innovative minds dream up? Would the Kardiac Kids pull out another heart-stopping last-minute miracle win? Would they get conservative and take another shot at a short-range field goal? After all, a field goal—if made—would win the Browns the game.

Coach Rutigliano called out the full name of the play: Red Slot Right, Halfback Stay, 88. The scrappy quarterback turned toward the field, eager to get back in the arena. Sam shouted: "Brian—just don't get sacked."

Sipe assured him: "No problem, coach," and ran out to join the huddle. The pass was supposed to go to wide receiver Dave Logan. But in Cleveland's offense, Sipe was trusted to adjust mid-play, based on what the defense was doing.

On second and 9, with 49 seconds left in the game and possibly the Browns' season, the ball was snapped.

Sipe eased back, surveying the field. Cleveland's quarterback saw Oakland safety Burgess Owens break toward his intended receiver, Dave Logan. Sipe decided to target his big tight end. Ozzie Newsome was deep in the end zone, running right to left. Sipe put the ball up. Willie and Tyrone had the perfect vantage point: both Newsome and the ball were headed toward them, from two different directions.

"It's goin' to Ozzie!" Willie instinctively threw his arms out to his sides, the way you do when you're driving and hit the brakes and try to hold your passenger from falling forward. Willie, Tyrone, and everyone else in the stadium, plus millions more at home, watched the play unfold. Oakland's Mike Davis, who was not as deep in the end zone, shadowed Newsome.

The ball, possibly knocked down by the wind, was not deep enough for Newsome to have a chance. Davis reached out. The frozen pigskin that had bounced off so many receivers' hands this day nestled into his. Newsome lunged, but he couldn't dislodge it. It all happened so fast, the players and fans weren't quite sure what had happened for several frozen seconds.

A deafening hush. Still life on the field. A frozen moment on a frozen day. Then Oakland players rushed to the end zone. A celebration ensued. They'd picked it off. They'd just won the game. They were going to the AFC Championship Game.

For the Browns and their fans: Kardiac arrest. The final, fatal play's name would be etched in the annals of Cleveland sports infamy: *Red Right 88*. Art Modell stared blankly into the distance. He remembered the 1968 playoff game against the Colts in kicker Don Cockroft's rookie season. He'd wanted to fire Cockroft back then. He'd ended up having a nice career with the Browns, but he wished his injured veteran kicker could have made just one more field goal. Today.

## 20

# CHARLES WHITE LINES

(Don't Do It)

*Before the 1980 season, the Browns had spent their first-round pick* (number 27) on University of Southern California running back Charles White. While playing for the Trojans, he'd blown away the records of all previous University of Southern California running backs, including those of O.J. Simpson. His 6,245 career yards are nearly 1,500 more than Marcus Allen's USC career total! Simpson and Allen are both in the NFL Hall of Fame. Was there any way Charles White's bust would not join theirs in Canton?

If White had managed to become a premier running back—even if never reaching Hall of Fame caliber—the Browns may have won against the Raiders in the *Red Right 88* game. Who knows how far they'd have gone in the playoffs this year? Had they beaten Oakland, league MVP Brian Sipe and his star rookie running back would both have made it back to where they grew up, in Southern California, for the next round of the playoffs. Maybe they'd have beaten San Diego on the Chargers' home field and finally gotten to the Super Bowl.

But White would never play like a premier running back, at least not until late in his career in one glorious All-Pro season while playing for his hometown Los Angeles Rams. In his first three years with Cleveland, he only started half the games and never eclipsed 350 yards rushing over the course of a season.

In White's third year with the Browns, after being confronted by Coach Rutigliano, he checked himself in to rehab for his addiction to cocaine. He'd first sampled the drug as a junior at USC. The negative effects didn't show up on the field until he went pro, and the professional football player money enabled him to fully fuel his habit.

In 1983, White had broken an ankle and was on Cleveland's injured reserve list during his fourth season. After his stint in drug rehab, he was one of several players participating in the Browns' pioneering Inner Circle addiction treatment program that Coach Rutigliano instituted with Art Modell's blessing and support. Players enjoyed anonymity not just from the outside world but also from teammates, with retired players Calvin Hill and Paul Warfield running the program and shielding the participants from prying eyes.

Rather than keep his addiction hidden, White wanted to let others benefit from his struggles. So far, he hadn't provided much value on the field. But addiction doesn't just wreck a playing career; it wrecks your life. And White was determined not just to improve his life but to prevent others from derailing their lives by getting started with drugs in the first place.

In the first half of the twentieth century, pioneering Swiss psychologist Carl Jung developed the theory of synchronicity. In this concept, two seemingly related events occur simultaneously. Neither event causes the other. The result is what looks like an astonishing coincidence, which is what happened on October 29, 1983. On that day, Melle Mel from the early rap group Grandmaster Flash and the Furious Five released a song called "White Lines (Don't Do It)":

*Ticket to ride, white line highway*
*Tell all your friends, they can go my way*
*Pay your toll, sell your soul*
*Pound-for-pound costs more than gold.*

On that same day, twenty-five-year-old Charles White spoke about the dangers of drug addiction—specifically, cocaine—to an assembly at Cleveland Heights High School. A student asked the former Heisman winner how much he spent on his habit.

"Over $75,000."

The assembled students let out a collective gasp.

"If I didn't have the money, I'd have sold my piano, my stereo, my car, socks, anything," White said. "That's the hold it gets on you. Your best friends are not the guys who tell you, 'Let's do a little of this and that.' I had one I thought was my best friend. I know now what he was—a hypocrite. Your best friends are the ones who tell you NO!"

*The longer you stay, the more you pay*
*My white lines go a long way*
*Either up your nose or through your vein*
*With nothing to gain except killing your brain. . . .*

"I haven't been using for the last year and a half," White told the assembly. "It's so good to be stripped of all that crap. You can get up in the morning and see the sun, all the good things around you. On drugs and alcohol, you're in a haze. You think you can see, but you can't."

A student asked what his reaction would be if someone put a little cocaine in front of him now.

"I don't know. I can't take the chance. I'm going to have to go to meetings the rest of my life."

*A million magic crystals, painted pure and white*
*A multimillion dollars almost overnight*
*Twice as sweet as sugar*
*Twice as bitter as salt*
*And if you get hooked, baby*
*It's nobody else's fault, so don't do it!*

Charlie White's addiction had cost him some serious dinero. But he was an NFL first rounder; he could afford to burn the cash. The tolls it took on his life and his football career were another story. The damage was profound. In five years with the Browns, he'd totaled only 924 yards rushing for a lame 3.4 yards per carry average. After Coach Sam was fired and Marty Schottenheimer took over, White's playing days with the Browns were numbered. He was cut before the 1985 season.

21

# RIP KARDIAC KIDS

EARLY EIGHTIES

***In the immediate aftermath of the 1980 playoff loss to the Raiders,*** nobody knew anything about the struggles Charles White was having and would continue to have. But White wasn't the only one who'd struggle on the football field. Brian Sipe and the Kardiac Kids' pulses would plummet the next season (1981) as they slid to 5-11. 1982's season was shortened by a strike, and the Browns might have been better off if it had been canceled altogether. Sipe won only two of the six games he started that year.

In 1983, the Browns were 9-7, but didn't make the playoffs. The most notable thing to happen in Cleveland in 1983 was the January filming of *A Christmas Story*, featuring Ralphie and his pursuit of the Red Ryder carbine action, 200-shot range model air rifle.

By 1984, Brian Sipe—the very heart of the Kardiac Kids—left to play for Donald Trump's New Jersey Generals in the U.S. Football League (USFL). Cleveland was now quarterbacked by Paul McDonald who led them to a 5-11 record. The other pillar of the Kardiac Kids, Coach Sam Rutigliano, was fired halfway through the season, having won just one game. The Kardiac Kids era's heart had stopped beating.

22

# BERNIE'S BEGINNING

1985

**Red Right 88** *on January 4, 1981, was a knife to the heart of the Kardiac Kids.* The team that had been so exciting in the two years leading up to that game was mortally wounded. The team that was an AFC-best 12-4 in 1980 won 23 games and lost 35, including their lone playoff appearance, over the next four years. 1980 Coach of the Year Sam Rutigliano and 1980 MVP quarterback Brian Sipe were gone. There hadn't been any songs sung about the team since Oakland's Mike Davis made that fateful interception.

In 1985 the Browns drafted (in the most circuitous way possible) Boardman High School and University of Miami product Bernie Kosar. Bernie was an All-American in high school and had grown up a rabid Browns fan. The fact that Kosar had grown up a Browns fan was something of a minor miracle.

Boardman is situated almost exactly midway between Cleveland and Pittsburgh. Bernie was born a year before the Browns' last NFL championship and clearly would not remember it. But he would have witnessed the Steelers winning four Super Bowls during his impressionable formative years in the seventies. Many of the neighbor kids flipped to the dark side. But not Kosar.

In college, Kosar led the Hurricanes to their first National Championship by beating a juggernaut Nebraska team in the Orange Bowl in his first year. Then he followed that by getting the Hurricanes to the Fiesta Bowl, narrowly losing the next year. He set a slew of passing records along the way.

Kosar wasn't picked in the 1985 NFL draft. At least not the normal NFL draft. Officially, he didn't meet the NFL's requirements of eligibility to be drafted in time for the regular 1985 draft. Namely, he was less than three years out of high school and hadn't graduated college. There is a "supplemental draft" that is occasionally held. The normal NFL draft is held in April. The supplemental draft, when there is one, is typically held in the summer. It is for players who, for one reason or another, are not eligible for the regular NFL draft.

Looking through the list of players who came into the NFL via this method, there are reasons they were not eligible for the regular draft. Most of these reasons are along these lines: academic ineligibility, suspension from team for rules infraction, suspension by the National Collegiate Athletic Association (NCAA) for testing positive for steroids, suspension from their team for drug arrests, issues with high school and junior college transcripts, improperly signing with an agent. . . . In other words, there is usually some sort of dark cloud under which these players are striving to make the NFL.

Kosar's reason for entering the supplemental draft? He *graduated* college with two years of eligibility left. He just hadn't graduated in time for the regular draft in April. But by taking eighteen credit hours in the spring semester, and another six in the summer, he qualified to graduate in June—after the regular draft but before the supplemental. And he (intentionally) did not inform the NFL of any desire to enter the regular NFL draft by the appointed deadline. Oh, and he didn't just graduate. He graduated with *two* degrees: finance and economics!

Kosar's path to the NFL was fraught with controversy. Virginia Tech's Bruce Smith had already been signed and was headed to Buffalo at number one overall in the draft. But after that, the hot commodity was a quarterback who could emulate the Dolphins' Dan Marino, who in 1984 had been the first NFL player to throw for over 5,000 yards in a season. And the quarterback who played Saturday afternoons in Miami's Orange Bowl Stadium—Bernie Kosar—was believed to be the same kind of quarterback as Marino, who played there on Sundays.

Teams attempted to maneuver into the number two slot, hoping or believing that Kosar would qualify for the regular April draft. The Browns wanted Kosar desperately, but Houston, who held the second pick, being from the same division, would never aid a rival. With that avenue closed, the Browns' General Manager Ernie Accorsi hatched a creative scheme.

Accorsi worked out a trade with the Buffalo Bills for the number one overall pick in the 1985 supplemental draft. His thinking was that Kosar would not be eligible for, nor declare for the regular 1985 draft, but *would* be eligible (by taking classes and graduating during the summer) and would declare for, the supplemental draft.

At one point in the run-up to the regular draft, Accorsi heard yet again from Ladd Herzeg, the Houston Oilers' GM. Every previous time they'd talked, Ladd had raised the price above Accorsi's offer to acquire Houston's pick in the Browns' bid to be the team that would land Kosar. This time Herzeg told Accorsi, "We traded Bernie to Minnesota."

Accorsi replied, "No, you traded your *draft pick* to Minnesota. I just made a trade with the Buffalo Bills for their number one pick in the *supplemental* draft." Then, as Accorsi would relay later, "All hell broke loose."

Herzeg: "What the hell are you talkin' about? I already made a deal with the Vikings!"

Accorsi: "The Vikings will have the number two pick in the April draft, that's true. But Kosar won't be eligible for the regular draft. I just dealt for Buffalo's pick in the supplemental draft. And they pick first overall."

Herzeg: "Are you tellin' me Kosar won't be draftable in the regular draft, but he will be for the supplemental draft?"

Accorsi: "Ladd, you're catching on really quick."

Herzeg: "You sonofabitch! That's dirty pool! I'm gonna call the commissioner about this," and he slammed down the phone.

It wasn't just Herzeg who was furious. Once this maneuver came to light, the Minnesota Vikings were apoplectic that they wouldn't be getting Kosar. Herzeg and the Oilers were upset that they would not be getting a pair of Minnesota's draft picks. Minnesota threatened lawsuits against the Browns and the NFL. Ultimately, NFL Commissioner Pete Rozelle summoned representatives from the Browns, Vikings, Oilers, and Bills to his New York office.

After careful deliberation, Rozelle informed all assembled of his decision: He would simply let Bernie Kosar decide whether he would make himself eligible for the regular draft (on April 30), in which case

Minnesota would select him, or whether he would instead opt for the supplemental draft, which would send him to his favorite team, the Browns. But Rozelle mandated a stipulation designed to offer Minnesota a chance.

The stipulation was that the Vikings would get one week of contact time during which they could try to recruit Kosar. And they had an impressive delegation: Bud Grant, longtime coach of the Vikings, who had been to the Super Bowl four times, and Marc Trestman, who was now with Minnesota, but had been a good friend of Kosar's while working with him as the offensive coordinator at the University of Miami. If anyone had a chance to wrest Kosar from his hometown team's grip, it was Trestman and the Vikings.

Meanwhile, Cleveland's Marty Schottenheimer would be countering Bud Grant's resume with his own. So far Marty had been head coach for a grand total of eight games in the NFL, winning four. And those games were as the *interim* head coach, just hoping to hang on for another season. It was Schottenheimer's four NFL wins vs. Bud Grant's four Super Bowls, and the innumerable wins that had gotten him and his Vikings there.

Minnesota had the more stable and compelling coaching staff and a clear desire to sign the precocious quarterback. Meanwhile, the Browns had a *defensive* coordinator turned *interim* head coach. The commissioner should have sold this plot to reality TV! Each team would make their case, but it would up to Kosar to decide where he'd play.

In his address to the media at the University of Miami, dressed in a blue "muscle" shirt, and with sunglasses propped on his head, Kosar made his intentions known: "I'm going to finish out this semester, which . . . which will end in about 10 days, and then in all likelihood, make myself available for the supplemental draft." The *New York Times* interpreted his comments and put it succinctly in its April 25 headline: "Kosar Chooses Browns."

In 1984, the Browns had finished third in their division at 5-11, the fourth disappointing season in a row. Art Modell had brought in Ernie Accorsi—previously with the Baltimore Colts—as his GM. They fired Sam Rutigliano halfway through the campaign, promoting defensive coordinator Marty Schottenheimer to head coach, even if it was initially just in an interim capacity. Accorsi convinced Modell to make Schottenheimer the full-time coach as the 1984 season drew to a close.

The defense was second best in the league by the "yards allowed" measure. The original Dawgs, Hanford Dixon and Frank Minniefield, were considered the best pair of cornerbacks in the league. The first-round pick of the 1984 draft, safety Don Rogers, would win the NFL's Defensive Rookie of the Year Award, giving the Browns a stout defensive secondary.

The offense, under quarterback Paul McDonald, was one of the league's worst. Only Ozzie Newsome really had a good year, earning All-Pro status with his 89 receptions and over 1,000 yards receiving. Accorsi knew he had to draft a quarterback. The need was as acute, and the stakes were as high, as when he'd pursued John Elway in 1983 as the GM of the Baltimore Colts. Due to meddling from his then-boss, Colts owner Bob Irsay, Elway had gotten away then. Accorsi, with the blessing of his new owner had gotten *highly creative* and had landed his quarterback this time.

It was no wonder the Browns had pursued Kosar with such fervor. Sending their 1985 first- and third-round draft picks and 1986 first- and sixth-round draft picks to Buffalo was expensive. But most everyone thought it was worth it to land the pride and joy of Boardman, Ohio. And the twenty-one-year-old Bernie Kosar did not disappoint!

Statistically he didn't knock your socks off. He started ten games (forced into action before the team brass wanted, because of injuries to starter, longtime NFL veteran, Gary Danielson). The Browns improved to 8-8 with Kosar firmly entrenched by the season's end. The Browns even won the division, despite not having a winning record.

The most notable element of the Browns' 1985 offense was the running game. For the third time in NFL history, two running backs on the same team—Kevin Mack and Earnest Byner—each ran for over 1,000 yards. The only other times this had happened, the teams ('72 Dolphins, '76 Steelers) each won the Super Bowl!

In the first round of the 1985 playoffs, the Browns went back to Kosar's collegiate stomping grounds, the Miami Orange Bowl, to play the AFC's hottest team, Dan Marino's Dolphins. Giving any kind of edge to the Browns because their rookie quarterback had played in the Orange Bowl as his home field for the last three years would have been misguided, to say the least. The Dolphins' record at home in this venerable old stadium over the last two years was 17-1. Good luck, rookie Kosar and underdog Browns!

The Dolphins had represented the AFC in the Super Bowl after the 1984 season, losing to the dynastic San Francisco 49ers. During that season, Marino had obliterated passing records, crushed the opposition's defensive backs' psyches, and destroyed the sleeping patterns of the other teams' defensive coaching staffs. By the time the 1984 season was over the Dolphins had amassed a 14-2 record and scored over 500 points. Marino had thrown for an NFL record 48 touchdowns and NFL record 5,084 yards.

The 1985 season was almost as strong for the Dolphins, who finished 12-4. Marino returned to earth a little but was still one of the best in the business. This is the team that rookie Bernie Kosar would have to face after playing in only a handful of NFL games.

23

# ORANGE BOWL IN THE NFL

JANUARY 4, 1986 – MIAMI ORANGE BOWL – DIVISIONAL PLAYOFF GAME

*In Cleveland, it was freezing. Literally. Thirty-two degrees with snow,* with a windchill bringing it down to 15. In Miami, it was 80 and humid. Not so bad for the fans, but tougher and tougher for the out-of-town football team as the game ground along through four steamy quarters. The Dolphins scored a field goal on their first possession after the Browns had gone three and out.

The Browns would not get their first first-down until their third possession. But what a possession. They were true to their regular season form. Rush left, rush right, rush up the middle. Rush Earnest Byner, rush Kevin Mack, rush Curtis Dickey, and then from about the 16-yard line: Bernie Kosar hits Ozzie Newsome for a touchdown! PAT is good and the Browns lead 7-3. Raucous cheering indicates there are plenty of Browns fans in the Orange Bowl.

After some back and forth, the Browns got the ball back. Again, they were pinned back, deep in their own territory. Miami punter Reggie Roby's booming kicks and tremendous hangtime made for long fields for the Cleveland offense.

Kosar would throw an interception on an attempted slant to Brian Brennan. The rookie quarterback's eyes had followed the receiver the whole way. That might have worked for Kosar in this stadium last year when he was playing against college defenses. But this was the NFL. They made him pay for being so obvious. Dan Marino would have a short field to traverse in an attempt at scoring the Dolphins' first touchdown.

Miami put together positive plays and made a first down. Gifting Marino's team with a turnover was usually a recipe for disaster. It felt like the momentum was with Miami now. Past the halfway point in the second quarter, the Dolphins had third and goal from the Browns' 8-yard line. Marino dropped straight back and fired over the middle.

Safety Don Rogers broke on the ball, nabbing it at the goal line. He sprinted upfield before getting tackled at the Browns' 45! Big players make big plays in the biggest situations! Rogers single-handedly prevented the Miami touchdown and restored the momentum to the spunky Cleveland Browns. Cleveland methodically drove down the field, deep into Miami territory. With under a minute left in the half, Byner would turn a counter-draw play into a 22-yard touchdown run. Matt Bahr's extra point put the underdawgs up 14-3.

Cleveland went into the prevent defense. It was tough watching them allow Marino to get on a roll. Was preventing this last-minute, first-half touchdown via the prevent defense worth allowing him to find a rhythm? The early returns said yes! Capping the near perfect (from a Browns fan's perspective) half, Dolphins kicker Fuad Reveiz missed a field goal with time expiring in the first half. The Browns, picked by some outlets as a 14-point underdog, led by 11 going into the refuge of the relatively cool locker rooms for halftime.

Someone who looked more like a businessman than a locker room equipment manager was walking rapidly away from the visitors' locker room at the Orange Bowl as the Cleveland players approached. He had a cashmere coat draped over his left forearm. Had any of the players stopped to wonder about it, they'd have found that to be very strange in the heat and humidity of Miami. Could it be that Miami was a bit cooler than where he was from?

Rogers got to his assigned locker, tore off his jersey and shoulder pads, and set them down. Like all the players, he wanted to hit the showers or at least get to a sink to douse his overheated head. But something caught his eye at the locker. It was a small glass cylinder with a silver screwcap. It was the length of a AAA battery and maybe two-thirds the diameter. It was filled with a white powder.

Rogers grabbed it and bolted to one of the bathroom stalls. He closed the door behind him, but instinctively looked over each shoulder before unscrewing the cap. Once it was open, he licked his right index finger and rubbed it over the opening of the cylinder, picking up some of the powder. He brought the powder to his tongue to taste it.

It was the sensation he was used to. The one he'd first experienced three years prior, halfway through his time at UCLA. *Man, who put that there?* Had some close friend of his somehow gained access to the locker room, and known which locker was his? His mind raced. Then he reflected how good this had made him feel. Invincible. And so far as he could tell, it had never hurt his performance on the field. It had made him more fearless. More focused. And had made him feel no pain.

He poured the contents into a rough line in his left palm. A cast covered his forearm and engulfed his lower thumb, making the task harder. He brought his nose down toward his palm . . . then hesitated. He entertained inverting his hand, spilling the powder, and then flushing it down the toilet that sat in front of him, ready and willing to conveniently facilitate the right thing. But the little angel on his right shoulder lost out to the little devil over his left shoulder, and in the blink of an eye, he'd snorted the powder up his left nostril, having used his right index finger to press the other one shut. He then licked his palm, as much to eliminate any evidence as to glean the last of the magic dust.

He ripped off an arm's length of toilet paper, just in case his nose started to run. He stuffed it into the side of his waistband and headed to the closest open sink. The visitors' locker room had only one temperature of running water. It wasn't heated, but you couldn't call it cold. He splashed it on his face repeatedly, like he was trying to wash away a stain, though his original intent was just to cool off. He then doused his hair and neck and made no attempt to dry off before grabbing his shoulder pads and jersey to go listen to what Coach Schottenheimer had to say.

Cleveland's defense continued to confuse Miami on the Dolphins' first possession of the second half. The Browns' offense continued their winning ways. On their first drive of the second half, the Browns converted a third and 11 on a 12-yard pass and catch: Bernie Kosar to Clarence Weathers. On the next play Byner gashed Miami up the middle for a 66-yard run for a touchdown! Matt Bahr added the PAT. The Browns had been dominant on both sides of the ball and had earned a 21-3 lead!

Miami's legendary coach, Don Shula, suffered a flashback. The team he then coached, the Baltimore Colts, had been favored to beat the Cleveland Browns in the 1964 NFL Championship Game. Instead, he saw Jim Brown set a Browns playoff rushing record en route to a Cleveland blowout win. Now Shula was coaching the Dolphins. His legacy as a legend was already established. But as Byner scored to put Cleveland up 21-3, the 66-yard scamper, added to his 62 first-half yards, set a new Browns playoff rushing record. Was history repeating itself?

On Miami's next possession, the Browns were keeping the Dolphins under wraps. On a long third down, Marino heaved it downfield into double coverage toward wide receiver Mark Clayton, who hadn't made a catch all afternoon. Frank Minniefield made a great play, knocking the ball away. Minniefield's momentum sent him rolling down onto the turf. When he popped up, he pumped his arm in triumph! He hadn't seen what had happened after he'd knocked the ball away from Clayton.

The Browns' first-half defensive hero, Don Rogers, who'd clearly seen Minniefield neutralize the threat, continued his trajectory for three more strides, and rudely applied his right elbow to Clayton's helmet. The resulting unsportsmanlike conduct penalty turned triumph to tragedy as suddenly Miami went from needing to punt the ball away to having a first and 10 with improved field position. Then Marino strung together a succession of long third down conversions. It was on this penalty-extended drive that Marino finally connected with a wide receiver . . . over forty minutes into the game.

On first and goal, Marino fired for his receiver in the end zone. Rogers knocked it away. On second and goal, nickelback Felix Wright forced the tight end to break inside. Rogers was waiting at the goal line and again knocked the ball away. Rogers was doing his best to atone for putting the Browns in this position they never should have been in. Finally, on a third and goal Marino passed to Nat Moore in the end zone, and Miami's TD drought was over: 21-10 Cleveland.

The crowd noise ratcheted up to jet engine level. The officials refused to start the game clock until it quieted back down to rock concert level. Kosar fired a bomb down the left sideline to speedster Clarence Weathers. The throw was perfect, but Weathers couldn't haul it in. Then two more incompletions. Very little time burned. Miami held the Browns to a three and out. The momentum swung, and the crowd was deafening. Cleveland punter Jeff Gossett uncorked a 28-yarder. Miami had the ball on Cleveland's side of midfield to start their drive.

On their ensuing possession, Miami systematically progressed down the field. Forty-eight yards in five plays. The last 31 were on a run by Miami rookie Ron Davenport off the left side. He steamrolled the Browns' Don Rogers and continued unmolested all the way to the end zone for the touchdown. Fuad Reveiz made the extra point, and Miami tightened the score to 21-17. What had been a lopsided blowout mere moments earlier was now a nail biter . . . with *all* the momentum on Miami's sideline.

Cleveland's Glen Young, who led the league in return yardage during the year, made a great return of 34 yards to the Browns' 42-yard line, striving to win back some of the momentum. After the nice start, the Browns would implode, first with a holding penalty and then by allowing a sack. They had to punt after four plays.

With thirteen minutes left in the game, the Browns' defense finally made a second-half stop of Miami. After just three plays, the Dolphins had to punt it away. Brian Brennan fielded the punt under duress, but instead of calling for a fair catch, attempted to return it. He held onto the ball but only made about 1 yard of progress. The risk didn't pay off as Felix Wright got flagged for illegal use of hands. Brennan's effort to provide a spark instead sent the Browns in reverse.

Bob Trumpy alerted the NBC viewers that the Cleveland Browns led the NFL in fumbles lost after Byner made two carries to get the Browns from their own 9 to the 20. This was a minute after Don Criqui advised the viewers that the Browns had led the Dolphins in the fourth quarter of a playoff game in 1972, only to lose. That Cleveland collapse enabled the Dolphins to achieve the NFL's only perfect season.

The Browns put together a nice drive (all runs), but then a busted sweep play resulted in a 7-yard loss on third and 2, and they stalled around midfield. Byner, exhausted and nicked up, had missed his block by running the wrong way, and poor Curtis Dickey was a sitting duck for the Miami defenders.

Gossett's punt was short, but Miami's returner fumbled it. The Dolphins recovered. Unable to hook up with his wide receivers all day, Marino continued to throw underneath. On second down Tony Nathan caught a short pass and ran after the catch for a 39-yard gain. Byner was on the Browns' sideline, sucking oxygen from a tank. He wasn't the only Browns player who was near exhaustion from the heat and humidity.

The Browns' defensive line was losing every skirmish now. Each Dolphins run was for plus yardage. The secondary was still shutting down the Marks: Duper and Clayton, on the outside. But Coach Shula and Dan Marino had adjusted the passing plays to hit the tight ends and especially running back Nathan out of the backfield. Those shorter passes were adding up to first downs.

When the Dolphins turned to the running game, Ron Davenport's 235-pound heft helped him smash through the line. Miami scored another touchdown. After the extra point Miami was up 24-21 with less than two minutes remaining.

Glen Young gave the Browns a decent start with a 25-yard return from the goal line. Kosar knelt on the sideline and made the sign of the cross before coming out on the field for the final drive that would either win the Browns their first playoff game since 1969 and extend their season or send them home 'til next year. Kosar stood at the 20—5 yards behind scrimmage—in shotgun formation. He received the snap, backpedaled 5 yards, then hit the workhorse, Earnest Byner, on a slant of 7 yards on first down. Byner came back to the huddle huffing.

On second down, again in the shotgun, Kosar called for the ball. It was a bad snap, and Kosar fumbled. The gangly quarterback jumped on the ball. It was a loss of 4 yards. Third and about 7. Kosar approached the line of scrimmage to give the offensive line a chance to hear his signals against the deafening Orange Bowl din. He retreated and the snap came. Under pressure, he rolled to the right and made a low pass to Byner. Byner caught it but, doing so, fell down. He scurried up and made it to the 33-yard line before being tackled.

On fourth and 2, Kosar was under center for a change. The ball was snapped, and he backpedaled to pass. He faked the throw, then ducked his head and loped, giraffe-like, across the line of scrimmage, then ahead for the first down! Lying on the ground, Kosar worked his hands feverishly to call time out! Forty-six seconds remained, and 30 more yards to go to get into field goal range to tie the game.

The ball was batted down on a first-down pass attempt. On second down, Kosar had to start scrambling, then he flung it, almost underhand, for a completion to Ozzie Newsome. But Newsome was tackled before he could get out of bounds.

The clock was ticking off the seconds double-time. The Browns snapped the ball with sixteen seconds left. But rather than toss it away to stop the clock, Kosar looked downfield. With nobody open and with pressure coming, he scrambled in the backfield. He found Byner well behind the line of scrimmage and shot it to him. Byner caught it on his knees, got up and ran to the Dolphins' 45. He was tackled with the clock at four seconds left and counting down. Byner didn't even make it to his feet before the game clock got to double zeros. Miami 24, Cleveland 21.

If ever you could give the game ball to a player on the losing team, this was that time. Byner had left it all out on the steamy Miami turf today. It was fitting the game ended with the football in has grasp. It's just a shame he wasn't buried under a pile of jubilant teammates in the end zone. His stat line was gaudy, but the tenth round pick of the 1984 draft would have traded all the stats for the win.

A more experienced quarterback, better clock management by the coach, less fatigue on the part of the Browns' players, and avoiding a couple mental mistakes might have secured the win. But overall, this was as close as you could come to a moral victory. Cleveland went into the reigning AFC champs' stadium as a huge underdog. Yet they were ahead for the lion's share of the game and had dominated the first half. All this with two young running backs and a rookie quarterback! Another talented youth brigade infused the defense. Things were definitely looking up. Wait 'til next year!

After the game, Don Rogers was glued to the visitor's bench, head in hands. He was a competitor, and the loss stung. But it was more than just that. He couldn't revel in the first half interception he'd made, which accounted for a 14-point swing, robbing Miami of a touchdown and leading to one for Cleveland. He was fixated on the bonehead cheap shot he'd made on Miami's Mark Clayton. Rogers's own teammate had already prevailed on the play. The Dolphins had to punt. Until Rogers's penalty undid it. This was not aggressiveness, it was aggression. Why hadn't he controlled it? He was afraid he knew the answer.

The 1985 divisional playoff game against Miami was a microcosm of the season as a whole. Namely, a prodigious running game, coupled with a conservative, underwhelming passing attack. The trend in the league was toward pass-heavy offenses. That is why the Browns had contorted themselves to win Bernie Kosar in the 1985 supplemental draft. And yet there wasn't even a passing resemblance between the Browns' offense and that of Dan Marino's Dolphins, Joe Montana's 49ers, or Dan Fouts' Chargers. Marty Schottenheimer, a lifelong defensive coach, didn't have the juice. Newly hired offensive coordinator Joe Pendry wouldn't last beyond one year, despite the team's success running the ball.

Once back in Cleveland after the Miami playoff loss, Kosar expressed frustration to the press. "We need to improve our passing philosophy," he said. "It's not at a professional level." Kosar went on to say the Browns just didn't have the personnel yet for an NFL-worthy passing attack. One of the sportswriters opined, "What Bernie wants, Bernie gets." That would come true. In the 1986 draft with their first pick (second round), the Browns selected wide receiver Webster Slaughter. Meanwhile, with the collapse of NFL rival the United States Football League, Lindy Infante, formerly the head coach of the USFL's Jacksonville Bulls, became available and was hired as Cleveland's offensive coordinator.

In 1986, the Browns would morph from a running team to a passing team. They also transformed from being a .500 ball club to the team with the best record in the entire AFC at 12-4. Under Infante's tutelage, Kosar was adapting well to the pro game. Rookie Slaughter and 1985 seventh-round wide receiver Reggie Langhorne were establishing themselves. Ozzie Newsome was just past his prime but still a reliable target. They could keep defenses honest with Kevin Mack and Earnest Byner, who had both eclipsed 1,000 yards rushing just the year before. Oh, and Byner and reserve running back Herman Fontenot were great receivers coming out of the backfield.

## 24

# DON ROGERS

JUNE 20, 1986

*With training camp still nearly a month away, Don Rogers hopped a* plane in Cleveland bound for Los Angeles. He had some momentous occasions awaiting him in the Golden State. He had a few days of classes to complete to secure enough credits to graduate from UCLA. He'd knock the studies out, then drive to the family home in Sacramento. Up there, the plans were laid out: He'd attend his bachelor party one night, the rehearsal dinner the next, and then on June 28th marry Leslie Nelson, his college girlfriend and mother of his four-year-old son Donny.

The budding defensive star read a *Plain Dealer* sports page that someone had left folded in the seat pocket in front of him on the plane. The headline was hard for him to wrap his head around. It was hard for anyone to wrap their head around: "Basketball Star Bias, 22, Is Dead." Len Bias, who had just been drafted by the National Basketball Association champion Boston Celtics earlier that week, had "died unaccountably of an apparent heart attack," reported the Associated Press. The article went on to mention the number two pick of the draft had passed a physical given by the Celtics just days earlier. University of Maryland athletic director, Dick Dull, stated that the school had performed regular drug tests on Bias and other members of the team and "We've never had absolutely any kind of indication that there was excess of alcohol or any kind of drug involvement by Lenny Bias."

Rogers, a recent first-round pick professional athlete who was not yet twenty-four himself, couldn't believe this was possible.

Toward the bottom, the article mentioned that police detectives became suspicious because the room where Bias collapsed at around 6:30 a.m. was spotless and appeared to have been recently cleaned. Washington, DC, television station WDVM reported that unidentified police and hospital sources stated that traces of cocaine had been found in Bias's urine, but it was not known if that was a factor in his death.

As Rogers deplaned in the City of Angels, he hoped for Len Bias's family's sake that it wasn't the drugs that had killed their loved one. That would just be too cripplingly sad. A freak heart attack, probably the result of a lifelong though undetected physical defect, was hard enough to take. But if the heart attack was caused by drugs? That seemed so preventable. So unnecessary. So selfish.

Rogers slipped back into the mode of student athlete for a few final days. With the courses completed, his path to graduation was clear. It was one more thing he'd done for his family. He'd bought his mother her house once he got his NFL signing bonus and had purchased cars for his siblings. He'd been happy to do it all. He just wished he didn't always feel this weight on him. The self-imposed weight of responsibility.

With his father hardly ever around as he grew up, he'd been the man of the house. He grew up fast, constantly helping his mother and looking after his siblings. Now he was setting the standard by graduating from college. Trying his best to make the family proud with his play on the field. And in a matter of days, by marrying the mother of his child.

### Thursday, June 26, 1986

In a Sacramento hotel, Don, his brother Reggie, and nearly two dozen friends, including some Cleveland Browns teammates, gathered for a low-key bachelor party. By most accounts it was a pretty quiet affair. The hotel was a classy, sophisticated place. According to those in attendance, neither Don nor anyone else was swinging from the chandeliers or doing anything crazy.

The boys were enjoying a great meal, some laughs, and sure, plenty of adult beverages. Some of those seated at the long table had been Don's high school teammates. As the drinks flowed, old friends got sentimental. "Man, I always knew you'd get to the NFL." Another one roasted: "Even if it's just the Cleveland Browns!" Somewhere toward the third hour, Don and Reggie got up to relieve themselves. Don got to the bathroom first. Before Reggie could follow him in, a distinguished man in a cashmere overcoat did. Reggie, remembering the bathroom was only a "two-holer," waited outside.

The older gentleman must not have had to pee too badly, because he was out of the bathroom in seconds. Reggie went in and sidled up to the urinal. He turned his head in the direction of the stall where Don was. "Man, I can't believe you're getting married, bro! I'm glad all your boys was able to make it here tonight. You shouldn't have to pay for the dinner though, this is *your* bachelor party."

Before Don answered, Reggie heard him sniffling. He wondered if his brother was overcome with the emotion of the night and was crying or something. "Hey man, you alright over there?"

Don: "Yeah, yeah, I'm alright. Uh, just blowing my nose. Yeah, hey man, don't worry about me payin' for the dinner. I'm just happy to have everybody out tonight. It's so cool. Thanks for helpin' to pull it together." They finished their business and stood at the twin sinks washing their hands. Reggie had had enough drinks to not notice any change in his brother. Had he been more observant, he might have noticed his brother's dilated pupils.

Rather than rejoin the party at the hotel, Don snuck out quietly and headed back to his mom's house and went to bed.

Friday morning, the day before he and Leslie were to be married, he awakened at around 10 a.m., got to his feet, then collapsed, letting out a scream. In the cool Sacramento morning air, he was drenched in sweat as he lay on the floor. His mother rushed into his room. "Donnie, Donnie, what's the matter? What happened?" When he couldn't respond verbally, only clutching his chest, she called an ambulance. He had slipped into a coma by the time it arrived.

Donald Lavert Rogers died later that day in the hospital. His rehearsal dinner was supposed to have been taking place in just a few hours. He was only twenty-three. He died the same way Len Bias, age twenty-two, had died just eight days prior. Days later, Leslie Nelson would be standing by a grave near the body of her betrothed for his funeral rather than standing beside him at the altar for their wedding. The coroner's report stated that he had enough cocaine in his system to kill an elephant—more than five times the toxic amount in a human.

25

# 1986 PLAYOFFS

JANUARY 1997

*The 1986 Browns reeled off five consecutive victories to close the regu*lar season. In their final two games, they had outscored their opponents 81-20. Earnest Byner, who had been hurt earlier in the season, was back, and with him the running game. Cleveland amassed over 100 yards rushing in each of those five victories. The Browns had a tough defense, good special teams, and a powerful, balanced offense. They were peaking as the playoffs approached. Going into the playoffs, the Browns had earned home field advantage throughout the postseason and were the favorites to represent the AFC in Super Bowl XXI.

### DIVISIONAL PLAYOFF ROUND: SATURDAY, JANUARY 4, 1987

The New York Jets flew a strange route to the postseason. They started off the year 10-1, but then lost their last five games and backed into the playoffs the coldest team in the NFL. They heated up at the right time and spanked the Chiefs 35-15 in the wild-card round to get to the divisional matchup against the odds-on favorite to reach the Super Bowl: the Browns. Which Jets team would show up in Cleveland? Answer: the good one.

Though the Browns were favored by 7 points, they were down by 10 with just 4:14 left in the fourth quarter. Complicating matters further was the fact that Cleveland only had one timeout left. On their first offensive play after receiving the kickoff, the Browns were called for holding. Then they got sacked. On second and 25, the Jets' injured but seemingly possessed pass rusher Mark Gastineau bore down on Bernie Kosar. Kosar got the ball off, but it was batted down at the line of scrimmage. Gastineau drilled Kosar in the back after he released the pass. What would have been third and 25, was, courtesy of the penalty, now first and 10 at the Browns' 32.

Kosar showed why the Browns traded away all those draft picks to secure him. He completed passes for successive first downs, getting to the Jets' 22. With the clock at 2:32 and ticking, Kosar connected with Brian Brennan at the 3, where he was ruled down by contact. A few plays later, Kevin Mack smashed into the end zone! Mark Moseley made the PAT, and the Browns were down by only 3 points.

Cleveland's defense would stiffen and, with around a minute left, the Jets would punt. Cleveland started at their own 32-yard line, 53 seconds left, with no timeouts. The Jets got called for a pass interference penalty, costing them 26 yards. First and 10 from the Jets' 43-yard line. Kosar backpedals, throwing off his back foot for Webster Slaughter, who makes the catch and is tackled at the 5-yard line! The Browns are celebrating the great play; meanwhile, time is running off the clock, down to 23 seconds and ticking!

NBC's Don Criqui tells the audience, "They're gonna congratulate themselves right out of a football game."

His partner, Bob Trumpy, shouts what is on every fan's mind: "Throw the ball outta bounds! Throw the ball outta bounds!"

Finally, with fifteen seconds left, Kosar threw into the end zone for Slaughter, who was open to the outside. The ball was underthrown and almost picked off. Despite the cold, the fans were sweating; they knew they had just dodged a bullet. The incompletion stopped the clock with eleven seconds. It was only second down, but the Browns decided to go for the tie with a field goal.

Marty Schottenheimer sent his veteran kicker out onto the frigid field. Moseley's kick went up and snuck just inside the right goal post. Field goal good! Score tied with seven seconds remaining. By the time the Jets' returner was tackled on the ensuing kickoff, the fourth quarter was over. The game headed to overtime.

The Jets called tails and the coin landed tails up. In 1986, the overtime period was a sudden-death affair; the first team to score wins. The Browns' defense caused the Jets to punt after going three and out.

The Browns started at their own 26. Kevin Mack and Herman Fontenot—the running backs—are gaining yards catching passes and taking handoffs, as the Browns maneuver down field to the Jets' 39 for another first down. Kosar throws deep for Reggie Langhorne, who got behind the defensive back. Langhorne makes the catch and is tackled at the 5!

Rather than risk a fumble or interception, or any other calamity, the Browns decide to send Moseley out on first and goal to attempt the chip-shot field goal to win the game. The thirty-eight-year-old, who had already missed twice that day, shanked it badly to the right—not even close!

The Jets took possession but would punt. The Browns would punt. The Jets would punt again. The Browns would mount a drive. The clock would strike zero. The game would not end. At least not yet. Entering the second overtime, the game would simply continue; no kickoff or anything. So, the Browns had the ball, third down and 3 at the Jets' 35-yard line. Mack surged up the middle for 15 yards to the Jets' 20. Rather than attempt the field goal, Marty played Martyball. Mack up the middle for 4. Mack up the middle for 7, and it was first and 10 at the 9-yard line.

First and goal, with plenty of time. Schottenheimer decided to bet on his field goal kicker not missing another point-blank field goal. Cleveland fans' minds went back to January 1981, when Sam Rutigliano decided not to send in Don Cockroft to attempt the field goal. It was right down at this end of the field, going toward the Dawg Pound. The result of that decision five years ago was the interception on the infamous *Red Right 88* play. Still, Moseley had just missed from 23. This would be from 26. Maybe the Browns should try running a few more times?

Too late. The team was lined up. The snap made, the hold, the kick . . . GOOD! Moseley made it! The Browns had won a playoff game for the first time since 1969! It was official: The Browns had won a playoff game! For the first time in eighteen years, the Browns had won a playoff game!

In their loge, Art Modell hugged his wife, Pat, and gave a thumbs-up to the camera. Art was quoted after the game. "I do not recall in my twenty-six years in the National Football League any game that would equal that comeback."

## 26

# 1986 PLAYOFFS CONTINUED . . .

### AFC Championship Game: Cleveland Stadium – Sunday, January 11, 1987 – *The Drive*

*"Can you believe this?! Can you frickin' believe this? If we win this* game, we go to the Super Bowl!" Chris was screaming at the top of his lungs. He had to shout if he wanted to be heard. The noise was loud and constant. He and his high school buddies were back from college for the game and were intoxicated with the prospect that their team could actually be headed to the Super Bowl in three hours or so. (Of course, they were primarily intoxicated from tailgating in the Muni Lot since 8:30.) Just like last week's crowd in the Jets game, everyone was chanting "SU-PER BOWL! SU-PER BOWL!"

Chris, Tony, Mick, and Pete launched into a reprise of what they and seemingly all tailgaters had been singing all morning: "Bernie Bernie, oh, yeah (mumble, mumble, mumble)" "Bernie Bernie, oh, baby, Super Bowl!" Just like with the 1960s Kingsmen song, "Louie Louie," everyone knew the chorus, but nobody knew a single word of the verses. It didn't matter. For the first time since the Kardiac Kids days, people were singing about the Browns and believing they could make the Super Bowl. That they could *finally* make the Super Bowl!

Just like the gangly quarterback leading the team, these guys had all been born but were all too young to remember the last time the Browns had gotten this far. Last week's game was the first Browns playoff victory any of them had ever experienced. Today, the Browns would try to do what they couldn't do in last year's playoffs: beat a future Hall of

Fame quarterback from the draft class of 1983 to advance deeper into the playoffs. Last year it was Marino. Today it would be John Elway.

The Browns stopped Elway and the Broncos on their first drive after four plays, forcing them to punt. "Woof, woof, woof" (a stupid thing for grown men to say, but after copious Bud Lites, and with the atmosphere in the stadium, it just felt right). Hey, a Dawg's got to bark. The Browns' offense was inspired. On a third and 12, Bernie Kosar completed a pass to Reggie Langhorne for 13 yards on the Browns' fourth play. And the Browns were off to the races. Bernie made passes, the receivers made catches, Kevin Mack churned upfield.

"They look awesome today!" Pete yelled.

"They're picking right up where they left off last week," added Tony.

A few minutes in, and the Browns were already at the Denver 4-yard line with a first and goal! With two running backs in the backfield, Kosar tried a pass for reserve tight end Harry Holt, the most unlikely of targets, but they couldn't connect. On second down, Mack bulldozed ahead, but—fumbled! The Browns' Travis Tucker averted the disaster and recovered. On third and goal, now from the 6, Kosar dumped the ball to Herman Fontenot in the right flat. Fontenot made Tony Lilly miss and walked in for the touchdown!

Tony and Chris high-fived. Mick and Pete tried, but failed, falling over their seats in the process. They didn't care. They and 79,000 others were delirious! With Mark Moseley's PAT the Browns were up 7-0 over the Broncos.

"Look at Reeves down there, it looks like he should be walking to work on Wall Street or somethin'." Tony had a good point. Denver's coach with his glasses, his suit, and today his heavy khaki trench coat looked like he was more likely to review a financial ledger than coach a bunch of testosterone-drenched athletes in a gritty football game. The guys cut short this insightful dialogue to bark some more. "Woof woof, woof!"

The Browns' defense caused Denver to punt on their second possession. Intrepid 140-pound Gerald "Ice Cube" McNeil made a nice return ... but fumbled! "No, Cube!" everyone shouted. Luckily, the Browns recovered.

"Man, *that* was a lucky break!" Pete exclaimed.

One play later, under pressure from Rulon Jones, Bernie threw an interception to Ricky Hundley, who returned it to the Cleveland 35.

Chris shot a look at Pete. "Lucky, huh? Looks like our luck just ran out."

"Damn, Bernie, what are you doing?" Mick demanded.

"Bernie had the lowest interception rate in the NFL this year," Pete told his friends. "He only threw ten all season."

A few plays later, the Browns had the Broncos at fourth and 10, a little too far out for a field goal attempt.

"What the hell are they doing?" asked Tony. "They're going for it on fourth and 10?"

Elway was out there. He proceeded to quick-kick it after the snap. The Browns got the ball back at their 17.

A few plays later and it was first and 10 for the Browns at their 27. Bernie tried forcing a pass . . . but the Broncos intercepted!

"What the fuuuuuudge?!" the whole stadium asked at once. (Only they didn't say *fudge.*)

In his last three attempts, Bernie had thrown two interceptions. The Broncos' Jim Ryan returned the pick to the Cleveland 9-yard line. The Browns' defense would rise to the occasion, and the Broncos would have to settle for a field goal. Browns 7, Broncos 3.

"Alright, let's get back on track," Pete shouted. "Let's go!"

Ice Cube took the kickoff at the 7 and returned it all the way to the 37.

"That's it! Yes!" Maybe the Browns' offense would take a cue from the fearless flea they called the Ice Cube.

Kosar made the handoff to Mack. Mack fumbled at the line of scrimmage, and Denver's Ken Woodard recovered, then rumbled all the way to the end zone.

"No!" cried Tony, smacking his gloved hands to his forehead.

The officials ruled that Woodard was down by contact where he made the recovery. No touchdown, but the Broncos still had the ball.

"Damn, what's happening?" Mick said. "We started out like we were gonna dominate today, and now we can't do anything right."

Art Modell in his loge, who'd started out so gleeful after the Browns raced out to the early advantage, began feeling queasy. Something was wrong. The Browns had fumbled *three* times already. His league-leading quarterback had thrown two interceptions in his last three throws. "He normally goes three games without throwing two interceptions!" Art griped to a guest in his party. "I don't like what's going on down there. Something doesn't seem right."

"Let's stop 'em here!" Tony exclaimed.

The crowd started chanting "DEE-FENSE! DEE-FENSE!"

Elway silenced everyone on first down by scrambling for 33 yards and got out of bounds at the Cleveland 4.

Chris punched the railing that was there to keep fans from falling from the second deck. "What the $%#@," he screamed.

What really hurt was watching Elway limp back to the huddle, demonstrating that the sprained ankle he suffered the previous week was hampering him, yet he had still gashed the Browns for the long gain. Gene Lang took the handoff up the middle but was turned back at the 1. On second and goal Sammy Winder tried diving over the pile but was stopped for no gain.

"Hold 'em out! Hold 'em to a field goal," Chris implored.

On third down, Elway opted to pass but was pressured by Clay Matthews. He threw wide for Matt Sewell. Fourth down.

"All right, D! Way to go!"

The crowd was expecting Broncos Coach Dan Reeves to send in the kicker, but Elway and the offense remained on the field. Apparently, the Browns coaching staff and players were surprised too. Cleveland only had ten defenders on the field. Marty Schottenheimer noticed the shortage and furiously signaled for a timeout. To no avail. The officials didn't call one. Elway took the snap and pitched to Gerald Willhite, who jumped, twisting in the air as defenders tried to stop him short. But he prevailed and just got into the end zone. Touchdown Denver. After Rich Karlis's kick, the score stood at Denver 10, Cleveland 7.

Karlis kicked off again, after the chilly wind blew the ball off the tee. The lightest man to ever play in the NFL took it at the 6 and surged up to the 31.

"Man, that Ice Cube is fearless," Tony marveled.

"Yeah, he's the only one doing any good out there since the first drive of the game," groused Chris. Chris's words were prophetic. The Browns had started the game in overdrive but had been stuck in neutral since. This drive stalled too.

In turn, the Broncos could only muster three plays then a punt. A short 32-yard punt and a nice 12-yard McNeil return and all the sudden the Browns were in Broncos territory! But not so fast. A penalty against the Browns moved the ball back to their own 35-yard line with around four minutes left in the first half.

After some clunkers, Kosar threw a gorgeous pass to Clarence Weathers to get the Browns to Denver's 20. The Browns drove the ball and eventually had first and goal. They'd get as close as the 2-yard line. Finally, on fourth down, Schottenheimer made the decision to send Moseley out to attempt the short field goal to tie the game.

The guys remembered him missing from about this distance last week in the first overtime. "C'mon, make it . . . make it . . . make it," Pete implored.

The 29-yarder was up and good! At the end of the first half, the teams had played to a draw: 10-10.

Chris and the crew went to stand in the beer line at halftime with seemingly everyone else. Well, okay, they all had to visit the bathroom first. The talk in the beer line was that the Browns still had a chance. They had committed three turnovers and yet were tied. If they could just avoid turnovers in the second half, or maybe even force a couple, they should be in great shape, right? "Man, I never wished for warm beer before, but I don't know if I need an ice-cold beer right now, I'm still shivering from the first half," Mick confided.

"Come on, suck it up, you wimp," Chris said, and put Mick into a friendly headlock.

Back at their seats, Pete offered some perspective: "Boys, we are one half of football away from the Super Bowl." With that, they started chanting "Super Bowl! Super Bowl!" By degrees, the chant spread, and soon the entire stadium was reverberating with the wish that could finally, at long last, come true.

Art Modell looked stoic in his loge, but inside his heart was burning. It was twenty-two years since the Browns last won it all. Would this be the year? He braced himself against the wind and cold and hoped along with the 79,000 others around him that confetti would be littering his stadium in about two hours. But still, he had seen some unusual, uncharacteristic things in the first half, and felt like some force was arrayed against him and his team.

The Broncos and Browns would each punt on their first possessions of the second half. On Denver's second possession, they had a herky-jerky drive. Every time it appeared they were stopped; their cause was aided by a penalty on the Browns. They made it to midfield. On third and 5, Elway tried to hit Mark Jackson on the right sideline. Browns defensive back Mark Harper maneuvered to get the inside position. He dove and made a great catch, landed, and rolled out of bounds. The officials ruled: no catch. The crowd voiced its displeasure in no uncertain terms: "Bull$7it!" . . . After review, the officials overturned their call: interception Cleveland!

"Finally, we get a turnover!" Chris celebrated, pounding his comrades' fists with his own. The crowd came to life. On first down, Kosar threw long for Webster Slaughter, everyone held their breath, and the stadium grew silent. But the pass was too long. Another couple disappointing plays and a lousy punt. Well, the punt itself was fine, but the fact they had to punt was lousy.

"Man, we killed that opportunity," Pete lamented.

Denver would take over at their 31. Elway and company put together a string of successful plays and ultimately sent barefoot kicker Rich Karlis in to try a 26-yard field goal. Karlis put it through, and Denver reclaimed the lead, 13-10, with less than 3 minutes left in the third quarter.

Karlis' subsequent kickoff sailed to the 17, where Herman Fontenot received it. He ran up through the middle, shifting, making defenders miss; with every move the crowd got louder. He was out past the 35, the 45, finally taken down at the 50.

"That's the spark the Browns needed!" Tony exclaimed.

But it was all for naught.

"Holding, return team," boomed the referee's voice over the PA system.

"Man, I hate that friggin' phrase," Mick said.

"Every time we make a good return, we go backwards," complained Chris, although he was just stating what everyone felt. So, the Browns would have to go 83 yards instead of 50.

After a 4-yard Mack march, Kosar hit Slaughter for 20 and Langhorne for 22. In three plays the Browns were back in business, down to Denver's 38-yard line. Two more Mack runs and a first down at Denver's 21-yard line as the third quarter clock ran to zero.

As the teams switched ends, the guys all agreed: "This is like the first drive . . . we're movin' the ball again."

"We gotta punch it in," Chris added. "We need touchdowns."

With the fourth quarter starting, the Browns would be driving with the wind, toward the closed end of the stadium.

Mack ran off the left side for 7, to make it first and 10 at the Denver 14. For the fifth play in a row, Bernie handed the ball to Mack. He took it up the middle for 3 yards.

"Man, I like this!" Pete yelled. "We are wearing them down!"

Once again, Mack trucked the ball, up the middle for about 4 yards. On third and 3, Kosar snapped the Mack streak, surveyed the end zone for an open receiver, then slung the football harmlessly away.

"Damn!" Tony said. "We couldn't seal the deal."

As Moseley ran out on the field, Mick observed: "We can tie it up here. Our O-line is starting to wear 'em down. We just need to stop 'em on defense."

With around 12 minutes left, Moseley tied the game at 13.

"Just like you drew it up, Micky!" yelled Tony, as Denver quickly went three and out and had to punt.

"We just need to keep doing what we did on our last possession, take some time off the clock and score," Pete professed as if it was just as easy as that.

"Yeah, a touchdown, not a field goal," Chris clarified.

The atmosphere was electric as the ball sailed off Karlis's foot toward Gerald "Ice Cube" McNeil. The Cube, fearless again, made a move or two, but, like always, surged north and south and got out to the Browns' 41.

"Great field possession! Let's go Browns!"

Denver recorded its first sack of the day on the Browns' first-down play, a 3-yard loss.

"Why aren't they running it?" Pete questioned. "We ran it down their throats last possession."

Kosar hit Brian Brennan, bringing up third and 2. Mack got the handoff, but was hit at the line of scrimmage and only gained 1 yard. Fourth and 1 at midfield.

"What do they do here—punt, or go for it?" Pete threw out the question.

"Go for it!" Chris and Tony screamed, their adrenaline affecting their judgment.

Mick disagreed. "There's still nine minutes left, and we're tied. We can't give them the ball at midfield."

The decision wasn't up to them anyway. Coach Schottenheimer sent the offense out on the field.

“They better make it,” Mick warned.

Before the snap, right tackle Cody Risien moved backward. This caused the Denver defender to launch through the neutral zone into the Browns’ backfield. The Browns had intentionally not lined up a receiver or tight end outside of Risien, leaving him as the last player on the right side of the line. In theory, this allows that player to move—just like a tight end or wide receiver will often motion off the line of scrimmage, and through the backfield, prior to the snap. Of course, nobody watching the game knew this.

“He jumped! Denver jumped!” Chris (and half the crowd) shouted.

“No, we moved first. The penalty will be against us,” Pete replied.

Coach Schottenheimer and the Browns were expecting the penalty to go against Denver, giving the Browns a first down in Denver territory. What Schottenheimer didn’t know was that, even though it was true that Risien *could* move pre-snap, he would have had to do so while in the act of a legitimate play (as in truly going in motion as a receiver would). League rules don’t permit someone on the line to move for the express purpose of causing the opponent to jump offsides. Long story short: Schottenheimer and the Browns outsmarted themselves. The Browns were penalized, pushed back 5 yards, and really did have to punt.

After the punt, Denver started at the 12-yard line. One yard by Winder, then a great pass break-up by Frank Minniefield on second down, and it was third and 9. Elway took off on a designed run and made 15 yards. Offensive holding negated the play. Third and 15—and a pass play to Sewell netted 13 yards. Now the Broncos would have to punt. Under 7 minutes remained in the fourth quarter. After Denver’s punt and Gerald “Ice Cube” McNeil’s return, the Browns had the ball on their own 48-yard line.

Kosar hit Mack with a screen, but Mack took his eyes off the ball and dropped it. Second down and 10. Fontenot ran for 4 tough yards, making it third and 6. Kosar backpedaled into a 7-step drop and threw long for Brian Brennan. The pass was well short, but Brennan made a great adjustment and caught the ball at the 15. In all the twisting and turning, Brennan caused the defender to fall. Brennan navigated around him and waltzed into the end zone! Touchdown—Cleveland!

Whatever Chris, Tony, Pete, and Mick were screaming was drowned out by the roar of the crowd. Finally, the Browns had broken through for another touchdown! Moseley kicked the extra point, and Cleveland led 20-13 with 5:43 to go before they were Super Bowl bound.

Moseley's kickoff was short, bouncing at around the 15-yard line. It tumbled past Gene Lang, who was set up around the 10. Lang scurried back and from one knee tried to gather it in around the 2, rather than letting it trickle in the end zone for a touchback. He mishandled it, but finally secured it just as four Browns landed on him. The ball was Denver's, but they would have to start from their 2-yard line. First down and 98 yards to go!

"Super Bowl!—that's it! We're going to the Super Bowl!" Chris beamed. Chris saw nothing but sunshine now. He hugged his buddies. His buddies hugged him. Everybody hugged everyone, or at least high-fived them.

"Hey, maybe we can get a safety here," Tony commented.

"That would remove all doubt," Mick said. There was still time, but the odds were looking awfully long against the Broncos emerging victoriously from this predicament.

The Broncos opted to risk the pass on first down, Elway retreating deep in his end zone, then throwing in the left flat to Winder, who made it out to the 7. On second down, they ran for 2, making it third and 2. Timeout Denver.

"Oh, man! If we can hold them here, they'll have to punt," Mick observed. "They can't risk going for it on fourth down."

On third and 2, Elway handed to Winder who ran over center and was met by resistance. It looked like it would be close. When the officials measured, it was apparent that Denver had made the first down by one length of the football. First and 10 with 4:11 left.

"Guys, I hate to say this," Tony said, "but last week the Browns were down by 10 points with 4 minutes left . . ."

"Shut up Tony!" shot Chris. "We don't wanna hear it."

Winder for 3 on first down and a big hit by a wall of Browns. On second down, Elway took off and gained 11 yards for another first down.

"Oh man, I'm not feeling so good about this." Pete's giddy confidence from moments ago was flagging.

"Pete, they need a touchdown, and they still gotta go 75 yards," Chris said. "We got this."

The entire right side of Elway's white pants and orange jersey were now deep-dyed dark brown with mud. On the next play, Elway used his arm instead of his legs. He connected over the middle for a 23-yard gain to Sewell to the Denver 48.

Now even Chris was getting nervous.

The clock was ticking, now less than two and a half minutes remained in the fourth quarter. Elway made a connection to Steve Watson at Cleveland's 40 as the two-minute warning gave the teams a brief respite.

"Man, this is getting ugly. I don't like it," Tony blurted. "This stupid prevent defense; they're letting 'em go right down the field."

"Man, we could sure use Don Rogers out there right now," Peter commented.

It would have been deadly silent in the stadium, except everyone was nervously venting about the momentum swing.

First and 10 from the Browns' 40. Elway threw a bomb to the goal line, but well over the receiver's head. Cleveland's Ray Ellis was closest, but not close enough to pick it off. On second and 10, Elway dropped back, then up into the pocket, and started to scramble, but was stopped dead in his tracks by reserve defensive lineman Dave Puzzouli.

"Finally—*that's* what we needed!" Pete shouted, but his voice was lost in the roar.

The sack gave new hope to the crowd and made it third down and 18. Third and a whopping 18! Denver called their second timeout.

With 1:47 left, Denver lined up in a T formation, with a running back to Elway's right and wide receiver Steve Watson to his left. Prior to the snap, Watson goes forward, then right, cutting in front of Elway, headed toward the right side of the line. The center snaps it before Watson is clear, and the ball glances off his backside, sapping some of the energy off the ball. Elway must reach down and pick the ball off the ground. He deftly snags it and backpedals to the Broncos' 40 and fires a missile to Mark Jackson at the Browns' 28 for a completion. First down, with the clock running.

"Ahhhh! They just converted a third and 18!" Pete blurted.

Elway hustles the team to line up and then throws the ball away to stop the clock at 1:19. On second and 10, the Browns have two defenders bearing down on the backpedaling Elway. It is a perfectly set up screen, and Sewell gains 14 yards but stays in bounds near the left sideline. With under a minute, Elway fires to the right side of the end zone for 6'4" Steve Watson, who is being covered by 5'9" Frank Minniefield. Watson catches it, but not in bounds. Second and 10 from the 14 with 49 seconds left in the fourth quarter.

Elway, bad ankle and all, calls his own number and runs toward the first down marker on the right sideline. He picks up 9 yards and gets out of bounds with 42 seconds still on the clock. Third down and 1 from the 5-yard line.

By now none of the guys can talk. If anything, they are muttering silent prayers under their breath.

From the shotgun, Elway makes the pass to a slanting Mark Jackson in the end zone. Jackson makes the catch. Touchdown, Broncos.

The Broncos have just driven 98 yards.

Elway had just written *The Drive*, as it will simply be known from then on, into the annals of football lore. *The Drive* would drive a stake into every Clevelander's heart and cause decades of anguish. But it didn't even hurt yet, because the fans were all still in shock. The Broncos were a PAT away from tying the game at 20.

Karlis who grew up in Salem, Ohio, and had given away fifty tickets to friends and family for today's game, would try to boot the extra point into the Dawg Pound—barefoot. The snap and hold were good. With thirty-seven seconds, Karlis knotted it up.

The Browns pulled off the miracle finish last week. Now the Broncos were returning the favor.

"Hey, it's not over yet," Chris said, trying to cheer himself up as much as anyone else. "We'll get a shot here . . . and then overtime if we need it."

Art Modell felt like he was falling backward into a black hole. His heart was racing, and beads of sweat appeared on his brow despite the icy temperature. Modell was a driving force in marketing and televising the NFL. The Super Bowl was the marriage of his two worlds: football and advertising. His team was destined to be a part of the big show. The Browns had had the lead with mere minutes left. They'd had the opponent backed up against their own end zone. Now the game was tied.

All the momentum was against them. Against him. Something felt wrong about this game. All those turnovers. As he swirled backward into the abyss, the sneering face of that stranger kept flashing in Modell's mind. He had wanted nothing more than to beat the Colts in the '64 championship. And they had. But at what cost?

Karlis's kickoff sailed out of bounds. He re-kicked from the 30. It bounced before Gerald "Ice Cube" McNeil could catch it, right at him, then off him. Ice Cube finally got control at the 4-yard line and only made a few yards before getting out of bounds at the 16-yard line. With 31 seconds, Kosar threw a safe screen pass to Fontenot, who gained only 3 yards and didn't get out of bounds. Timeout Browns.

During the timeout, the Browns decided they would wait for overtime rather than force anything risky here. Kosar took a knee and ran out the clock.

"Ah man, I don't know about this call. . . . Why not try a couple passes, and just throw it away if the guy's not open?" Pete seemed to make a good point.

But now the fourth quarter was over. For the second week in a row, Cleveland's fans would get extra playoff action for the cost of admission.

The teams' captains came out for the coin toss. Denver called heads. The coin came up tails. The Browns elected to receive. That is what you need to do in sudden death.

Someone in the owner's loge patted Modell on the shoulder. "That's a good break, Art." Modell barely heard it and offered a faint smile and a vague look in his acquaintance's direction. His mind was focused within. *What did I sign? Who was that strange man in 1964? When will we win again?*

As the intermission drew to a close, Modell snapped out of his musings, regarding them as strange, irrational, unwelcome thoughts.

Karlis kicked toward the closed end of the stadium into the waiting arms of Gerald McNeil at the 15. Ice Cube raced forward and disappeared into a forest of Browns blockers and Denver defenders. He was tackled at the 30.

"No turnovers!" Tony bellowed.

He was right. A fumble here, and Denver would immediately be on the edge of Karlis's field goal range.

On the overtime's first play from scrimmage, Kosar faded back to pass . . . plenty of time, but nobody was open. He loped forward and picked up a couple yards.

"He's no Elway, he runs like a wounded giraffe," someone behind them said.

On second down, Ice Cube was lined up in the slot for a rare offen-sive appearance. He ended up being a decoy as Kosar hit Brennan, who made it out of bounds around the 38. Third down and 2 yards to go. Fontenot received the handoff but was met by Mecklenburg in the backfield and did well to avoid the loss. Fourth down and the Browns could not risk trying another play. Gossett came in to punt it away. Willhite took the kickoff at the 21, was hit an instant later by Felix Wright, and was downed at the Denver 25.

"Our D needs to step up here!" Chris exclaimed.

"How 'bout a turnover . . . a pick six?" Mick had the right idea. Whoever scored the next points was going to the Super Bowl!

Behind good blocking, Winder picked up 5 yards on first down. Elway went to the air on second down, throwing a laser to big tight end Orson Mobley at the Cleveland 48-yard line.

"Oh no. No. No." Pete wasn't shouting. It was more like mumbling. His nerves had seized up his body.

Elway pitched to Winder. He was almost tackled 6 yards back but broke one tackle and ended up losing only 2. Second and 12 at midfield. The Browns' defensive line put pressure on Elway. The fans got excited until they realized the offensive line had allowed the Browns' defense to penetrate so easily. It was a screen play. Elway lofted the ball toward his receiver but had to arc it high to get over college basketball's Pittsburgh Panthers' all-time leading rebounder Sam Clancy's extended arms. Incomplete.

"Ahh yes! Hold 'em. Hold 'em, hold 'em!" Chris's jaws still worked. This play was critical. "Hold them here, and we'd get the ball back on offense. A field goal is all we need."

On third and 12, Elway stood in the pocket. The Browns' pass rushers forced him out to the left. He was running away, toward the sideline, then turned to run north-south. It looked like he might scramble like he'd done so many times for a first down. Just before he reached the line of scrimmage, he fired downfield, high for the 6'4" Steve Watson. Watson jumped and came down with the catch at the Cleveland 22. Suddenly Denver was in field goal range. The Browns called timeout.

"This is terrible," Chris said. "We're gonna lose."

"Chris, he could miss the field goal. It's not a sure thing," Pete advised.

"Hey, we gotta look to strip the ball, and get a turnover," Tony offered.

Winder carried it for 5 yards on first down. The chances of Denver missing the field goal were decreasing with every yard they gained. Clay Matthews and Bob Golic penetrated, and made a hit on Winder in the backfield, but he managed to pick up another yard. The defense would need to go all out to force a turnover here on third down. Winder ran once more. He didn't make any yardage, but he centered the ball to make the field goal try easier for Karlis.

"They could miss! They could miss! Last week the Browns were kicking from this same spot, *in overtime* to try to win the game, and Moseley missed. I think it was even shorter than this." Mick was right. Karlis had made eight field goals in a row, but his bare foot had been out in the cold all day. Maybe he *would* miss! Karlis measured out his steps after tamping down the turf with his bare toes. The snap was placed, the kick was up . . . it was . . . good!

The Broncos were the AFC champions. The Broncos were going to Pasadena. Days of wine and roses. Fame and fortune. The Broncos were Super Bowl bound.

The Browns' season was over.

27

# WILL THE BROWNS FINALLY STRIKE GOLD?

1987 Season

*Doesn't it just figure . . . the Browns almost make it to the Super Bowl,* and the next season the league goes on strike.

The Browns made the divisional round of the NFL playoffs in Bernie Kosar's first year. In his second season, they made it to the AFC Championship Game, and only *The Drive* prevented them from reaching the Super Bowl. The year 1987 was supposed to be *their* year. But in August the NFL Players Association (NFLPA) authorized a strike to start after the second game of the year. The key concession the NFLPA was seeking was the right to free agency, which would give players much more clout in negotiating with teams.

The first two weeks of games proceeded normally. The Browns were 1-1 at that point. Then the strike hit. There were no games the third week, but by week four, the owners had lined up teams of replacement players, with the intent of playing out the rest of the regularly scheduled season. Teams of bartenders, firefighters, construction workers, and unemployed former USFL players competed against each other as the regular NFL players formed picket lines. The Vikings even had a chemical engineer playing defensive end. He had to leave the team early because he ran out of vacation days from his engineering job.

The players' union lost leverage as some of its members crossed the picket lines and began playing for their teams. Each week more regulars suited up. After three weeks, the union called off the strike. In week seven, all the regular players were back (and all the bartenders were back serving drinks). The league had decided that all the "replacement player" games would count toward the teams' official records, and all the statistics would be official, recorded for posterity. The replacement Browns didn't fare too poorly, going 2-1. Coming out of the strike, the Browns were in a three-way tie for first place in the AFC Central at 3-2.

On October 25, it was all systems go!

"Man, I am glad this strike is over! Now we can get to the Promised Land!" Pablo felt the same way most Browns fans felt.

"Yeah, we shoulda beat that horse-tooth dude last year, man. We shoulda got there last year," Jaime added. "Plus, Byner is healthy now, and we got Mack, Brennan, Ozzie, Langhorne, Slaughter, and Fontenot."

"Don't forget Bernie, Jaime!"

"No duh, Pablo, of course Bernie."

"Yeah, remember his first year, when Mack and Byner both got a thousand yards, and then last year Bernie turned the Browns into a passing team."

"Yeah Jaime, whaddya mean?"

"Byner's back healthy again, man. I love that dude. We'll have Byner and Mack, and Bernie has all his receivers back. The other teams won't know how to stop us, man!"

"Yeah, that sounds good, they won't know if we're gonna run or pass," Pablo said, then paused to take a sip. "How 'bouts the D, Jaime?"

"We got the Dawgs, man," Jamie said, punctuated his remark with a bark. "The best cornerbacks in the league."

"What about Chip Banks? Man, that hurts." Pablo was worried about the impact of losing the perennial Pro Bowl linebacker.

"Man, we got Clay Matthews, he's a Pro Bowler," Jamie said. "And we just got Mike Junkin in the draft. Marty says he's like a mad dog in a meat market. And we got Golic. He's another Pro Bowler, man. We're gonna be tough on D, man. No way we ain't goin' to the Super Bowl. Bro, we're gonna win the Super Bowl!"

The rest of Cleveland felt the same way, from Art Modell down through the coaches and players and throughout the fan base. Somehow, almost miraculously, the strike didn't undermine the good fortune that finally appeared to be the Browns'. By the time the regular season was over, the Browns stood alone atop the AFC Central at 10-5. Unlike last year, they didn't compile the best record in the entire AFC, but at least they made the playoffs for the third year in a row. And they would be playing the first round at home.

## 28

# 1987 AFC DIVISIONAL ROUND PLAYOFFS

CLEVELAND STADIUM – JANUARY 9, 1988, 1 P.M.

*Not that there had been an overwhelming sample size, but the weather* for this January football game in Cleveland was much like the others: below-freezing temperatures with a west wind making it feel just above zero. Flurries in the air. Ice on the lake. NBC sideline reporter Ahmad Rashad described the playing surface as "neither Astroturf nor grass. It is green-painted frozen dirt."

Bookmakers put the Browns as 7.5-point favorites over the visiting Indianapolis Colts.

Art Modell sat in his frosty loge, ready for the game to begin, reflecting back to just over twenty-three years ago. Back then his Browns had defeated the Colts—the *Baltimore* Colts—to win the biggest game in football: the NFL championship. So much had changed since then. The Colts ownership changed from Carrol Rosenbloom to Robert Irsay. Then Irsay moved the Colts from Baltimore to Indianapolis. Modell mused aloud, "Who would move a football team? I mean who would *do* that?"

Modell's mind compulsively flashed back to that strange man and his deal, whether he still "owed" anything in that "deal" he'd made in 1964. Was he beholden to the Colts? Or to Baltimore? If there ever really was some kind of voodoo debt to be worked off, was it now null and void? Since 1984, the Baltimore Colts had ceased to exist. Modell considered it: *The Colts were in Indianapolis now. Baltimore had no team. That had to be significant, didn't it? Baltimore had no team!*

The first half of today's game was a seesaw affair. The Browns scored a touchdown, then Indianapolis scored a touchdown. The Browns went up again, 14-7, then the Colts tied it up again, 14-all. Those scores came on a Bernie Kosar touchdown pass to Earnest Byner and a touchdown on a bomb to Reggie Langhorne, who caught it and fell down at the 3. He had been so wide open he was able to scamper into the end zone. Modell could be seen beaming on that one.

The Colts' Jack Trudeau—who as a junior at Illinois in the 1984 Rose Bowl had thrown two interceptions to UCLA's Don Rogers—had been Kosar's equal in today's game with two touchdown passes of his own. At halftime, Modell again harkened back to 1964. The title game was tied at halftime too. He wondered for a half-second, *If I were to see that strange man now, would I beg him to let us win this game?* The thought was barely formed in his mind when he forced himself to banish it and talked with his loge guests.

In the second half, the Browns scored on a touchdown run by Byner and a field goal by Matt Bahr, making it 24-14. Then, from the Colts' 47-yard line, Byner burst through the line on third and short and rumbled for over 20 yards before being tackled. As he's tackled, the Colts jar the ball loose. Modell groans as he sees Byner has lost the handle. Fortunately, Herman Fontenot makes the recovery at the 5-yard line. It is first and goal. One pass from Kosar to Brian Brennan and the Browns are up 31-14 with time getting short in the fourth quarter!

Maybe it was the "prevent" defense, but the Colts were able to drive down the field for the first time in the second half and scored a touchdown with 1:34 left in the game. After the extra point, the Browns led, 31-21. The Colts lined up for the on-sides kick. It looked like Colts player Craig Swoope recovered the ball while one of his feet was still behind the 10-yard marker, meaning he contacted it before it traveled 10 yards, and the possession should have gone to Cleveland.

That is how it was originally called, but the refs reversed it. Art and many of the fans flashed back to last year. In both of those playoff games, the team that was behind late in the game made a stunning comeback and won in overtime. Suddenly, this presumed feel-good victory was in question.

The Browns' Al Baker sacked Trudeau on first down, dropping him for a big loss, knocking his helmet off and knocking him out of the game for good measure. Eventually it was fourth and 19. Most NFL fans would be feeling rather good right now. Every Browns fan, though, remembered last year when they had Denver in a third and 18. What happened next in that game would go down in infamy as *The Drive*.

Nobody in Cleveland felt safe. True, there was only one minute on the clock, and the lead was 10 points . . . but . . .

Finally, the ball was snapped. Sean Salisbury, who'd replaced Trudeau, had to go for broke and threw deep downfield. Frank Minniefield picked it off and ran it all the way—48 yards—to the end zone! After Matt Bahr's PAT, the Browns were up 38-21 with just 39 seconds left. And that's how the game ended! Cleveland was moving on!

There was no doubt who had been the game's Most Valuable Player: Earnest Byner. He did it on the ground, with 122 rushing yards and two touchdowns on 23 carries. He did it in the passing attack with four receptions for 36 yards and another touchdown. And as always, he played with heart, quietly inspiring his teammates as he'd done for years. Sure, he'd fumbled once, but even that had helped the team, as the ball was recovered by a teammate a yard closer to the end zone than where he'd have been tackled.

Modell stood in his loge looking out over the field. He just held the gloved index finger of his right hand up, quietly but resolutely indicating that his team was number one. It felt good, it felt right, to be in this position as the clock ticked down to zero. No overtime required. The Browns won in a landslide. Next stop: the AFC Championship Game. After winning the last three games of the regular season and dominating today, Modell, like Browns fans everywhere, had reason to feel good about this season. You might say they felt *Super*!

Tomorrow the Broncos would play the Oilers. If the Oilers won, they would travel to Cleveland. If Denver won, the Browns would play in a rematch against the Broncos, but it would be in Denver this year. While many fans and likely some players savored the chance to avenge last year's heart-stomping loss, most would be pulling for divisional rival Houston to earn the victory tomorrow. (Spoiler alert: Denver would win.)

## 29

# THE FUMBLE

1987 AFC Championship Game – Mile High Stadium, Denver – Sunday, January 17, 1988

*"All I'm sayin' is it's nice to see clear blue sky for a football game for a* change," Alice told her husband.

"You're tellin' me you wouldn't rather be back in Cleveland right now?" Ken kidded her. "You'd rather go on the road?"

They'd flown out just for the game, getting in on Saturday and planning to fly out on the red-eye Sunday night to be at work Monday morning. It wouldn't be so bad if they knew the Browns were headed to San Diego in two weeks for the Super Bowl. They'd be flying high—with or without the plane (on wings of sheer happiness).

Ken and Alice had been at the previous week's playoff victory against the Colts in Cleveland. There, they had been surrounded by friends, family, and a joyous brown and orange brotherhood. Here in Denver, they were outnumbered and feeling a little on edge. They wondered if they should cheer in full-throat mode if the Browns took the early lead or whether to play it a little cooler.

Denver, despite all the sellouts, didn't seem like a football town to Alice and Ken. Maybe it was all the sunshine. But they couldn't ignore the Broncos were legit. And they had won more home games than any other team over the last four years. And man, was it loud! Revenge, if the Browns would taste it, wouldn't come easy.

Though they were nervous, Alice and Ken were also happy to be here. What a year it had been for the Browns. *The Drive* by these

Broncos to end the Browns' playoff run a year ago, lofty expectations all off-season. Then a strike during the season, seeming to derail what was supposed to be *their* season. Replacement players holding their own. The strike ending, and their regulars coming back to the field to win the division, scoring the most points in the AFC and allowing the second fewest. Winning big last week in Cleveland, and now: facing the team with the AFC's best record. The team that kept them out of the Super Bowl last year. Maybe it was just the thin air, but they felt like the Browns had been building toward this moment for a long time. It seemed the team was poised on the edge of history and about to break through.

The reverie didn't last. Gerald McNeil was only able to return Rich Karlis's opening kickoff to the 12-yard line. On first down, drowning in an ocean of noise, Bernie Kosar was flushed from the pocket and sacked at the 4-yard line by Simon Fletcher. Byner made a nice gain on second down to get almost to the original line of scrimmage.

On third and 12, Kosar took a quick drop, then passed to Webster Slaughter. Kosar led him well, but Slaughter's churning thigh popped the ball out of his grasp and into the air before he could secure it. A Bronco batted the ball, and the Bronco's big defensive lineman Freddie Gilbert came down with it for an interception. The Broncos had the ball at the Browns' 18-yard line. Everyone surrounding Ken and Alice was ecstatic. The Cleveland fans had to admit it: This stadium was LOUD!

Four plays later, Denver scored on a John Elway pass to Ricky Nattiel. Karlis kicked the extra point, and the Broncos had a 7-0 lead. Ken started to feel a little sheepish about wearing his doghouse-shaped hat with the stuffed animal dog sticking its head out the door. It tends to make one feel a little self-conscious when everyone around you is mocking you in a chant: "All bark!" [clap, clap] "no bite!" "All bark!" [clap, clap] "no bite!" Only three and a half minutes in, and already the Browns had turned the ball over and the Broncos had scored a touchdown.

Art Modell, watching from the visiting owner's suite, did not like how the game had started out. He thought about vanquishing the Colts last week. It seemed a horse of a different color was the new monkey on the Browns' back. *Bucking Broncos. Buck-toothed Broncos.* Art's mind flashed back to the mystery man. If he were to see him now, he'd almost want him to put a hex on Elway and the Broncos—whatever the cost.

Karlis kicked off, but this time Ice Cube made a nice return, all the way out to the Browns' 35. Three straight runs by Mack and Byner and the Browns had a first down.

"I like this," Alice said. "They are making yards on the ground. No need to take too many risks." The next play was a pass, on an ugly, broken play, but it netted 6 yards. Byner carried it to just shy of another first down, near the Broncos' 45.

On third and short, Kevin Mack surged beyond the first down marker and got 5 more yards. Ken high-fived Alice. Mack was stood up around the 40. Before his forward progress was stopped, a Bronco knocked the ball out of Mack's grasp. The Broncos recovered the ball.

Ken took his hat off as the Broncos fans kicked into maximum decibel mode again.

Modell grimaced. He knew this Broncos team would be tough to beat if the Browns played well. But to keep giving them back the ball? That was begging to be beat. To be embarrassed. Exasperated, Modell let out a long sigh. It was like he could feel the nation looking at him. Laughing at him. He felt like a pretender. *Why all these turnovers*?

These sinking feelings only worsened as Cleveland nearly sacked Elway, but he scrambled for 7 yards on first down. The bottom nearly fell out on the next play as Gene Lang ran for 42 yards, down to the Browns' 11. To Alice and Ken, the delirious Denver fans seemed like an ugly mob. A few more plays, and after an Elway keeper, the Broncos had first and goal at the 1-yard line. "C'mon D," yelled Ken. "Stop 'em here!"

Sammy Winder got nothing. Second down and goal. Elway fumbled the snap! Ken squeezed Alice's arm in anticipation of the possible turnover. The ball bounced around in Denver's backfield, there for the taking. Of course, it was Elway who corralled it.

"Damn!" yelled Ken. "That Elway always gets the breaks."

Ken had a point. How many times did the Browns have him dead to rights. Sacked. Only to have Elway break out of the grasp and scramble for a first down. And last year! How did he cleanly catch that snap on the defining third and 18 play on the famous Drive?

"He's a backbreaker, Ken, that's for sure."

The Browns' tough goal line defense stopped Denver on third down. Before Alice and Ken could cheer, the flag came out. It was against an irate, protesting Frank Minniefield. Denver had a fresh set of downs. A couple plays later and Matt Sewell hit pay dirt on a reverse. Karlis did his part, and the Broncos were ahead 14-0 in the first quarter.

"Wow, I wish we recovered that fumble," Alice said dejectedly.

"I wish Mack never fumbled in the first place," Ken replied. "Maybe we'd be tied up by now. Or just down 7-3."

Somebody behind them yelled, "Looks like your dogs' got no fight in 'em!" and everyone laughed. The Brown fans' disappointment was joined by a vague feeling of danger in this crowd.

"Everything's stacked against us," Modell muttered under his breath.

Karlis once again kicked off such that Ice Cube would have to fight the brilliant sun to find the ball before he even started his return. Since Ice Cube regularly practiced and played in Cleveland, it is a safe bet that his eyes had no experience going against the sun. But he handled it and got the ball out to the 30-yard line.

It was still only the first quarter, but the Browns felt they were almost in desperation mode. On first down, Bernie threw long and connected with the Wizard for 25 yards. Bernie tried another pass to Ozzie, but it was batted away. "Interference!" screamed Ken, but the officials didn't call it. "That shoulda been a 20-yard gain." On second down Byner busted up the middle for 9, to the Denver 36.

The Browns would get the first down, then after an intentional grounding call make another on a 19-yard pass to Clarence Weathers on third and 17.

"We're driving," Ken said. "We're showing we can move the ball on 'em if we just don't turn it over."

The quarter ended, and the Browns would need to try to finish this drive in the noisy closed end of Mile High.

On third and 3 from the 7, Kosar couldn't find a receiver in the end zone. He threw it perfectly into the right flat for Byner. Byner felt the defensive back waiting for him and dropped the pass. It would have been a first down. Matt Bahr picked up the pieces and redeemed at least something for the effort. Denver 14, Cleveland 3.

"We need to show we can stop them here," Modell told someone in his party. "If we can make them punt, and then score before halftime, we'll be right back in it."

Instead, the Broncos marched down the field. A combination of runs, passes, Elway scrambles, and penalties on the Browns, and Denver was on the Browns' 1-yard line with a first down. "Pound the puppies! Pound the puppies!" The crowd around Alice and Ken sent up a cheer that would have made the ASPCA blanch. Ken and Alice didn't care for it, either. Elway handed off to Gene Lang. Touchdown, Denver. Karlis hit the PAT. Twenty-one-3 Denver.

"Every time they touch the ball, they score a touchdown!" Modell yelled. "We allowed the fewest touchdowns in the NFL this year! What's going on with our defense?" If he'd had a hotline to the sideline, somebody would be getting chewed out. Meanwhile the Browns offense couldn't get into the end zone and had more turnovers than field goal attempts. The crowd noise was like a jumbo jet. Modell felt like he was being sucked into the vortex. His head was spinning. He saw flashes of that mystery man from 1964. Was there anything in that contract that said he'd *never* reach a Super Bowl? Was the 1964 NFL Championship the last time Art and his team would win it all?

On the next series, the Browns started from their 20. Three plays and a sack later, and they had only gone backward. Barefoot Lee Johnson's 58-yard punt from the end zone was the bright spot of this gloomy series.

"It might be a long trip back to Cleveland tonight," Alice said.

"Yeah, and a long day at work tomorrow, with no sleep."

The Browns hadn't stopped Denver all game, and now the Broncos were getting the ball back again with an 18-point lead.

Once again, the Broncos drove up the field. Somehow Elway threw three incompletions in a row, and Karlis was called on to attempt a 50-yard field goal. Nobody needed to remind Alice and Ken that the last time Karlis attempted a field goal against the Browns it was in overtime and sentenced the Browns' 1986 season to a sudden and painful death. Karlis shanked it badly to the left.

"Why couldn't he have done that last year?" Alice wanted to know. Ken just shook his head.

The Browns' offense took over and promptly gained 23 yards on a run and a pass. Second and 1 became third and 1 became fourth and 1. The Browns gambled and made it. First and 10 at the Denver 33. Bernie threw over the middle for Slaughter. The ball glanced off his hands, in and out of a defender's hands and fell incomplete. Denver's Lilly knocked into Slaughter. No official saw that. They *did* see a frustrated Slaughter take a swing at Tony Lilly. The Browns were pushed back 15 yards.

"Ugh, just what we need!" Alice lamented.

On second and 25, Bernie looked to pass, was flushed from the pocket, and completed an ugly connection to Brian Brennan fought to regain Denver territory. The ball popped out, almost simultaneously with his helmet hitting the turf. The refs called it a fumble. A review was ordered. Denver fans were sure it was a fumble. Alice and Ken were positive the call would be reversed—it had to be—it was clear Brennan was down. The referee made his proclamation:

"Upon further review . . . the play stands as called on the field . . . recovery Denver. First down."

Modell seethed. *We had the fewest turnovers all season and now we have three in the first half. What is going on here? These turnovers are killing us! I swear it's like someone has it out for us.*

Denver would have to wake up their punter, Mike Moran, who was finally being called to duty now with less than a minute to go until halftime. The Browns' offense would look better in hurry-up mode than they had for most of the game. They navigated 34 yards in a matter of seconds and stopped the clock to give Matt Bahr a chance at another field goal. The 45-yarder would be a challenge to the kicker who'd injured his knee and hadn't attempted anything much beyond 30 yards in half a season. The Browns would have done better to attempt a Hail Mary. His kick sailed wide right.

At halftime, the Broncos held a 21-3 lead. Total yardage and time of possession were nearly even for each team. The glaring difference was in turnovers. Denver didn't commit any. The Browns had given the ball away three times. Modell looked out at the cloudless sky. It certainly seemed to be Bronco blue today. Everything was going their way.

Modell then noticed a propeller plane pulling an advertising sign and had a slight chuckle. "Well, there's one thing that didn't go right," he mumbled. The sign had become twisted midway. It was meant to display "Diablo's Pizza 999." To the intended audience, directly across the stadium from Modell's perch in the visiting owner's box, it was now hard to divine its message. "Diablo's" was still mostly right-side-up, though the last few letters were hard to make out. "Pizza" was illegible, totally folded over on itself. The price presented as upside down and backward to those across the field from Art. To Art and those on his side it read, plain as day: "666."

Ken and Alice, bathed in sunshine in the stands, squinted out onto the field, which now was almost completely enshrouded in shadow. "I like the weather out here," Ken said. "I don't even need my jacket."

"Yeah, well, I'd rather freeze through a blizzard but have the Browns win," Alice replied. As if the lopsided score wasn't bad enough, the Broncos would be receiving the ball to start the second half.

It was hard for Ken to keep his mind on the game instead of the red-eye flight, the early morning arrival in Cleveland, and the long, sad day at work that would be here soon enough—and the credit card bill that would have an expensive flight and a hotel room on it.

Ken was brought back to the here and now as Lee Johnson's second half opening kickoff landed in Ken Bell's arms and was returned to the Denver 25. Denver went backward after two plays thanks to a penalty and eventually faced third and 11. The dastardly John Elway dropped way back inside the 5-yard line to avoid the Browns' rush and threw long over the middle.

As the ball flew through the rarefied air Modell felt like he'd seen this movie before: near disaster for Elway, followed by an improbable escape and a backbreaking reversal of fortune at the expense of the Browns. The ball whistled its way into the hands of Felix Wright! The Browns' safety looked like a centerfielder making a basket catch. He returned it to the Denver 35. Alice and Ken embraced. They were happy, but their happiness was muffled by the deep hole the Browns were in.

On first down Mack took the handoff, bounced outside, and surged 13 yards to the Broncos' 22. Hope dawned in Alice's heart. Maybe the Browns had a chance. The Broncos hadn't really stopped them all game. The Browns had stopped themselves all game, by turning it over. Maybe it was time for the turnovers to even out. If they did, the Browns had a good shot. That was her little mental flight of fancy, anyway.

Byner followed with a 4-yard run. The Browns were heading toward the closed end of the stadium. It was deafening. Bernie approached the line, then had to walk left and right while yelling, just so half the players might hear what he was calling. Gregg Rakoczy snapped the ball to Bernie who took a short drop and threw off his back foot. The ball was in Reggie Langhorne's hands, and Langhorne's feet were in the end zone. Touchdown Browns! Bahr's extra point made the score 21-10.

As quickly as the Broncos capitalized on the Browns' miscue at the start of the game, the Browns had similarly returned the favor to start the second half. Modell felt a sudden surge of possibility just as Alice had moments before. "Who's to say we can't dominate the second half, the way Denver did in the first half?" Modell asked one of his guests. "We outscored the Colts 24-3 in the second half last week." The Browns fans could breathe again in this thin air.

The Broncos ran a few plays and again found themselves at third and 11, just like on the last series. Elway dropped back, and under a heavy rush, scrambled, knocking into one of his own players. Like in the last series, he retreated back inside his 5-yard line, and finally threw in desperation toward Mark Jackson. Jackson caught it short of the first down but shed the would-be tackler at the 25. He juked another Browns defender at the 30 and raced down the sideline. Fifty, 40, 30, 20, 10 . . . Ray Ellis dove and brought him down, but it was too late. Jackson fell into the end zone. Touchdown Denver. Karlis restored the lead to 18 points, and the Broncos had negated the Browns' only touchdown.

Alice hung her head low. "Just when I thought we had a chance."

"I wonder if that will break the Browns' spirits?" Ken pondered. "They finally do something good, and Denver comes right back and scores another touchdown."

"We still have Bernie, and we still have Byner!" Alice exclaimed. "They'll fight to the end."

Ken knew Alice was right. He just hoped it would matter.

After a pair of Mack runs, Kosar hit Byner on third down to pick up 11 yards to their 37-yard line. Then a 29-yard pass to wide-open Langhorne, who got drilled in the back by Dennis Smith's helmet (with Smith's head inside it and full bodyweight and momentum behind it).

"They're driving again," Ken said, almost whispering so as not to jinx it. First and 10 on Denver's 33. Kosar dropped back to pass. Feeling a little pressure, he galloped up toward the line of scrimmage, and, just short of it, lofted a touch pass, perfectly leading Byner, who was running full steam toward the end zone. No Bronco could stop him. After Bahr's kick, the score was Denver 28, Cleveland 17.

Ken looked at Alice with eyebrows arched and the hint of a smile on his face, his shoulders held in a partial shrug. The look said it all: The Broncos really couldn't stop the Browns. They would have shouted it from the rooftops, but they knew that so far, the Browns couldn't stop the Broncos either. With the sun setting behind the opposite field stands, they now felt a ray of hope flickering. "We really need to stop them on this possession if we want a chance," Ken said.

Cleveland's Lee Johnson kicked off to the same spot on the field that Karlis had been kicking to in the first quarter. Karlis had chosen that "flight plan" to make Ice Cube lose the ball in the blinding sun. Denver's return man, Ken Bell, wouldn't have the sun to contend with anymore. As the ball descended toward Bell, he stepped up to receive it at the 6. He bobbled and fumbled it out of bounds at the 14-yard line. A player can't advance the ball on a fumble out of bounds, so the Broncos would be pushed back to their 9-yard line to start this drive.

The Broncos could not advance the ball—at all! They were faced with fourth and 10 and had to punt. Alice stole a look at Ken with the same expression he had worn moments ago. Hope. Ice Cube received the punt inside the Broncos' territory and returned it to their 42.

"We couldn't ask for much better than that," Ken said. "Three and out, and now we are right back on their side of the field!"

Either the few hundred Browns fans were making more noise, or the 77,000 Broncos fans were becoming eerily quiet.

On first down, Kosar connected with Mack on a swing pass that gained 9 yards. Next the Broncos jumped offsides. First and 10 at the Denver 27 for the Browns. Kosar to Slaughter on a comeback pattern. Slaughter bobbled it, but still made the catch, good for another 15. On the next play Mack would sneak out of the backfield, and Kosar would find him for another 8 yards. The Browns were down to the Denver 4-yard line.

Alice smiled broadly now and showed Ken the crossed fingers on both her hands. "We're keeping them off balance. They don't know if we are gonna pass or run, and they can't stop us either way!"

All these successful offensive plays were like an intoxicant to Ken. His inhibitions were falling away. He was starting to cheer openly and loudly. The hat with the doghouse on top was again proudly adorning his head.

On second down and 2, from the 4-yard line, Byner took the handoff and burst up the middle. By the time he was taken down, the upper half of his body, including the ball, was in the end zone. Earnest was pinned there and punched the ground. It wasn't in frustration or anger. It was the only way he could celebrate until everyone got off his back.

From NBC's broadcasting booth, Merlin Olsen said it all: "Earnest Byner is a money player. Money players know where the goal line is." Matt Bahr made the extra point. The Browns now trailed by only 4 points! Ladies and gentlemen, we have a ballgame. Denver's fans may have been in shock. Their team had only allowed 21 or more points in an entire game three times throughout the season. The Browns had just scored 21 in the third quarter. Momentum was clearly with Cleveland.

"Art, it's beginning to look like we could win this thing," someone in the loge said. "The offense looks great!"

"Well, I sure hope so, I would love to get revenge for *The Drive*," Modell grumbled. "I don't want to hear about the damn *Drive* anymore."

*The Drive* was already—in just one year—a term that was instantly recognized by football fans everywhere. Like the "Immaculate Reception," it was shorthand for an improbable and legendary turn of events in NFL playoff action. *The Drive*, though, was something more. It somehow encapsulated the feeling of inevitable *whoa* that the Browns had been experiencing ever since that 1964 Championship.

It resonated beyond the Browns. Cleveland had been a mighty industrial power when the Browns were at their most dominant. Ever since, the team and the city seemed intertwined in a slow death march. In 1979, Cleveland became the first major city since the Great Depression to face financial default. *The Drive* finally put that into stark relief. Like the Cuyahoga River fire in 1969, it sharpened the world's focus on what had only been a vague unnoticed feeling to that point. When Modell wanted his team to avenge last year's loss, he didn't just want to beat these Broncos. He wanted to undo *The Drive*—and everything it stood for.

"All right, defense! Just like last time!" Ken was completely unabashed now.

The Broncos would be starting at their 20 after a touchback on Johnson's kickoff. Between Winder's run and a facemask penalty on the play, the Broncos had first and 10 at their 35. Then a 2-yard run. On second and 8, Elway had all day to throw and hit Jackson on the left sideline. Like last time, he made a tackler miss and picked up a bunch of extra yards before being pushed out at the Browns' 40. Browns fans' hope began eroding. Denver's team was not imploding.

Denver would pick up another first down. Then try a few plays including a crack at a bomb to the end zone but would have to settle for a Karlis field goal. The score with under a minute to go in the third quarter was Denver 31, Cleveland 24.

"Well, at least we kept them out of the end zone," Alice said with a smile.

"I actually think we have a shot," Ken said. "Denver's defense really hasn't stopped us all day." And he made some sense. If they could keep scoring touchdowns—and why wouldn't they?—they could avenge *The Drive* and play in the Super Bowl!

Bernie made the sign of the cross on the sideline before coming in for the Browns' first drive of the fourth quarter. Announcer Dick Enberg was moved to announce that, "Interestingly, Art Modell, when he traded all those number ones to get Kosar, thought he was Jewish. Well, he's quite happy with his religion, and his talent."

Right now, Modell wouldn't care if Kosar emulated Moses parting the Red Sea or Neil Armstrong shooting for the moon, just as long as he got the Browns to the Promised Land. "C'mon Bernie," Modell said in his Brooklyn accent. "Tie up this game."

Mack picked up 6 yards on first down, and the Browns faced second and 4 at their 19. Kosar threw over the middle for Ozzie Newsome. Five Broncos defenders had him surrounded, and the badly thrown ball hit one of their helmets. Alice covered her eyes as it looked like one of that quintet might make the interception. The ball fell harmlessly to the ground. It was Kosar's first incompletion in nine second-half attempts. "We can't take any stupid risks," Ken pleaded. "No turnovers!"

Kosar went to the air again. Third-quarter hero Earnest Byner had snuck way downfield and caught a long pass in full stride. By the time the Broncos corralled him, he had picked up 53 yards, all the way to the Denver 27! Enberg announced to the millions watching the NBC broadcast that "Coach Marty Schottenheimer has said, 'When the going gets tough, we want the ball in Earnest Byner's hands.'"

Kosar to Newsome for 8. Mack for half a yard. On third and a long yard, Mack smashed up the middle for 14! First and goal at the Denver 5-yard line. Alice and Ken held hands and squeezed tight in anticipation of the tying score.

Byner gained only half a yard on first down. Kosar, backpedaling, threw into the end zone for Fontenot. It was catchable, but Herman didn't pull it in. Alice and Ken knew a field goal would not do it here. They wanted the touchdown. They wanted to see the game tied up. On third and goal, Bernie went back to the air. Slaughter slanted across the end zone, underneath the coverage. Bernie hit him, and Slaughter didn't disappoint. Touchdown, Cleveland!

Merlin Olsen: "Kosar perhaps answering *What can we do to answer* The Drive *from last year that kept us from going to the Super Bowl?*"

Matt Bahr came on to try to tie this game. He succeeded. With just under eleven minutes in regulation, they were back where the game had started. After 62 points had been scored, each team had an equal share of them.

Euphoria surged through the Browns players and their fans. Impossible as it seemed in the first half, or in the third quarter when Jackson scored the 80-yard touchdown, the Browns had tied the game. Better yet, they now had a tidal wave of momentum carrying them toward the end of the game. Carrying them toward the Super Bowl.

Modell was buoyant in the box, talking comfortably to everyone. They had seen all second half that the Browns could score almost at will. At present it didn't occur to anyone that Elway had authored *The Drive* just one year ago. That he might rally the Broncos at any time. The swelling tide had lifted Cleveland's spirits. It felt like the tide was still coming in. That it wouldn't turn. Though the tide always does turn, eventually.

On first and 10 from the Broncos' 20, Elway connected for 22 yards to—who else—Mark Jackson. Sammy Winder gouged the Browns for 6 yards. Sewell ran for just 1, and it was third and 3. Elway was about to spring his patented soul-crushing, demoralizing play on the Browns' defense. He took the shotgun snap, took a step or two back, indicating a pass play. The trap set, he sprang it. He sprinted forward—a quarterback draw! His cleats sawing through the chewed-up field were no match for the power of his legs, and he lost traction. Third-string defensive lineman Daryl Sims got Elway before Elway got the first down. Alice and Ken high-fived, then hugged. "We got him! We stopped him!"

But Denver's punting unit didn't come on. Elway and the offense were out there with fourth and 1 yard to go, about a foot into Browns territory. Elway had grown into a myth since this time a year ago. He was now the bogeyman who haunted the imaginations of Browns fans everywhere. It is not hyperbole to say terror descended on Browns fans universally. Would Elway do a quarterback sneak, or go into a shotgun formation and throw, or try another quarterback draw? Would he just try to draw the Browns offsides? Anxiety replaced the brief elation of thirty seconds earlier.

Elway was in shotgun. The ball was snapped. He pooch-punted it! A warm blanket of instant relief melted the frozen terror in each Browns fan's heart. On top of that, the short punt took a terrible bounce from Elway's perspective and netted only 18 yards.

"Great field position!" Alice exclaimed.

The Browns would get to third down. Then Kosar connected with Brian Brennan for 12 yards and a first down at the Browns' 45. But the Browns could not advance it into Denver territory. Lee Johnson punted 38 yards. Denver would be taking over at their 23-yard line. Last year trailing by a touchdown, Elway took over from inside his 2-yard line with between five and six minutes remaining in regulation.

Now, from the 23, Elway would be taking over with between five and six minutes left in regulation. This time he was tied, and he was playing at home. Modell had felt the tide coming in all second half long. Was it starting to recede? "We need to keep them out of the end zone here," Modell, grim-faced, uttered to nobody in particular. "We don't need another Drive."

On the first play from scrimmage, Elway fired for Ricky Nattiel, who ran an out pattern. Nattiel had to drop to his knees to make the catch. He then rolled out of bounds and inside Browns territory. A few plays later, Elway reconnected with Nattiel for another first down. Again, he got out of bounds. Suddenly the Broncos were well inside Karlis's field goal range.

"This dawg-g one Elway, he's shredding us like last year!" Ken would have loved to see the Broncos make a field goal on this possession, even though that would put the Broncos back on top. His gut told him a Denver touchdown was coming, so a field goal sounded good in comparison.

On first and 10 from the Browns' 20, Elway threw a short pass to Sammy Winder. Winder broke tackles and ran into the end zone. It took just over a minute for Denver to reclaim the lead. Karlis made the extra point, and again the Broncos had a 7-point lead: 38-31. Nobody had processed it yet, but Elway had just put together another *Drive.* Last year it covered 98 yards and tied the game. This year it was only 77 yards, but it put his team up by a touchdown.

The question was: Could Kosar spoil the dreams of the home team's fans with a *Drive* of his own? He'd already put together four touchdown drives in this game's second half. With under four minutes left, could he lead a fifth?

On first and 10 from the 20, Byner ran for 20 yards. "Man, that Byner, he's the man!" Ken exclaimed. Along with Kosar, Byner had shown amazing fortitude in leading the Browns back when their spirits could easily have been broken. Here he was again, starting the drive with a big gain to near midfield. After a 2-yard gain by Byner, it was back to the other offensive hero: Kosar. He completed a 14-yard pass to Brennan. First down at the Denver 44. Kosar to Brennan again, and the Browns were to Denver's 24-yard line at the 2-minute warning. After encroachment on Denver, the Browns would try from the 19-yard line, first down and 5.

Kosar handed off to Byner. He juked and jived his way for 6 yards and another first down. Bernie threw to Byner, who'd gotten free in the back of the end zone. The pass went through his hands, but he'd have been out of bounds anyway. His exhaustion was obvious as he slowly ambled back to the huddle. On second and 10, Kosar threw incomplete to Langhorne, but an offsides call against Denver gave the Browns second down and 5 at the Denver 8-yard line. One minute and 12 seconds remained.

Modell stood silent in his suite, his hands clasped so tightly that he was literally white-knuckled.

Kosar handed the ball to Byner. He went off left guard, then angled outside and found plenty of daylight! Byner cut back up the field, toward the end zone, his ball-carrying left arm flinging away from his body slightly. Jeremiah Castille approached Byner at about the 1-yard line, where Byner had already gained the first down. Byner's momentum carried him into the end zone, where he was knocked down by another Bronco. Browns fans everywhere leaped in celebration!

But there was a problem. As Castille was closing in on Byner, he had punched the ball out at around the 1-yard line. From just inside the goal line, Byner looked back from whence he had just come. That's where the party was. And not just a party. A ball. The football. And he wasn't invited. Castille had not only knocked the ball loose, but he had also fallen on it, just inside the 3-yard line.

The big gulp of thin air that Ken and Alice had inhaled in preparation for belting out the loudest exultation of their lives was now stuck in their throats. They were choking. They felt like they had been leaning over the bow of a sailboat, feeling a tropical breeze caress their bodies, and the warm water splashing their faces, then suddenly they were underwater, drowning. Once they recovered from the shock, they'd feel the pain seep in.

The one man—besides Bernie Kosar, whose steely will and stellar skill had dragged the Browns back from oblivion—had proven himself mortal after all. Like Moses, he had gotten his chosen team to the brink of the Promised Land. But he could not enter.

Earnest Byner wandered back to the sidelines, exhausted. His teammates approached him as he sat alone, atop his helmet. Each man said some version of the same thing: "We love you." "We wouldn't have even had a chance without you." "No matter what, I'd always want you by my side." Byner heard every one of them, but somehow, even though he knew they meant it, he still felt like he had let them all down. The enormity of it couldn't be comprehended, especially now, so soon. But it could be felt. A new "The" was born into the sports lexicon: *The Fumble*.

In the visiting owner's box at Mile High Stadium, Modell hadn't yet realized the full scope of what had just happened. He knew the Browns had lost; knew they would not reach the Super Bowl—again. He knew that John Elway's team had stolen his birthright. It would only dawn on him later that *The Fumble* was yet another emblem of the Browns' ineptitude. Was it really ineptitude? Or was it a *curse*?

He thought back to the improbability of all that had to go wrong for the Broncos to win this game. Three uncharacteristic turnovers in the first half to put the Browns in a deep hole. A few critical missed tackles. Then a big gamble on Castille's part to punch at the ball rather than to go for the touchdown-saving, game-tying tackle. His "money" player, who'd carried the team all game—all season—on the back of his quiet, strong example, had dropped the ball at the most important time imaginable.

Modell thought back to the previous year. He thought that game was won. First and 98 to go for the Broncos. Then it was third down and 18, and the center snapped the ball off the running back's backside. Deflected, the ball still made its way into Elway's waiting hands. Elway made the pass. The receiver made the catch. *The Drive* made its way into football lore. That game went into overtime and ended in crushing defeat. So many things had to go exactly right for the Broncos, and go all wrong for the Browns, to prevent the Browns from winning.

Modell thought about the Super Bowl that his team would not be in. That his team had never been in. Modell was alongside NFL Commissioner Pete Rozelle in the mid-1960s when the decision was made to rebrand the "NFL Championship Game" into the "Super Bowl." It was the nexus of football, television, and advertising that would turn the Super Bowl into the must-see popular culture event of the year. The biggest party. The biggest stage.

It was Modell who'd come to own an NFL franchise after conquering the worlds of television and advertising. It was Modell as much as anyone who created the climate that made the Super Bowl so big. His team should be there. He should be there. It was his rightful place. Modell, like every Browns coach and player, like every Browns fan, was tired of waiting until next season.

## 30

# COVERT SUMMIT

SUMMER 1988, WEST POINT, NEW YORK

*"So, what does the middle linebacker do when you're in cover 2, and the* slot receiver adjusts his pattern to the outside?" Nick inquired of his lunch companion. His normally passionate voice was hushed. They were in public, and on a secret mission. Bill, who like his counterpart, normally was monomaniacally focused, glanced uncomfortably to his left and right, and drew a diagram on the napkin, talking through the intricacies of his defensive scheme.

"Hey, could we get the check, we're in a hurry," Bill asked the waitress. They were both eager to get back to the hotel, to privacy. West Point generals were less paranoid about their old wartime enemies discovering their military planning than these two assistant coaches were of being found out. After all, the Meadowlands was just an hour away.

Bill wondered, *What if Coach Parcells somehow spotted me talking strategy and tactics with a coach from the Houston Oilers?* He didn't want to find out the answer.

Bill Belichick. Nick Saban. To even the most casual football fan, these names are more than mere names. They are shorthand. There are implied meanings attached to both names. Significance that is understood by both the speaker of the name and the hearer, or the writer and the reader. But in the summer of 1988, Bill Belichick was simply the defensive coordinator of the New York Giants. Nick Saban was only the defensive backs coach of the Houston Oilers.

Dawning with the new millennium and forever forward "Bill Belichick" has been, and will always be, shorthand for "Bill Belichick, six-time (and counting?) Super Bowl–winning coach of one of the greatest dynasties in the history of professional sports. A no-nonsense, gruff, intensely competitive, mad genius who may be the greatest NFL coach of all time."

"Nick Saban" is shorthand for "Nick Saban, coach of seven college football champions (and counting). Winner at LSU, and right up there with Bear Bryant in creating an NCAA dynasty at Alabama."

But, in 1988, in this little restaurant in West Point, they were just Bill Belichick and Nick Saban. Granted, they were both respected (if not yet revered) in coaching circles, particularly by their head coaches, Bill Parcells and Jerry Glanville, respectively. As they left a fistful of crumpled singles on the table for a tip and made for the door, a man stood up from his table.

Oddly for a summer day, he was wearing an immaculately tailored overcoat. He greeted the coaches with a smile. "It certainly sounds like you men really know your football. I am sure you are each destined for great things." Belichick and Saban stole sideward glances at each other.

"You know what really surprises me, though?" the man continued. He paused, but both men were too stunned, too afraid that they had been found out, to answer. "I can't believe Coach Parcells, a man who won't even allow his assistants to talk to the press, and Coach Glanville, a coach who's so paranoid that he forbids his assistants from giving football clinics to schoolboys, would permit you two men to meet and discuss such high-level strategy."

Belichick dropped his car keys, then, crouching to pick them up, dropped a folder of notes and plays, papers flying all over the checkerboard floor. Saban stood dumbstruck with a look on his face normally reserved for mugshots and driver's license photos. He felt the blood drain from his face. Belichick felt his egg salad sandwich threaten to come back up. Each man's first thought was, *I could be fired.* Their second thought was, *Who is this guy?*

The man chuckled. "Oh now, what's the matter, gentlemen? You look like you've seen a ghost." Bill was the first to speak. He stammered out, "You, uh . . . we're not going to get in, um . . . who are you?" The man, utterly at ease, in great contrast to the coaches, relished the moment, like a cat toying with two terrified mice.

"I am just someone who can see that the two of you are exceptionally good at what you do," he answered. "You are here today because you have the ambition to be great. You both realize that in meeting with each other, you will each become better. That is, if your bosses don't find out about your sneaking behind their backs. Am I right?"

It was as if their sandwiches or iced tea had been laced with some kind of hallucinogenic drug. Each coach had approached this meeting on a firm foundation of coaching wisdom and skill. Over lunch they had each edified the other with a few more building blocks of knowledge. That which had already been rock solid was now gaining prominence. They had begun to feel the certainty of future success. But suddenly this stranger had replaced the bedrock beneath their foundations with quicksand. It was disorienting. Could their nascent fortresses be turned to castles of sand and so quickly melt away?

The man unclicked his briefcase. There was just one piece of paper inside, legal size, and crisp white save for the sparse typed copy.

**-CONFIDENTIAL-**

**We agree to the following: Apart, we will work together, and in so doing we will make each other better. We will have unparalleled success. However, together, we will eventually work apart. One's success will not be the other's, and though we each will succeed often, we will never fully succeed at the same time. The secret will be all ours.**

______________________________ **Signature**

______________________________ **Signature**

______________________________ **Signature**

**-CONFIDENTIAL-**

Two of the generation's most adroit tactical minds were stumped. *What the hell was this?* Had they not been so disoriented, they'd have laughed at this kook and been on their way. *What kind of weird riddle was this? Who would try to pull such a cockamamie move as this? How could a "contract" such as this be enforced?* Then again, how was it that this strange man had this paper in his briefcase? *How did he know we'd be here? How does he know who we are?*

The man handed Belichick a pen and remarked, "I hear Bill is enjoying his vacation on Martha's Vineyard." Belichick interpreted this comment about Coach Parcells to be a veiled threat; it was this strange man's way of saying "Sign this or I will tell your boss that you are deceiving him, being unfaithful." Belichick, seeing no other option, but also seeing no harm, immediately scrawled out his signature on the top line. He handed the pen to Saban, nodding to him to follow suit.

After Saban signed, the man affixed his signature to the third line. Both coaches looked but couldn't make out the stranger's name.

"I'll send you copies of this," the man said, looking pleased. "Good afternoon, gentlemen. Thank you." And he headed out the back door.

The coaches left by the front, got into their car, and drove the five minutes to their hotel in shocked silence. That afternoon they didn't talk any football . . . they just exhausted themselves and each other trying to figure out what had just happened.

31

# SPORTS ILLUSTRATED COVER CURSE

1988 SEASON

*When the 1988 NFL Preview issue of* **Sports Illustrated** *hit newsstands* in late August, Bernie Kosar's image dominated the cover. Next to his action photo was the title of one of the stories inside: *Cleveland's Bernie Kosar – Last of the Great Quarterbacks?* Text toward the bottom of the cover said: "Dr. Z's Super Picks: Browns and 49ers." *Sports Illustrated* wasn't going out on a limb here; most of the other football magazines picked the Browns to go all the way.

When a Cleveland *Plain Dealer* reporter asked Art Modell whether he was concerned about a possible *Sports Illustrated* cover jinx striking down the Browns, he quipped, "I sure as hell would rather be on the cover than on the obituary page." He continued, "I don't think it will add any more pressure than we've imposed on ourselves. We've had it in our hands two years in a row, and we blew it. That's pressure enough."

Modell—like all of Cleveland—was excited for the 1988 season to get underway. *The Drive* after the 1986 season and *The Fumble* after last season both still stung. On the bright side, though, Denver had a lousy draft in 1988, and they were not expected to be a nemesis to the Browns this year.

With a top-flight defense, first-rate offense, good special teams, Pro-Bowlers at several positions, strong coaching, and consistent playoff experience, this seemed to be the "next year" that they'd been waiting for since 1964. "*Sports Illustrated* jinx," Modell mumbled under his breath. "We'll show them we don't believe in any *Sports Illustrated* jinx."

Lindy Infante, the excellent offensive coordinator who came to the Browns before the 1986 season, had accepted the head coaching job at Green Bay during the off-season. Both years with Marty Schottenheimer as head coach and Lindy as O.C., the Browns had won the AFC Central and reached the AFC Championship. When Infante departed, the defensively minded Schottenheimer decided not to hire a new O.C. He would take on those duties himself. No one knew it yet, but this would be his undoing.

In the second quarter of the season opener in Kansas City, a Chiefs defender blitzed from his safety position and sacked the *Sports Illustrated* cover boy and odds-on NFL MVP candidate. Bernie Kosar suffered a "bruised right [throwing] elbow." The "bruise" turned out to be a sprain and Kosar wouldn't return to action until the seventh game. *Sports Illustrated* jinx, anybody? Besides Kosar, six other Browns starters were hurt in the game. The only good news was the Browns won. It wasn't pretty—no touchdowns, with a final score 6-3—but it was a win. The first season opening win in six years.

In the home opener the next week, the backup quarterback who had replaced Kosar the previous week was the new starter . . . not that he wasn't old. Gary Danielson was 37 and seeing his first significant action in years. Or so he thought. He broke his ankle in the third quarter, and it turned out to be a career-ending injury.

"Maybe there's something to this *Sports Illustrated* jinx," Modell confided to his wife that evening at home. "Or maybe, maybe it's really that old curse."

Pat didn't know what Art was talking about.

Art didn't sleep well that night. What sleep he found was spoiled by nightmares; he was falling backward into oblivion and everything he reached for getting further and further from his grasp. Flickering images of a strange man in a cashmere overcoat. When he woke up, he'd be agitated, sweating profusely, and exhausted.

Third-string quarterback Mike Pagel finished that second game, a 3-23 loss to the Jets. He managed to start and finish three more games, winning two, including the Browns' fifth win in a row against Pittsburgh. Schottenheimer's record against Chuck Noll and the Steelers at that point was 6-2. It would run to 7-2 by the end of the season. Was journeyman Mike Pagel more powerful than the jinx, or the Curse, or whatever had afflicted the Browns? No. Pagel was carried off on a stretcher after his shoulder was separated in the second quarter of game 6 against the Seahawks. The Browns would lose with Don Strock at the helm in the second half.

Strock had backed up Hall of Famers Bob Griese and Dan Marino and barely started a game in his fifteen-year NFL career with the Dolphins. When the Browns' quarterbacks started dropping like the stock market did on Black Monday the previous October, they picked up Strock, whose stock had fallen in Miami. Strock's stock rallied, and the Browns beat the Eagles 19-3.

The Browns' defense was more responsible for the win than the latest Browns quarterback, as they sacked the mobile Randall Cunningham nine times. Frank Minniefield picked him off twice for good measure. Strock made it through the entire game without injury! The Browns didn't escape unscathed, though. Webster Slaughter, their best receiver, broke his arm, and doctors expected him to miss eight to ten weeks.

Strock would not start the next game. But not because he was hurt. Bernie Kosar was back! This was the eighth game of the season and the fifth time a different quarterback had started the current game than the previous one! Kosar showed why he was the starter: he completed 25 of 43 passes for 314 yards, three touchdowns (and three interceptions).

Reggie Langhorne played well, catching two touchdowns, as the Browns won their second game in a row. Best of all, Kosar remained uninjured throughout the game. They would need him to stay healthy to have a chance against division-leading Cincinnati the next week.

Between Kosar, the defense, and the special teams, the Browns beat the Bengals, to even their record with Houston and pull to within a game of Cincinnati.

"It's been a tough season so far, but we're in good shape," Coach Schottenheimer said. "I like where we are right now. We still have some guys banged up, but Bernie's back, and we're playing well in all phases of the game."

Modell, for his part, was feeling the same way. His nightmares had subsided. He felt now that his fixation on a "jinx" or a "curse" was receding, retreating underneath a rock in his imagination, hopefully to disappear forever when the Browns won the Super Bowl at the end of this season.

A loss in Houston to the tough—and, most would say, dirty—Oilers pushed the Browns back into third place.

The following week was a rematch of last year's AFC Championship, back in Mile High. What was anticipated to be a good game and was hoped to offer a measure of retribution for the Browns and their fans didn't work out so well. The Browns' Tim Manoa fumbled on the first play. The Broncos quickly scored. Like last year, the Browns committed more first-half turnovers, and the Broncos turned them into touchdowns. Unlike last year, the Browns never mounted a comeback. The Browns lost for the *tenth straight time* to Denver, 7-30.

Modell harkened back to early this season when he laughed at the *Sports Illustrated* jinx. He told the reporter that the Browns had held their fate in their own hands the last two years, when they blew it. Well, they had just blown it again. Blown out by Denver. The loss dropped the Browns to a 6-5 record. This loss didn't eliminate them from playoff contention, but it made the odds longer.

Modell wondered again about the jinx or the Curse, or whatever it was, or wasn't. With all the injuries this season, then returning to Mile High, just to be embarrassed—to a Broncos team that was supposed to be in decline—maybe there was a *Sports Illustrated* jinx. Art thought about *The Fumble*, *The Drive*, *Red Right 88*, and all the other misfortunes that had befallen him and his team. All these things happened *before* Kosar appeared on that cover. But *after* that mystery man made him sign that contract.

The Browns would recover, reeling off three straight wins to improve to 9-5, again tying them with Houston for second place in the division and keeping their playoff hopes intact. It was a weird year. There were so many injuries, so many chances for the ship to sink. Yet every time they took on water, they would bob up above the waves and right the ship.

The coach, the players, the fans, the owner—all harbored a feeling that maybe this *was* the year. Maybe *Sports Illustrated* and the other magazines were right. The Browns were so powerful that even with so many storms, they'd sail straight into history, finally getting to the Super Bowl, and possibly even winning it.

Unfortunately, they would lose the next game—the second to last one of the regular season—back in Kosar's college home. In fact, they lost more than the game. They lost their hold on second place in the division. Worse yet, they lost Bernie Kosar! For the second time this year, he was knocked out of a game with an injury serious enough to make his return this season questionable—even for the playoffs, on the off-chance they would even make the playoffs.

Don Strock was summoned once again and played well in the Miami Orange Bowl where he'd been the Dolphins' backup for so many years. He led a great comeback, with two quick touchdown passes in the fourth quarter to tie the game. Dan Marino put together the game-winning touchdown drive to add insult (of defeat) to injury (of franchise quarterback).

Houston came to Cleveland for the regular season finale with a one-game lead over the Browns. The Browns had Webster Slaughter back from his broken arm, but they didn't have Kosar to throw to him. His sprained knee would keep him out of this must-win game. Essentially, this was a one-game play-in to make the playoffs.

Strock threw three interceptions in his first six passes in the worst start imaginable. Houston went up 23-7. Fans behaved badly. The weather stank: heavy snow and swirling winds. Against all odds, Strock turned it around! Slaughter had his best game ever! And the Browns prevailed! They punched their ticket to the playoffs—for the fourth straight year.

Next week's wild-card opponent: the Houston Oilers.

The season's final regular-season game was a microcosm of the season: the dejection of being down and seemingly out for the count, followed by the Browns rising from the ashes. From looking like there was no way to make the playoffs to looking like they would triumph. Indeed, they did. They made the playoffs. But, unfortunately, the other major theme of the season—losing the starting quarterback to injury—played out in this game too.

The joy of surmounting this season of pain to make the playoffs was tempered with losing Kosar once again. Considering the Oilers had squandered a big lead to lose the game, and they would need to play in Cleveland—in the freezing cold, again—next week and considering next week's starting quarterback Don Strock had just beaten them, things were not looking so good for Houston in the impending wild-card matchup with the Browns.

Dozens of the mangier denizens of the Dawg Pound had fired snowballs at the Houston players during the regular season finale. A pair of particularly rabid fans poured beer on a defenseless TV cameraman knocked senseless in the snow just short of the Dawg Pound. (The camera operator was unconscious because two players had just smashed into him, just out of bounds.)

Modell was angry that the actions of a couple drunken idiots could cast a pall over his team and their accomplishments. "This should be our moment!" he said. "We could make the Super Bowl, and all anyone is talking about across the country is these 'criminal' Browns fans!"

The Washington (D.C.) Touchdown Club had informed Modell earlier that week that he'd won their first-ever Lifetime Achievement Award. This was a huge honor, of which he was justifiably proud. His team was in the playoffs for the fourth straight year and had a shot at finally winning it all. This was finally a chance for Modell to take a victory lap.

Yet all he heard about on the news was those snowball-throwing, beer-swilling idiots. When he should be basking in the warm floodlights of respect and admiration, he was instead the owner of a classless team with classless fans from a classless city. It was hard not to feel cursed.

32

# AFC WILD-CARD GAME VS. THE OILERS

December 24, 1988, AFC Wild-card Game – Cleveland Stadium

*Somehow 77,000 fans managed to convince their families that they* should go to the Browns game rather than stay home or accompany their family to Christmas Eve worship. Since the game was sold out, it would be televised locally, so all fans not at the game could watch from their living room or favorite watering hole—if any were open on Christmas Eve. All last week's snow had melted. There would be no snowballs thrown at this game. But mud . . . now that could be a problem.

Neither team was in a charitable spirit. There would be twenty-two penalties, many of them unsportsmanlike conduct infractions and personal fouls. Houston had a reputation as a tough (dirty) team under Jerry Glanville. Their home stadium, the Astrodome, was known as the House of Pain. In the end, the Browns fell into the trap of trying to match Houston, cheap shot for cheap shot. It wasn't the Browns' style of play, and they weren't good at it.

Cody Risien and Earnest Byner were normally hardworking but not hot-headed. But today emotion got the better of them. Their penalties knocked the Browns out of field goal range on at least one occasion. The Browns lost 23-24. In a game of inches, those penalties—more than anything else—are what lost the game for Cleveland. True, their starting quarterback, Don Strock, was knocked out of the game (why should the playoffs be any different than the regular season?). But that was not the reason they lost. Mike Pagel, just back after healing for nine weeks due to his injury, played great.

Whatever the ultimate reason for defeat, the loss was more than just a lump of coal. It was the sixth time the Browns had reached the playoffs in the 1980s. And each trip ended in a loss before they reached the Super Bowl. Each game had been winnable; only strange circumstances prevented a Browns win. And with each loss, something painful, iconic, and enduring was attached. Something that diminished the team and diminished the city.

Three of these losses even had shorthand nicknames. Nicknames that are universally recognized by even casual fans: *The Drive, The Fumble, Red Right 88*. Although each of those games also had a winning team, the very mention of any of those terms immediately conjures up the losing perspective. Futility. *The Drive, The Fumble,* and *Red Right 88* are a refutation of the American Dream. The basis for humiliation, fatalism, resignation. They are each an emblem of decline. Together, can they be anything other than proof of an oppression of a supernatural dimension?

Worse yet, the era these games defined would prove to be the days of wine and roses compared with the next thirty years. The decades of desolation.

## 33

# MARTY MOVES ON

### End of the Schottenheimer Era

*What do you do with the coach who's compiled the third-best winning* percentage in team history, right after he's made the playoffs for the fourth of four full years that he's coached the team?

A. Give him a big raise?
B. Name him general manager in addition to being head coach?
C. Make him part owner of the franchise?
D. None of the above

True, the Browns had just lost the wild-card round playoff game to Houston. But the Browns had practically lost more quarterbacks than games during the season (and playoffs)! To even make the post-season was something of a miracle. On December 27 (three days after the loss and exactly twenty-four years since the Browns last won the NFL Championship) Art Modell called Marty Schottenheimer in for a meeting.

"Marty, you've done a great job since you've been the head coach. We made the playoff every year and won the division twice. But we couldn't get to the Super Bowl, and we couldn't get past the Oilers this year."

"Well, Art, we had a couple injuries this year. I don't know how many coaches could salvage a season where you can't keep a quarterback on the field for more than a game before he gets hurt." His voice elevated, the vein on the right side of his forehead raising, his face flushing. "I mean, c'mon, Bernie only played, like, four games all year!"

"Marty, since we lost Lindy, the offense hasn't been the same."

"You're kidding, right?! You think it's my play calling? Art, I don't know that Infante would have been able to do any better if he was still here. You can't win in this league without a quarterback, and we went through four of them this year!" Marty was hot!

"Maybe with some better coaching on the offensive line, and some different play calls, we could have protected the quarterback."

"Ha! I can't believe this! You are beating me up after I took this team—that could barely walk—and got 'em to the playoffs. Art, I—"

"Marty, you are a great defensive mind. But I want you to hire an offensive coordinator, like I told you after Lindy left."

"I told you, hiring an O.C. would do more harm than good. We've had so much success these last few years. It doesn't make sense to bring in a new system."

"Well, I demand it. I want an offensive coordinator, and I want several other changes, too. I want you to relieve your brother from his special teams role—"

"What the hell is this? Did you wake up on the wrong side of the bed? You're telling me *I* am not good enough and my *brother's* not good enough. You want me to fire my own *brother*?!"

"Marty, the window of opportunity is closing. Cincinnati has a great team now. Houston is strong and getting stronger. We can't stand pat. We need to do everything in our power to win now."

"I want you to reconsider. The game was just a couple days ago. Why don't we take a break and meet again later. Right now, I can't see how we can agree on anything."

"Fair enough. You know where to find me. But Marty—I want you to take a step back and swallow your pride. I am not likely to change my mind."

Schottenheimer started to protest but knew it was futile. It was his suggestion to take a break, so he would drop his retort and hash it out with Modell later. Whether that meant later today or sometime later in the week hadn't been defined. Schottenheimer thought to himself, *The gall of this man! Telling me to swallow* my *pride.* As he drove from the suburban Berea headquarters to his suburban neighborhood he argued in his head with an imaginary Art Modell.

At home, Schottenheimer stewed. The time away from Modell didn't serve as a cool-down period. *He wants me to fire half my coaching staff, and my brother, my BROTHER! No way in hell am I gonna stand for that. And I am not hiring anyone to be my offensive coordinator. Dammit, if Bernie had stayed healthy, we'd probably be going to the Super Bowl this year. I don't see any need for a big change.*

Schottenheimer was dug in deep. He was resolved not to reconsider. He was ready to call Modell now and tell him so. He hesitated, wondering whether Modell might change his mind and relent on all his demands once the sting of the Houston loss had worn off for a couple of days.

Modell, meanwhile, back at his house, was not as hot and bothered. Sure, he was bothered, but it was more of a steely resolve. Schottenheimer was a great defensive coordinator and had been a great head coach—when he had a great offensive coordinator calling the plays beside him. The defense was fine. But the offense needed an overhaul. Well, actually, the offensive players were fine. They just needed to be better coached, and there was no reason that Schottenheimer shouldn't be able to see that.

Schottenheimer didn't have the patience to wait for Modell to possibly come around. He called Modell, and they agreed to meet back in Berea later that same day. When they did, neither side budged.

Modell didn't have to fire Schottenheimer, as Schottenheimer quit, not being willing to accept Modell's demands. The two men agreed to go their separate ways. There was not a tremendous amount of animosity; they were just two headstrong men who were convinced of the merits of their philosophy and they agreed to go in different directions. After the most successful four-and-a-half-year stretch in over two decades, the coach who'd been there, making it happen, was now no longer with the Cleveland Browns.

In his four full seasons as Browns head coach, Schottenheimer's Browns won the division twice, got to the AFC Championship Game twice, and made the playoffs the other two years, all while compiling an overall record (including the 4-4 stint as interim head coach after Rutigliano was fired in 1985) of 46-31 (.597).

Around town, fans' loyalties were split.

Half bashed Modell: "How can you fire a coach that gets you to the playoffs every year, especially this year, with all the injuries!?"

Others bashed Schottenheimer: "He was too stubborn. The offense took a big step back when we lost Lindy. Plus, he could never win the big one. Time for a new coach!"

Be careful what you wish for.

After promises of an exhaustive search, and rumors of several big-name head coaching candidates, the Browns hired former Jets defensive coordinator Bud Carson as the eighth head coach of the Cleveland Browns. Carson was the architect of the Steelers' dominant Steel Curtain defense in the seventies, so he seemed a great choice to replace Schottenheimer. Oh, and you'd better believe they hired an offensive coordinator: Marc Trestman. Remember him? Bernie Kosar did. Trestman was Kosar's offensive coordinator at the University of Miami. And they were close friends.

With another defensive guru as head coach and a respected offensive mind coordinating the offense (one with a proven track record of getting the best out of Kosar), things were looking promising as the Browns approached the goal line of the 1990s. Maybe the Schottenheimer-bashers were right. The Browns experienced tons of success throughout the eighties. But they could never win the big one. They couldn't even *get* to the big one. Maybe this new regime was just what the Browns needed.

The year 1989 might be the one. Maybe the Browns would finally play in a Super Bowl just weeks after the calendar left the 1980s behind. Heck, the nineties might prove to be the best decade since the hallowed days of Paul Brown!

34

# DIFFERENT SPORT, SAME STORY FOR CLEVELAND

## The Shot

***The year 1989 might be the one for the Cavaliers, as well. The Cavs had*** eked into the playoffs after the 1987–1988 season. It was the first time they'd made the playoffs since the *Miracle of Richfield* era in the mid-seventies, other than an embarrassing stint under George Karl in 1984 when they made the playoffs with a record ten games under .500.

After the 1987-1988 season, Michael Jordan and the Chicago Bulls quickly dispatched the upstart Cavaliers. But it hardly mattered. Boston and Detroit were dominant in the East, and the Los Angeles Lakers were still a power in the West. When the playoffs were all said and done, Magic, Kareem, James Worthy, and the Lakers downed Isiah, Rodman, Dumars and the Bad Boys from Detroit 4-3.

The next year, Detroit and Los Angeles were both stronger. The Cavs has surged. Having limped into the playoffs last year, they shared the league's second-best regular season record (57-25) with the Lakers, behind only the Pistons (63-19) in the whole NBA. Meanwhile, Chicago's record (47-35) had receded to ten games worse than the Cavaliers'.

If there was ever a year for the Cavs to master the Bulls, and challenge Detroit for supremacy in the East, this was it. For the second year in a row, their first-round opponent was the Bulls. As last year, it would be a best-of-five contest.

The Cavs, without point guard extraordinaire Mark Price, who'd been out for a month with a groin injury, found themselves down 0-1 after the first game. Price came back and helped Cleveland even the series at a game apiece after two. Chicago gained the series lead again, and the Cavs were in a must-win situation in game four.

By the end of game 4's regulation in Chicago Stadium, the outcome hadn't been decided. This series had been billed as Cleveland being the better team and Chicago being a bunch of guys with one great player. When that player is Michael Jordan, though, the otherwise inferior team always has a shot. Jordan scored 50 in this contest. Even so, the Cavaliers won in overtime! The Cavs had the momentum and were headed back home to the Richmond Coliseum for the deciding game 5.

## May 7, 1989, Richfield Coliseum, Richfield, Ohio

Like the whole series, this game was tight: down to the final quarter, 11 seconds to go. Cleveland led by a single point, 98-97. Inbounds pass to Jordan. He'd been cold in the first half but had erupted for 26 so far since intermission. Jordan took the 10-foot jumper from the right side of the paint and banked it in for his 27th and 28th second half points, giving the Bulls a lead with 6 seconds remaining. Timeout: Cavs.

Coach Lenny Wilkins drew up a play. From half-court, six-foot-six guard Craig Ehlo, who'd been tasked with defending Michael Jordan despite having a sprained ankle, inbounded the ball to Larry Nance. Nance underhanded the give-n-go back to the surging Ehlo, streaking in from the left sideline toward the basket.

Jordan abandoned his post in the middle of the paint to help on Ehlo. Ehlo leaped, and Jordan did too, coming in from Ehlo's right in a bid to block his shot attempt. The Cavs' guard maneuvered midair, avoiding Jordan's defenses. He banked in the layup with three seconds on the clock! Ehlo had come to compete! Injured and all, he'd guarded the best player in the league and had scored 15 points for the Cavs in this fourth quarter. When Ehlo came back to earth, he collapsed to the floor. Fellow wounded warrior Mark Price helped his backcourt mate to his feet.

Chicago's time for a timeout. Doug Collins drew up a play for his team to try to win it in the end. Bill Cartwright picked off Ehlo to initially free up Jordan, who was quickly picked up again before Brad Sellers could inbound the ball to him. Jordan worked himself free and got the ball. He was midway between the midcourt line and the foul line extended, about ten feet from the right sideline.

Jordan took two left-handed dribbles. Initially it looked like he'd drive toward the basket, but then he glided leftward to the top of the key. Jordan jumped and Ehlo reacted, jumping from Jordan's right side, looking to swat away Chicago's only shot at winning the series.

Ehlo reached his apex and was on the down elevator as Jordan seemed to levitate. His air-ness shifted the ball from his left to his right hand as gravity finally decided to begin pulling him earthward.

Jordan launched the jumper. As the ball back-spun off his fingertips and reached its zenith, exactly halfway to the basket, the red light illuminated. Time had run out. The outcome literally hung in the balance. Time would have run out on Chicago's season if the ball clanked off the rim and fell harmlessly away. Time would have run out on Cleveland's season if the ball made its way through the hoop.

As the ball approached its date with destiny, it was obvious this would not be a "nothing but net" swish. The ball would contact some metal. The ball grazed the inside of the rim between the 10 and 11 o'clock positions. It slid in, giving Jordan his 43rd and 44th points of the game. He'd willed Chicago to the 101-100 win. In perhaps the defining image of Michael Jordan's brilliant career, he jumped and pumped his fist as Craig Ehlo fell to the floor.

In the last three years, Cleveland fans had endured *The Drive*, *The Fumble*, and now, at the hands of Michael Jordan, *The Shot*.

The unfortunate news for the Cavs and their fans was that the period of their resurgence aligned with the Michael Jordan era. It was like a total eclipse of the sun. The Cavs made the playoffs eight out of nine seasons, starting in 1987-1988. They never beat the Bulls in a playoff series in that era. Cleveland was eliminated by the Bulls five times in that stretch, including in the conference finals in 1991-1992 after the Cavs had beaten the Celtics in seven games.

The very next year, the Bulls ousted them in the conference semi-finals.

Just as John Elway had single-handedly foiled excellent Browns teams, repeatedly blocking them from the league championship, Michael Jordan was anointed by the basketball gods at just the right time to block the Cavs from ever reaching the NBA Finals. At least until long after Jordan had retired, and his "air-apparent" LeBron James came to define excellence in the NBA.

35

# DAWN OF THE BUD CARSON ERA

1989 Season

*The first game of the Bud Carson era almost made fans forget all about* Marty Schottenheimer. Schottenheimer had resounding success against the Pittsburgh Steelers as Cleveland's head coach, but nothing like what the Browns did to the Steelers in Three Rivers Stadium to open the 1989 campaign. By the time the Steelers limped to their locker room, they had fumbled six times, five of which had been recovered by the Browns, and three of which were returned for touchdowns. Further, the Browns had intercepted quarterback Bubby Brister three times. Cleveland's defense sacked Brister another six times!

The Steelers only managed 36 yards rushing for the game. But that was their strong point, as they were limited to just 17 net yards passing! Cleveland crushed Pittsburgh 51-0. The next day the Cleveland *Plain Dealer* printed the following:

"Records set in the Browns' 51-0 victory over the Pittsburgh Steelers yesterday:

- 51 points – Largest margin of defeat for a Steelers team.
- 51 points – Most points scored by an opponent at Three Rivers Stadium.
- 53 total yards – Fewest allowed by a Cleveland defense and fewest gained by a Pittsburgh offense.
- 5 first downs – fewest by a Pittsburgh offense.
- 51-0 – Largest shutout in Browns' history."

After the game, the team tried to give the game ball to Coach Carson. (Had any coach, anywhere, ever had a better debut?) The rain-soaked and disheveled first-time head coach wouldn't hear of it, instead announcing to the team, "This was a total team effort. Everyone will be getting a game ball!" If Art Modell was ecstatic after this historic win, he certainly hid it well: "I'm happy for Bud Carson, but I'm not euphoric," he said. "But I know we lost sixteen in a row here once. Do you want the scores?"

The Browns' offense had a field day in game 2 against Coach Carson's most recent team, the Jets, and won 38-24.

Reality would slap the Browns in the face in week three as they saw that they could lose after all. This one was to division rival Cincinnati—one of the teams whose ascendance had scared Modell into wanting to rid himself of Schottenheimer after last season.

Undefeated Denver came to town in week four. The Browns' defense harassed John Elway into his worst game ever. They sacked him four times, picked him off once, and held him to just six completions all game. *Six* completions all *game*! The Browns also forced four Denver fumbles and recovered two. Still, it took a last-second field goal to secure the win.

Following the Broncos' game with two straight losses, the Browns found themselves at 3-3 after playing six games. They had even lost to the Steelers—at home—during this stretch. This was the team they shellacked 51-0 at Three Rivers a month and a half before. In this topsy-turvy season, Cleveland would find themselves leading the division at 7-3 after four straight wins. The Browns were again looking like they would fulfill the promise of glory that radiated magnificently in the first game of the season.

But that wouldn't last.

Starting the second half of the year, Bernie Kosar wouldn't throw a touchdown pass in twenty straight quarters! Lingering elbow soreness and a subdued running attack—Kevin Mack had been out all season so far because of his arrest and incarceration on drug charges—may have held Kosar back. The Browns went winless during this stretch, and their record sagged to barely above .500 after fourteen games, at 7-6-1. Cleveland would beat Minnesota in the penultimate week to set up a showdown in the Houston Astrodome against the Oilers in the season's final week.

Cleveland jumped out to a 17-0 lead in the House of Pain. The Oilers mounted a comeback. On one Houston series, the snapped ball whistled right past quarterback Warren Moon, who was aligned in the shotgun formation. Veteran Browns linebacker Clay Matthews recovered the fumble. Inexplicably, rather than run toward the goal line or drop to the turf, he lateraled the ball backward in a panic. To nobody!

Houston recovered this completely unforced error. On the next play, Moon threw a touchdown strike to Drew Pearson to put Houston into the lead! For Browns fans shell-shocked by *Red Right 88*, *The Drive*, *The Fumble*, and *The Shot*, there now seemed to be a new term that might live in infamy: *The Lateral*.

The Oilers held the lead late in the fourth. The Browns turned to Kevin Mack down the stretch. Mack was an unlikely hero, having only recently returned from the NFL suspension stemming from his arrest on drug charges during the off-season. But Mack drove through Houston's defense play after play and finally hit pay dirt with forty-five seconds left in the game.

The Browns emerged victorious and, in so doing, won the AFC Central Division for the fourth time in the last five years. *The Lateral*—sapped of lasting power by the win—never joined *The Drive* and *The Fumble* in the dictionary of defeat, the lexicon of losing, the vernacular of the vanquished.

It had been a very strange season. At times, the Browns dominated. Then they could look bad for a month. In one game, the offense would spark them as the defense slept. Other times, the defense would carry an impotent offense to victory. The Browns had destroyed the Steelers in Pittsburgh, while taking the ball away eight times. Then they gave the ball away seven times at home and lost to the Steelers. Weird season.

It was also weird that no team in the division had a losing record, and yet the Browns won the division with a mediocre 9-6-1 mark. Last year's AFC Central champion, Cincinnati, was the only division team not to make the 1989 playoffs.

The 1983 NFL draft is considered the finest one for quarterbacks in league history. Six quarterbacks were taken in the first round. Three of those would eventually be enshrined in the NFL Hall of Fame. The Browns had already met two of these quarterbacks in their playoff runs of the late eighties: the Dolphins' Dan Marino, and, of course, the Broncos' John Elway. This year, they would again encounter Elway. But first, they'd have to get past someone they hadn't yet faced in the playoffs: Jim Kelly and his Buffalo Bills.

In the leadup to the game, star defensive end Bruce Smith insulted the Browns' house, giving the Browns' locker room some grade-A bulletin board material: "The only advantage they have is playing on that terrible field. It's a beach with sand painted green. It's the Sahara Desert. The field is horrible, and it ought to be banned from the league."

Now, this was a very insulting thing to say . . . although completely accurate (except for the part about it being Cleveland's *only* advantage). By the end of the game, Smith's words would prove prophetic.

36

# AFC DIVISIONAL PLAYOFF VS. BUFFALO

JANUARY 6, 1990 – CLEVELAND MUNICIPAL STADIUM

*The Bills scored first on a 72-yard pass from Jim Kelly to Andre Reed.* Scott Norwood's extra point was good. Cleveland tallied a Matt Bahr field goal, after he had missed one earlier. Buffalo led 7-3 after one quarter. Bernie Kosar threw two touchdown passes in the second quarter: a 52-yarder to Webster Slaughter and a 3-yarder to seldom-used Ron Middleton. These were sandwiched around Buffalo's 33-yard touchdown pass from Kelly to James Lofton. Bahr made both of Cleveland's extra points, and Norwood made his for Buffalo. The Browns led at halftime 17-14.

Sisters Mary and Martha were among the 77,454 at the game. Sisters as in nuns, not siblings. Getting ahead of herself, Sister Martha confided: "Oh, how I want to beat the Broncos this year!"

"Are you kidding me?" Mary said. "We've got to pull for Pittsburgh tomorrow. If the Steelers win, they must come here. If the Broncos win, we have to go to Denver."

"I know, but I cannot bring myself to root for the Steelers, I just can't do it. Besides, we handled that twerp John Elway pretty well earlier this season, he could barely get off a pass."

These nuns knew their football . . . and loved their Browns.

In the third quarter, the Browns went big play, and the Bills went small ball. Kosar hooked up again with "Web-Star" Slaughter, this time for a touchdown of 44 yards. Kelly repeatedly found crafty running back Thurman Thomas down field for dink and dunk completions.

Eventually one was for a touchdown. This brought the Bills back to within 3 points of the Browns, at 24-21.

Just as the Bills and their ball control passing attack seemed to wrest the momentum from Cleveland, rookie running back and kickoff returner Eric Metcalf showed what speed and moves can do—even on "sand painted green."

Charlie Jones alongside fellow NBC announcer Merlin Olsen picks up the action:

"Metcalf at the 10. To the 20! 30! 40!" And then when Metcalf was still 40 yards out, but had obviously vanquished the Bills' special teamers, Jones continued with a lusty cry, "Ninety yards!" What he said next was amazing. Nothing.

Charlie Jones and Merlin Olsen let the delirium of the crowd tell the story. For a full minute, there was no narration. The camera panned the stadium showing the devout duded up in doggie duds in the Dawg Pound, Art Modell hugging someone else in a camel-colored cashmere coat in his loge, pompons pulsing like pistons in the stands, and Browns players hugging, jumping, and celebrating like the game was won.

Jones and Olsen didn't resume talking until after the extra point was made, when a Bills player was penalized for running into Bahr. Lesser announcers would have fallen over themselves ratcheting up the superlatives to describe the play everyone had just seen. But their silence told the story more eloquently.

The Browns had again stretched the lead to 10 points, 31-21. Browns fans were hoping Bahr wouldn't be needed for a last-second field goal; he had limped off the field after the penalty.

The Bills couldn't match the sudden strike scoring on the ensuing kickoff. Instead, they started at the 20 after a touchback. Thurman Thomas seemed to get better as the game wore on. Time and again, he was there to bail out Kelly and seemed to always get the first down when the Bills really needed one.

Eleven plays later, on a third and a foot from just outside the Browns' 11, the Bills had taken Thurman out of the game, opting instead for a two-fullback set. Larry Kinnebrew took the handoff, but linebacker Mike Johnson stopped him in the Bills' backfield. Marv Levy sent Scott Norwood to attempt the short field goal. It didn't make it very high or very long, but it made it. Early in the fourth quarter, the Browns led by a touchdown, 31-24.

Eric Metcalf returned the kickoff, making three Bills miss. Could he break another one? Not this time, as he was tackled at his own 33 after picking up 26 yards. Cleveland would methodically drive down the field with runs and short passes. They had taken 7 minutes off the clock by the time the Bills stopped them at the Buffalo 30-yard line and sent Bahr in to attempt the 46-yard field goal.

Thus far Bahr had made a 45-yarder and missed a 45-yarder. Both of those were prior to his last-made kick, the recent PAT. The one on which he'd been run into, causing him to limp off the field. This kick started wide right but curled nicely through the uprights. With 6:50 remaining, the Browns again had a 10-point lead!

Wagner returned the kickoff from the 9 to the 22-yard line. The Bills would need to go 78 yards for a touchdown. Kelly would take advantage of Bud Carson's prevent defense. Little arcing lollipop passes to Ronnie Harmon, and especially Thurman Thomas, each went for positive yardage, if not directly for a first down. Harmon caught a short pass and made a big gain before being tackled inside the Browns' 5-yard line. The Browns' Tony Blaylock was injured and after a lengthy delay was removed from the field on a stretcher. Once play resumed, Kelly went back to Thomas for a 3-yard touchdown. With the point after, the Bills would trail by just a field goal.

But Scott Norwood would not make the extra point. He kicked the ball into the backside of one of his offensive linemen. The "beach" that Bruce Smith had talked about had come to bite the Bills. Norwood's left foot slid as he tried to plant. His kicking foot didn't really kick the ball. It kind of slid in parallel with his plant foot and never gave any propulsion to the football. Home field advantage, indeed! This was huge, as the Bills—if they could stop the Browns and get the ball back—would need to score a touchdown. A field goal was no longer an option.

Buffalo attempted an on-sides kickoff, but the ball went out of bounds. After the 5-yard penalty, they kicked again but kicked deep this time. Mike Oliphant sacrificed a long return attempt for ball security. With 3:48 remaining, the Browns' offense started the drive just over their 30-yard line. If they could make two or three first downs and burn clock, they would be headed for another AFC Championship Game, their third in four years.

After just three plays, and not much time, the Browns had to punt. The Browns fans who'd suffered through *Red Right 88, The Drive, and The Fumble*, all during the previous five years, could feel the hand of fate clutching their throats. Would the Browns choke yet again? What would future generations call this failure? Or could the Browns somehow escape with the victory? Would Jim Kelly emulate his fellow "Class of 83" quarterback, John Elway, and engineer more misery for the Browns and their fans? Time would tell. In two minutes and forty-one seconds of game time, the demoralizing, or joyous, outcome would be known.

Kelly and company took over at the 25-yard line. A field goal was of no use, it would be pay dirt or bust. Two plays, two completions to Ronnie Harmon out of the backfield for 18 yards. The Browns were getting no pressure on the quarterback. Nor had they figured out how to stop a running back from asserting his will in the passing game. The two-minute warning offered a chance for the Browns to make defensive adjustments.

Maybe the Harvard man, Bills coach Marv Levy, anticipated the Browns finally clamping down on the running backs after eight straight completions to Thurman Thomas or Ronnie Harmon. He dialed up a bomb. Kelly overthrew James Lofton, and the Bills faced second and 10.

Finally, the Browns applied defensive pressure. Kelly avoided it, and threw downfield, high for his receiver. Reserve defensive back Kyle Kramer got his hands on the football but couldn't make the game-icing interception. Third and 10. Again, the Browns forced Kelly from the pocket. He set and threw an arcing pass toward his receiver in a sea of Browns defenders. The ball hung up long enough for another Ohio college rookie defensive back, Robert Lyons, to knock it away.

The Bills season came down to this play. Fourth and 10 with 1:36 remaining. A first down, and they would play on. Anything short of that and Cleveland would play once again in the game that would send its winner to the Super Bowl. Kelly backpedaled, then broke out of the pocket and headed toward the line of scrimmage. He pulled up and fired a laser to Don Beebe, who caught it for a 17-yard gain and a season-saving first down.

As time ticked down under 1:20, everyone in the stands remembered how Elway had converted on a third and 18, amid *The Drive*.

Fate's grip tightened, and the fans couldn't cheer. You can't cheer if you can't breathe.

With 1:16 left, and the ball on the Cleveland 41, it was the Browns who called timeout. It aided Buffalo, but Bud Carson must have believed his defense needed some substitutions. On second and 10, Kelly again found Thomas, who made 9 yards and got out of bounds with 1 minute remaining. The Browns had to burn another timeout to get some personnel off the field before Buffalo quick-snapped the ball.

On third and 1, the Browns finally got pressure on Kelly. He was too elusive to be sacked, but he had to throw the ball away, and was lucky the refs didn't call him for intentional grounding. Again, the Bills faced fourth down, this time with just 1 yard to go.

Andre Reed ran a short slant and made the catch for another first down. Kelly then clocked the ball with 35 seconds left. Second down and 10 from the 23-yard line. Art Modell fidgeted in his loge. A 4-point lead was so tenuous. A Buffalo touchdown would put the Bills up by at least 2 points . . . and leave almost no time on the clock.

After an incompletion, Kelly went back to Thomas, who caught it and spun out of a couple tackles, eventually being downed after picking up the first down at the 11.

Kelly clocked it with 14 seconds remaining. The Bills would have three chances to go 11 yards. If they could do it, they would be going to the AFC Championship Game. If the Browns could stop them, the Browns would have that honor. The Browns used their final timeout. The first-year Browns coach exhorted his team to clamp down.

The Bills' Ronnie Harmon got open, streaking into the left side of the end zone. Kelly led him perfectly. The ball arced down into Harmon's hands. But it glanced off them harmlessly. Third and 10, with 9 seconds in the game.

Thomas lined up in the right wing. Would he come through yet again, as he had all second half? Kelly took his drop and stood tall in the pocket, the offensive line keeping the Browns defenders at bay. Kelly pulled the trigger, looking for Thomas, who was over the middle, 1 yard deep in the end zone. Kelly's throw was short. Clay Matthews closed on it and made the interception, falling immediately to the sandy "turf" at the 3-yard line!

The game clock showed three seconds, but the linebacker had sealed the deal. The same man who had nearly lateraled away the

Browns' season in Houston two weeks ago was now the hero. The Browns' offense ran one play to run the clock out, and the Browns had weathered the storm. The Browns won 31-27. The Cleveland Browns were again headed to the AFC Championship Game!

In the owner's box, Modell embraced Ernie Accorsi, each of them swaddled in camel-hair overcoats. Another man, dressed in a full-length dark cashmere coat, emerged from the darkness of the suite. He approached from behind Accorsi to congratulate Modell. It was awkward, as interactions in the delirium of exultant happiness often can be. Art reached toward the man in the dark coat. Ernie, stuck between the two men, was swallowed up in the ungainly embrace, becoming an Accorsi sandwich. As the man reached for Modell, Modell reached toward the man's face, to pull him in.

Modell was confused by the presence of this man, who wasn't an invited guest. What was he doing here? But joy overwhelmed Art, and he didn't protest his trespasser's presence. This was not the mystery man from 1964. This intruder was a former nemesis of the NFL and no friend of Art Modell's. This was an interloping guest from minority owner Al Lerner's box next door. This was the man who had stolen Brian Sipe from Art Modell and the Browns in 1985, who brought the Kardiac quarterback to the USFL's New Jersey Generals. This was Donald Trump.

## 37

# THREE STRIKES AND YOU'RE OUT APPLIES TO FOOTBALL, TOO

JANUARY 14, 1990

*Heading into the third AFC Championship Game in four years against* the Denver Broncos, the Browns and their fans had reasons to be optimistic that this third time would be the charm: The Browns had beaten Denver already this year. It may have only been a 3-point win, but the Browns had harassed John Elway into his worst game as a pro. Secondly, Denver barely got past Pittsburgh in the divisional round, needing overtime to defeat the Steelers.

Speaking of Elway, although Bernie Kosar was banged up, his statistics throughout the season were better than the Denver quarterback's. In fact, Elway had thrown as many interceptions as touchdowns. Finally, Bud Carson had been here before and had prevailed. As defensive coordinator for the Steelers and the Rams, he had stymied his opponents' offenses and led his teams to the Super Bowl on three occasions.

Of course, there were reasons to be pessimistic too. The Browns were 0-2 against the Broncos in championship games. They would be playing at Mile High—doubly tough because it was the Broncos' home field, but also because of the altitude, which takes a toll on low-landers' lungs by the end of the game. Most concerning was the lackluster defense the Browns had been playing over the last month. The last two opponents, Houston and Buffalo, had each gained over 400 yards. The defense was getting weaker when they would be needed the most.

## 1989 AFC Championship Game – Mile High Stadium, Denver January 14, 1990

Like two years ago when these two teams tangled in a Mile High matchup to decide who would represent the AFC in the Super Bowl, the Broncos got out to the early lead. Today Denver led 10-0 by halftime.

Behind Bernie Kosar and Brian Brennan's two touchdowns and a short Tim Manoa touchdown run after Felix Wright returned a fum-ble 26 yards to the Denver 1, the Browns erupted for 21 third-quarter points. These would be the only points the Browns scored all day. Lead-ing by 3 entering the fourth quarter, Denver would end up scoring 13 points to close out the game.

In the end, it was a blowout: 37-21. There was no *Drive*, no *Fumble* to define this game. Elway had simply flourished during the chaos of defensive pressure and broken plays. Denver just plain won—and decidedly. A trilogy had just concluded, and Denver had won each time. For a Browns team just embarking on the 1990s, it was three strikes and you're out.

## January 14, 1990 – Mile High Stadium – Browns locker room (after the loss)

Art Modell talking with reporters about his head coach: "I'm proud of the job Bud did, but we have to improve. We had a good defensive scheme, one that Bud was comfortable with. But Elway was just too much."

Referring to three Super Bowl–denying losses in four years to the Broncos, Modell continued: "It hurts, but we will do whatever we have to do to win. We will be going over the organization from top to bot-tom very soon." Just then Modell's banged-up quarterback came by, and Modell gave Kosar a big hug.

The embrace was one of affection; Modell almost felt like Kosar was a son. But the owner was also clinging to his fervent hope that his quarterback would yet help him realize his Super Bowl aspirations.

Bud Carson's first game as head coach had been a blowout victory over archnemesis Pittsburgh. The rest of his first season never matched up to that initial glory, but he did get the Browns back to the AFC Championship Game. Just as with Marty Schottenheimer before him, Bud Carson failed to defeat the Broncos and make it to the elusive Promised Land of the Super Bowl.

38

# THE ASCENDANCE OF THE INDIANS AND CAVALIERS

## Baseball and Basketball Take Center Stage in Cleveland

*In the mid- to late-eighties, Art Modell, Ernie Accorsi, and the rest of* the Browns' front office had been trying to build a championship-caliber team. Bernie Kosar came of age, flourished, and then started getting beat up; his performance, though always gritty, had started to slip. The talented wide receiver corps transitioned from Dave Logan and Reggie Rucker to Reggie Langhorne and Webster Slaughter. The Wizard, Ozzie Newsome, kept on playing, from the time of Sipe, Logan, and Rucker, through the Kosar, Langhorne, Slaughter, and Brennan era, extending his Hall of Fame career.

But Newsome's playing days were numbered. Coach Marty Schottenheimer had gotten so close, so many times, and then quit in a power struggle with ownership—that is, Art Modell. Browns players and fans who had gotten used to winning the division after decades of losing started seeing success ebb away again, somewhere out into the swirling gales of Lake Erie. Things were not standing still around them. The world was turning, the city was changing.

The Cleveland Indians had played at Cleveland Municipal Stadium since it was built in 1932. The Browns were later to the party, joining the Indians at the hulking structure in 1946, the year of their founding within the All-America Football Conference. As the decades progressed and the stadium's condition regressed, the City of Cleveland, which had been the stadium's owner, couldn't afford badly needed repairs, and in 1972 leased it to Cleveland Stadium Corporation. The president of the Cleveland Stadium Corporation was Browns majority owner Art Modell. From that point onward, the Indians had been his tenant. Kinda crazy, when you consider the Browns played eight home games per year and the Indians played eighty-one.

Although Modell had shelled out $28 million over the years in renovations, by all accounts, the stadium was not just rough around the edges but thoroughly ragged through and through. Modell had made some bad financial moves in the 1970s, forcing him into procuring a loan at the prime rate plus 1 percent. As the prime rate skyrocketed to 20 percent during the Brian Sipe years, Modell needed to drum up revenue wherever he could and slash costs any way possible.

Bear in mind, the Cleveland Browns (and the related Stadium Corporation) were Modell's only businesses (save for a stint of ownership in some Cleveland radios stations until 1987). He wasn't like most owners who were making big bucks in oil or real estate. The Browns and the Stadium Corporation had to make money for Modell and his family to stay solvent. Some of Modell's moves put Browns minority owner Robert Gries at odds with Modell to the point of lawsuits and strained his relationship with his prime tenant, the Indians.

Modell wasn't competing only against the Steelers, the Oilers, Paul Brown's Cincinnati Bengals, and the rest of the NFL. He was competing against the Cleveland Indians, and, although he may not have known it yet, against the Cleveland Cavaliers. The battle wasn't being waged so much to win the devotion of the fans of Cleveland; as the next several decades would prove, the Browns would always be foremost in the hearts of Cleveland fans, even when they were putrid. As Cleveland journalist Roldo Bartimole pointed out in an article after Modell died, the battle was for political pull.

Right in the thick of the Browns run of AFC Central domination, in 1986, Dick and David Jacobs bought the Cleveland Indians. Dick Jacobs was the prime mover and face of the ownership team. The Tribe was a sad sack club that hadn't made the playoffs since their last World Series appearance in 1954—a full decade before the last Browns NFL Championship.

The Indians played to tiny crowds through much of the long season. Season after season, they were renters in Modell's enormous, deteriorating stadium. Now this new owner, who made his money building malls and being a landlord, was going to be Modell's tenant. Class A real estate this was not. It didn't take long for Dick Jacobs to begin banging the drum for a new ballpark of his own.

Major League baseball had long been cajoling the various Indians ownership groups to build a more intimate baseball-only park. The visiting American League teams' owners were not recouping their travel and lodging costs when playing to the anemic "crowds" in Cleveland. Dan Coughlan summed it up best in his 2010 book *Crazy with the Papers to Prove It: Stories About the Most Unusual, Eccentric & Outlandish People I've Known in 45 Years as a Sports Journalist*: "On the night that Hank Aaron broke Babe Ruth's all-time home run record in 1975, Bowie Kuhn was at the Stadium Club in Cleveland speaking to the Indians official booster organization, the Wahoo Club, stressing the importance of a new ballpark. This was in 1975!"

Coghlan continued: "Kuhn's successor as commissioner, Peter Ueberroth, brought the same message to the City Club eleven years later in 1986. American League president Bobby Brown added to the cacophony when he came to Cleveland and said a small, cozy ballpark was preferred for baseball. 'Cleveland will lose the Indians if they do not get a new ballpark,' Brown said bluntly."

While the principals—Art Modell and the various Indians owners—and Major League leadership alternately negotiated and waged battle, the city and county business leaders and politicians had been working up various schemes to improve the state of the stadium(s) where the Browns and Indians would play. Further, it was thought that this momentum would lure the Cavaliers away from their exurban Richfield Coliseum, back to Cleveland.

In the early 1980s, the vision was to build a domed stadium for football and baseball and possibly basketball. In May 1984, the ballot proposal (which would have paid for the stadium by raising property taxes), despite backing from Art Modell and Ohio Governor Richard Celeste, failed by a two-to-one margin at the polls.

Undaunted, in 1985, local architect Robert Corna drafted plans for a six-sided retractable dome dual-purpose stadium called Hexatron. (Just think about the fun the ESPN anchors could've had with that name ... "The Big Hex.") It would be situated away from the lake, freeing up the site of Cleveland Browns Stadium for a new convention center. The convention center, new hotels, the Hexatron, and even the huge International Exposition Center by the airport would all be connected by rail.

There was even a plan to finance the project: a fifteen-year "sin" tax on alcohol and cigarettes. This funding mechanism was promoted by a young lawmaker from the Ohio House of Representatives named Jeff Jacobs. Jeff Jacobs was the son of future Indians owner Dick Jacobs. As city and county government transitioned to new administrations, these ambitious Hexatron plans were never seriously considered.

The public-private Greater Cleveland Dome Stadium Corporation was formed by Governor Celeste and Cleveland Mayor George Voinovich. Cleveland Tomorrow, compossed of top executives from the city's biggest firms, raised money and acquired land and buildings in downtown Cleveland's historic market district. By 1989 the city had leveled buildings, making way for parking lots and a future stadium, or stadiums. No funding was in place, however.

As the Browns were inhaling their last gasps of sustained success and the calendar was turning to the decade of the 1990s, the city's leadership was in transition. Republican Mayor George Voinovich had ended his ten-year run and was replaced by Democratic candidate Mike White. Mayor White quickly inserted himself into the effort to bring the stadium(s) to fruition.

Along with new City Council President Jay Westbrook and several county commissioners, this political powerbase allied itself with the business leaders of Cleveland Tomorrow. The sin tax idea was resurrected to collect the funding. Proponents hoped the prospect of paying 1.9 cents more for a beer, 1.5 cents more for an ounce of liquor, and 4.5 cents more per pack of cigarettes wouldn't scare people like the threat of higher property taxes. It would be put to a countywide vote as Issue 2 in the May 1990 gubernatorial primary election.

Once again, Major League Baseball weighed in. A lockout over salary arbitration and free agency had truncated the spring training season and caused the regular season to get started about a week late. Some of the concessions made to the players could hurt a small-market, poorly drawing team like the Indians. As the May election approached, Clevelanders were deluged by advertising both for and against supporting Issue 2.

Days before the vote, MLB Commissioner Fay Vincent was invited to Cleveland to attend a city council finance committee meeting. His message was ominous: "Should this [cozy, new] facility not be available in Cleveland . . . should the vote on [Issue 2] be a negative one, we may find ourselves confronting a subject we want to avoid." The threat was real. If the Tribe didn't get a new home, Major League Baseball could take the team from Cleveland.

On May 8, 1990, there was a massive turnout for what was originally scheduled to be just a state gubernatorial primary election. Issue 2 (and good weather) drove turnout that rivaled the 1984 presidential primary, according to Robert E. Hughes, the chairperson of the Cuyahoga County Board of Elections. When all the votes were counted, Issue 2 prevailed—narrowly—with 51.7 percent in favor.

Two wheels were now simultaneously set in motion; one that would make Gateway and its new baseball park and basketball arena a reality; and one that would roll all the way to Baltimore, carrying Art Modell and the Browns with it.

"What the hell is going on? How is this fair?" Modell yelled, pacing, as his wife Pat sat on their sofa. "After everything I've done throughout the years, and they never gave me anything. And now this . . . this . . . *strip mall king* wants a new stadium, and they give him everything!"

Pat sighed.

"When the city couldn't afford the stadium, I took it over. I spent my money . . . money I didn't even have . . . I took out loans to pay to fix it up, and this is the thanks I get?! What are they going to give *me*? How am I going to be compensated for losing the Indians? They subsidize their new park, and they don't give me a dime when they steal my tenant?"

Pat had heard Art rant before, but nothing like this. She didn't try to stop him. Not only would it not have worked, but her heart was breaking for her husband. The financial aspects of this new development would hurt and were unfair. More than anything, her heart hurt because his heart was broken. Betrayed. She had seen him give everything to this team, to this city. Now the Indians, who couldn't draw a crowd without a nickel beer night promotion, who hadn't been to the playoffs in thirty years, had inherited the bounty.

It was unfair that the city and county officials had fallen over themselves to accommodate Indians owner Dick Jacobs and the Cavaliers and their owner, Gordon Gund. What had the Cavs ever done for Cleveland? They played out in the suburbs. They weren't drawing people downtown. Now they were getting a new stadium, too? The politicians who couldn't find money to fix up a stadium they already had all of a sudden could afford not just one but *two* brand-new stadiums?

But Pat knew what really grieved her husband's heart, even before he said it.

"How could they do this to me? How could they vote for this Issue 2? What kind of fickle fans do we have in Cleveland? We've taken the Browns to the AFC Championship Game three times in the last four years. If it wasn't for two lousy plays, we'd have been in the Super Bowl twice! I have put a good football team on the field. A lot better than the lousy Indians. And the damn Cavaliers. Now the fans vote to give them new stadiums? Pat, I've never felt so unappreciated in my life. They take me for a fool. They must take me for a fool."

For those keeping score at home, this new decade was not shaping up well for the owner of the Cleveland Browns. Art Modell had watched his team lose in the AFC Championship Game for the third time on January 14, 1990, and then watched his influence and relevance in the Cleveland community vaporize, as politicians and fans put their faith in a cozy new ballpark for the Indians and a new downtown arena for the Cavaliers. Art was left with an aging team, an ancient stadium, and a vacancy sign instead of an 81-games-a-year tenant.

Art poured another glass of scotch and switched off the TV. As Pat headed off to bed, Art switched off the lamp and sat in the dark, alone.

39

# SOPHOMORE SLUMP

BROWNS' 1990 SEASON

***The 1990 season, again, opened against the Steelers. Like in Bud Car-*** son's first year, he came away with a victory. But instead of a blowout, the final score was 13-3. The next three games were all losses, with the third being a 34-0 shutout at the hands of Marty Schottenheimer and his Kansas City Chiefs.

The Browns returned to Mile High Stadium in week five. On the eve of the game, Art Modell had a fitful night of sleep in his hotel room in Denver's thin air. When at last he slumbered, the lack of oxygen mingled with memories of Broncos games past. He was assailed by a nightmare:

*He was on a high desert plain. Mountains loomed off in the Western distance. A tumbleweed rolled across the ground until it got temporarily caught on a scrub brush nearby. Then from afar, approaching from the west: rolling thunder . . . and a low cloud rising. A dust cloud. The thunder was the galloping of hooves. They were getting closer. Closing in on him. Then he saw them: One white, one orange, and one—blue! They roared in closer then began to circle him, the wild horses stampeded in a tightening noose. Closer and closer they crowded. Art convulsed in terror. Dust coated his body, invaded his mouth and nostrils. The sun glinted off the eyes of the horses; they had no fear in them, no feeling. They whirled around him, mesmerizing him. He was dizzy, disoriented.*

*Suddenly the thunder ceased, the three horses stopped. The thick dust cloud parted like a pair of curtains. A fourth horse, pale in color, approached*

*Art and locked eyes with him. Art's eyes betrayed the terror in his heart, while the horse's revealed a knowing confidence.*

*The pale horse reared up and Art fell to the ground on his back. The pale horse's front legs fell toward Art's prone body, and Art instinctively threw his arms over his face as he curled into a fetal position. He saw a horseshoe stamped with #7 E.L. Way & Co. descending toward him, and he knew it was all over for him. He sealed his eyes shut. But the horse splayed out its legs, one hoof landing on either side of Art's head. Art was spared. But when he squinted open his eyes, the horse was braying over him. Its eyes were rolled back. The mouth was wide open, showing huge teeth and fully exposed gums. This image was seared into his mind. Art gasped for breath like a drowning man just bobbing to the surface.*

Modell was now awake, soaking with sweat in the hotel's king bed.

Though conscious now, he couldn't shake the dream. Images exploded into his mind. The three horses circling. The pale horse rearing, its eyes cold, like a killer's. The enormous horse teeth. The hooves raised high, descending toward his prone, helpless body. The horseshoe, branded with #7 E.L. Way & Co. Modell wondered, why would a wild Bronco even be wearing a horseshoe? The horseshoe image brought his mind to Baltimore and the Colts.

Art had never considered this before. His twin tormentors—Baltimore and Denver—were both named for horses. Certainly, facing John Elway and the Broncos was fuel enough for a nightmare. But now Art wondered if his subconscious mind was pulling from deeper in his past. Was tonight's dream and all these intermittent "encounters" with the strange cashmere-coated man all a hangover from 1964? Was all this business about Baltimore's revenge also still psychologically haunting him?

Things were much better on Sunday afternoon than in the dreams of Saturday night. The Browns squeaked out the win 30-29. The mild satisfaction of beating the Broncos was eclipsed by the reminder that the Browns never could beat them when it really mattered.

Modell, normally buoyant and effusive after a victory, sat silently in the visitor's box, alongside the team's general manager Ernie Accorsi.

"Art, what gives?" Accorsi nudged his friend. "Show us a smile. We won!"

"Ernie, why couldn't we have beat this guy in '86 or '87, or '89?"

Accorsi knew Modell meant the AFC Championship Games. And he also knew by "this guy" he meant the Denver Broncos team, not just John Elway. Accorsi understood all too well why Modell would have felt that way, and why he had phrased it that way. It had been Elway's singular excellence that had beaten the Browns. Well, that and *The Drive* and *The Fumble*.

"Art, that guy is my white whale. Elway. Ever since I saw him when I was scouting the East-West game as the Colt's GM, when he was coming out of Stanford, I wanted him. There was no question in my mind. He was the guy I was gonna draft. I told Kush, the coach there in Baltimore, 'We are picking him. Period. No discussion.'"

Modell was familiar with the saga, as was any football fan in that era. "But Elway refused to play for the Colts," Modell commented. "He said he'd go play baseball instead of football if the Colts drafted him. I didn't like that attitude. But I gotta admit, he turned out to be a helluva quarterback."

"True," Accorsi said. "Elway let it be known that he didn't want to play for the Colts; [Baltimore's owner, Robert] Irsay had made the Colts into a mess. But I drafted him anyway. After I drafted him, Elway called me. He wanted to patch things up. Getting drafted into baseball was just a bluff. He would have played for us; I know it."

"That's when Irsay screwed it up?" Modell asked.

"Without talking to me, Irsay called Denver and pulled off the trade," Accorsi said. "Never breathed a word of it to me or Kush or anyone. I know Elway would have played for us! I strongly believe that Elway would have kept the Colts in Baltimore. He'd have turned the team around. We would have won. Attendance would have picked up. Fan enthusiasm would have picked up. I really think it could have turned around the political will. I think they'd have built a new stadium down there."

"And Baltimore would have had a football team these last seven years," Modell said. "I can't believe Irsay stealing the team out of town in the middle of the night, like a bandit. How could anybody do that to the fans?"

"You don't know Irsay like I do," Accorsi said. "Try working for him. This is a guy that started a company to run his own father out of business. Yeah, his dad had an HVAC business for thirty years. And Robert

Irsay starts a company to try to run his own father out of business! His own mother called him 'a devil on earth.' The guy couldn't tell the truth if he tried and would do anything for a buck."

"Well the joke's on him," Modell said. "That Elway is a helluva quarterback. If Irsay never made that trade, and Elway went to the Colts, who knows, he might have taken them to a bunch of Super Bowls. Or maybe, maybe we would've played Baltimore in the AFC Championship Games all those years. Who knows? Maybe we would've won a couple of 'em. Nothing would have made me happier than to beat the Baltimore Colts and John Elway at the same time and get to the Super Bowl because of it."

Art stared off in the distance lost in reverie.

After the Denver victory, Cleveland would again slide to three consecutive losses. The latest loss came on the road against the defending league champion San Francisco 49ers. The score had been tied until a last-second field goal. Bud Carson, desperate to keep his job, had pulled Bernie Kosar with the Browns down by 14. Mike Pagel led the team back to tie it up in the fourth quarter. Joe Montana, who'd had a lackluster second half, rallied San Francisco in the final minutes. The 49ers kicked the game-winning field goal with five seconds remaining. If the Browns could almost beat the 49ers on the road, maybe they weren't so bad? Still, their record stood at an ugly 2-6 halfway through the season.

It was gut check time. The Buffalo Bills were coming to town to start the second half of the season. They had built on their strong 1989 season—which ended in a playoff loss to the Browns—to become one of the AFC's best teams this year. A win against Buffalo could set the Browns back on the winning track. A win against the Bills would serve notice that Cleveland was still a team to be reckoned with in the AFC power structure. A win against the Bills would assuredly save Bud Carson's job.

The Browns lost 0-42.

It was the Browns' worst-ever defeat at home. The sellout crowd had thinned to about 10,000—all Buffalo fans. They serenaded the fleeing Browns fans with, "Na na-na-na, na na-na-na, hey hey hey, goodbye!" Homemade signs, brought in by Cleveland fans, were left displaying their messages at the highest reaches of the nosebleed sections. Referencing their placement several stories above the parking lot, the signs read: "Jump Art."

Carson, on the sidelines, was trying to disappear, embarrassed by his team's performance. Modell, in his loge, was humiliated. The media were speculating whether the Buffalo fans' "Hey, hey, hey, goodbye" chant indicated Modell's intentions toward his head coach.

After the game, Coach Carson told the media he might quit but he needed to go home and think about it. Modell, when asked whether he would fire Carson, told reporters, "I want to go home and reflect on this. I hope to get up fresh tomorrow and have a fresh perspective."

Around town fans and sportswriters didn't pin much blame on Carson. Instead, they held Modell, General Manager Ernie Accorsi, and Director of Player Personnel Mike Lombardi responsible. The prevailing feeling was that the team just didn't have the players. These were the men who were supposed to draft and trade for players to keep the team strong. Fans felt that no coach could have done much better than Carson had done.

The porous line had undermined the offense all year, making quarterbacks Bernie Kosar and Mike Pagel, as well as the running game, ineffective. When pressed about this critical deficiency, Modell claimed he and his brain trust were blindsided by the "startling retirement" of two offensive line stalwarts, Cody Risien and Ricky Bolden, right before the season started.

The Cleveland *Plain Dealer*'s Bill Livingston countered that "Risien and Bolden were walking Red Crosses. Reporters knew Bolden was considering a[n imminent] new career in the ministry." Besides that, Risien had already retired once, then had come back for another try, before finally hanging up his cleats for good. Modell had commented then that "It's always in the back of your mind that if a player says he's going to retire once, that he may say it again." So, players, fans, and the media all supported Carson, and looked at ownership and the front office as the culprits and the ones who should be replaced.

The next day the front-page headline on the *Plain Dealer* was "Modell Fires Carson as Head Coach."

Accorsi and Lombardi were retained. Of course, Art Modell wasn't going anywhere . . . at least not yet. So, ten months removed from making the AFC Championship Game, the Browns' head coach was gone.

Pro Bowler Michael Dean Perry's comments were consistent with those of other players: "This is a shock to me. I think he got a raw deal. All the players think Bud got a raw deal. I was behind him 110 percent. . . ."

Art informed the media that, as expected, offensive coordinator Jim Shofner would be the interim coach.

Like any interim coach, Shofner would really have to distinguish himself if he wanted any chance of staying on beyond this season. If he could run the table, which would include inflicting four losses upon AFC Central rivals, the Browns would be playoff-bound once again. They'd be one of the hottest teams, having won seven straight games. With that head of steam, who knows, maybe they could finally get over the hump and into the Super Bowl. Heck, maybe even win it?

Instead, Shofner's Browns won one game and lost six. The Shofner era was over. Neither Bud Carson nor Jim Shofner would ever serve as head coach again in the NFL. And the Browns had to crack down on signs being carried into the stadium. Art didn't want to suffer any more humiliation. Some enterprising fan floated a large balloon over the south stands; one side read: "2-14"; the other, "Jump Art." Yes, the natives were getting restless.

Meanwhile, Marty Schottenheimer coached the 1990 Kansas City Chiefs to an 11-5 record and into the playoffs. Schottenheimer had quit the Browns after feeling he didn't have enough control. Bud Carson felt much the same way, stating to reporters the day he was fired, "Coaching here is a tough job. Your hands are somewhat tied. A coach of the Browns doesn't have much power."

Maybe the fans and sportswriters were right. Maybe the problems facing the Browns started at the top. The Browns and their owner, Arthur Modell, were again in the market for a head coach.

# COACHING SEARCH

JANUARY 6, 1991

*"Well, Marty went down again last night," said Mike Lombardi, trying* to lighten the mood.

"Yeah, he's a helluva coach 'til he gets to the playoffs," Ernie Accorsi added.

Lombardi and Accorsi joined Art Modell and Jim Shofner—who was now director of player personnel—at Tower B at Cleveland Municipal Stadium on a Sunday night, when they'd rather have been watching a Browns playoff game. They were referring to Kansas City's playoff loss to Miami last night.

Modell wasn't in the mood to be cheered up. "Well, at least they made it to the playoffs," he said. "We were 3-13, a total disaster. Less than a year ago, we were licking our wounds after the AFC Championship Game. This season we were an embarrassment. We've got to get this right." Modell meant the coaching search.

"Somebody hand me the coaching list," he said.

Accorsi, Lombardi, and Shofner had compiled a list, and an assistant distributed copies to everyone at the table.

## - Prospective Coaches -

### Top Prospects

<u>MIKE WHITE – 55</u>

Special projects with Raiders

**Pros**

- Assistant with 49ers in late '70s. Highly recommended by Bill Walsh
- Consensus solid head coaching candidate

**Cons**

- No NFL head coaching experience
- Not a "name"

<u>BILL BELICHICK – 38</u>

Defensive coordinator for NY Giants
Extensive assistant coaching experience in NFL

**Pros**

- Heir apparent to legend Bill Parcells at NY Giants
- Demonstrated skill as defensive coordinator
- Super Bowl winner as DC in NY
- Family near Youngstown

**Cons**

- Similar background as Cowher, but Cowher played here and assistant-coached here
- No head coaching experience at any level

<u>BILL COWHER – 33</u>

Defensive coordinator, LB coach for Kansas City Chiefs

**Pros**

- Played here, assistant coached here
- Great motivator
- Get to steal him from Marty

**Cons**

- Young!
- Had some defensive lapses, like against Houston this year
- No head coaching experience at any level

GREG LANDRY – 43

Offensive coordinator for Chicago Bears

**Pros**

- QB coach for Browns previously, worked with Bernie Kosar here
- An offensive version of Cowher – enthusiastic, motivator
- Learned from Mike Ditka

**Cons**

- Not sure he wants to become head coach at this time
- No head coaching experience at any level

BOBBY ROSS – 54

Head coach – Georgia Tech

**Pros**

- Led team to Citrus Bowl victory, 10-0-1 record, #1 ranking in UPI, #2 AP
- NFL experience – Assistant with Chiefs for 4 years

**Cons**

- May not want to leave the collegiate level

HOWARD SCHNELLENBERGER – 56

Head coach – Louisville University

**Pros**

- Crushed Alabama in Fiesta Bowl, 10-1-1 record, #12 UPI, #14 AP ranking
- National champion while HC at University of Miami
- NFL head coaching experience (Colts)

**Cons**

- Signed five-year contract extension at Louisville, wants to win championship there
- May want coach/GM type of control

LOU HOLTZ – 54

Head coach – Notre Dame

**Pros**

- Head coach of perennial college powerhouse program
- Great motivational leader

- Top-tier name
- NFL head coaching experience (Jets)

**Cons**

- Stint as NFL coach did not go well (3-10 record, resigned with three games to go)

## Other Strong Candidates

MIKE HOLMGREN – 42

Offensive coordinator/QB coach – San Francisco 49ers

**Pros**

- 49ers – top organization in the NFL
- Top offense in NFL under his coaching
- Worked with Joe Montana and Steve Young as QB coach
- Super Bowl wins last two years

**Cons**

- Signed two-year contract with San Francisco that would be tough to break

RICH KOTITE – 48

Philadelphia Eagles – offensive coordinator and QB coach

**Pros**

- Former receivers coach here in Cleveland
- Familiarity with Jim Shofner, would work well with front office
- Also OC for New York Jets

**Cons**

- Eagles lost yesterday in playoffs to Redskins
- Fired from New York Jets after last season
- Not a "big name" coaching candidate

JOHN MACKOVIC – 47

University of Illinois – head coach

**Pros**

- Native of Barberton, OH
- NFL head coaching experience (KC Chiefs 1983-1986)
- Other NCAA Division 1 head coaching experience

**Cons**

- Lost bowl game to Clemson 30-0 last week
- Players nearly revolted in KC under his leadership
- Not a "big name" coaching prospect, despite resume

### Long-Shot Candidates

DAVID SHULA – 31

Dallas Cowboys – offensive coordinator and QB coach

**Pros**

- Considered good head coaching prospect by many
- Great pedigree

**Cons**

- Dan Marino, Troy Aikman supposedly disliked him
- Very young

BILL PARCELLS – 49

NY Giants head coach

**Pros**

- 1986, 1990 Super Bowl winner as head coach of Giants
- Great motivator
- "Big name" coach

**Cons**

- One year left on contract, could be tough to break
- May want high degree of control to leave NY Giants

BUDDY RYAN – 56

Philadelphia Eagles head coach

**Pros**

- Success as head coach in NFL
- Highly experienced

**Cons**

- 0-3 in playoffs
- Personality could be off-putting
- Not disciplinarian

STEVE SPURRIER – 45

University of Florida head coach

**Pros**

- Motivator
- Great track record at major NCAA program
- "Big name"

**Cons**

- Says he's committed to staying at Florida

DAVE ADOLPH – 53

LA Raiders – defensive coordinator and linebackers coach

**Pros**

- Born in Akron
- Coached at Akron and Ohio State
- A top 10 defense and 12-4 record in 1990

**Cons**

- Not a "big name"
- Not much buzz about him as head coaching candidate

VINCE TOBIN – 47

Chicago Bears defensive coordinator

**Pros**

- Other than '89, always a top defense in the NFL
- Disciple of Mike Ditka
- A finalist during search that yielded Bud Carson

**Cons**

- Why did we not hire him in 1988?
- Not a "big name"
- No head coaching experience

TOM FLORES – 53

Seattle Seahawks president and general manager

**Pros**

- .628 winning percentage as head coach of Raiders
- Won two Super Bowls as Raiders' coach
- Qualifies as a "big name"

**Cons**

- Currently president and general manager; would want a lot of control, if interested at all

Modell looked around the room before perusing the list. "Gentlemen, we have *got* to get this right. I cannot emphasize this enough. We've been going backwards since we parted ways with Schottenheimer."

Catching himself, Art turned to Shofner and said, "No offense to you, Jim."

Shofner quickly demurred. "No offense taken. I didn't compile a very good record."

Modell's retort was an attempt to lighten the tension: "No kidding, you only won one game!"

Like savvy employees, everyone laughed. Modell looked through the names, skipping past the brief biographical sketches to see who was out there, his head slightly cocked backward so he could look through the "reader" part of his bifocals.

"I want someone who's a great motivator," Modell said. "And someone who can control the team, a disciplinarian. I need somebody that the team is going to get behind. To believe in and raise their level of play. I don't just want to get back to the playoffs and lose. I can't stand the thought of being left at the altar again, like against Denver all those times!" He pounded the table, reflexively. "I want somebody that will take us all the way. I have been trying to get to the Super Bowl for twenty-five years. With the history of this team, with the legacy here, there is no reason we should not have gotten to a Super Bowl. We *need* to *get* to the *Super Bowl*! This next coach might be the last one I ever hire. I am not getting any younger, you know. We've got to push hard to get the best possible person for this job. With the Browns' legacy, we should get the pick of the litter. Let's not forget that. We should shoot the moon."

"We think we have compiled a comprehensive list of the best candidates out there," Accorsi said.

But Art was studying the list, not listening.

"Art, as you can see, many of these guys are still in the playoffs," Accorsi said. "We'll have some time over the next week or two to really investigate the men you wish to consider."

Accorsi was right. These guys were hot candidates because they were successful. That meant most of the NFL candidates were still in (post)season.

"There are some college coaches on here," Accorsi said. "We could talk with them immediately. I know Bobby Ross—"

"Ernie, last time I listened to you, I got Bud Carson, so make sure you are *sure* before you recommend anyone," Modell said.

Accorsi raised his eyebrows.

"Ah, I'm sorry Ernie. That was harsh. I am just on edge. I feel desperate to get this right. Let's go through this list name by name and get this search started."

As the days passed, Modell became more and more convinced that Mike White was the man for the job. He'd gone so far as to draw up a contract. He'd had open conversations with White, and the deal was all but official. But Accorsi asserted that Belichick was far and away the better choice. Accorsi urged that Modell wait and interview the young defensive wunderkind.

## 41

# THE WEDNESDAY BEFORE THE SUPER BOWL, TAMPA

JANUARY 23, 1991

*In the glare of the TV lights, with an armada of microphones thrust in* his face, reporters hurled a salvo of questions at the defensive coordinator of the New York Giants. He dutifully answered the questions about how he planned to stop the surging Buffalo Bills offense that had scored 95 points in two playoff games.

Bill Belichick's patience wore out when the head coaching questions became the main focus. In his mind, every minute in front of this rumormongering paparazzi was another minute he couldn't be in the film room, figuring out a way to stop Jim Kelly and the Bills.

Reporter: "Bill, would you be more inclined to take the job in Tampa, or in Cleveland, if you are offered both positions?"

"I have not talked to anybody about a head coaching job with any team, okay," Belichick said, raising his voice. "That's it. We're [expletive] focusing on the Buffalo Bills, which is plenty enough for me to think about. I'm not smart enough to think about eight things at the same time, all right? There's no more questions about head coaching offers, period!"

Between the uncertainty over his future and with the weight of winning the Super Bowl on his shoulders (the Giants would need to win on defense—Belichick's responsibility—they'd never beat the Bills in an offensive shoot-out), it was no wonder Belichick was testy.

Just days later, Cleveland interviewed the Raiders' Mike White, and it was reported that he was the front-runner to get the Browns job. Tampa had also interviewed Mike White. Tampa, like Cleveland, planned to interview Belichick after the Super Bowl. The Buc's primary aim, however, was to lure legendary former 49ers coach Bill Walsh out of the broadcasting booth to become general manager/head coach.

# THE FATEFUL FAX

WAITE HILL, OHIO, JANUARY 28, 1991

*Art Modell was sitting at home the day after the Super Bowl, worn out* from all the research, debates, interviews, phone calls, finagling, and apprehension over possibly making the wrong move in selecting his team's next head coach. Bill Cowher was coming in tomorrow for a round of interviews, to boot. Modell sat there in the back room, not watching TV, not seeking companionship with Pat, just sitting, worrying. The phone rang. On the third ring, since apparently no one else was going to answer, he picked up.

"Art, you must be facing quite a dilemma in your coaching search." The voice was vaguely familiar, cultured, yet somehow taunting. It was like the speaker reveled in Art's discomfort. Voices are often so when words of help are offered. "Mr. Modell, you would be wise to consult the contract we signed, all those years ago. There may be some guidance there to lead you in the right way."

Modell knew right away: this was the same man—that he frankly still wasn't convinced *wasn't* just a figment of his own imagination—who helped the Browns win the 1964 championship, in return for a generation's worth of misery. Modell surmised this mystery man seemed to only appear when he was under great duress. Maybe "the man" was some psychosis that was conjured into being only when Modell's nervous system was on overload.

"Listen, if you're so smart, why don't you just tell me who to choose," Modell said involuntarily. He was surprised to see that he had actively engaged in conversation with someone he wasn't even sure was really there.

"No, I don't think I should be so bold, Art. After all, you can just go by your own best judgment after rereading the relevant part of our little contract."

"I don't have the contract; I don't know where it is," Modell shot back, his face flushed. "I don't know if it really even exists, or if I am just dreaming it all up." Modell had enough self-awareness to be glad now that nobody else was around, realizing that he must sound unhinged.

"Well, Art, I still have a copy of the contract, and I can tell you, it is very real."

"Well, send it to me. I've lost my copy."

"Art, that is very disappointing. You should keep something so important safe."

"The part about the coaches. Just send me that part now. I'm sure the contract will turn up sometime, but right now, I need the part about what coach to pick." Modell sounded desperate. He was.

"Art, I will cut you a break. I will email you the relevant page of the contract. What is your email address?"

"Uh, well, I know I have one, but I—"

"That's okay, Art, I know what it is. I will send it before you arrive in your office tomorrow. Goodbye Art." And before Art could respond, the man had hung up.

The next morning, Art arrived early at the office. Bill Cowher would be coming in for an interview. But Art's mind was on the email. He asked his receptionist, Margie, to check to see if he had indeed received an email (or maybe the whole conversation was a delusional dream)?

"Mr. Modell, it looks like someone tried to send you something, but I don't think it came through."

"What do you mean, what does it say?"

"Well, there is an email here, addressed to you, but it just says 'Mail Daemon – undeliverable.'"

"What? What the hell is that? Male Demon? Who's the Male Demon?"

"I don't know, that's just what it says."

"Well, why can't he fax it, like everybody else, dammit! Margie, can you call him and ask him to fax the information over?"

The phone rang. Margie had to attend to people calling on behalf of Bill Cowher, inquiring about interview logistics. She put the Cowher party on hold to straighten out her befuddled boss:

"Mr. Modell, just click on the 'Reply' button, and type, 'Please send fax to 216-555-1212' and then hit the 'Send' button. Oh, and the fax machine is on the fritz. It still works, but the faxes come through blotchy sometimes."

She then returned her attention to the phone call, cheerfully giving instructions to Cowher's people as Modell methodically hunted and pecked his way through his email reply.

A few minutes later, Modell dolefully watched Margie as she continued with the Cowher phone call. Modell was like an old hound dog laying on the foyer floor, waiting to be let out, silently imploring his master with a lugubrious face. Modell perked up when he heard a fax coming across the machine. Maybe he didn't need to wait for help from Margie.

To his amazement, the contract was indeed being faxed over; line by line it was appearing like magic. Eagerly, Modell pulled it out of the tray as soon as the fax machine quit squawking. "Margie, this fax looks like some seagulls used it for target practice," Modell said and went back into his office and closed the door.

Modell sat at his desk, but held the fax firmly in both hands, at an angle so he could easily read it through his bifocals. He dug in like it was a treasure map. Would this document reveal the coach that would lead him over the rainbow to the pot of gold, the elusive Super Bowl? Modell was bogged down immediately, though, as if mired in quicksand as the first coach's name he saw was not one of the new prospects, but Blanton Collier's, his coach for the 1964 NFL Championship (Modell's only championship).

This name was an invocation down memory lane. Modell was reminded how this whole odyssey had begun: his desperate pursuit of the 1964 NFL Championship. Was this twenty-six-year period in the desert really a result of this contract? Would the Browns have beaten the Colts in '64 even if they had never signed this stupid thing? Whether or not the Browns won in 1964, in the era before the Super Bowl, and all the fame and money and prestige that comes with it, would the Browns have won the intervening years? Modell read on:

TELEFAX TO:216-555-1212 FROM:(666)666-1212 DATE: 2-01-1991 08:17:34

Clause XVII

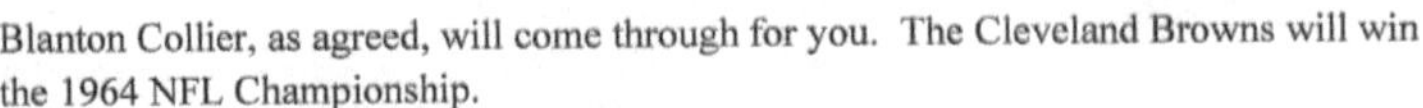

Blanton Collier, as agreed, will come through for you. The Cleveland Browns will win the 1964 NFL Championship.

Mr. Collier will not prevail again. In fact, you will hire and fire many coaches before the Cleveland Browns or Art Modell ever win it all again. The price, quite admittedly is high, but you want and deserve to win so badly now, don't you Arthur? You'll show the world that Paul Brown wasn't the exclusive key to success for the Cleveland Browns.

In the future, you will be faced with decisions as to who should coach your team. Let me offer you some insights. (By the time you are likely to read this, you will have suffered greatly, along with the fans of Cleveland).

At the appointed season, beware of Mike White. He will bring you only trouble. Don't make a big move you will forever regret because of Michael R White.

In your searching hour, a coach of great power will become available. He will rule his era. By the time he is done, many will say he will have eclipsed the brilliant results of Paul Brown. He may be gruff, he may not play to the media, nor to the fans, but he will achieve like almost no other coach in the history of the game. His name is Bill Belichick. He will lead this team, [illegible]land, to more NFL championships than Paul Brown ever did.

Belichick's team will dominate for years, winning its division (AFC [illegible] seventy (70) percent of the years he coaches it, over a period measured in decades[illegible]

I guarantee, you, Arthur B. Modell, will hoist Lombardi's trophy with B[illegible] B[illegible]k as your coach.

And remember, choose wisely, as not choosing the right coach is as bad as choosing the wrong coach.

BC initial 12/26/64

Once Art had returned from his reminiscence of yesteryear and returned to the fax, he felt like he had hit the jackpot! *Wow, this is giving me the names of the coaches we are looking at right now.* He had practically already hired Mike White, but for the protestations of Ernie Accorsi, who really wanted Bill Belichick. Over the last week Accorsi had been pulling Modell toward his point of view. But, after reading the fax, Modell was convinced Belichick was his man.

Now he wished it was Belichick who was coming in today instead of Cowher. He'd have offered him the job on the spot. "Looks like Mike White is out," Art said aloud. When he noticed Bill Belichick's name being mentioned in a favorable light, even comparing favorably to Paul Brown's, that was it! He was convinced Belichick was the man they'd been searching for . . . forever.

Modell stormed out of his office, his wide grin something nobody had seen in weeks. "Margie, are Ernie, Mike, Jim, and the others all in yet?"

"Yes, they are all getting settled in the conference room—oh and remember, I just confirmed plans for Mr. Cowher to be here around noon for lunch before you meet this afternoon."

Modell had almost forgotten about the impending Cowher interview. "Ah yes. Bill Cowher. It will be good to see him again."

Modell was making a beeline toward the conference room. He couldn't wait to show them all the fax, citing it as proof that he knew the right guy to pick as the next Browns coach. The last man Modell would ever need to hire to coach the Cleveland Browns. But then, Modell stopped in his tracks, a look on his face like someone dropped an anvil on his head. *I can't show these guys this fax. They'll think I've lost my marbles when I tell them where it came from.*

Modell hastily folded the fax and put it in the interior breast pocket of his sport coat. He burst into the conference room. The small talk subsided as the men got up from their seats. He didn't wait for an exchange of pleasantries.

"Gentlemen, I have made up my mind on our next coach," Modell said. "I am as sure of it as I've been of any decision in my life." He could have let his front office staff marinate in anticipation and savored the secret for a few tantalizing moments, but his excitement wouldn't allow for it. "I want us to begin immediately to get in touch with Bill Belichick. I want to make him our next coach before someone beats us to it."

His staff was speechless. They were all there today to talk through the shortlist of candidates and to interview Bill Cowher, due to arrive in a few hours. The men were caught between congratulating their boss on his epiphany and urging more due diligence about this momentous decision.

Finally, Ernie Accorsi spoke: "Uh Art, I thought you liked Mike White. What made you—"

"Did you see Belichick's defense stop the Bills?" Modell cut him off. "The Bills were scoring a million points on everybody, and he held them to two touchdowns and a field goal. And the week before he held the 49ers to 13 points."

Modell continued, feverishly: "I saw that press conference before the Super Bowl. The reporters were asking him about head coaching opportunities. He shot them down immediately. He's a no-nonsense man. He wanted to keep his focus on stopping Buffalo. He is there to coach football. I don't think he cares about the limelight or anything else. He's just a tough SOB coach, and I think he's just what we need."

"Art, that makes him a great defensive coordinator," Mike Lombardi weighed in. "But a head coach needs to be able to communicate with the media, and the public. Do you—"

"I have a feeling this is the last coach I will ever hire for the Cleveland Browns," Modell said, emphatic. "Mark my words, he will go down in history as a great coach."

"So, you're decided, then?" Accorsi asked, secretly wanting to jump for joy.

"Yes. I am certain."

"Is it too late to stop Cowher from coming?" Jim Shofner inquired.

"Well hold on," Mike Lombardi interjected. "We haven't hired Belichick yet. He could sign with someone else or stay with the Giants. I have information that he's headed to Tampa later this week to interview for their head coaching job. We'd better keep all the fires burning until we have our coach signed, sealed, and delivered."

"In the meantime, I want no stone left unturned in getting Belichick here as soon as possible," Modell said. "I want to make him an offer before Tampa or anybody else gets the chance."

Bill Belichick had a busy week: Sunday: win the Super Bowl. Wednesday: meet with Art Modell at his home. Thursday: meet in the Browns offices with Art and the front office staff, then fly to Tampa for dinner with the Buccaneers brass. Friday: interview with various Tampa Bay executives and ownership. It was an unbelievably hectic schedule but likely not any more intensive than a typical workweek for Coach Belichick. The following week would not be any less eventful.

## January/February 1991

| Sun | Mon | Tues | Wed | Thurs | Fri | Sat |
|---|---|---|---|---|---|---|
| 20 | 21 | 22 | 23 | 24<br>M. White in Cleveland | 25<br>M. White in Cleveland | 26<br>M. White in Tampa Bay |
| 27<br>Belichick at Super Bowl | 28 | 29<br>TB not interested in M. White | 30<br>Belichick at Art Modell's House | 31<br>Belichick with Browns.<br>TB interviews<br>B. Ryan & G. Stevens | 1<br>Belichick with TB<br>Cowher in Cleveland<br>Walsh says no to TB | 2<br>Belichick with TB<br>Cowher in Cleveland |
| 3<br>Plain Dealer reports Browns close to hiring Belichick | 4<br>TB sticking with Williamson;<br>Belichick visits Modell home with his wife | 5<br>Belichick named as Head Coach of Cleveland Browns | 6 | 7 | 8<br>Scouting Combine Indy, IN | 9<br>Scouting Combine Indy, IN |
| 10 | 11 | 12 | 13<br>Belichick names Saban as DC (first assistant hired) | 14 | 15 | 16 |

## 43

# MODELL PICKS HIS COACH

MONDAY, FEBRUARY 4, 1991

*Art Modell and Bill Belichick were seated in the back room of the Modell* home in Waite Hill. Their wives, Pat and Debbie, were talking in the kitchen. Debbie was all ears as Pat relayed stories from her time in Hollywood, before abandoning her acting career to marry Art and coming to live in Cleveland—former capital of the football universe. Art was swirling the melting ice cubes in his glass of scotch. Belichick had laid his cards on the table. He wanted control. The kind of control Marty Schottenheimer had sought and was denied, causing Schottenheimer to part ways with the Browns.

In truth, Modell was mostly trying to *look* like he was playing hardball. True, Tampa Bay was out of the running when they revealed they might vest control in an *experienced* coach—like Buddy Ryan, or Bill Walsh, but not in the young first-time head coaching aspirant Bill Belichick. Maybe Tampa had a point.

But Modell was smitten. In everything he had seen in interviews and press conferences, in the way Belichick's defenses performed on the field, in the way Coach Parcells and the Giants players talked about him, and in every interaction that Modell had with Belichick personally, Modell was convinced: Bill Belichick had to be the next Cleveland Browns head coach. (A certain fax may have colored his perceptions as well.)

Belichick then softened up, revealing a more even-tempered side, usually reserved for when he was hanging backstage at a Bon Jovi concert. "Art, I don't know if you are aware, but I was on the sidelines at Hiram College watching training camp in your first year with the Browns in 1961. I was nine years old."

"What? Why on earth was that?"

"My dad coached Hiram back then. My mom was a Spanish teacher there. I was a nine-year-old, but even then, I knew I was witnessing greatness when I watched Jim Brown."

"Ah, that's right! Your dad did coach there. How about that!? I guess this is a homecoming for you then!"

"Well, it took me nearly thirty years, but I guess I'm back where it all started."

For Art, all other coaching candidates had faded to insignificance as Belichick came into sharper and sharper focus. Meanwhile, from Belichick's perspective, the other potential suitors—Tampa Bay, the New York Giants (where he could be head coach in waiting for a year until Parcell's planned retirement), and every other possibility—fell away.

Maybe Modell could have held back some measure of control, over roster, over drafting, over selection of assistants . . . but he was in love, and love can be blinding.

Modell finally sipped his drink, firmly placed it on the table, and stood up. Belichick rose to his feet in turn. Offering his hand to seal the offer, Modell said, almost solemnly: "Bill, I have great faith in your abilities and judgment. I want you to be the next head coach of the Cleveland Browns."

When the ink was dry, Belichick was signed to an "almost unheard-of" five-year contract worth an estimated $2.5 million. The next day, at the press conference, Modell explained his rationale for such a long, lucrative deal: "I wanted to make a statement of confidence in Bill, despite his age. I also wanted to make a statement as it relates to continuity and stability. I thought it was appropriate to start fresh and give him as much visible support going in as I possibly can." (One wonders if Art considered the irony in the fact that the only other time he signed a five-year contract for a coach was a renewal for Sam Rutigliano and that he fired Rutigliano one year into the deal.)

Modell told the media that Belichick would "have all the authority he needs to run the team." Modell indicated this would include a major role in the upcoming draft and full authority over hiring his staff. For his part, Belichick was equal parts assertive and humble and showed aplomb in dealing with the reporters, betraying none of the prickly peevishness that would come to forever vex the media and fans.

"I feel I've been coaching for thirty years," Belichick said. "It's ingrained. I've done all the jobs in an organization you can do: typing, driving people to the airport, liming the fields, coaching, period. I think I'm ready to be a head coach, but it's a question that still has to be answered."

When Modell compared Belichick with another coach who got his head coaching chance at a young age and who had boyhood roots in Northeast Ohio, Belichick answered with humility, class, and textbook savvy: "To be compared to Don Shula really is a joke," he said. "I mean, the guy's a Hall of Fame coach and I have yet to coach one game in this league. I hope he's not insulted."

Thus, the Belichick era in Cleveland was underway. Owner, coach, and most of the media and football cognoscenti considered it a perfect marriage: an up-and-coming coach and a historically mighty football franchise bound again for glory.

The week before the Super Bowl, Bill was consumed with preparing to limit the stampeding Buffalo Bills' onslaught. The week after the Super Bowl, he was the NFL's hottest head coaching commodity, jetting from city to city, interviewing with Tampa and Cleveland.

This week was shaping up to be just as hectic.

Monday, he had met with Art at his house and was offered and accepted the job. Tuesday was the big press conference announcing his anointment to the world. Tuesday and Wednesday, he interviewed holdovers from the Bud Carson regime. Thursday, it was off to Indianapolis with the rest of the Browns' talent evaluators for the annual combine (and assistant coach instant-dating service).

By early the following week, Belichick had hired his first coordinator: Nick Saban. Nick was brought in as defensive coordinator as well as to handle the defensive secondary. This hiring was put into motion before Belichick had even been offered the Browns head coaching job. He just knew that—wherever he landed—he wanted Saban on his team. Saban, happily coaching at the University of Toledo, had told Belichick that he would only leave Toledo to go to the Browns. No other destination in the NFL interested him. Imagine that!

44

# BELICHICK BEGINS

August 6, 1991, Cleveland and Cincinnati

*On the sidelines, as the head football coach—at any level—for the first* time in his life, Bill Belichick took one fleeting second to allow himself to savor the moment. This was the same team—the Cleveland Browns—that he had watched during training camp at Hiram College when he was nine years old when his dad was the coach there. Something about those plain orange helmets had made an impression on him, and now he was a part of it. He was *leading* it. True, it was only a preseason game, but he was the *head coach of the Cleveland Browns.*

True, many of his starters were banged up and wouldn't play tonight, but there were 65,000 fans in Cleveland Stadium ready to cheer his team on. Belichick also thought about Art Modell, who had been a rookie owner back when Bill was that wide-eyed nine-year-old. The legendary Paul Brown was the team's coach. Now here he was, Bill Belichick, hired by Modell to be the one to return this franchise to prominence. It felt like fate.

Though Belichick didn't know it, something similarly monumental had also happened this day. The founder and namesake of this organization, the team's greatest figure, the genius innovator in modernizing the NFL, Modell's first coach, and the first one he fired, the man who had since founded a second NFL team and coached them to a division title a few years later, the legend—Paul Brown—had died.

Belichick was glad he didn't know until after the game. He didn't really know Paul Brown, but somehow, he suddenly felt alone. It was disorienting, like one of the pillars that supported the equilibrium of football life had collapsed. Was that it? Or was it that Belichick had lost his living rival for what and whom he hoped to become—a second Paul Brown, Cleveland Browns and NFL all-time coaching legend.

Belichick felt like a kid being dropped off at college. Feeling the sudden clean, cold break from family and familiarity. When you know you'll go back home but that things will never really be the same again. Pangs of sadness and loneliness swell like sudden waves, and you feel like you'll be dragged out to sea and drowned.

But then, you realize a new and exciting life is awaiting. Freedom. New friends. College girls. In Belichick's case, now looking to the future, he wondered if a torch had been passed. Could it be Paul Brown, or perhaps a higher power, had acknowledged that a worthy steward had now taken the reins? That the legacy was secure in the cradle of professional football, with a new innovator, master, a new legend installed to reassert Northeast Ohio as the center of the football universe?

Belichick felt something like a divine hand on his shoulder on his car ride home. He felt sadness at the passing of a master. But he felt confirmation that he would one day join his predecessor in the pantheon of coaching greatness. He almost forgot that the Browns lost the game. *Almost.*

Belichick and the Browns didn't fare any better in the actual season opener, losing to the Cowboys 26-14. The Browns were banged up coming into the game. Before Belichick would win his first game as a head coach, he would reveal his true colors in his monomaniacal approach to coaching, as relayed by Cleveland *Plain Dealer* reporter Bill Livingston, who was trying to do his job in the leadup to the Browns' game against the New England Patriots:

> We know our place in the media and it's not to jeopardize the team effort in wartime.
>
> Yeah, war. I mean, weren't Patriot missiles manufactured somewhere near Boston? Would Gen. H. Norman Schwarzkopf have told Saddam Hussein where the Pats were deployed? You think his lips would budge when asked about Kevin Mack, either?
>
> I know, I know. This is just a football game. What, you ask, do the New England Patriots have to do with Patriot missiles

other than in New England owner Victor Kiam's sleazeball jokebook? But hey, loose lips sink ships, as Browns coach Bill Belichick learned from his daddy, Steve, when the elder Belichick was an assistant coach at the Naval Academy and young Bill was charting convoy routes, er, plays for him.

Don't expect any observations from us media types about Mack's practice time this week, either. Coach B. says no and that's the way it's gonna be.

We'll sit in our little box at the practice field, touch-typing because of the blindfolds. Nobody can report what happened at practice, either. Nobody can print much of anything Belichick doesn't want printed or practice will be closed....

Something else transpired the week after that first loss that would be a hallmark of Belichick's time with the Browns. Art Modell declared in a newspaper report that he "felt much better about the Cowboys' loss after sitting down and watching film with Bill." Modell had considered Bernie Kosar to be almost like a son since the Browns first considered drafting him. But Modell was *smitten* with Belichick. Further proof would come when Belichick would convince Art to have the Browns fork over $500,000 to change the turf on the fields at their practice facility/team HQ in Berea, Ohio. Bear in mind that this facility was only opened the previous year!

Belichick would earn his first NFL coaching victory in his next game, his second ever. His win would come in a 27-0 shutout over—of all teams—the New England Patriots!

The 1991 season would unfold in much the same way as the first eight days of the season: Belichick would have a prickly relationship with the media. He would maintain and strengthen Modell's full faith. And there would be ambiguity as to whether Belichick was a good head coach. His first season as head coach in the NFL would end with a record of 6-10. Not good. Or was it? Belichick had only won six games, but that was twice as many as the Browns had won the previous year.

By November, despite a losing record, Modell went on record with the *Plain Dealer*'s Mary Kay Cabot: "I'm more excited today about the future of the Cleveland Browns than I was in training camp, because I see things developing with a masterful head coach who's going to be around a long, long time. He may not know it himself, but he's got the potential to be a Chuck Noll or a Don Shula."

Be that as it may, the coaching prospect they had passed over with barely a consideration would be hired a year later, in 1992, by Pittsburgh to replace legend Chuck Noll. Though a legend, in fact, Noll had barely squeaked out a winning record at 93-91 over the last dozen years. The Steelers finished 7-9 in 1991. Bill Cowher would lead the team to an 11-5 record and win NFL Coach of the Year honors in his first season.

"People say they are alike, Marty [Schottenheimer] and Belichick," said wide receiver Reggie Langhorne around this time. "Marty was somewhat of a dictator. But I could talk to Marty. Most guys on the team could talk to Marty. This guy [Belichick], no. Players have a certain feeling about their head coach. Do they respect [Belichick] as a coach? Yeah. Can they carry a conversation with him and talk to him and understand? Or go to him with a problem? Or ask him for advice? Or take suggestions to him? No. Communicate with him? No."

45

# BELICHICK'S SOPHOMORE SEASON

## Browns 1992

*Despite the Browns having one of the NFL's worst offensive lines in* Bill Belichick's rookie year of 1991, resulting in Bernie Kosar being sacked forty-four times, resulting in a rotating cast of injured quarterbacks; and despite Art Modell's comment that picking an offensive lineman high in the draft was "an automatic," and despite Executive Vice President Ernie Accorsi's admission one week prior to the draft that "my biggest mistake in recent years was not taking offensive linemen high enough" in the draft, the Browns did not select any offensive linemen in the 1992 draft.

They, instead, picked Stanford fullback "Touchdown" Tommy Vardell. Though he scored highest of all running backs entering the draft on the NFL's Wunderlich (intelligence) test, he betrayed the naivety of a rookie when addressing a reporter's concern about his new team's shoddy offensive line: "I don't think that's always as serious a problem as people might think. I know it's not the same level, but in high school our offensive line averaged about 170 pounds. I was bigger than they were. You can take advantage of different strengths. I'm not worried about that." ("Touchdown" Tommy would go on to score a total of five touchdowns—three rushing, two receiving—in his four years with the Browns.)

Incidentally, other teams drafted offensive linemen with three of the next four picks. It was no secret: There was a bonanza of high-quality offensive lineman. When the media asked Accorsi about not selecting an offensive lineman, he commented that he "was surprised too." This betrayed that he'd been pushed aside in this year's draft and that the two men whom Accorsi had helped bring to the Browns, Bill Belichick and Mike Lombardi, were now running the show.

The day after the draft, Belichick sent popular and productive receiver Brian Brennan packing. Later that day, Modell accepted Accorsi's resignation. "I believe in runs," Accorsi said. "And I've had my run there."

Tony Grossi of the *Plain Dealer* captured what franchise quarterback, local hero, and fan favorite Bernie Kosar felt about the recent draft and shoving aside Accorsi:

"When we have done well offensively, I've always deferred the attention, notoriety, and praise to the people around me. And when things haven't gone well, I've stood up and taken the blame and criticism for many things completely out of my control, and for other people's mistakes. As a quarterback and leader of this team for eight years, I feel it was my responsibility to my teammates, the organization and our fans to do that for the sake of trying to devote my life to making the Cleveland Browns a winning team. With all that in mind, and without many positive things to say, I think it's best for all concerned that I don't comment."

Before the 1992 regular season had even gotten underway, Belichick had:

> Hired eleven new assistants for a league-high total of thirteen. Reorganized the scouting staff, hiring seven new scouts. Overhauled the roster, keeping fewer than twenty players from when he first arrived. He'd let go of veterans such as Brian Brennan and Reggie Langhorne. He'd replaced the indoor and outdoor fields at the new facility at a cost of about $1 million. He'd moved training camp to Berea from Lakeland Community College.
>
> The team did not fill Ernie Accorsi's position as executive vice president of football operations after he left. [Belichick] closed practices to the media. Belichick acquired players with previous substance abuse problems such as John Rienstra, Terry Taylor, Barry Wilburn, and George Williams. He acquired high-priced veterans such as Mark Bavaro, Jay Hilgenberg, and James

Brooks. Took charge of the draft and Plan B free agency. Brought in in more Plan B tryouts (seventy-eight) than any other team.

Belichick, a hard rock fan, would watch Van Halen and Pink Floyd concerts from the loge in Cleveland Stadium during his tenure. His close friendship with Jon Bon Jovi has been well chronicled over the years. But perhaps no song by any rock star could capture Belichick's credo like a song Frank Sinatra made famous: "My Way."

The *Plain Dealer*'s Mary Kay Cabot quoted Belichick as saying this in September 1992:

"I've tried to look at a lot of coaches in in the league that were successful and kind of catalogued a lot of things I thought they were doing well, but I think it's important—for better or for worse—that I try to be myself and not emulate Al Davis or Don Shula or Chuck Noll or whoever. They were successful being themselves and they all had different styles. I've had success in my career and I feel comfortable with the way I've been doing things. I'm not saying there's no room for improvement, but I would be insincere if I went out and tried to be a Sam Rutigliano or Bum Phillips."

The NFL is a results business, measured in wins and losses. So far, the jury was out on Bill Belichick. He'd only won six of sixteen games. Not good. But he'd doubled the win total in his first year. Not bad. Players, fans, and the media all tend to extend the benefit of the doubt in such probationary periods when the coach is playing by the unwritten rulebook, doing things the *expected way*, not *MY WAY*.

MY WAY is only cherished, indeed only tolerated if it results in unparalleled success. Then MY WAY is eccentric, not mad. MY WAY is genius, not folly. But absent that track record of success, MY WAY will meet its enemies. And Belichick was adding more to the ledger every day.

Among the team's leaders, almost everyone, save Kevin Mack, was unhappy. Star quarterback and hometown hero Bernie Kosar wasn't vocal, heeding his father's advice not to say anything if he had nothing nice to say. Michael Dean Perry, probably the best player on defense, said he'd "never seen eye-to-eye" with the head coach. Eight players had held out, deep into training camp. Two of them, star receiver Webster Slaughter and running back Eric Metcalf, had gone on record that they would rather play elsewhere.

The media felt about as appreciated by the second-year coach as the players. Locked out of practices and treated to only a few grudging moments of contact time with Belichick, the reporters used their typewriters, radio waves, and TV slots to unload on the coach. Understandably, the fans, who could see (albeit briefly) for themselves, the monosyllabic, clearly uncomfortable head coach duck routine questions, became more and more convinced that Belichick was not the answer for the Browns.

But the man whose opinion truly mattered, the man who had signed Belichick's five-year contract, the man who owned the team—was behind him 100 percent. This was true when Art Modell hired him. It was true coming off a 6-10 first season. It was true when the Browns started the 1992 season 0-2. It was especially true on December 6 after the Browns beat Cincinnati 37-21, giving the Browns a 7-6 record on the year. It was even true after the three-game skein that ended Belichick's second season at 7-9.

Seven and nine. It's a losing record. But it is almost playing .500. Just one game shy of a non-losing season. One lousy game. Maybe one missed field goal. Possibly just a ref making one bad call was all that had prevented a non-losing season. Heck, starting quarterback Bernie Kosar had missed nine full games because of a broken ankle. Had he been healthy, who knows? Maybe two or three narrow losses would have been wins!

Seven and nine just sounds way, way bigger than a one-game improvement over 6-10. Other than the difference between 16-0 and 15-1 (or 1-15 and 0-16), a one-game difference never seems so stark as the difference between lousy, losing 6-10 and practically neutral 7-9. Somehow, Coach MyWay had again managed to finish a season where he hadn't succeeded, yet he hadn't really failed, either.

After starting 0-2, the Browns had bobbed to a winning record three different times, most recently at 7-6 before dropping the season's last three games. Coach MyWay built onto last season's win total. Good! But didn't achieve a winning record. Bad! He hadn't bowled anyone over with a historic worst to first. Yet, he had kindled hope that maybe, just maybe, he was building something that would last. Even if players were skeptical and fans were split, Modell was still firmly convinced he had his man, the last coach he would ever need to hire for the Cleveland Browns.

"Bill, we need to strengthen the offense," Modell said. "The media is killing us, and I agree with them." He went on to mention that maybe the team would benefit from having an offensive coordinator.

"Art, I don't think we are that far off," Belichick said. "Bernie was hurt early in the season, and he just broke his ankle again against Pittsburgh. He'll have surgery and have all off-season to recover—"

"Still," Modell said, "Bill, I think you should consider some help on that side of the ball."

Modell summed it up for the media the next day: "We have to retool the offense. We have to address the offensive side, but what we do is up to Bill. It's his call."

There is probably nothing better at conveying Modell's faith in and dependency on Belichick than Tony Grossi's *Plain Dealer* article "Modell's Jokes Fail to Hide Sadness as Chances Slip Away" published on New Year's Eve 1992:

> Art Modell called it his "rambling, disjointed, unconnected, incoherent, articulate overview" on the state of the Browns.
>
> It was so entertaining. So enlightening. And so very sad. . . .
>
> But like the aging comic, Buddy Young Jr., in Billy Crystal's "Mr. Saturday Night," Modell could not conceal the sad soul behind his smile.
>
> At sixty-seven, Modell seems to have come to grips with the likelihood that he might never celebrate the joy of competing in a Super Bowl, much less winning one.
>
> He pretty much assured that by pledging that he will "pick up stakes and leave town" if he and Belichick "do not get the job done" in the last three years of Belichick's contract.
>
> "He is the last head coach I've hired. I will not hire another head coach," Modell said. . . . Modell's legacy is now left in the hands of Belichick. Together, they will write the final three chapters of a fascinating, but so far unfulfilling, era in Cleveland sports history.
>
> "Nobody has that luxury," Modell said, when asked what he would have done differently. "I've made so many mistakes. I think I guessed right more often than not."

## 46

# THIRD TIME A CHARM FOR COACH MYWAY?

Browns' 1993 Season

*There were some good signs heading into the 1993 season—Bill Belichick's* third with the Browns. The head coach/de facto general manager had picked up free agents at key positions of need prior to April's draft, allowing the Browns to, as Belichick noted, "take the best player on the board—whoever that may be," instead of potentially having to reach for a position of dire need. The free agents they picked up were starting left guard Houston Hoover, starting cornerback Najee Mustafaa, starting wide receiver Mark Carrier, and quarterback Vinny Testaverde. The Testaverde pickup was a prudent move to add depth and didn't raise too many eyebrows at the time. But it sure would cause a tidal wave of tumult midway through the season.

Belichick drafted a center, Steve Everitt, in the first round, and he was a day-one starter. In the second round, he picked up a defensive end, Dan Footman, who would end up starting regularly in his third season. Nothing glamorous, but not a disaster. There was generally optimism that Belichick was shoring up some key areas and was now firmly established after two foundational years. Good things could happen this season.

In July, on the eve of training camp, there was another good sign. The ever suspicious and grumpy coach had invited area reporters into his world for an informal (though off-the-record) chat session, followed by an invitation to the staff picnic! The players reported that their coach seemed more relaxed and approachable than they'd ever seen him.

"I'm a lot more comfortable heading into this season," Belichick said. "I just think we're way ahead of where we've been the last two seasons. It's not even close. I feel a lot better about the talent of the players and the attitude they're coming in with." Yes, things seemed to be looking up in 1993.

Then the regular season hit. And it started off great! Whereas Bernie Kosar had been sacked 11 times in last year's opener, the Bengals only bagged him twice in 1993's debut. The Browns won. In week two, Kosar and the Browns beat the mighty 49ers and reigning MVP Steve Young, picking him off three times. The Browns went to 3-0 after a comeback win against the LA Raiders. Kosar had had a tough first half in that game and was replaced by new pickup Vinny Testaverde. Kosar was immediately named the starter for the next week, but the seed was planted.

Week four, the Browns were again down against Indianapolis at halftime, 6-0. Kosar was 4 of 8 for 53 yards in the half. On one occasion during the first half, Kosar had improvised and called his own play. Looking to spark the team, Coach MyWay yanked Kosar and started the second half with Testaverde.

The Browns led 10-9 entering the fourth quarter but suffered their first loss of the season to the Indianapolis Colts. Whereas the papers were praising Belichick's "Midas touch" for making the quarterback switch in the previous game, now they were lamenting a brewing quarterback controversy. Funny how a loss will change everything.

In game 5, versus the Dolphins, Kosar again started. The savvy veteran called his own play on the game's first drive that went for a 14-yard touchdown to receiver Michael Jackson. After that, the offense bogged down. Coach MyWay was dinking and dunking, calling the most conservative game possible. Kosar drew up another of his own plays.

"Bernie, what the hell was that? That is not the play I called! I call the plays I call for a reason. And that's the second time you changed a play today."

"Well, the last one I called went for a touchdown. *Coach.*"

"I'm the coach of this team. I'll call the plays."

"Coach, I want the same as you, to win. I know what I'm doin' out there. I've called plays for years. I even called plays in college."

"Well, you are not in college now, and you're not playing the rest of this game. I'm benching you."

It was all Kosar could do to keep from throwing his helmet.

Talk about a quarterback controversy. Take a look at this excerpt from Tony Grossi's piece "Belichick, Kosar Aren't in Sync" in the *Plain Dealer*:

> Kosar is not the first quarterback to be yanked. But he might be the first one to be yanked after completing 79% of his passes (15 of 19) and not committing a turnover. Of course, many of the completions were nothing more than extended handoffs. Seven of Kosar's 15 completions gained 3 or fewer yards. Four times, the play called for Kosar to throw on the run, bootlegging right or left, something he is not adept at doing. Two of those plays netted gains of 6 and 3 yards, one produced a loss of 2 yards, and one resulted in a sack.

Vinny Testaverde did not save the day, throwing one interception and no touchdowns, as the Browns lost the game to the Dolphins 24-14.

After the game, reporters caught a divergence of opinion between the longtime starting quarterback and the coach. Grossi reported:

> On three occasions in his carefully worded postgame remarks, Kosar said that all he could do was execute the plays "at our disposal." Asked if Kosar called his own plays, Belichick said, "Play-calling has been the same as it's been the past three years."
>
> It's the first time Belichick has confirmed Kosar has no greater latitude in calling plays than before. Yet, giving Kosar more latitude in calling plays was Belichick's rationale in the off-season for not hiring an offensive coordinator.

A couple days after the game, it would be revealed that Kosar was yanked after changing a play—a deep pass for wide receiver Michael Jackson that was batted away (an earlier changed play by Bernie resulted in a touchdown pass to Michael Jackson). Coach Belichick was showing it was MyWay or the bench. This same week, star receiver Michael Jackson was quoted saying:

"Belichick can't communicate with his players," among other disparaging remarks made to the Browns Backers Club in Mansfield, Ohio. He even asserted that the ultimate legend himself—Jim Brown, who'd been hired by Belichick—was acting as a spy, reporting back to Belichick what the players were saying.

Another quote published in the *Ashland Times-Gazette* on October 14th and cited in the *Cleveland Plain Dealer* the next day, sums up the situation:

> "The whole thing is a power play between Bernie and Belichick," star receiver Michael Jackson was quoted as saying. "Bill has brought a lot of commotion between the players, and actually every day we expect it. If you question Bill, you're out of line. Bernie will tell Bill if he doesn't like the offensive game plan . . . and if you question Bill, he'll write you right out of the game plan. That's what's happened to Leroy Hoard and why he's not playing much."

Finally, Jackson brought Modell's name into the conversation:

> Things probably won't change. Art is supporting Bill because Bill's the man he chose to lead his team. I really thought Art would speak out on the Bernie thing because Art loves Bernie Kosar.

The next game, Testaverde started at quarterback. Kosar remained on the bench. Jackson would not get many reps, after stirring up all the controversy in Ashland. Regardless of what Jackson or the other players felt about him, or what the reporters wrote about him, Belichick came off looking like a genius. The Browns jumped out to a 21-0 lead on three first-half Testaverde touchdown passes. The Browns won (against 0-6 Cincinnati) 28-17. It was the most points they scored to that point in the season, and the most rushing yards they'd had in six years.

47

# EXECUTED OR EXTENDED?

Thursday, October 21, 1993 – Cleveland Browns Headquarters

***"Come on over, have a seat right here." Art Modell was in a conference*** room at the Berea complex and instructed his coach to have a seat across the table from him. Modell was dressed in slacks and a sweater, he seemed to be in a good mood, but Coach wondered what might be in store for him. Was he about to get a lecture warning him to warm up to the media, like Modell had made him promise to do so many times before?

"Bill, you've been getting a lot of grief from some of the players and from the media, especially these last few weeks—"

"I know, I know," Coach started, "you want me to play nice with these reporters—"

"That's not why I called you up here today," Modell cut him off. "I think you are on the right track. I believe in you, and I want to double down on that as we head into this game against Pittsburgh."

Belichick sat there, just looking at Art, not sure what to make of his boss. He was waiting for a "But," or a "However," and then a bunch of stuff he didn't want to hear—especially with precious time ticking by and the Pittsburgh game coming up.

"Bill, we are halfway through that contract we signed at my house, did you realize that?"

"Uh, no, I guess I wasn't keeping track."

"Well, it's true. I gave you, a rookie coach, a lengthy five-year contract, because I believed you were the man that could turn us around."

Belichick started sweating, involuntarily clenching his fists and teeth, instinctively girding for a battle. Before he could speak, Art continued.

"I believe in you now even more. I called you up here because I want to extend your contract for an additional two years."

With that, Modell clasped his hands behind his head and leaned back in his chair. He had seen his coach begin to squirm and knew Belichick wasn't sure what he had in mind. The relief that surged through Belichick's being spread a smile across his face. Automatically he sprang to his feet, approached Modell, shook his hand, and thanked him.

"In my view, you've earned it," Modell said. "I just want to show you that you've got my full support. Now let's get ready to beat Pittsburgh!"

Game 7 was a battle against the co-leaders of the AFC Central—the Steelers—in Cleveland. Jackson burst out of the doghouse with a 62-yard touchdown reception to open the scoring. Eric Metcalf would electrify the stadium by returning not one but two punts for touchdowns! This win put the Browns in sole possession of first place. Best of all, it came at the expense of archrival Pittsburgh!

Despite the victory, Belichick was not celebrating. His newly minted starting quarterback, his recently validated choice to pilot the Browns through the rest of the season, Vinny Testaverde, had his shoulder separated, straining for a first down, late in the game. Of course, it was the one attached to his throwing arm. It was uncertain whether he'd play again this season.

In sole possession of first place, the Browns had a bye week and thus two weeks to prepare for the team that had been Kosar's archnemesis—even more than Pittsburgh—the team that denied the Browns' entry to the Super Bowl three times in four years during Bernie's career: the Denver Broncos. The Broncos and Browns would each enter the game at 5-3. The Broncos still had future Hall of Famer (and Browns arch-adversary) John Elway at quarterback. But Denver's pass defense was terrible. And, the Browns had the home field advantage.

Despite Denver's weakness in defending the pass, Belichick opted to run, run, run. When that didn't work and the Browns were forced to throw, the Broncos inserted seven defensive backs and cranked up the pass rush. Kosar couldn't do enough to carry the team, though he did throw two touchdowns and no interceptions. He was sacked six times. The Browns' defense was mostly just a rumor. Down by 22 points with under a minute to play, Kosar's final play was one he drew up in the dirt as the Browns huddled: It was a 38-yard touchdown pass to Jackson.

It would be Kosar's last play as a Cleveland Brown.

# EXCOMMUNICATED—BYE, BYE BERNIE

NOVEMBER 1993

> In their most shocking and controversial move since Paul Brown was fired as head coach in 1963, the Browns yesterday waived nine-year quarterback Bernie Kosar, saying he was washed up.
> —Mary Kay Cabot, *Plain Dealer,* November 9, 1993

*"Man, what the hell is Belichick doing?" Marlon yelled, crumpling his* newspaper and throwing it down in disgust. "Vinny's hurt, he's out for the season, and he cuts Bernie! This guy is a maniac! It's one thing to cut Bernie if Testaverde was healthy, but he's hurt!"

His wife was upstairs getting the kids ready for school. "What's going on down there? You're scaring the kids!"

But Marlon wasn't the only fan disturbing his family's tranquility. This scene played out all over town. It was louder than New Year's Eve, though a lot less joyful.

As Marlon began his commute to work, his brother Tevin called him, car phone to car phone. "What the hell was that?" Tevin began.

An eavesdropper might have thought Marlon had shown up drunk at their mother's house for Sunday dinner and relieved himself on the dining room table, such was the disgust and anger in Tevin's voice.

"This is unbelievable," Marlon said. "It's like he was sent here to destroy the team."

"The $%&#-ing Rooneys are probably paying him more than Modell is," Tevin said. "He's like a Pittsburgh spy sent here to destroy us."

"And what the hell is Modell doing?" Marlon said. "I thought he loved Bernie. He extends Belichick's contract for two more years, and then Belichick axes Bernie, and Modell's okay with that?"

"Yeah, and he cuts him when Testaverde's hurt," Tevin said. "He's probably out for the year!"

"I know, that's what I said this morning. Maybe it's Elway's fault. Maybe Art was sick of seeing us lose to that horse-toothed—"

"Hey man, I'm at work now," Tevin cut him off. "I gotta go."

Bill Livingston summed it up in the November 10, 1993, issue of the *Plain Dealer*:

> If you react with your heart, and this city's huge heart loved Bernie Kosar more than any other athlete of his generation, it is hard to endure Bill Belichick today.
>
> You probably saw the tape of the news conference in which Belichick fired Kosar. The contrast with Bernie's agony was striking. This was the Belichick who unifies his players only in their animosity to him.
>
> The mumble. The monotone. The eyes shifting uneasily away from questioners, looking for a way out. Richard Nixon had body language like this. It is why so few people trusted him.

"Hey, pass me the cream cheese," Strongsville police officer Bob Burly commanded his partner Tony Strang.

"Man, what's wrong with you?" Strang shot back. "And what's up with these bagels? Don't you know us cops are supposed to eat donuts?" He let out his trademark laugh, then threw back some more black coffee. The two were in their cruiser outside Bill Belichick's suburban house. The Cleveland Browns were paying Strongsville police for surveillance and protection for the Belichick family since the release of Kosar.

"Man, how many more days we gotta babysit this guy?" Strang said.

"I hear we'll be here 'til the 18th—Thursday," Burly said. "Damn, I kinda feel like we should just let the fans have their way with this guy. I'm a fan. I know I wanna wring his neck."

Strang just laughed. "Maybe we should make a police escort, and escort him—and his family—outta town." He chuckled, then decided a bagel didn't sound so bad after all.

Finished with their morning snack, and with the Belichick kids off to school or their activities, Strang worked on a crossword and Burly read the sports pages.

"Hey d'ya see this?" Burly's thick index finger pointed to an article on page 5. "Says Browns minority owner Al Lerner is looking to start a team in Baltimore."

"Man, how long has it been since they lost the Colts down there, poor suckers?" Strang inquired of his partner.

"Hell, I don't know, Strang. We got enough to worry about with our own team. Hey, I tell ya what. If this Lerner does start a team in Baltimore, I hope he takes Belichick with him."

"Yeah, but we'll lose all this overtime for baby-sittin'," Strang said, letting out another goofy guffaw.

Although most people in Cleveland would have liked to have wrung Belichick's neck, not everyone was sad to see Kosar go (even if they didn't like the way it was handled). TV5 WEWS in Cleveland asked fans whether the Browns should or should not have cut Kosar loose. In six-and-a-half hours an amazing 33,600 phone calls flooded in. When the results were tabulated, it was surprisingly close: 51 percent "Don't Cut;" 49 percent "Yes Cut."

Kosar was picked up by the reigning Super Bowl champs, Dallas, whose future Hall of Fame quarterback, Troy Aikman, was injured. The next Sunday, Kosar started for the Cowboys, leading them to victory. Meanwhile, the Browns, down to backup (and former third-string) quarterback Todd Philcox, lost their next three games. In the most biting irony, Belichick ceded play-calling duties the very next game after releasing Kosar—to his quarterbacks and running backs coach.

Kosar—universally regarded as a supremely intelligent quarterback—had been strictly prohibited from calling or changing Belichick's plays, despite being one of the most adroit minds to play the game . . . and as soon as he's gone, the head coach's iron grip on play calling loosens. Wow!

The Browns had been tied with Pittsburgh at the top of the AFC Central when Kosar was cut. Now they were in third, with only one-win Cincinnati worse. The Browns would finish Belichick's third season 7-9. Vinny Testaverde would return more quickly than most had thought and play the final five games, going 2-3. In Belichick's three years so far with the Browns he had three losing seasons and no playoff appearances. And yet, he had the unwavering support of Art Modell.

Meanwhile, the Cowboys moseyed on through their season and galloped through the playoffs. Kosar headed to the bench as Aikman returned to take the reins. By the time the 1993 NFL season was over, the Cowboys rode off into the sunset, repeat NFL champions. Kosar had a Super Bowl ring and a smile that gleamed like a pair of silver spurs in the Texas sun. Kosar thought about sending Belichick a note of thanks, something along the lines of "Your actions are directly responsible for getting me to the Super Bowl. You are a one-of-a-kind coach. Thank you!" But he didn't want to waste the stamp.

By the final month of the season, Belichick was proclaiming 1993 as a "rebuilding year." Just four months earlier, Modell and the organization had proclaimed this was the best Cleveland Browns team since 1986. This slide, coupled with fans' disillusionment with Belichick and with Modell, had taken some of the bloom off the rose of the city's relationship with its favorite sports team. Solidly a "football town" for the last four decades, problems with the Browns were allowing seemingly unrelated developments set the stage for the looming ultimate expression of the Curse.

49

# ONE DOOR CLOSES, ANOTHER OPENS

1993

*In October 1993, the NFL Expansion Committee selected Charlotte as* the winner of one of two expansion teams, to begin playing in 1995. The announcement of the second expansion city was delayed until the end of November. The front-runners in that race were Baltimore and St. Louis. Memphis and Jacksonville—which had earlier pulled out of contention, before jumping back in on a wing and a prayer—were considered long shots.

When the smoke cleared, the city with the smallest media market—Jacksonville—had won out. It wasn't shocking to most people that Memphis hadn't gotten a team. St. Louis—which had a brand-new domed stadium being constructed—was shocked that they were not selected. Baltimore was denied as well. The long-dormant fans in Baltimore wanted to come out of hibernation and were furious that the NFL didn't award that second team to their city.

Imagine if the NFL had awarded one of the expansion teams to Baltimore. The Browns wouldn't have moved there to become the Ravens. Would they have pulled up the stakes for some other city? Or would Art Modell have grudgingly settled for a refurbished stadium on the shores of Lake Erie? Would Jonathan Ogden, Ray Lewis, Ed Reed, and Joe Flacco all have written glorious chapters in Cleveland's history?

Outside of football, something was growing in Cleveland. Growth is usually thought of as beneficial. To almost everyone, this new growth was a positive development, but to Art Modell it was a growing tumor.

The growth was baseball fever. Something the fans of Northeast Ohio had been inoculated against since the mid-1950s. Though amid a bleak midwinter, the germ of hope for the normally sickly Indians was alive. It was made tangible by the rising new concrete-and-steel Gateway area baseball stadium. By December 1993, it was really looking like a ballpark. During this Christmas season, it was enough to make Modell say, "Bah humbug!"

He was preoccupied with thoughts of Dick Jacobs and the Gunds and fuming at the outrage of these newcomers being handed the keys to the city. Meanwhile, his team was the one that had always drawn the crowds and inspired the most rabid devotion. Modell himself had always played nice. He was never demanding. And now he and his team were being taken for granted.

The 11 o'clock news had said goodnight over thirty minutes ago. Modell didn't even know what he was now watching, so consumed was he in his ill thoughts. In his La-Z-Boy, he slid into a restless slumber. Soon he was dreaming:

*A woman gives birth to two sons. The firstborn has the head of a ram. The second has a humanoid head, though slightly elfin. The "camera" in his mind's eye pans way out and their white baby blanket becomes a map of Ohio. The birthplace of these twins is a dot on the map labeled "Cleveland."*

*Audio comes in while he clearly sees the birthplace of the Rams and Browns. He notices a labeled dot on the map for Canton. The audio echoes. It says, "Truly Northeast Ohio is the cradle of professional football."*

*His mind's eye zooms back in on the twins. The Ram and the other son both are now wearing crowns. The Ram wears only two, and they are golden. One is inscribed with: "C.R. NFL '45." The other: "L.A.R. NFL '51."*

*The elfin son is wearing a stack of four 14-carat gold crowns, engraved in turn: "C.B. AAFC '46"; "C.B. AAFC '47"; "C.B. AAFC '48", and "C.B. AAFC '49." Four 24-carat golden crowns are stacked on top of the 14-carat gold crowns, inscribed with, "C.B. NFL '50"; "C.B. NFL '54"; "C.B. NFL '55"; and "C.B. NFL '64".*

*It was amazing; between the Rams and the Browns, there was a professional football champion from Cleveland every year from 1945 through 1950. Then another from the Rams the very next year, in 1951, after they'd relocated to Los Angeles. Then a "drought" of two years. The Browns reclaimed the NFL crown in 1954 and kept it in 1955, then added one last crown in 1964. Art thinks to himself,* I guess Northeast Ohio really is the cradle of pro football, *and he swells with pride knowing it is he who owned the current Cleveland franchise.*

*The dreaming sixty-eight-year-old Art Modell squints, focusing closely on the elfin boy's top crown. He sees something staring back; it is his reflection but it's the thirty-nine-year-old Art Modell from 1964. He looks so confident. So cocky. So enthusiastic. So certain of a glorious life laying out ahead of him.*

*Now he sees himself in the Cleveland Stadium locker room. Champagne is being sprayed in the dank, drafty cave. Quarterback Frank Ryan takes a swig and passes the bottle to coach Blanton Collier. Coach grins from ear to ear and enjoys some bubbly, his eyeglass lenses dotting with droplets of the spray. Coach gets the team's attention and exclaims, "To the owner of the Cleveland Browns, a toast to Art Modell!" Players cheer. Some spray champagne on him, and he has to fight back tears.*

*It feels so good to be loved, to be respected. Like the Grinch at the end of the Dr. Seuss book, Modell's heart seems to grow, nearly bursting with pride out of his heaving chest. He proclaims, "Congratulations on winning the 1964 NFL Championship! This is the first one the Browns have won on my watch. But it won't be the last! Not if I have anything to say about it!" The players cheer, and someone shouts, "Hip, hip, hooray!"*

*Art becomes conscious in his dream that he is seeing this scene in a kind of mirror. As he draws back his gaze, the crown comes back into focus, and this locker room scene recedes into its gleam. His vision pans out wider and he sees the boy with the eight crowns in full, one elfin foot on either side of the dot on the map labeled "Cleveland"—but he no longer sees the twin with the ram's head. "Where is your brother?" Modell asks. The boy is mute.*

*Modell now notices that the boy has lost his youthful vigor. He has gotten old, tired, shabby. He asks again, "Where is your brother?" The "boy" just looks up at Art cheerlessly. Modell seems to levitate and is now looking downward on the crown from above. The crown he looks down upon has lost its luster, turning from brilliant, radiant gold to a pale ochre. It then morphs from round to oblong, with one side straight.*

*Modell realizes now that he is looking down on Cleveland Stadium. As if riding on the coattails of the ghost of Christmas past, he is conveyed down from his aerial viewpoint, through the frosty air, to the surface of the field. It is empty, cold, dark. He half expects tombstones to protrude up through the playing field.*

*Modell scans the stands, desolate in the moonlight. The place looks dilapidated, abandoned. One of the advertising signs looks to Modell like it said "Vacancy." Up higher, Modell sees the numbers designating the championships the Cleveland Browns had won: 1946, 1947, 1948, 1949, 1950, 1954, 1955, 1964.*

*"Eight championships in the team's first nineteen years," Art mumbles, almost inaudibly.*

*"Ah, but nothing in the thirty years since."*

*Terrified, Modell spins around to see who'd said that. It is the man in the cashmere coat. He looks exactly the same as when Art had seen him in this very stadium thirty years ago, almost to the day.*

*"Art, you aren't surprised, are you?"*

*"Well, you startled me. I didn't know anyone was here."*

*"Arthur, I mean about the championships. You are not surprised that they all have dried up, are you? After all, that was the deal. You really beat the pants off those Baltimore Colts in 1964, though, just like I promised."*

*Modell stammers, "But, but, I—"*

*"Oh, but nothing!" shouts the man. "You are simply paying me my due."*

*He turns and begins to walk away.*

*Modell begins to protest, "But I don't even know what the deal is. When will it end? When will it end?" He falls to his knees on the field.*

*The man approaches Modell as he rises again to his feet. "Let me show you something," the man says, then slowly extends his arm toward the south. Art notices that the two of them are now perched on Cleveland Municipal Stadium's roof. In the distance is a brightly lit structure. It shines almost like a beacon. Presently, Modell realizes that he and the man are floating toward it. Vibrant blue-and-red neon beckons, complemented by the Christmas lights all around the city, and in stark contrast to the gloomy, forlorn stadium they had just left.*

*Now they are directly above this gleaming gem—a new ballpark. No games had been played here yet. But the floodlights shine down on the field. A perfect green carpet of natural grass surrounds the infield. Modell hates to admit to himself that "diamond" seems an apt term for this field of dreams.*

*Presently they descend onto the pitcher's mound. The stands are so close. They seem to hug the field. Modell can see this park is a retro design. It wasn't a cruiseliner, surrounded by an asphalt ocean of parking spots. It wasn't round or oval. It was oddly shaped, to accommodate the city around it, which reminds Modell of going to games at Ebbett's Field in Brooklyn with his dad. The nostalgia and the intrinsic beauty captivates Modell, but only for a second, as he realizes all the taxes that made this possible could have been used to fix his stadium and keep the Indians playing there.*

*"The mayor and city council and the voters have really done a wonderful job, haven't they, Art?"*

*Before Modell can reply, the man continues: "Not only is this a beautiful baseball park, but the new, next-door basketball arena is top-notch, too. Meanwhile your old stadium is falling to pieces. If I were a sports fan, I know which venues I would rather visit to watch a game."*

*"But wait a minute," Modell sputters. "The Indians haven't won anything in years. They're a laughingstock. The Cavaliers played in Akron, practically; now they've got a new palace in Cleveland?"*

*The man starts walking away, but Modell doesn't notice, ranting as he is.*

*"Two new stadiums! Not one, but two new stadiums. They could have fixed up my stadium for pennies on the dollar! After all the good I've done for the city! They roll out the red carpet for Gund and Jacobs—"*

*Consumed in his screed, Modell finally registers that the man is no longer by his side and has been shouting something from the stands.*

*"He moved, Art; he moved away."*

*"What, what are you talking about? Who moved?"*

*"Art, earlier you were asking the boy with eight crowns where his brother had gone. Art, you remember, he moved to Los Angeles. He knew there were greener pastures out there. In fact, he added another crown out there in '51 . . . Art . . . you know this. What you don't know is that boy will move again and add a Super Bowl crown in St. Louis, then move to Los Angeles once again and equal your Browns with a fourth NFL Champion's crown. Arthur, cradles are quickly outgrown. Have you not seen the signs? If you want to progress, you can't sit still. You've got to move."*

Modell awakened in his chair, disoriented, agitated. He was relieved—as we all are after an unsettling dream—that it had, in fact, only been a dream. On his TV the credits were now rolling to a movie adaptation of *A Christmas Carol*. Modell chuckled when he thought to himself that this nonsensical flying from stadium to stadium in his dream must have only been his subconscious mind following Dickens' story, even while he slept.

A steady undertow was nagging at him, though. He made his way up to bed. The minutes, then hours passed, and Modell realized the dream wasn't just some silly caprice. He had aligned with the majority of owners and voted to grant the two expansion teams to Charlotte and Jacksonville mere weeks ago. Three other cities were out there, hungry for a team. Some of the other owners talked at the meetings about moving their teams. By the time Modell finally fell asleep, he was resolved. He had to beat the other owners to the punch . . . he had to go where he'd be appreciated. He had to *move*.

50

# CLEVELAND CATCHES BASEBALL FEVER

APRIL 5, 1994

*The most powerful person on the planet, decked out in an old Block-C* cap and blue-and-red nylon Cleveland Indians jacket, toed the rubber, wound up, and let 'er rip. The southpaw's pitch was right down the middle. The president of the United States of America, William Jefferson Clinton, had nailed his part in this very grand opening. The president then chatted with other dignitaries, such as Ohio Governor George Voinovich and Indians owner Dick Jacobs.

An Indians legend, Hall of Fame pitcher Bob Feller, then threw out his ceremonial first pitch. Fifty-four years earlier Feller had thrown the only Opening Day no-hitter in baseball history. This was already a red-letter day in Cleveland history, and the inaugural Jacobs Field Indians game hadn't even started yet.

The game wouldn't disappoint, either. One of the most dominant pitchers of the era was pitching for Seattle, 6-foot-10 Randy Johnson. He had just retired the heart of the Tribe's order in the seventh inning. He was getting close to joining Feller in the history books: He was hurling a no-hitter. The Tribe finally got to Johnson in the eighth and tied the score at 2 apiece. The Cleveland fans missed out on witnessing pitching history, but the Indians were now positioned to possibly win.

The game was tied after nine innings. The first game in Jacobs Field history was going to extra innings. Then Seattle scored in the top of the tenth. The magic didn't end there. The Indians knotted the score in the bottom of the inning. In the bottom of the eleventh, reserve outfielder Wayne Kirby singled in the winning run. The Indians were undefeated in their new home!

"Browns Town" was catching baseball fever. About the only person in Cleveland immune to it was Arthur Modell. Nor was the enthusiasm confined just to Indians Nation. Nationally, Cleveland and the Indians were getting universally favorable press regarding their new gem of a ballpark. Comments like Richard Justice's in the *Washington Post* were equally adept at conveying the prevailing sentiment and of plunging a dagger into Modell's wounded heart:

> After 61 years at baseball's worst address, at a cavernous old stadium that was dark and cold and utterly depressing, the Indians now have a home that can stand beside any of the game's other showcases . . . . Jacobs Field has the cozy feel of Wrigley Field, the urban backdrop of Camden Yards and the nooks and crannies of Fenway Park.
>
> —Richard Justice, *Washington Post*

As the weather warmed, so did the fever. By mid-July, the Indians had sent two players to the All-Star Game and boasted the American League's best record. The Indians were on a trajectory to win 100 games! This was the same team that hadn't been to the playoffs since their 1954 World Series loss to the New York Giants. (Why they played a football team, I don't know.) Forty years in the desert—or the nearly deserted Cleveland Municipal Stadium—was a thing of the past.

Delirious baseball fans packed Jacobs Field. The Tribe had found an oasis and were prospering. Around Cleveland, ever since Modell had been in town, abetted by poor-performing Indians teams, mid-July had always meant the start of the NFL year, and the fans' excitement was for training camp to start. By the looks of it, nobody was wishing away the summer to get to football season this year.

*Plain Dealer* reporter Mary Kay Cabot summed it up in a July 17 story, "Modell Unworried About Tribe Run," that quoted the owner as saying:

"The sports heart in Cleveland is bigger than anywhere else in the country. There's enough room for everybody—the Indians, the Cavs, the Browns. The Indians are having their first legitimate run in years.

They're playing very good baseball and I'm very, very happy for them and the people who follow them. We have our followers, too, and I'm extremely confident we'll reward our fans this year."

Belichick was also quoted by the same reporter, same day, different article: "New Season, New Talent, Old Goals: Belichick Starts Fourth Season Full of Confidence." Belichick continued the storyline that he and Modell had both started in January, fresh off the team's fourth (and Belichick's third) consecutive losing season: "This is the best team I've had, and I'll be extremely disappointed if we don't make the playoffs. It's a very realistic goal this year as opposed to a hope. We can't have another 7-9 season. We're better than that."

Art Modell was in lockstep with his coach: "I don't want to get my hopes up so high that I'm disappointed. I've been disappointed before, and I don't want it to happen again. But I don't think it will. This is an outstanding football team from top to bottom. It's a playoff-caliber team. Now, we just have to go out and prove it on the field."

You could argue that Art and Bill were playing pitchmen. The Indians were the new sporting darlings. The Browns had to do something. But were they just selling snake oil, or were the Browns really poised to return to glory—or even respectability? In a few months, everyone would know for sure. But for now, the coach backed up his assertions with facts and a line of reasoning that seemed to make sense. Belichick had even officially hired Steve Crosby as his first-ever offensive coordinator. The fact that the heretofore secretive coach was so forthcoming with the media about his rationale and hopes lent an additional measure of credence to Belichick's and Modell's claims.

Modell also divulged that "Browns officials were in negotiations with the City of Cleveland for a new or refurbished stadium!"

51

# ONE STRIKE AND THEY'RE OUT!

August 12, 1994

*"I wanna go! I wanna go!" The words came out haltingly, wedged* between the full-throttle sobs that only a very unhappy and terribly determined four-year-old is capable of. "Why can't we go?"

"I told you honey; I know I promised, but they aren't playing their game tonight. We'll go to Honey Hut and get some ice cream instead." Kenny's mom used the old ice cream ploy to try to change the subject. But it was no use.

"I don't want ice cream; I want to see the Indians! I want to see Slider! I wanna dollar-hahdog!"

The truth is, most fans felt the same way Kenny did, even if they weren't quite as articulate in expressing the depths of their frustration. Kenny's parents hadn't yet been born the last time the Indians had been this good. Heck, even Kenny's grandparents could barely remember the last time the Indians were this good. And now the magic was over!

Major League Baseball was on strike.

Modell had nothing to do with the MLB strike, and he'd gone on record over a month ago claiming he hoped there would not be one. But all the sudden, his Browns were the only game in town. The timing was perfect! Three games left to go in the NFL exhibition season, then the real season would begin. If only the strike could last, and the Browns could get off to a strong start—as Coach Belichick kept telling him they would—the Browns would again be foremost in the hearts and minds of the fans. And Modell might sell a few thousand more season tickets.

On the eve of the NFL season opener, Cleveland sportswriter Tony Grossi likened Belichick's situation to facing fourth down on the football field. Grossi wrote what most people felt: After failing to make the playoffs in his first three seasons, this would be the do or die season for Coach Belichick—despite repeated affirmations from owner Art Modell that there was no such sword dangling over his coach's head.

Only six players who predated Belichick's reign remained on the team. Coach MyWay finally really had everything his way and finally felt confident enough to assert, "We've got a core of players in their fourth to eighth years in the league and nobody due to leave after this season." So, with his fourth season dawning, he really had no excuses, nor did he feel that he'd need any. It was playoffs or bust!

In the first eight games of the season, the Browns would only lose twice: to archrival Pittsburgh, and to arch nemesis John Elway and his Denver Broncos. Mark Rypien would play quarterback against the Broncos and start three more games due to a concussion suffered by Vinny Testaverde. Even losing their starting quarterback wouldn't slow down Cleveland. The Browns went 3-2 in Rypien's starts. Vinny returned for the last five games and went 3-2 to close out the regular season.

Adding it all up, the Browns finished the season 11-5, in second place behind Pittsburgh in the AFC Central. Finally, Belichick and the Browns had done it: For the first time since 1989, they were going to the playoffs!

Of all the teams Belichick could face in his NFL head coaching playoff debut, the football gods would have some fun with history. Looking back from today's vantage point, there is one team that would make an ironic and uniquely interesting opponent for Belichick's Browns: the New England Patriots.

In facing the Patriots, Belichick would be squaring off against his former boss, Bill Parcells. Together in New York, Parcells had been the head coach and Belichick the defensive coordinator for the Giants' two Super Bowl victories. Since then, Parcells had moved on to coach New England, and his protégé was now the top man in Cleveland. Pretty remarkable that his first taste of the playoffs would pit him against his mentor.

This master/protégé angle was well understood at the time. But nobody could have known the historical significance of Belichick coaching against the Patriots in the 1994 playoffs. How crazy that he'd be trying to beat the team that he would one day coach to dominance!

The sole Browns playoff victory during Belichick's regime would be Cleveland's last playoff victory for 28 years.

52

# 1994 WILD-CARD PLAYOFF GAME VS. NEW ENGLAND

JANUARY 1, 1995 – CLEVELAND MUNICIPAL STADIUM

*The Patriots were the hottest team in the NFL heading into the postsea*son. They had reeled off seven straight victories to close the season. The last time they had lost was to the team they would be facing today. That early November loss hinged on a controversial pass interference call against New England that led to the Browns' only touchdown. The Browns won that game 13-6. So, in addition to the Browns playing the NFL's hottest team, they were playing one that sought revenge.

Nick C. and Josh M. were fresh off their senior seasons playing quarterback for their high school teams, University School and Canton McKinley, respectively. They bonded while being recruited on the campus of John Carroll University, ten miles from Cleveland Municipal Stadium where they both were now delirious with anticipation.

"Man, the Browns are gonna crush the Patriots today!" Nick said.

"I hope so," Josh replied. "But I don't know if Belichick can match up to Parcells. Tuna is a freakin' great coach, and Belichick had three losing seasons before this one. I seriously think I could coach better than Belichick."

"Man, you are insane! I can't wait to beat your ass out for starting quarterback at JCU."

"Yeah, the only time you'll get in is when they pull me and the rest of the starters after I put six touchdowns on the board."

"Dream on, Josh!"

A half-hour before kickoff, on the field during warmups, the "Bills"—Parcells and Belichick—met near midfield.

"I know we've been friends for, what, thirteen, fourteen years," Parcells said. "But I want you to know I will hate your guts for the next three hours and will do everything I can to crush you and your lousy team."

"And I hate yours," Belichick replied. "I would like nothing more than for the papers tomorrow to say, 'The Student Has Schooled the Teacher.'"

With that exchange, the two genuine friends, who also happened to be apex alpha competitors, shook hands then parted company to join their respective teams.

Like during most games in Cleveland in the dead of winter, the sky was gray. The grass was somewhere between tan and brown (or maybe there was no grass, maybe it was all just dirt). At least it was warm: 40 degrees at game time. But the air was damp, and the 10 mph wind could saw right through you if it found you. The game was a seesaw affair. The Browns drew first blood on a Matt Stover first-quarter field goal. On New England's first drive, Browns safety Louis Riddick intercepted Drew Bledsoe and returned the ball to the Patriots' 33-yard line. The crowd, sensing blood, roared in excitement.

But the Browns' conservative play calling only netted 1 yard and they had to punt.

"I told you I could coach better than Belichick!" Josh said. "We'd be up 10-0 right now if I was on the sideline!"

"I am gonna switch to defense next season so I can knock your head off when I sack you in practice," Nick replied.

In the second quarter, the Patriots would take the lead on the game's first touchdown, a Bledsoe pass to Leroy Thompson, followed by former Browns kicker Matt Bahr's PAT.

Vinny Testaverde would connect with fellow former 'Phin, Mark Carrier, with Matt Stover punctuating the touchdown with the extra point.

"These Miami boys have adapted fast to Cleveland winters!" Josh noted.

New England's Matt Bahr evened things up with a field goal for New England. Matt Stover's 50-yard field goal attempt at the end of the first half was blocked. The teams were knotted up 10-10 going into halftime.

Nick and Josh spent the bulk of the intermission in the line for the bathrooms. A place that you'd go out of your way to avoid with anything other than an overfilled bladder sure becomes popular when duty calls! Josh spent the time lecturing Nick how he would have run different plays in the various situations if he was in charge. Nick threatened to dunk his counterpart's head in the toilet when they finally got into the latrine.

When Leroy Hoard ran in for the touchdown from 10 yards to put the Browns up 17-10 (after Stover's PAT) in the third quarter, fans spontaneously erupted into a chant, "Whoomp! There it is! Whoomp! There it is!" (if that sounds familiar, it's from the 1993 rap/hip hop song by the Tag Team, a single that in 2024, *Billboard* ranked as number fourteen in "The 100 Greatest Jock Jams of All Time").

The fans upped the ante when the Browns widened the lead to 10 points in the fourth quarter. Josh and Nick shouted themselves hoarse: "We want Pittsburgh! We want Pittsburgh! We want Pittsburgh!" The chant boomed and reverberated through the old stadium. There were still four minutes left in the game. Didn't these people remember *The Drive*? Drew Bledsoe, who had already thrown three interceptions, guided the Patriots down the field and took a couple shots into the end zone that fell incomplete. On fourth and 10, and needing two scores to tie, Parcells sent Matt Bahr onto the field to try to kick a field goal into the Dawg Pound. Bahr did so, and the Browns led by 7. The Patriots attempted an on-sides kick that failed . . . BUT . . . wait a minute! A penalty on the Browns gave New England another shot.

Art Modell began feeling pains in his chest. His poor heart could not take another playoff collapse. *Red Right 88*, *The Drive*, *The Fumble* . . . enough!

Again, Bahr kicked to the left. This time the ball slowly tumbled diagonally toward that 10-yard marker. The Patriots had time to progress beyond 10 yards and sealed off the Browns players. The ball now continued in its path beyond 10 yards, and a Patriot was able to scoop up the ball. The Patriots had recovered! Nick and Josh and about a quarter of the crowd let out the same expletive simultaneously. (The same one that got Ralphie's mouth washed out with Lifebuoy in *A Christmas Story.)*

Around 1:30 remained on the game clock. New England needed to go 65 yards and score a touchdown and extra point to tie. Not probable.

But as the silence in the previously raucous stadium attested (and which memories of *The Drive* confirmed), there was certainly a possibility the Browns hadn't won anything yet.

Two quick Bledsoe passes, and the Patriots had a first down near midfield. Timeout was called with about a minute left. On first and 10, Bledsoe threw it away to the right sideline. On second and 10, he connected on a toe-touch sideline reception to the Browns' 35-yard line for an apparent first down. But the receiver hadn't gotten both feet down. After another incompletion, it was fourth and 10 from around midfield with around forty seconds remaining in the game.

"I hope this kid doesn't pull an Elway on us," Art Modell muttered in his loge.

Under heavy pressure, the young New England quarterback backpedaled, surveying the field for an open receiver. The Browns' pass rush bore down on him and he had to fire early. The pass fell harmlessly to the ragged turf. Josh and Nick, two young quarterbacks destined for big things in football that they (incorrectly) assumed would culminate at John Carroll University, embraced each other, then everyone around them.

Belichick had won his first playoff game as a head coach! The student had beaten his friend and former master. The Browns had won their first playoff game in five years. Belichick was vindicated in choosing Vinny Testaverde to be his quarterback and letting Bernie Kosar go. Testaverde's mistake-free game had made the difference. On to Pittsburgh!

"How do you like Belichick now?" Nick asked his friend. "If the Big Tuna is such a great coach, and Belichick just beat him, what's that say about Billy B.?"

"Hey man, I love it," Josh replied. "But if I was coaching, we'd have won by three touchdowns instead of one!"

"I can't wait to beat you ragged at JCU this fall. I may transfer to Mount Union and play defense so I can knock your block off!"

After the game, TV cameras were rolling, flashbulbs from newspaper camera crews were popping, and media personnel were buzzing as Belichick entered the interview room. Holding up a football, the normally gruff coach exclaimed: "We brought a home playoff game to Cleveland and there were a lot of people yelling for us and giving us a lot of support. I really appreciated it."

Belichick said the game ball would be displayed in the lobby of the Browns' facility in Berea.

Out of the limelight for the moment, Art Modell beamed. His faith in his coach was now paying off. Not only had his head coach won a playoff game, he was now also playing nice with the fans and the media.

To nobody in particular, Art decreed, "We're back baby, we're back!"

He was overheard by reporter Mary Kay Cabot. She asked him about the Browns' return to the playoffs and how he felt.

"It has been an elusive, horrendous thing in this organization, the inability to get to the big game, starting in 1980, '85, '86, '87, coming so close each time. In fact, in 1985, Don Shula told me we gave them the toughest game they had all year when we lost down in the Orange Bowl. Of course, you know about '86 and '87, when we came a play away, a tackle away, a tipped ball away from going to the big game. The big game became an obsession here in this organization, starting with me, and I made changes to try to get over the hump—struggling to find the formula that might get us there. Maybe this is the formula, I don't know yet."

On his drive home later, Modell reflected on all those heartrending eighties playoff losses. He wandered back through time further, to his lone championship game victory. Now knocking on the door of seventy years of age, Modell considered his younger self naïve after winning in 1964. He had assumed then that his Browns would be a regular fixture in championship games, just as coach Paul Brown's (and owner Arthur McBride's) Cleveland Browns had been in the forties and fifties.

"I didn't know it would be so hard to get back."

"What's that, Art?" Pat asked from the passenger seat.

Not realizing he had mused aloud, Art told her: "Nothing, it was nothing. I guess I was just talking to myself."

53

# DIVISIONAL PLAYOFFS IN THE PITS

Saturday, January 7, 1994 – Three Rivers Stadium, Pittsburgh

*The Browns had already lost to the Steelers twice during the 1994 season.* In their early September tilt in Cleveland, Vinny Testaverde threw four interceptions, and the Browns lost 10-17. In the second-to-last game of the season, Testaverde threw two picks, and the Browns were beaten 7-17. All told, the Browns had committed eight turnovers. The Steelers hadn't turned it over at all.

Browns defensive lineman Michael Dean Perry challenged the offense to stand up to the Steelers. He claimed the Steelers' defense had intimidated the Browns' offense. Perry implored the team to attack Pittsburgh right out of the gate, just as Pittsburgh's offense had come out strong in their last two games.

As always, Three Rivers Stadium was a swirling sea of gold. Terrible Towels were foisted and flung by everyone. Even the Steelers players were twirling them pregame, getting themselves and their fans fired up. As pregame introductions were being made over the boisterous crowd noise, Ernest Byner made his way over to the Steelers' side of the field. Unfortunately for Cleveland, it was the only evidence all day that they were not intimidated by the men in black and gold. Steelers defensive lineman Brentson Buckner dropped one of his Terrible Towels in the revelry. Byner stomped it into the turf. That move only added more fuel to Pittsburgh's desire to beat the Browns.

Perry's exhortations didn't work. The offense didn't start fast. They didn't even start slow. They just plain didn't start. It didn't help that their leading receiver, rookie Derrick Alexander, dropped two passes on the first series. But it wasn't just the offense that fizzled. The defense stayed in the locker room deep into the first half as well. The Steelers' runners waltzed through the Browns defenders', who offered all the resistance of cotton candy.

By halftime, the Browns were down 3-24. The Browns wouldn't score a touchdown until late in the fourth quarter, long after the game had been decided. The Browns managed to force one turnover, a fumble. But they lost a fumble themselves and Testaverde threw two more interceptions. Final score: Cleveland 9, Pittsburgh 29.

Linebacker Pepper Johnson, who led the Browns with sixteen tackles, sounded in awe of the Steelers' offense. "They treated us like little kids," he said. "They spanked our bottoms and sent us back to Cleveland."

Inside of a week, Bill Belichick had savored sweet playoff victory and tasted bitter playoff defeat. Pittsburgh would lose to San Diego in the AFC Championship Game. San Diego would then lose the Super Bowl to San Francisco. So, the Browns had climbed the mountain, and made the playoffs, only to see there were higher peaks that they were ill-equipped to scale, at least this year.

## 54

# THE FATEFUL YEAR BEGINS

MID-JANUARY 1995

*Art Modell squinted. He wanted to just shut his eyes. The brilliance was* blinding. He sat at the restaurant table, facing the lake from a lofty perch on an upper floor of one of downtown Cleveland's tallest skyscrapers. It's amazing how Cleveland's weather can be dreary gray, day after day, almost all winter through. Then one random day, not a cloud, pure blue above, and out in front, extending over the frozen lake, nothing but blinding white as far as the squinting eye can see, which, even on this day isn't all the way across to Canada. Maybe Modell thought there could be an allegory there. Maybe all the years past were the gray days. Maybe this was a foreshadowing that the days that lay out before him would be brilliant.

Modell stood up and walked to the edge of the window, so he could get a better look at the city at his feet. Straight ahead of him on the lakeshore, some bulldozers and excavators were peeling back the blanket of white snow, pulling up frozen brown clay until they got below the frost line. Modell knew a shiny new jewel—the Rock & Roll Hall of Fame and Museum—would soon grace the site.

Immediately west of the future site of the Rock & Roll Hall of Fame was vacant land. There was already a plan to build the Great Lakes Science Center there. The next parcel of land was Modell's tired old stadium. The gleaming snow hid the patchwork roof that ringed the open field, but also accentuated the dirty brick edifice the way a freshly starched oxford shirt collar highlights nicotine- and coffee-stained teeth.

Modell was painfully aware that the view to the south would reveal a pair of brand-new sparkling gems: Jacobs Field and Gund Arena. It was as though there was a giant necklace surrounding him. The only shabby, stained, and faded jewel was his stadium.

Then Modell's eyes were drawn back to the horizon. Maybe this shining January day was presaging a new era for the Cleveland Browns. Maybe this year, 1995, would be the year he got to (and maybe even won!) his first Super Bowl. Whatever he was thinking, his reverie slowly dissolved when someone addressed him:

"Jump, Art!"

Modell turned to face the man who'd addressed him, and who now was chuckling. He could tell by the voice that it wasn't his expected lunch companion from the Cleveland Clinic—one of Modell's philanthropic causes, as well as the institution that kept him and his feeble heart alive. Yet, it was a voice he recognized. Turning to look at the man didn't help. Modell's pupils were the size of pinholes, and the interior of the restaurant seemed as dark as a cave.

"It's the dawn of a new year . . . I bet this one will end differently than any since you've been in Cleveland, Mr. Modell. It's been a long time since 1964, Art. Thirty years. Don't you think it's curious that you and your team have not made it back to another NFL Championship Game, and never gotten to the Super Bowl since we made our little deal? Art, by the time this season ends, if we can make another deal, I think the whole league will be surprised how *far* the Browns will go . . . farther than anyone has ever imagined. Arthur, don't be shy about making a real *move*!"

"Come over here, I can't see," Modell implored. "I'm snow blind or something."

"I'm sorry, Art, as *charming* as it is to see you, I need to be going. But I will be in touch. When you are ready to make your move, I am sure we can work out a deal."

"Wait a minute, what are you talking about? Where are you going?"

It was too late. The man had left.

By the time the calendar turned to February, the Los Angeles Rams had announced their intentions to move to St. Louis. Not only did this understandably upset the fans in Southern California, where the Rams had played for forty-nine years (after moving from Cleveland), it also depressed NFL-starved fans in Baltimore, who'd hoped to land an expansion or existing team back in Maryland after an eleven-year hiatus.

It also unsettled Cleveland sportswriters, such as the *Plain Dealer*'s Paul Hoynes, who speculated that Modell must be paying attention to the windfall that the Rams' owner Georgia Frontiere would be set up for if the other NFL owners ratified her plans to move. In baseball, the news had not been encouraging, and it looked like the strike would continue into the 1995 season.

On February 15, 1995, a special expansion draft was held to begin the process of stocking the two teams that would make their debuts this September. Each existing NFL team had to make six players available to be awarded to these new teams: the Jacksonville Jaguars and the Carolina Panthers. Each new team was required to select a minimum of thirty players and a maximum of forty-two, in this way. Once one of the new teams selected a player from a given existing team, that team was allowed to remove one of the remaining players from the available list of six.

Deeper into February, the baseball situation didn't improve, and replacement players opened spring training instead of the superstars who'd put butts in the seats during previous years. Not that it bothered Modell in the least. In the NFL, expansion teams Carolina and Jacksonville held their first expansion drafts, including snatching wide receiver Mark Carrier from the Browns. During free agency, the Browns would let defensive linemen James Jones and Michael Dean Perry depart for Denver. The Browns would start courting perennial Pro Bowl receiver (and thorn in the Falcons' coaching/management/ownership's side) Andre "Bad Moon" Rison.

March's Major League Baseball talks between the owners and the union broke down, making it inevitable that the regular players would not open the season. Somehow Belichick thought it would be a good idea to hire forty-year-old ex-Giants quarterback Phil Simms out of the broadcast booth to become a backup quarterback. After some back and forth, Simms did the sane thing and renewed his contract as an announcer with NBC.

The Browns went all-out and hauled in Andre Rison. He and Art Modell traded autographs! Art and Bill felt like Andre was one of the top wide receivers in the game, and, teamed up now with Derrick Alexander and Michael Jackson, that the Browns had the best receiving corps in the league.

The NFL owners rebuffed Georgia Frontiere and her plans for moving out of Los Angeles. Modell explained his "No" vote to the media: "You can't have clubs jumping for the big buck and deserting a marketplace at a whim." He further went on to say that his Browns met the criteria for moving better than any other team in the league. Modell did not say he would move the Browns, but if his demand for renovations was not met that he may be forced to sell the team, and there was no telling whether a new owner might bolt.

Atlanta and Cleveland were busy in March. Once the Rison deal was done, the Browns traded Eric Metcalf and their first round (number 26) draft pick to the Falcons in exchange for the Falcons' first round pick (number 10). "This is the most dramatic twenty-four hours of activity since I purchased the Browns," Modell said. "We've taken a giant step forward in two days and it will be even more so after this draft. I'm going for bust. I feel we're on the verge of doing something big this season."

April dawned, and all the key management, coaching, and ownership staff were busy preparing for the draft. Modell took a moment to summarize where they'd gotten to since last season.

"Bill, you finally got us to the playoffs last year, and we even won a game. We've got Rison now. Our passing game will be hard to stop. Who are they going to cover? Jackson, Alexander, and now Rison! It's almost unfair to the rest of the league! We lost Metcalf, but we just never could get him meshed in with the offense."

"Don't forget about his punt returns, those can turn a game," Belichick said. But he didn't push the point. He knew Eric Metcalf was talented, but the Browns just could never seem to unleash his talent in a consistent way. And he'd pushed for the trade.

"Lombardi assures me there will be an impact player available with the tenth pick," Modell said. "Bill, this is our chance; I want to pull out all the stops. I'm not getting any younger. My health is not the best. If baseball ever gets its act together, the fans will flock to the Indians' brand-new park. I'm telling you, Bill, if that bastard Jacobs ever got to the World Series before I get to the Super Bowl! I think, I don't know, I think it would kill me!"

"Art, we'll be fine," Belichick said. "We've got a good plan. We know what we need to complete this team, and we'll have some good options on draft day."

In early April, a nineteen-year-old amateur golfer from Stanford University made his debut at the Masters. Eldrick "Tiger" Woods would go on to have a pretty good career as a professional golfer. In baseball, the strike officially ended on the eve of the original Opening Day date of April 2. However, replacement players took the field for a few weeks until the regulars could get back in game shape. The regulars resumed playing in late April, and the teams were all now scheduled to play an abbreviated 144-game schedule.

The harsh reaction of fans to MLB's labor dispute tamped down attendance in many stadiums throughout the country. But that didn't extend to Jacobs Field. The Indians fans were rabid, and every game was selling out. Before the regular Big Leaguers were back in action, the NFL's annual spring rite—the draft—played out.

One thing sports has taught us is that money talks. The NFL owners had voted (on principle) in March by the count of 21-3-6 to disallow the Rams' move out of Los Angeles. In April, after the Rams upped their payout offer to the league by $21 million and threatened to sue the league if it prevented the move to St. Louis, twenty owners had a change of heart.

The Los Angeles Rams would soon be the St. Louis Rams after all. For the record, Modell was one of the owners who now supported the move. The man who just last month had said "You can't have clubs jumping for the big buck and deserting a marketplace at a whim" was now, on a whim, voting to allow that to happen.

The people of Baltimore were not happy. After having missed out on landing the expansion Panthers or Jaguars, and now the relocating Rams, the Maryland Stadium Authority was actively considering suing the NFL.

Almost every year, the NFL draft produces at least one and sometimes several eventual Hall of Famers. The 1974 draft produced five, and 80 percent of them were selected by the Steelers! Maybe the Browns could have such luck, or even a dose of it this year. If not an eventual Hall of Famer, the Browns, and especially their owner, were champing at the bit to land an immediate contributor. (Even if Coach Belichick had gone on record with local media on the eve of the draft that "Tomorrow's draft [class] is the second worst in my five years.")

In the *Plain Dealer,* Mary Kay Cabot quoted Modell: "We're looking for a starter with that No. 10 pick who's going to make an impact right away. We want a player who's going to make a lot of music in 1995."

In other words, the Browns wanted a player who could help them get to the Super Bowl in 1995. Potentially a defensive lineman.

"We want to make a real run for the roses this season," Modell said. "That's why we went after Andre Rison in free agency and that's why we're close to signing [running back] Lorenzo White. It's why we traded Eric Metcalf to Atlanta to get the No. 10 pick."

55

# DRAFT CRAFT

BROWNS HEADQUARTERS – BEREA, OHIO, APRIL 22, 1995

*As they watched all but one of the few players Belichick deemed worthy* of a top 10 pick (predictably) get drafted, the Browns' cabal mentally locked into pursuing a player whom they'd desired/admired all along: Penn State tight end Kyle Brady.

Already possessing three standout wide receivers and Earnest Byner, Tommy Vardell, and almost surely Lorenzo White at running back, the addition of a solid tight end was the obvious move to make on offense. The Jets were the only team left to pick before the Browns got their chance.

Seconds after Seattle made their (number 8) pick, Mike Lombardi asked Coach Belichick, "Alright, the Seahawks just grabbed Galloway and Westbrook is already off the board, so do the Jets go with J.J. Stokes, or do they pick a lineman?"

"Who cares, as long as they don't take Kyle Brady," Belichick shot back in an offhand manner, a smirk on his unshaven face. Everyone knew the Jets wanted a wide receiver or a big interior lineman. They had no designs on a tight end.

The Browns brass had decided their areas of greatest need were defensive line and tight end. With defensive ends Mike Mamula and Kevin Carter already gone, that left just defensive end Derrick Alexander, whom Belichick and his crew didn't have rated as a top 10 pick, and the tantalizing Warren Sapp, who scared many teams away when multiple reports of failed marijuana and cocaine tests were released right before the draft. The decision was, therefore, simple. Just take Kyle Brady.

Fifteen minutes before the Browns needed to submit their selection, the Jets had to make theirs. "With the number nine pick in the 1995 NFL draft, the New York Jets select ... Kyle Brady, tight end, Penn State University."

"What the #@$%," Belichick blurted out. His eyes seeing only red rage, burned through the others in the Browns' "brain trust." "That's not supposed to happen! What are the Jets doing?!"

Nobody had any answers. The phone rang. Another team's general manager, seeking to acquire the Browns number ten draft pick, asked to speak with "whoever's authorized to make a trade."

Belichick ripped the phone from the staffer's hands. "What's the deal?" Nobody in the room heard what the other team's GM offered: not the ESPN reporter, not Lombardi, not Modell. But nobody could miss the maelstrom unleashed by the coach whose foundation had just cracked open, sending him tumbling into the abyss.

"You mother_____r! What do you think I am, some kind of an a__hole idiot?!"

After that opening salvo, the fury only increased. The volume was louder, so loud that the words were distorted, unintelligible. Nobody could doubt that they were not kind words. We still don't know what that GM had offered in exchange for the Browns' number ten pick. Nor do we know who that GM was. If there's a former GM whose been hearing-impaired since the mid-nineties to due to a ruptured eardrum, chances are that's him.

The room, this brain trust who'd considered themselves better prepared this year than in any of their four previous drafts, that considered themselves to have done more homework than any other NFL front office, was shell-shocked. Belichick's temper had gone from zero to100 in one second flat, but it would take more a lot than fifteen minutes to cool back down. And fifteen—now thirteen—minutes was all he had. History would one day report that there were six Hall of Famers in this "second-worst draft class" that Belichick had ever seen.

Unbeknownst to anyone, *five of the six* were still on the board.

Utterly unprepared after Brady was taken, the Browns panicked. (Imagine how different NFL history would have been if Belichick had gotten *Kyle* Brady in the 1995 draft but missed getting *Tom* Brady in

2000!) Their giddy intentions after trading away Eric Metcalf was to draft an impact player and securing Atlanta's number ten pick was thought to be the lynchpin of that plan. Now there was no plan. No fallback.

Like the calculating, opportunistic Mr. Potter during the run on the bank in *It's a Wonderful Life*, San Francisco, the era's most dominant team, traded their 1995 (number thirty overall) first-round pick, their first-round pick in 1996 (sure to be at the very bottom of the round), and some mid-round picks to secure the Browns' number ten pick.

With the trades, the Browns had ping-ponged from pick twenty-six to ten, and now to thirty. Along the way, they picked up a few draft picks but had lost a dynamic punt returner (Metcalf) who had the potential to shine as a runner or slot receiver in the right offense and had abandoned their primary objective of picking an impact player high in round one.

Had the Browns stuck with pick number ten, they would have had their choice of any of the five remaining eventual Hall of Famers: Tampa picked defensive tackle Warren Sapp at number twelve, New England grabbed defensive back Tajuan "Ty" Law with number twenty-three, Tampa struck again two picks after the Browns' initial position at number twenty-eight, selecting linebacker Derrick Brooks. Curtis Martin remained undrafted until the third round when the Patriots joined the Bucs in each picking two Hall of Famers in the 1995 draft. And finally, with the 196th overall pick in the sixth round, Denver selected running back Terrell Davis.

As for the Browns? They'd had their eye on defensive back Devin Bush since before the trade with Atlanta and were considering taking him with their original number twenty-six pick. Atlanta did take him at number twenty-six. The Browns went with Ohio State linebacker Craig Powell. Art Modell had been quoted as saying he wanted a player who was going to "make a lot of music in 1995." Well, all Powell would do is sing the Injury Blues. For the record, in his NFL career, Craig Powell was credited with making a total of one tackle. One. Solo. Tackle!

With no second rounder, the Browns would pick Georgia quarterback Eric Zeier in the third. He would start an average of two games per season over his six-year NFL career.

In a cursed way, Belichick was right: This was the second-worst draft class that he'd ever seen. But only for the Browns!

56

# BASEBALL RETURNS—WILL FOOTBALL DEPART?

1995

*As the cruel grip of winter finally loosened for good and the leaves came* back out of hiding, real baseball was again underway. Opening Day 1995 debuted for the second time this year. The first time, it was with replacement players. This time it was for real. May seems so much more reasonable a time than early April in cities like Cleveland to fire up the national pastime.

The Indians returned home with a record of 5-3 in the new, official season, and were greeted by adoring fans. This was in stark contrast to the rightfully disgruntled masses that booed the returning Big Leaguers at other parks. So it is when you're a winner. By the time May was over, the Indians' record was 22-9, and Manny Ramirez had won American League Player of the Month honors with a .349 batting average, 23 runs, 8 doubles, 11 dingers, and 27 runs batted in!

The other Ohio baseball team reached agreement with the City of Cincinnati and local business leaders that the Reds would be building a new baseball-only stadium of their own—which leads directly to football news.

The Bengals' Mike Brown demanded either a refurbished Riverfront Stadium or a new football-only stadium. The threat was in the air that if that didn't happen, he'd start looking at relocating to recently jilted Los Angeles or long-vacant Baltimore. Meanwhile NFL Commissioner Paul Tagliabue was trying his darnedest to coax the irascible

Al Davis to keep his Raiders in LA in a yet-to-be built stadium complex in Inglewood.

Tagliabue was trying to find a second team, representing the NFC, to play there as well. This news and persistent rumors out of LA that the Browns would be that second team prompted Art Modell to deny all rumors. Pressed for his feelings on the Cleveland Stadium renovation progress by Cuyahoga County, who was mulling a sin tax extension, Art could only muster: "No comment."

Modell was home. It was a sunny Sunday May morning. He normally devoured the morning paper—a habit formed in his early thirties as a young NFL team owner and eligible bachelor about town—to see how many times he was mentioned. Today, he avoided picking it up. He didn't want to read any opinions on how bad the draft had been or any other stupid things the press had to say. He tried to convince himself that the draft was good.

Modell reflected on the strong free agent pickups and the progress his coach had made in molding the team in 1994. He fashioned the fantasy that as excited as Cleveland might be about the upstart Indians, they'd all be rallying to the Browns again come fall. And by this time next year, with any luck at all, he'd still be basking in the afterglow of a Super Bowl victory.

This happy daydream was shattered by the ringing of his desk phone. Another longtime habit caused him to instinctively answer on the first ring. For thirty years, he'd been taking calls that way. Usually, to provide a witty quip for a glowing sports story, or to commit to a worthy cause where he would be a speaker at a future gala, or possibly even be honored for past contributions. Like Pavlov's dog, Art had been conditioned by the ringing of Ma Bell. Only this wasn't one of those kinds of calls.

"Hello Arthur, you must have the utmost confidence in your team this year." It was that worldly, beguiling voice. Art recognized it right away, though he had not been expecting it. Uncharacteristically, Modell remained silent.

"After all, Arthur, you had traded for the number ten pick so you could select an impact player."

"Now listen," Modell said. "I'm comfortable with my coach's and my personnel man's picks. We were 11-5 last year, and we'll be better than that this season." Every time he talked with this character, he felt like a defendant being grilled by the prosecution and needing to justify himself, to clear his name.

"And what if that doesn't happen, Art? Have you seen how quickly the fans have warmed up to the Indians—despite that ugly strike? Do you think these fans will be so kind to you if you don't deliver the championship? And worse yet, Arthur, what if you do win the elusive Super Bowl this season? Will that solve your stadium issues? Will that solve your financial issues?"

Modell sat silently, the receiver held to his ear. The eternal extrovert, Modell didn't even fumble for words. He felt woozy. His mind was ravened by incoherent thoughts. He was deeply confused, but in that confusion, he could sense that maybe his energies this last year had been misspent in the wrong direction.

*Was this quack right? What if the Browns did win the Super Bowl?* It would be the crowning glory of his professional and personal lives. But it's not like they hand you a new stadium with the Lombardi Trophy. It's not like they waive the inheritance tax your heirs must pay when you die and bequeath your football team to your family.

As Modell sank deeper into these contemplations, the man spoke, "Remember what I said when we saw each other in January in that top-floor restaurant?"

"I remember you said, 'Jump Art!'" Art quipped in a clipped retort, then confided. "I don't remember much else, we barely said ten words to each other."

"I advised you that if we could make a deal, you and the Browns would go farther than anyone ever expected, and in doing so, you would shock the league. Shock the fans. Shock everybody."

"Oh, that. Well, forgive me, but last time we made a deal it didn't work out so well for me."

"Did I not follow through? Did not the Browns win the 1964 NFL World Championship as I promised?"

"But I haven't won anything since!" Art protested.

"Well, Mr. Modell, perhaps you should have negotiated a better contract," the man said teasingly. "I assure you we are strictly adhering to its terms." The man's voice became instantly matter-of-fact: "Sometimes the only way out of a bad contract is to sign a new one. Art, opportunity is tap, tap, tapping at your window, but soon that window will close. You must make a bold move, then I can assure, these present problems will bother you nevermore."

"What in the name of heaven are you talking about?" Modell was peeved.

He heard the phone click.

"Hello? Hello, are you still there?" Modell inquired. *Nevermore? Nevermore? Who the hell says nevermore? Whoever that is, he's totally off his rocker.*

Modell went about his day, and, after an hour or so, had finally shaken the echo of this strange phone call. Later, after dinner and a drink, he went off to bed.

A storm awakened him in the dead of night. The winds whipped a branch, or something, repeatedly against his bedroom window. Tap, tap, tap. On and on it went. Tap. Tap. Tap. Art fixated on it and could not sleep. Tap. Tap. Tap. He remembered that morning's phone call. Hadn't that weirdo said something about opportunity knocking at the door? Or a window of opportunity? As badly as Modell wanted to discount anything that man said, it was the middle of a stormy night. Thoughts and words take on a foreboding significance upon a dreary midnight. Though those thoughts and words usually dissipate, like a dream, when day breaks.

In the morning, Modell, who'd finally fallen asleep, awakened feeling agitated. He threw open the bedroom curtains to let the slanting light into the room. It was peaceful outside. No signs of the storm other than a few leafy twigs littering the lawn. Nothing was stirring, except a large black bird perched on the alabaster birdbath below. The bird seemed to be staring up at Modell. "Window of opportunity," Modell mumbled.

He called the operator. "Hello, is it possible that you can trace a call? I received a call yesterday morning, and I don't know the person's phone number, but I'd like to talk with him."

"Well, do you have their name?"

"No, I don't know his name."

"Was it the last call you received?"

"No, the call came in yesterday morning, I'm sure we've gotten several calls since then."

"Well, sir, I'm sorry, but I don't think there is anything we can do to help you."

"Damn! The window of opportunity."

"Excuse me, sir?"

"Oh sorry, nothing. Uh, thank you."

That afternoon Modell sat in his office at Browns headquarters in Berea. *Rap, rap, rap* came a knock on his open office door. Looking up, Art saw his friend, the minority owner of his team, the banker and real estate mogul Alfred Lerner.

"Al, what a surprise! What brings you here?"

"Well, Arthur, I was in the neighborhood for some business with one of my properties. Plus, I needed to talk with you, so I figured, why not swing by instead of calling?"

"Well, I'm glad you did! Can I get you something to drink?"

"Oh, no, I'm good. Thank you."

"So, what's on your mind, Al?"

"Art, I got a call from someone. I don't know who it was. But he told me he had heard that Mike Brown is serious about moving the Bengals to Baltimore."

"Well, who was it? A reporter or something?"

"Art, I don't know. I didn't recognize the voice. When I asked him his name, he just said 'Art needs your Baltimore connections.' Oh, and he said, 'Make sure you tell Art the window of opportunity will be closing soon.'"

"He said *that*?" Modell tapped his right index finger to his chin, his eyes unfocused.

"What is it, Art?"

"What kind of a deal is Mike Brown getting out of Baltimore?"

"I have no idea, Art, but I know all the bankers there, obviously, and I know John Moag who's heading up the Stadium Authority there. I was tight with Bill Schaefer, the previous governor, and I am sure I could get to know this new one, Glendenning."

"Al, thanks for coming here today. I need you to snoop around and see what deal these Baltimore people are offering the Bengals. Hmm. I wonder if that's the window?"

"Window?" Al was puzzled.

"Of opportunity. I need you to help me find out if Baltimore is playing ball with Mike Brown. See what they are offering."

"I'm headed back to Baltimore this week. I'll make a point to meet with Moag, and I will snoop around with my banker cronies. This shouldn't be too hard to figure out."

"Thank you, Al. This is good. I'm so glad you stopped by."

"No problem, Arthur." Lerner turned and was headed out of the office.

"Al!" Art exclaimed. Al turned to face Art, who continued, "Don't get crabs in Baltimore."

Art smiled a goofy grin, as Al shook his head laughing under his breath as he departed.

57

# INDIANS SURGING, MODELL SEETHING

JUNE 1995

*Cleveland's love affair with the Indians was in full flower. On June 12,* 1995, the Indians sold out the first game in what would become an MLB record streak of 455 consecutive games, not ending until April 4, 2001. When June was over, they'd amassed a record of 41-17. On June 22, with the best record in baseball, the Indians set a franchise record for most tickets sold in a season—beating out 1948, the last time they won a World Series! Fans were buying up tickets for future games, realizing they'd be frozen out of the fun if they waited until anywhere near game day.

Art Modell read the gushing accounts of all the Indians' success, then crumpled the newspaper and threw it in the general direction of his living room's fireplace. Pat couldn't quite make out his mutterings, but thought she heard something about "all I've done for the city" and "this is the appreciation that I get" and "crappy old stadium."

On the southern end of the state, Bengals owner Mike Brown confirmed he'd be meeting in Baltimore with the Maryland Stadium Authority. When he followed through on those plans, then stated, "It is a fact that in professional sports today you need a first-class stadium to compete . . . I think Baltimore can provide that," it began to be reported that the Bengals would indeed bolt Cincinnati for Baltimore.

Meanwhile the Raiders' Al Davis signed a letter of intent to move his team back to Oakland after a thirteen-year run in LA, leaving the second-largest market with no NFL team! On June 28, just before midnight, the Cincinnati City Council voted 5-4 to join Hamilton County on a $540 million project to build two new stadiums: a baseball park, as previously agreed upon for Marge Schott and her Reds, and now a new stadium for Mike Brown and his Bengals.

Pat Modell nearly spilled her morning coffee as her husband's fist pounded the table and he dropped the newspaper. "Pat, why is everybody getting exactly what they want! Everybody except Art Modell?"

## 58

# PRESSURE BUILDING

SUMMER 1995

*"Mr. Modell, is this a good time to talk?"*

It was 11 p.m., and Art Modell was home. It was that urbane voice on the phone again.

"Well, I suppose the alternative is watching the 11 o'clock news, so I guess so." Recently, no news was the only good news to Modell's eyes and ears. And his aching heart.

"Actually, Arthur, timing is of the essence. I have been dropping hints for six months now, but I think now is the time I was direct."

"I can take straight talk."

"Mr. Modell, I think it's time we made another deal. I think it can solve a lot of problems you've been faced with over the years. But you need to act fast; 'supplies are running out,' as they say."

"Supplies are running out? Supplies of what?"

"Well, stadia, of course."

"*Stadia*?"

"The plural of stadium. Sorry, '*stadiums,*' if you will. You'd better believe Paul Brown's son would love to steal your chance at getting out from under your difficulties."

"You mean him taking the Bengals to Baltimore? I think he is bluffing to get a better deal out of Cincinnati. A better deal than I'll likely ever get out of Cleveland."

"Arthur, I wouldn't be so sure about Mike Brown and Baltimore. If they make him a deal he can't refuse, well, he won't refuse."

"Well, what are you proposing?"

"You are well aware that things have not been so well for the Browns and for Arthur B. Modell ever since you last won it all, aren't you?"

"Well. . . ." Art started off tentatively.

"Well, nothing! Your team has been left at the doorstep to the Super Bowl three times. The city fathers have thrown money around to perennially losing franchises to build them new palaces, stealing your tenant in the process, and you are left with an ancient stadium and mounting debts! I should say things are not going so well for you! Had you read our original contract, none of this would have come as a surprise to you."

Modell, per usual in these encounters, sat there, too dazed to reply.

"I am offering you the opportunity of a lifetime. It's simple, Arthur, you transfer the misfortune you've personally suffered to Cleveland and its other sports team, and you and your football team are released. The city that lost the championship to you in 1964—and subsequently lost their team, but that's another story—finally gets recompense. And the poetic thing is the two men who stole the game in 1964—that's you and me, Arthur—are the ones who bring them a new team!"

59

# THE BIGGEST WEEKEND ANYONE IN CLEVELAND COULD REMEMBER

JULY 1995

*In July, the Indians had their worst month so far, going "only" 18-9, to* run their record to 59-26. *Sports Illustrated*'s mid-July feature article "Full House: With Sellout Crowds and the Best Team in the Game, Cleveland Is the Major League Hot Spot" didn't bother Art Modell so much when Browns single-game sales got off to a brisk start. Also buoying his spirits was the fact that Peter King of *Sports Illustrated* picked the Browns to go to the Super Bowl and Bill Plascke of *The Sporting News* picked the Browns to win it!

What did gnaw at Modell and, to no less extent, his coach, was their first-round draft pick's contract holdout. Third-rounder quarterback Eric Zeier had signed quickly, but Craig Powell didn't sign until July 30, missing 18 days of practice and meetings. Whatever was happening in the world of baseball was irrelevant to Bill Belichick. Training camp was underway, and to him, it was football season.

During the summer, Modell had instituted a moratorium on discussing the stadium situation indefinitely, "to better focus on football." He broke his moratorium on July 22 to talk with Tony Grossi of the *Plain Dealer* about the new hot topic that was helping the expansion teams and the relocating Raiders to raise money to build new stadiums or refurbish existing facilities: Private Seat Licenses (PSLs):

"PSLs are a new phenomenon. It's fantastic. But I think it only works in a new marketplace. I find it impossible for me to conceive of charging a customer who's been sitting in the same seat for 45 years . . . charge him a premium for the right to buy that seat again. I can't see it."

How many customers did Modell think he would lose if he adopted the PSL concept? "I have no idea," he said. "I wouldn't put it to a test, because I think it's taking an unfair advantage of customers who've been supporting the Browns for years. They're ready to run me out of town now.'"

With these comments in the sweltering humidity of training camp in Berea, Modell seemed to be sensitive to the will of the fans and a sense of fairness, while also displaying business savvy.

In August, the Indians went 21-9, all but burying their so-called competitors in the race for the American League Central Division title. Their season's record by the end of the month was a staggering 80-35. While everything was going the Indians' way, life for Modell, Belichick, and the Browns was more of a mixed bag.

Starting quarterback Vinny Testaverde was in the hospital with a staph infection, missing precious time to mesh with new receiver Andre Rison, which was bad.

But rookie QB Eric Zeier showed flashes of brilliance in the first game of the preseason. Granted, it was against third stringers. But in the second preseason game, when Testaverde was laid up, Zeier started and excelled against a tough Bears first string defense, rolling up completions, yards, and points on way to a rout, which was good. But that set up a brewing quarterback controversy, which was bad. Modell had to tamp down rumors that he was planning to move the team to a new stadium in the suburbs, which was bad. But by the end of the month, they had finally signed their consensus best player, defensive back Eric Turner, which was good.

The Rock & Roll Hall of Fame threw open its doors on September 2, 1995. This was the culmination of years of work by scores of Clevelanders and lovers of rock 'n' roll. Against all odds, Cleveland won the honor over New York, Los Angeles, and other cities to host this prized museum and hall of fame. That DJ Alan Freed had coined the term *rock 'n' roll* and had held what many considered to be the first rock concert in Cleveland in March 1952 had been the clinchers.

The opening was being celebrated with a blockbuster benefit concert at nearby Cleveland Municipal Stadium. Art Modell (or at least his stadium) would be hosting rock royalty. This marathon extravaganza featured once-in-a-lifetime pairings and performances by greats such as James Brown, Bob Dylan, Jerry Lee Lewis, Aretha Franklin, Johnny Cash, Bruce Springsteen, and Booker T. and the M.G.s.

Besides the Municipal Stadium concert, the Hall of Fame's festive opening weekend featured a downtown Cleveland parade and a ribbon-cutting ceremony attended by Little Richard and Yoko Ono.

If there had ever been a curse on Cleveland, there was certainly no trace of it now. On September's first weekend, Harrier jump jets dazzled with their EXTREMELY LOUD vertical takeoff and landing ability a mile east of Cleveland Stadium. Skydiving Elvises descended from the blue yonder, while Jon Bon Jovi, John Mellencamp, Bruce Springsteen, and more the world's biggest living musical heroes meandered the grounds at Burke Lakefront airport. They were all in town to celebrate the long-awaited opening of the Rock & Roll Hall of Fame by playing a concert at Modell's Cleveland Stadium on Saturday night.

HBO would broadcast the six-hour concert live to their subscribers around the world. As for Modell and the Browns—they were not around for the biggest weekend anyone in Cleveland could remember, having flown to New England for their Sunday season opener against Belichick's mentor, Bill Parcells, and his Patriots.

If ever there was a time when the monomaniacal Coach MyWay felt a twinge of longing or a dose of what would one day be known as FOMO, it was now; he loved rock 'n' roll. He was close friends with Jon Bon Jovi, who happened to be playing in the biggest rock concert of the year, alongside and in duets with some of the biggest names in the history of rock 'n' roll. And this monumental concert was taking place in Belichick's stadium (well, Modell's stadium). And Belichick couldn't be there.

## 60

# CLEVELAND ROCKS

SATURDAY, JUNE 2, 1995, CLEVELAND STADIUM, BACKSTAGE

***Jules Belkin and his brother Mike co-founded Belkin Productions in 1966,*** almost on a whim. By the mid-seventies, their fledgling music promotion and booking company had (like Cleveland) grown into a major musical power on the national stage. Among hundreds of other important concerts, Belkin Productions was behind the famous "World Series of Rock" concerts that brought together the era's biggest acts to play at Cleveland Stadium.

Scheduling around Indians games, a total of fifteen dates were played between 1974 and 1980, and millions of fans were entertained. Thousands even remembered it. Imagine paying $8 to see a quadruple bill featuring Santana, The Band, Jesse Colin Young, and Crosby, Stills, Nash, and Young. The other dates featured similar star power. Tonight (as usual), Jules was backstage.

"Jules! How are ya, man?" Bruce Springsteen greeted the promoter, the fruit of whose six months of planning was now in full bloom. "Seems like everything is goin' off without a hitch."

"Thanks, Bruce. I thought you and Chuck Berry were great together. And thanks for being a part of this!"

"Are you kiddin' me?" responded Springsteen, dressed in a sleeveless flannel shirt and jeans. "I wouldn't miss this for the world. I get to play with Chuck Berry, Little Richard—"

"Hey, don't forget about me Mr. Springsteen," interjected Bob Dylan, wearing gold lamé. "Hey Jules—nice shindig you've got goin' here."

"So far!" Belkin said. "I'm sure you'll knock it out of the park, too. The two of you together—wow!"

"Was that on purpose, Jules?" Bruce asked. "Knock it out of the park . . . in a baseball stadium?"

Walking away, Dylan shot back, "Don't give the promoter too much credit, he's just a promoter, not a gifted writer like you, Bruce."

Jules didn't know Dylan well enough to know if he was being belittled by the "voice of his generation" or if Dylan was just being playful. Bruce wasn't sure if Dylan was being playful or subtly putting Springsteen in his place in the constellation of brilliant lyricists—in an echelon lower than Dylan himself. An enigma, that Bob Dylan.

"Seriously, I wouldn't miss it with all these legends," Springsteen said. "But also, I don't think I would even have broken nationally if it wasn't for you and for Cleveland and the whole scene here. WMMS played us on the radio. Man, you booked us at the Allen Theater to open for Wishbone Ash when we were nobody!"

"1974," Belkin said. "Yeah, we had a good thing goin' back then. John Gorman, Kid Leo, all those guys at [W]MMS played your records, and we booked your shows . . . it seemed like this was the center of the rock 'n' roll universe! It was a great time."

"That's what I mean," Springsteen said. "I feel like Cleveland put us over the top. Nobody outside of Jersey knew us before that, and you all broke us nationally—so I am glad to do it, man."

The joyous concert would go forty minutes beyond the scheduled six hours, well past midnight. Those watching on HBO missed out on the finale, as their coverage cut off at the appointed time. Still, it was a huge smashing success.

And the shiny new Rock & Roll Hall of Fame designed by I.M. Pei—the guy responsible for the Louvre Pyramid in Paris!—was just a block east along the lake. The concert was history, but this new gem was here in Cleveland to stay! The only mar on the weekend was that the Browns lost in the final seconds to New England. New England's third-r ound pick—the eventual Pro Football Hall of Famer—Curtis Martin scored the winning touchdown.

Derrick Alexander, one member of Cleveland's "best collection of wide receivers in the league" (as Modell and Belicheck had been telling fans all year), dropped a pass in the final seconds that would have set up a game-tying field goal. This time the teacher (Parcells) bested the student (Belichick) and last year's playoff loss to the Browns was at least partially avenged.

A hot new sitcom set in Cleveland and starring a native Clevelander would debut on national TV: *The Drew Carey Show*. The show opened to the strains of the song "Cleveland Rocks," written and originally performed by Ian Hunter. Talk about perfect timing. The series debuted while the last chords from the world's biggest concert reverberated through the Cleveland streets. Cleveland Rocks! Oh, and for the first time in forty-one years, the Indians won their division, just five days before ABC drew back the curtain on *The Drew Carey Show*. Cleveland Rocks, indeed!

Browns fans' enthusiasm still ran strong. The Tribe clinched the American League Central on Friday night; the Browns won their home opener on Sunday. Hey, if the Indians could return to the postseason and possibly make the World Series for the first time since 1954, why couldn't the Browns finally validate the predictions of the experts and break on through to a Super Bowl/NFL Championship berth for the first time since 1964?

The Browns would beat the Oilers in Houston on September 17, then finally get their vaunted offense in gear, winning 35-17 at home against previous coach Marty Schottenheimer and his Kansas City Chiefs. The only blemish in that game was first-rounder Craig Powell suffering a knee injury on a kickoff return.

By the time September wrapped, the Browns led the division at 3-1, were on a three-game win streak, and looked pointed in the right direction. The Indians had kept rolling since winning the division and finished September at 99-44 with one game left to go in the regular season. They would (of course) win that game, notching the elusive total of 100 wins! One hundred wins is rare and impressive in a "regular" regular season. This had been an irregular strike-shortened season in which the teams played eighteen fewer games than normal—and the Tribe still won 100 games! Cleveland rocked, and its teams were on a roll!

61

# STORM CLOUDS ON THE HORIZON

October 1995

*They say there is a calm before the storm. The weather in Cleveland is* most reliably beautiful in September. Gone is the humidity of the summer, not yet to arrive is the damp chill and ever-present cloud cover of much of the rest of the year.

Cleveland's spirit had soared all September, with few clouds, plenty of sunshine, and blue skies. The unveiling of a glimmering new lakeside Rock & Rock Hall of Fame. The major concert event of the year with more star power than most galaxies. A Browns team sitting in first place, with national media predicting a Super Bowl appearance. The Indians dominating baseball, barreling toward a World Series berth. Oh, and Drew Carey's new show was faring well in the ratings!

October is when the weather usually turns here. It is inconsistent, unpredictable. It is the best of months; it is the worst of months. It often starts out beautiful, then the skies grow dark ever earlier and the refreshingly cool air turns bitingly cold. Ominous clouds roll in from over the lake. Sometimes, as Gordon Lightfoot sang, the "gales of November" come early.

The Indians inaugurated the month winning for the 100th time by a football score 17-7 over Kansas City to close their regular season. Cleveland fans realized the more significant victory was in keeping the Indians in Cleveland by building them their gorgeous new home. Several Indians team members and their manager, Mike Hargrove, attended the Browns' *Monday Night Football* game, watching from the same seats where rock fans had cheered a month earlier.

ABC's *Monday Night Football* telecast kicked off with tie-in to the network's new hit sitcom. Drew sat front and center on a set supposed to be the "Warsaw Tavern," where much of the show was filmed, thronged by cast and crew. Everyone was decked out in Browns jerseys, with Browns pennants being twirled around.

Carey, in his trademark glasses, deadpanned, "Well, hockey and basketball haven't really gotten it started yet, so we just have one question for you." Then the entire cast and crew shouted, "Are you ready for some football?"

Dan Dierdorf, Frank Gifford, and Al Michaels provided commentary immediately before kickoff. Dierdorf had the final soliloquy: "Is this a Super Bowl team? You bet it is. Owner Art Modell may finally get his Super Bowl wish."

The loudest cheers during the football game came when the Indians contingent was announced after the first quarter.

"They deserve it, they deserve it," Art Modell muttered. "They haven't been to the postseason in forty-one years. I guess we have just spoiled the fans, and they start taking us for granted . . ." he continued, but more under his breath than out loud.

It was a tough brand of football, with many Browns sustaining injuries throughout the game. Or were Cleveland's players exaggerating minor bumps and bruises in an attempt to slow Jim Kelly's high-powered, no-huddle offense—one that had been to the last four Super Bowls?

The savvy quarterback Jim Kelly noticed when Browns cornerback Antonio Langham left the game with yet another Browns injury. Rookie Tim Jacobs came on in relief. On second and 2 from the Browns' 41-yard line, he sent his favorite target, Andre Reed, on a fly. The perfect pass landed in Reed's hands in the end zone, and the Bills took the lead 19-16. Steve Christie, who had entered the 1995 season as the NFL's all-time most accurate kicker—but had missed a chip-shot field goal earlier in the fourth quarter—came on for the extra point.

"And there's another hook by Christie!" bellowed *Monday Night Football* announcer Dan Dierdorf.

"And that's a huge, big miss," exclaimed Al Michaels, "because instead of a 4-point lead, forcing Cleveland to score a touchdown, it is a 3-point lead."

Frank Gifford chimed in: "We're going to have a head case on the sidelines for sure with Steve Christie. He was totally bewildered after missing that short field goal . . . this is hard to fathom."

Poor Bills fans must have had flashbacks to their 1991 Super Bowl loss where then-kicker Scott Norwood missed the Super Bowl–winning field goal against the Giants.

The Browns knotted the game at 19 with 3:49 to go on a Matt Stover 38-yard field goal. Andre Rison, who was having his first big game with the Browns, had a touchdown pass from Vinny Testaverde knocked away at the goal line by Bills safety Greg Evans. The Browns had been in situations like this before. Bills QB Kelly and Broncos QB Elway were both part of that magical 1983 draft class. Both had captained their teams to multiple Super Bowls. Both were well versed in engineering game-winning fourth-quarter drives, often doing so at the Browns' expense!

Indeed, Jim Kelly and friends did methodically pass and run their way down the field. With eight seconds left to play the formerly sterling, presently tarnished Steve Christie came on for the field goal attempt.

Browns radio announcers, Casey Coleman and Doug Dieken:

Coleman: "Okay with eight seconds left, trying to break the tie is Steve Christie. The snap, the kick. He missed it!"

Dieken, interrupting his partner: "He shanked it, just like the last one."

Coleman, interrupting Dieken: "Ahh, but wait—they are saying the Browns have called timeout before the kick."

And so, the suddenly shaky Bills kicker got a mulligan. When the kick actually counted, he nailed it, and the 7-point underdog Bills marred the magical fall that had engulfed Cleveland like a long overdue hug.

The Browns had lost a tight game to a good team. The Browns were still 3-2. But in that moment, something snapped in Art Modell. Bill Belichick was supposed to be the coach who didn't let his team be left at the altar on the national stage, as had happened under Marty Schottenheimer in the eighties. Belichick was supposed to be *The Coach*, and this was supposed to be *The Year*.

Before the Browns played next—on October 8—the Indians won their first playoff series. Once they won game 1, in Cleveland, in thirteen innings, and despite two rain delays and a confiscation of slugger

Albert Belle's bat, you just had the feeling they'd sweep Boston. And sweep they did!

In that same span, Buffalo Bills head coach Marv Levy leveled accusations against Bill Belichick that he had coached his players to overreact to their on-field injuries to attempt to slow down his offense. Belichick got into a firefight with Levy through the media denying the accusations. Oh, and the Browns first-round draft pick, Craig Powell was declared by the medical team as "out for the year" after undergoing reconstructive ACL surgery on his right knee. "The Browns lost to the Lions in the Silverdome 38-20 in a game that wasn't as close as the scoreboard indicated.

After a rash of injuries and losing two in a row to sink to a 3-3 record, the Browns limped into their bye week at the perfect time. The Indians enjoyed a short break, too. That's what happens when you sweep your opponent out of the playoffs. It took a full five games for the Yankees and Mariners to sort out who would be the Indians' American League Championship Series (ALCS) opponent—or victim. For teams facing the Indians in 1995, the terms "opponent" and "victim" were usually synonymous.

Alas, the mighty Randy Johnson, aka "The Big Unit," standing 6 foot 10 inches and looking 10 feet tall on the pitching mound, and Seattle slugger Jay Buhner beat the Tribe in game 1 of the ALCS. It took eleven innings, but the Mariners prevailed.

The Indians would win the second game in Seattle, but then drop game 3—the first ALCS game played in Cleveland. Just as the Indians were starting to seem human, to conform to the threadbare pattern of Cleveland teams dashing what turn out to be false hopes, they won games 4 and 5 in front of raucous crowds in Cleveland. Rocky Colavito threw out the first pitch for game 5. He'd been retired for thirty years, but he still loomed large in the hearts of Clevelanders.

A star right fielder for the Indians, Colavito was traded in 1960 to the Tigers. The trade stupefied Rocky, his teammates, and the fans. The Indians had been terrible ever since—up until this new Jacobs Field era. The trade, and the Indians' subsequent decline, became known as "the Curse of Rocky Colavito." With his return to Cleveland tonight, with his ceremonial first pitch, and with the Tribe's victory (with only one more needed to advance to the World Series), it looked like the Curse of Rocky Colavito just possibly may have been broken.

Was Art Modell in the stands or someone's luxury box at Jacobs Field to soak up the vibes that the rest of Cleveland was grooving on? Nope. On the biggest baseball weekend in Cleveland since the Eisenhower administration, Modell was checked out from Cleveland and checked into the Beverly Hills Hilton. Pinned down by *Plain Dealer* reporter Tony Grossi, Modell would not directly answer the question whether he was in Los Angeles to discuss the possibility of moving the Browns there.

Grossi continued the questioning: "Art, I gotta ask, did you leave town because of a kind of jealousy of the Indians and Jacobs Field and their success?"

> "The Indians deserve the spotlight," Modell said. "Hell, they've been waiting 41 years to get in that spotlight, and they should not relinquish it. We've had many days in the spotlight.
>
> It's their turn at-bat. I don't feel slighted by the position of Browns stories [in the newspaper] and coverage of the Browns. I've been around sports too long not to understand that. You can't sit there and say, "Oh, boy, we're being ignored.'" We haven't done anything yet to deserve the recognition I think we're going to get. In the meantime, the Indians have performed brilliantly. I think John Hart [Indians general manager] has done one of the great jobs in rebuilding a franchise I've ever seen in professional sports. A magnificent job. I have nothing but admiration for the Indians ballclub and its management. It's been brilliant. But it hasn't changed my lifestyle or my approach to my team one bit.'"

On Tuesday, October 17, the Indians got it done in Seattle. Behind a four-hitter by Dennis Martinez, Julian Tavarez, and the best closer in the Majors, Jose Mesa, the Tribe prevailed 4-0. The Cleveland Indians, yes, the CLEVELAND INDIANS had won the pennant! For the first time since that long-ago Browns victory over the Colts in the 1964 NFL Championship Game, a Major League team from Cleveland was going to play for the championship!

In "Browns Toast Tribe Pennant" Mary Kay Cabot of the *Plain Dealer* reported:

> After practice on Wednesday, Belichick gave the Indians their due to start his news conference: "I'd like to start off by congratulating [Indians manager] Mike Hargrove and the rest of the Indians organization on their American League pennant and wish them well on the World Series. They've got a good team. I was there [Saturday night] for their big victory. It looks like they've got a couple of guys that could play for us. A couple of big ones."

The Steelers lost to the Bengals on Thursday night, setting up the division such that a Browns win against the lowly Jacksonville Jaguars would put the Browns in sole possession of first place in the AFC Central. Andre Rison guaranteed a Browns victory, claiming the Browns would "bring the funk" for the game. "Bad Moon" was likely envisioning a big game for himself with some of the other starting Browns receivers still hurt and likely to miss the game.

It was simple: Win against an expansion team playing the eighth game of its existence and find yourself all alone in first place, or lose your third in a row and have a losing record on the season. But it was October in Cleveland. And even though the clear skies suggested that their opponent from the Sunshine State had brought the sunny weather with them, there were invisible clouds moving into place. After the game was played, the score was 15-23. The Browns had lost.

Morale sank. Quarterback Vinny Testaverde said it hurt as much as any loss he'd suffered. Jaguars' safety Harry Colon (not making that name up) was quoted as saying, "We talked about [Andre Rison's comment] all week and we talked about it again [yesterday]. Cleveland and Pittsburgh had been talking Super Bowl and we beat them. We have as many wins as they do. This time, Rison wrote a check he couldn't cash."

You can imagine how his new teammates felt about "Bad Moon" Rison now. Things among the players were getting ugly. Nor were they any better between coach and owner.

For the first time since Bill Belichick was hired, Art Modell did not give him an unswerving vote of confidence when questioned by reporters about his head coach's job security.

> Not going to get into that. I'll make my assessment at the end of the season. I'm not going to predict what I'm going to do down the line, until down the line is finished, until the fat lady sings.

> Ironically, we're tied for first with a 3-4 record. But yesterday's performance was not an aberration. It was a very, very poor performance by the entire team, the coaches, the players, everybody. I apologize to the public at large. It was an embarrassment to me. What's so distressing is that this is a better team than last year, based on the acquisitions we made. I've invested a lot of money in this ballclub this year, and I expected better results. I can't remember the last time I felt this low. I'm extremely upset. This was a bad one yesterday. I don't want to underestimate the impact it had on me and others in the organization.

The storm clouds had gathered. Fierce winds of recrimination blew through the locker room leaving destruction in their wake. Player relationships were upended like doublewides in a formerly tidy trailer park after an EF5 tornado. Gales lashed the monomaniacal Captain MyWay, who had weathered his share of misgivings from fans and local media, but up until now had always had firm backing from the USS *Browns* owner.

The White Whale—the Super Bowl—was escaping. The Browns' ship was sinking en route to Tempe, Arizona, where the manifest said the captain and crew were supposed to be sailing to play in Super Bowl XXX. (Despite this Super Bowl's designation "XXX," it is not the one where Janet Jackson's infamous wardrobe malfunction happened.)

Worse still for Cleveland and its fans, the Indians had lost World Series games 1 and 2 to the Braves in Atlanta. The second loss came the same day the Browns lost to Jacksonville. The Tribe's legendary offense could only muster two runs and three runs—one run fewer than Atlanta scored in each game.

The *Plain Dealer* had already brought up the parallels between 1954 and this season: The '54 Indians had tallied 111 victories to reach the World Series. The 1995 team had amassed 107 wins (including the seven playoff wins) and had reached the World Series for the first time since 1954.

That part of the story was all sunshine and rainbows. But then a sudden cloudburst doused the spirits with the rest of the story: The 1954 Indians lost the World Series, swept by the Brooklyn Dodgers. And now? And now the mighty feel-good Indians were halfway to being swept by the Braves, down 0-2.

The sudden downturn in the Indians' fortunes didn't buoy Art Modell's mood. But as October 24 slid into October 25, Eddie Murray's bat poked a hole in the gloom as he stroked a line drive single to center, scoring pinch runner Alvaro Espinoza. The crowd exploded in joyful exultation! The jubilation, the bright lights, the vibrant colors, the blaring of John Mellencamp's "Again Tonight" punctuated with fireworks, were all like knives in Modell's soul. How could he ever be expected to succeed in a bleak, gray, dilapidated cavernous relic of a stadium?

Modell had lost the unflagging faith in his head coach and now had a disgruntled quarterback in Vinny Testaverde. Art Modell, Bill Belichick, and Mike Lombardi had decided on October 24 to bench Testaverde, despite his number one passer rating in the NFL. They made offensive coordinator Steve Crosby break the news to Testaverde. It was a desperate bid to try to spark the team with rookie Eric Zeier, who admittedly had shown some flashes of potential in the preseason.

Modell knew the fans would turn on him as soon as the news broke in the morning. As he drove home from Jacobs Field, he resolved to call his friend and minority Browns owner Al Lerner first thing in the morning. Art was talking to himself: *I've done all I can do here. It's time to move on. I have no other choice. I just have to move on. I HAVE to move on!*

Modell called Lerner in his MBNA office in Baltimore first thing Wednesday morning: "Listen Al, we need to get down to see those Stadium Committee people in Baltimore as soon as possible. This week. I'd go today if it could be arranged!"

"Art, I am in the middle of some things here at work. Once I get through this, I'll circle the troops."

"Get everyone we'll need. I don't know if that means the mayor, the governor, the stadium people."

"Alright, Art, alright. I gotta go. I'll be back in contact with you after I arrange something."

Though the Indians were in the midst of the World Series, with a game in Cleveland this very night—October 25—the Browns' soap opera still claimed the bulk of the ink on the front page of the sports section. Tony Grossi opined that Testaverde would not be the last to fall, that those on the coaching staff and in the personnel department should be looking over their shoulders.

Later that day, during the press conference after practice, Testaverde unloaded on Coach Belichick. When asked if he was worried his loose lips would land him in the coach's doghouse, he quipped, "What's he gonna do, he can't bench me." Testaverde now knew what it felt like for a mistress who steals some wife's husband away to then fall prey to the philanderer's natural impulse when he then abandons the mistress for someone newer.

The just-jilted Testaverde said practically the same thing as Bernie Kosar two years earlier when he had been jilted to make room for Testaverde:

> I think there are bigger problems than the quarterback position. One of those is dropped passes by the receivers in scoring territory. There have been at least eight this season, including one by Andre Rison in the end zone in the loss to Jacksonville. I think we would have won at least two more games if we held on to some balls. [Dropping passes] is not sparking the team, because we'd be 5-2 and everybody'd be in a good mood.

The Braves and Indians faced off for game 4 at Jacobs Field around 8:30 that evening. Bob Feller, who pitched in the World Series the last time the Indians won it in 1948, threw the ceremonial first pitch. After five innings, the game was scoreless. The Braves drew first blood and wound up winning for the third time in four games. This time the game was not decided by a single run, with Atlanta prevailing 5-2. The Indians would need to sweep the remaining three games—the final two of which would be in Atlanta—if they were to win this Fall Classic.

On October 26, fans in Cleveland were nervous. Very nervous. Their Indians were down to their last chance tonight. Win or lose, this would be the last game played in Jacobs Field until 1996. They were also cautiously optimistic. They had watched the Tribe come back all year, with late-inning rallies, walk-off homers, and had seen the best closer in baseball hold precious leads forty-four times in a strike-shortened season. True, the Braves' pitching staff was one of history's best. But so were the Indians' batters! And those batters would need to show up, going against the era's best pitcher, game 1 winner Greg Maddux.

Another Hall of Famer threw out game 5's first pitch: "Cleveland's own" Joe Walsh. Okay, it was the Rock & Roll Hall of Fame, not Cooperstown, but still, he made it into *a* Hall of Fame! (As a member of the Eagles.) The fans' hopes were realized, their optimism rewarded. In yet another one-run game, the Indians came out on top. Whatever would happen in Atlanta, the Indians won the final game played at Jacobs Field! The fans forgot the decades of baseball misery, swept up in the rapture, each one really believing one of Joe Walsh's best-known lyrics: "Life's been good to me so far."

62

# INDIAN SUMMER FALLS SHORT

OCTOBER 28, 1995

***Though nobody would realize it for more than a week, in about eight*** hours something would be set in motion that would make possibly losing the World Series—and would even make *The Drive, The Fumble, Red Right 88*, and all other Cleveland sporting calmaities—look like minor annoyances. The bottom was about to drop out.

There is a saying in baseball that good pitching beats good hitting. That debatable statement was proven true in the 1995 World Series. Atlanta was the dominant team of the 1990s, chiefly because of their pitching staff, but could never seem to win it all . . . and now they were facing one of the best hitting teams in history. The Indians' team batting average against the Braves in this World Series was under .200. Still, the Tribe had prevailed in game 5 against Atlanta ace Greg Maddux. Maybe there was reason for hope.

In game 6, Indians starter Dennis Martinez scattered four hits and allowed no runs over four and two-thirds innings. Jim Poole relieved, got the last out in the fifth inning, but gave up a home run to David Justice to start the sixth. It was the only run Cleveland's gang of six pitchers allowed. But it was one more than the Indians' fearsome offense could muster. Tom Glavine, named the World Series MVP, threw a one-hitter over eight innings, and closer Mark Wohlers preserved the one-hitter, saved his fourth World Series game, and secured the World Series championship for Atlanta.

It was not the way any Cleveland fan wanted the magical season to end. But the ending couldn't undo the magnificent season. Losing to the Braves in the World Series didn't feel like losing to Elway's Broncos in *The Drive* game or *The Fumble* game. Nor was it as devastating as the 1954 World Series sweep after having won a record 111 games. After the initial sting, the loss didn't feel like a curse, just an unfortunate ending to an unexpectedly wonderful joyride of a season.

The fans' and the city's mood was best exemplified in how they greeted their vanquished heroes upon their return to Cleveland: Thousands of cheering fans thronged the airport in the middle of the night to greet the Indians' charter flight. Then, on Monday, the city held a rally and parade to thank the Indians for the season. Pride, gratitude, and happiness, mixed with some bittersweet, were the communal emotions. Let outsiders scoff at a community celebrating "losers." These Indians, these fans, this city were no losers!

## 63

# A BROWNS RESURGENCE?

October 29, 1995

*With Indians fever engulfing the city, football Sunday was almost an* afterthought. The Browns had lost three straight and were in Cincinnati to take on the Bengals. Somehow everything worked out for the Browns. Although they relinquished a 10-point lead with under three minutes left in regulation, Bill Belichick's newly anointed starting quarterback validated (at least for now) the decision to sit Vinny Testaverde in favor of Eric Zeier, who led the team to victory in overtime.

The Browns rolled up the most yards on offense in nine years! Andre Rison scored a touchdown on seven receptions for 173 yards. And the Browns were tied (with the Steelers) for first place! It was late October, but maybe, just maybe, the clouds were parting?

There was a renewed optimism in town. Fans, having just witnessed a historic Indians World Series run, allowed themselves to believe that maybe Zeier was the spark the Browns needed to ignite a Super Bowl blast. If Zeier indeed was the answer, then that meant Belichick, despite his idiosyncrasies, was a genius talent evaluator after all . . . and who knew what other diamonds in the rough he had just plucked from the draft?

The fans' optimism was matched by the players'. "I can't even tell you how big this was," said defensive end Rob Burnett, who had four sacks, including one that gave Bengals quarterback Jeff Blake a mild concussion and caused him to leave the game for a while.

“It was HUGE,” said Antonio Langham, who was flagged three times for pass interference that led to two Bengals touchdowns. “This victory brought some life back into this team. This might be the turning point of our season.”

It might also be a turning point in Browns history: namely, the start of the Zeier era. In his first pro start, Zeier completed 26 of 46 passes for 310 yards and one touchdown, a beautiful 17-yard strike to Rison into double coverage in the end zone. Zeier also ran eight times for 44 yards, including four times for first downs. He was picked off by Steve Tovar at the Bengals' 3 to waste a 59-yard pass to Rison in the third quarter.

“He was outstanding in his first at-bat in the NFL,” said Art Modell. “I think he'll captivate our city.” (Note Modell's use of “our city” instead of “Cleveland.”)

64

# SLUMBERING PROPHESY OF A FUTURE PARADISE LOST

HALLOWEEN NIGHT, 1995

*Johnny Milton was back home now after enjoying some spirits at a Hal-*loween party at a local watering hole. He'd worn his Albert Belle jersey and Indians ballcap and accessorized this standard fare with a homemade necklace. The central feature of which was a big rubber bat—not a baseball bat but the kind that could turn into a vampire. On the chain, to either side of the bat, at regular intervals, were a series of wine-bottle corks.

Most people got it immediately: a reference to the Albert Belle "corked bat" scandal from the previous season. It was met with mild amusement, although some fans thought it was "too soon!" coming just three nights after the Tribe lost the World Series. Johnny was proud of his creativity.

Home now, Johnny was still too amped up from partying with the ghouls and goblins (and naughty nurses) to hit the sack. "I may as well see what Casey Coleman has to say about the Browns," he muttered, flipping on the late TV news, before grabbing a bag of bite-size Snickers and plopping onto his couch.

"In national news," said the announcer, "the CIA today admitted that the damage caused by Aldrich Ames was far worse than originally thought."

"Traitor!" Johnny yelled. "Hang him!"

Then the anchors went on and on about other news, national and local, important and mundane. Then the weather came on.

"Come on, come on, get to sports!"

Then came the commercials. All the car dealers and their shouting and exaggerated hand motions. *Why does every frickin' car dealer act the same way?* Johnny wondered.

He started getting woozy. Could he suddenly be so tired? Was there something in those Jell-O shots besides ground cow parts, food coloring, and vodka? Had someone slipped him a mickey? And what, exactly, *is* a mickey? He waited for Casey Coleman to give an upbeat report on Eric Zeier and give him some hope after the tough Tribe World Series loss . . . but his lids were getting heavy.

He dozed off, and when he woke up the local news had been replaced by a retrospective on the glorious history of the Cleveland Browns. But this was not looking back to Paul Brown and the 1940s and fifties. This was something else entirely. It seemed like he missed the intro, but the show was basically just getting started.

The show's host, Faye Kass, narrated: *Perhaps no team has been so dominant in the history of the National Football League as the Cleveland Browns have been over the last twenty-five years. The reigning NFL champions have gone to the Super Bowl twelve times between 1997 and 2018, winning it eight times.*

Johnny's brow furrowed deeply as his subconscious mind detected the future dates of this retrospective program . . . but he kept dozing, though *he* didn't know that.

Kass reported: *And it almost didn't happen. It's hard to believe now, but for a while in 1995, there were reports in Cleveland that Art Modell was considering moving the team to Baltimore. Rumors also swirled that the sporting world's most successful and beloved owner was close to firing head coach Bill Belichick. That would have given Modell the distinction of firing possibly the two most dominant coaches in professional football history.*

*Instead, Modell kept the Browns in Cleveland, Belichick kept his job, and the rest as they say is history. In 2000 Belichick and general manager Ozzie Newsome used their sixth-round pick, number 183 overall, to pick Tom Brady in that year's draft. With Brady at quarterback behind an offensive line anchored by Newsome's 1996 first-round pick Jonathan Ogden, and with a defense anchored by the other Newsome 1996 first rounder, Ray Lewis, and 2002 first rounder, Ed Reed, it was no wonder the Browns found their way to the Super Bowl in half the seasons of the last quarter century.*

*Bill Belichick started his head coaching career in Cleveland, and he's just completed his twenty-eighth year there. It's shocking to think back now that he had a losing record and won only one playoff game through his first five years at the helm of this team—which would soon take off like a rocket and stay in orbit for two decades, with no sign of ever coming back to Earth.*

*Ozzie Newsome was a three-time Pro Bowler and two-time All-Pro tight end who spent his entire playing career in Cleveland. He moved to the front office immediately upon hanging up his cleats, becoming the NFL's first African American general manager as well as one of the most successful of all time. Between his playing and executive experience, Newsome has continually served the Cleveland Browns for a remarkable fifty years . . . and counting!*

*Art Modell moved from Brooklyn with zero sports ownership experience to buy the Browns at the age of thirty-five for $4 million, using only $250,000 of his own money. Until his 2012 death at age eighty-seven, he was part of Cleveland's "Holy Trinity," along with his coach and general manager. Without question, he is the one of the most recognizable and most beloved Clevelanders. Enshrined in the Pro Football Hall of Fame, he is revered throughout the sporting world as the consummate franchise owner. The name Art Modell is synonymous with the Browns, with football, and with excellence.*

*Tonight, we present for you some of the many, many highlights from this most dynastic of dynasties.*

The program went on to display and narrate highlights from all the following Super Bowls:

| | | | | | |
|---|---|---|---|---|---|
| Super Bowl XXXI | Jan 26, 1997 | Green Bay | 35 | Cleveland | 21 |
| Super Bowl XXXV | Jan 28, 2001 | **Cleveland** | **34** | New York Giants | 7 |
| Super Bowl XXXVI | Feb 3, 2002 | **Cleveland** | **20** | St. Louis Rams | 17 |
| Super Bowl XXXVIII | Feb 1, 2004 | **Cleveland** | **32** | Carolina | 29 |
| Super Bowl XXXIX | Feb 6, 2005 | **Cleveland** | **24** | Philadelphia | 21 |
| Super Bowl XLII | Feb 3, 2008 | New York Giants | 17 | Cleveland | 14 |
| Super Bowl XLVI | Feb 5, 2012 | New York Giants | 21 | Cleveland | 17 |
| Super Bowl XLVII | Feb 3, 2013 | **Cleveland** | **34** | San Francisco | 31 |

| Super Bowl XLIX | Feb 1, 2015 | **Cleveland** | **28** | Seattle | 24 |
|---|---|---|---|---|---|
| Super Bowl LI | Feb 5, 2017 | **Cleveland** | **34** | Atlanta | 28 |
| Super Bowl LII | Feb 4, 2018 | Philadelphia | 41 | Cleveland | 33 |
| Super Bowl LIII | Feb 3, 2019 | **Cleveland** | **13** | Los Angeles Rams | 3 |

After ninety breathless minutes of dialogue presented over countless video highlight clips, the narrator summarized:

*Twelve Super Bowls in twenty-three years. Eight NFL Championships. If not for one crazy helmet catch by the Giants' David Tyree in Super Bowl XLII, Cleveland would have gone 9–3 during this marvelous run. And although Tom Brady is moving on to Tampa Bay next year, nobody is betting against Coach Belichick and the Browns to keep the dynasty rolling into the 2019 season and beyond.*

The familiar NFL Films symphonic music played, and Johnny's lips curled into a contented smile. The strings swelled, and the horns came in. It was like a march, only more heroic, Wagnerian, like "Flight of the Valkyries." But slowly the music changed, the brass section dropped out and the strings became shards of jagged glass, thrusting like repetitive stabs. Like an irritating alarm clock, the strings penetrated his consciousness.

Unaware that he'd been sleeping, Johnny was now awake. The jarring music was blaring from the TV. He was now watching black blood spread across a white porcelain shower floor and swirl down the drain. It was 2 a.m., technically not Halloween anymore, but the network was showing Alfred Hitchcock's *Psycho*. He'd missed the sports report on the news and whatever had been on for the following two hours.

The movie is terrifying, but not nearly as scary as his realization that all this glory had been but a dream. His faculties fully restored, Johnny considered his slumbering reverie. How strange. He'd been dreaming twenty-four years in the future and looking back over a glorious past—a past that hadn't happened yet. What an unusual and detailed dream. Maybe this was some sort of premonition? Maybe this was a vision, foretelling the future, that for some weird reason he had been selected to see. Perhaps he was a modern-day prophet.

65

# THE ULTIMATE EXPRESSION OF THE CURSE

November 1995

*It was just one week since the raucous game 5 World Series victory at* Jacobs Field, five days since the end of the World Series, four days since the renewing Browns victory over Cincinnati, and three days since the Indians rally and parade on Cleveland's Public Square. And now Art Modell was being forced to address rumors of a Browns move or a possible sale of the team.

WBAL-TV in Baltimore reported that the Browns had made a handshake deal to move to Baltimore. No additional details about this rumored arrangement were provided. The station reported additional news, not involving the Browns, that the NFL owners would be voting in a week on which team of the NFL's choosing would be slated to relocate to Baltimore. The teams on the NFL list were the Seattle Seahawks, Tampa Bay Buccaneers, New England Patriots, Cincinnati Bengals, and Arizona Cardinals.

From Browns headquarters, Modell immediately and emphatically denied he was selling the team. He remained mum on the subject of moving the team, however. His spokesman, David Hopcraft, commented that Modell had not sold any additional interest in the Browns to minority shareholder Al Lerner (which somewhat deflated speculation in the *Baltimore Sun* that the Maryland banker would buy controlling interest and move the team to Charm City).

Hopcraft, when pressed on whether Modell may move the team without selling it, stated: "We're not going to confirm or deny or comment on any of it." Not exactly a categorical denial!

The Maryland political and Stadium Authority officials either declined comment or ducked phone calls altogether. Mayor Michael White of Cleveland dismissed the news as "rumors with a capital R," then, like any skilled politician, used his time in the spotlight to mention something to the effect of: "But they *will* leave if voters don't vote to extend the sin tax to fund either a new or refurbished Cleveland Stadium."

On the first Friday evening in November, Modell was at home responding to a pool of reporters from around the state via conference call.

Reporter: "Has a deal been struck?"

Modell: "I am not going to comment."

Reporter: "Will you be at a press conference in Baltimore on Monday?"

Modell: "I have not finalized my plans yet."

Reporter: "The *Baltimore Sun* will say that the deal is done."

Modell: "I have no reaction to that."

Reporter: "What is the outlook?"

Modell: "I've got some very, very serious, profound problems here in Cleveland that I'm trying to resolve and may be beyond resolution. Damn it! And I can't go any further than that right now, but I will have in due course a full disclosure."

The interjection of "damn it" and the overall tone of his voice testified to the fact that this situation (while of his own doing), was torture for him. It also demonstrated, as Al Lerner would later say, "Art Modell is not an emotional man. He is the *most* emotional man."

The balance of the group interview resulted in no concrete revelations. Modell only insisted that he was pushed into what he was about to do (if he did it) by an uncaring coalition of city, county, and business officials. He mentioned his "not standing in the way of Gateway" (which provided new stadia for the Indians and Cavaliers) yet being left waiting for the last six years for a similar largesse from the community he'd called home for thirty-five years.

Modell doubled down that he would not be selling the team. He asserted that since he lost the Indians as tenants in 1994 and since free agency hit the NFL in 1993, he'd been hemorrhaging money. He said that his previous pledge to sell the team before he would ever move it was null and void because of the changes in those circumstances. Modell claimed he was "not in this to make money. But I don't want to go broke either."

When pushed for details of a pending outcome, he steadfastly held to his position that he could not talk, that everyone would need to wait three days, and in due course all would be decided and disclosed.

Modell's mindset is laid bare in his answer to the final question. And his answer serves as a summary of the entire interview—a tacit admission that he's already gone, yet a tentative ray of hope that maybe he's not:

Reporter: "Can you be a happy man if you take the Browns out of Cleveland?"

Modell: "I cannot surrender thirty-five years of living in this town overnight and say I'm a happy guy. Of course not. But I have to do what I have to do. If I do that. If I go."

After Art hung up, the reporters hung around on the line. "What the hell was that?" "My head is spinning!" "What do we write? Is he leaving or not?" "It's a done deal, right? Isn't that the word out of Baltimore?" "So, do we just wait until Monday, and see what happens?" The normally competitive sports reporters were baffled. They'd never encountered something like this before. No one had.

The previous Friday all of Cleveland entered the weekend with its baseball team in the World Series. Its football team, though losers of three straight games, could (and did) find itself in first place in its division by the end of the weekend.

Cleveland entered the workweek with their football team in first place and apparently pointed in the right direction, and with a civic lovefest for their gallant baseball heroes. And now? Now it was faced with the possibility of not just a loss *by* their team, but the loss *of* their team. In fact, they were facing the possible loss of a core aspect of their collective identity!

Television, radio, and newspaper reporters kicked into high gear, trying to divine the true status of the Browns. Had an irreversible deal already been struck with Baltimore? Was there still time for Cleveland to rally for the win before (as Modell himself had said colloquially), "the fat lady sings"?

Meanwhile, Mayor Mike White and the city administration, along with county commissioners, the Cleveland Stadium, and the sin tax extension committees all burned the midnight oil, trying to do what they could to entice Modell to stay in Cleveland. Lawyers were consulted to try to enforce the lease that required the Browns to play their home games in Cleveland Stadium through the 1998 season. People reached out to the NFL trying to shore up support among the other owners to vote to disallow the move.

The only person who truly had control, Art Modell, said nothing more than he had on Friday night: "It's out of my control. I will provide a full disclosure Monday." The mayor argued that Cleveland would be able to put together a package that was "in the top third" of stadium deals in the NFL. Media reports were, by turns, hopeful and fatalistic. Some looked at the unparalleled support the fans had always given the team and couldn't fathom the NFL, or the city's offer, or Modell's conscience allowing him to leave. Others heard the rough dimensions of Baltimore's reputed offer—$30 million profit guaranteed per year in some reports, $50 million signing bonus in others—and couldn't see how Art could afford *not* to move.

It was all a lot like pregame analysis. Who'd win the big game? Except this time there was no manufactured B.S. disagreement between the sparring commentators as to why team A would win or why team B was much better and couldn't lose. This was real. This was raw. This was a potential divorce. The cheating husband (if he was cheating) had laid out his case that his cheating was justified (if he had done it), because of the inattentiveness of his wife (the city/county/business powers that be). Caught in the middle were the kids . . . the fans. They'd done nothing wrong. They'd been the best kids on the block, and they stood to be hurt the most. They always are. It would all come down to Monday.

On Sunday at home in Cleveland, the Browns got destroyed by the Houston Oilers. Bud Adams, owner of the Oilers, was actively contemplating a move of his own . . . prompting Browns receiver Andre Rison to say before the game: "What is this game, the Baltimore Browns vs. the Nashville Oilers?" (Instead of "Bad Moon," he should have been called "Nostradamus" as he nailed where both teams would land.)

The 37-10 drubbing was the Browns' worst loss since the 3-13 season in 1990. That 3-13 season was why Bill Belichick had been hired.

After five years at the helm, and with a Super Bowl–worthy roster—if this was all Coach MyWay could do, who needed him?

Monday, November 6th. Red and blue lights pulsed and Harley engines roared. A phalanx of motorcycle cops escorted a cavalcade of five black sedans through Baltimore's streets from the hotel to Camden Yards. Al Lerner, Art Modell, and Modell's son David were in one car (with a man who seemed to know Art Modell but who wasn't publicly recognized). Baltimore Mayor Kurt Schmoke and some giddy staff members were in another. Yet another car carried Maryland Governor Parris Glendening and a few aides.

Maryland Stadium Authority representatives, including head honcho John Moag, rounded out the short parade. As they emerged from the cars into the bright sunshine, a couple hundred fans cheered "Art! Art! Art!" A much smaller group held up protest signs: "Help Baltimore's Poor, Not Football Millionaires." The smallest cohort was Cleveland Browns fans. One had taken a magic marker to a piece of ratty cardboard and held it aloft: "$hame."

On the makeshift dais, the mood was universally joyful, triumphant. Except for one man. The one whose mounting professional problems were all about to vanish. The man whose personal and familial fortune was about to be secured. The man who'd been greeted by Baltimore as if a king. To them he seemed like Midas. But he felt like Judas. (And a few million people concentrated by the shores of Lake Erie and scattered in small bands throughout the world felt the same way.)

The TV camera was placed such that the lectern was centered in the frame. The lectern must have been the governor's because it was emblazoned with the seal of the State of Maryland. Behind it stood said Governor Parris Glendening, with an American flag behind him, to his right. In the background loomed Oriole Park at Camden Yards.

"Ladies and gentlemen, we have a signed contract in hand," the governor said, holding up some papers to punctuate the proclamation. He paused while most of those assembled cheered. "The Browns are indeed coming to Baltimore!" The cheers grew lusty.

Every TV and radio station in the Cleveland market had been delivering nonstop coverage of the sordid affair (and would continue doing so into the evening). Every person in Northeast Ohio heard the depressing news at the same time. Seismic equipment in Siberia could have picked up the resulting reaction. It was not a happy one. After an initial, almost interminable bout of profanity, all impugning Arthur Modell—and to some extent his deceased mother—some intelligible comments and questions spilled forth from the mouths of the jilted:

"Wow, I can't believe this is really happening. . . ."

"That liar! He's been stringing us along! He must have known for weeks he was out the door!"

Wailing, crying, gnashing of teeth . . . more profanity . . . still more profanity . . . sackcloth and ashes. . . .

"What else can we do? Nobody in the NFL gets more support from their fans! Everybody is either at the game or watching it on TV every week!"

Governor Glendening yielded the stage and Modell made his way to the lectern. Two hundred attendees cheered, while two million watching on TV in Ohio booed and labeled him a traitor.

As Modell prepared to speak, total silence descended on the small assemblies in Ohio's office buildings, barber shops, and bars as people huddled around TVs or even radios.

Modell squinted in the wilting brilliance of the sun. His lugubrious face betrayed an inner agony. His demeanor and his tone were a complete one-eighty from those of the governor and the others who would speak that day. The other speakers' audience was the fans (and voters) of Baltimore and Maryland. Although Modell could have addressed this same constituency, his initial words were instead a half-baked mea culpa to the people of Cleveland:

"This has been a very, very tough road for my family and for me."

He wasn't engaging with the camera, nor consulting notes. This extroverted man who had worked in television, had been a successful advertising executive, who'd always loved interacting with media and basking in the limelight, could not mug for the camera. Instead, his head hung low.

"I leave Cleveland, Ohio . . . and leave my heart . . . leave a good part of my heart and soul there . . . I can never forget the people . . . of Cleveland. The fans that supported the Browns for years. But frankly, it came down to a simple proposition: I had no choice. . . ."

Back in Cleveland:

"Bulls__t!"

"Oh, we feel so sorry for you, Modell!"

Then more profanity.

Modell received no sympathy from those whom he was in the act of traumatizing. He started talking to the Baltimore audience directly now, but his conscience kept steering him back to addressing those whom he was hurting:

"I know what you went through eleven years ago, because that is exactly what is happening in Cleveland right now," Modell said softly. "I am deeply, deeply sorry from the bottom of my heart."

A dispassionate observer could rightly be moved to tears by the tragic soliloquy. If Modell had been standing in a dark theater, under a spotlight instead standing in a parking lot under the sunlight, if speaking in Olde English instead of a Brooklyn accent, if instead of a blue suit and tie, he was dressed in period costume, he'd have made the most convincing Macbeth since Ian McKellen. It was a tragedy of Shakespearian magnitude.

But Cleveland fans are not dispassionate observers. The spilled blood was not that of some character on stage. It was their own blood. As it ran, orange and brown, down their pierced bodies to the floor, their pain rose up, and overwhelmed them.

Were the regularly scheduled soap operas to start airing as they did every other afternoon, their stories would have been relatively boring compared to the drama being broadcast from Baltimore. *Days of Our Lives* was about other, fictional characters' lives. This was real. This dramatic tragedy was happening live, on this day, to our lives, to us all.

And this is all while the nine-to-fivers were still at work. Nauseated and numb, Clevelanders turned off the radios and TVs in disgust. The U.S. Bureau of Labor Statistics probably showed a drop in U.S. productivity in the fourth quarter of 1995 owing to this one day in Cleveland when no work got done. The dip in productivity was offset by increased liquor tax revenues that evening.

While it was still afternoon, Cleveland Mayor Michael White, who had traveled to Baltimore, arranged a press conference of his own from Baltimore's Inner Harbor Marriott. "We are going to fight this fight," he said. "I can't say we're not going to lose, but when it's over, the other side's going to know they've been in a fight." White also called on Cuyahoga County voters to go to the polls (the next day) and approve Issue 5, an extension of the tax on cigarettes and alcohol to fund stadium renovations. The sin tax, White said, was the last piece of the financing package to fix up the stadium. With that in hand, he reasoned, Cleveland can argue in court and to the NFL that the Browns have no good reason to leave.

The Clevelanders who had tuned back in—since they couldn't concentrate to do their jobs anyway—began to feel a sliver of hope. But it was a tenuous hope . . . like being down three games to one in the World Series and knowing your team will need to win against the competition's best pitchers in their stadium twice if you even get that far.

66

# HOW THE DEAL WENT DOWN

NOVEMBER 1995

*Bernie Kosar, deposed favorite son of Cleveland, told the* Palm Beach *Post* that he would love to own an NFL franchise one day and was confident he could raise the capital. Cleveland would obviously be the ideal place for his franchise. The Bengals' Mike Brown, the son of deposed Browns namesake and coaching legend Paul Brown, said he'd jump at the chance to relocate his team to Cleveland if Cincinnati voters didn't back the 1 percent sales tax proposal that would hit the ballot in March 1996.

Amazing how another owner could be foaming at the mouth for the shabby relic Art Modell had "no choice" but to vacate. Mike Brown, when asked if he could really make a go of it in Cleveland, replied, "Oh yes, it's a bigger stadium, it's a bigger city, there are over 100 boxes, and you'd make more from local TV rights."

What was unfathomable even a week ago and dawned as a grim but abstract possibility over the weekend was now a fait accompli. A done deal. Something new would need to happen after the fact to change what had just happened. Only it hadn't *just* happened. The deal had gone down ten days earlier. The timing of it was insidious.

Groggy Clevelanders hit snooze for the third time on the morning of Friday, October 27, after getting mere minutes of sleep; it took a while for fans' adrenaline to recede and allow them to drift off to sleep after the Indians' game 5 World Series win over the Braves.

Meanwhile, Art and David Modell accompanied Al Lerner aboard his private jet that was now preparing to land at Baltimore/Washington

International Airport. They taxied to a stop off a back runway's beaten path, secluded from the commercial airliners. A limousine pulled onto the tarmac, next to their plane. A small delegation of Maryland Stadium Authority and elected officials boarded the jet.

"Well, you all are certainly up bright and early this morning!" declared Kurt Schmoke, Baltimore's mayor, as he boarded the aircraft.

"You know me, Kurt, I've been an early riser since my time in the Marine Corps, and probably forever to tell you the truth," replied Lerner. "Here, why don't you take a seat right here. Besides, Art insisted we get here as soon as possible . . . and when Art wants something, you won't hear the end of it until he gets it."

"I gave the pilot a few extra bucks to step on the gas," Modell added, playing along, lightening the tone before beginning the meeting in earnest. "So, we've been over the documents, and everything looks exactly as we've been discussing verbally."

Modell looked directly at John Moag of Maryland Stadium Authority. "I've got to hand it to you and your team, and the governor and the mayor," he said, shooting a glance at Schmoke. "You've put together a tremendous proposal. I think it is very fair, and will be good for the Cleveland Browns, err . . . let's just say 'the Browns,' and for the City of Baltimore and its fans."

The Baltimore team was silent for a few seconds, expecting Modell to say, "But," or "However," and then make some last-second demand or request. When that didn't happen, the mayor and Moag both started talking at once, agreeing with Modell's appraisal. Schmoke yielded the floor to Moag.

"Mr. Modell, we think we've put together a top-notch proposal. And let me tell you, I don't think you are wrong to think it is a phenomenal deal for you, and one which we can get done here in Baltimore and in Maryland. I think all sides come out winners in this deal."

The man seated behind Modell lowered his head slightly, the better to conceal the knowing smile spreading across his face.

"Well," Lerner spoke up, "I think it's time we got out some pens!"

Modell reached into the breast pocket of his suit jacket and retrieved the pen he had lifted over thirty years ago from the man seated behind him. He had no idea of its origin or significance. It was just a pen he sometimes carried around. He liked the weight of it, the "heft," as he said. Each party signed in the appropriate locations, and the deal was done.

## Timeline of events – October–November 1995

| Sun | Mon | Tues | Wed | Thurs | Fri | Sat |
|---|---|---|---|---|---|---|
| 22 | 23 | 24 | 25 | 26<br>World Series<br>Game 5 Indians Win | 27<br>Modell & crew fly to Baltimore and sign deal | 28<br>Braves win World Series, 4-2 |
| 29<br>Browns beat Bengals behind QB Zeier | 30<br>Parade for the Indians in Cleveland | 31 | 1 | 2<br>WBAL-TV reports Browns will move to Baltimore | 3<br>Modell addresses rumors with reporters | 4 |
| 5 | 6<br>MD officials and Art announce the move in Baltimore | 7<br>Mayor White in Dallas for NFL Owners meeting<br>Sin tax passes<br>Season ticket holders get mailing | 8 | 9 | 10 | 11 |
| 12 | 13<br>Browns Monday Night Football in Pittsburgh | 14 | 15 | 16 | 17 | 18 |
| 19<br>Baltimore Stallions win Grey Cup; Browns first home game since move news | 20 | 21 | 22 | 23 | 24 | 25 |

"Now remember, not a word of this to ANYONE until *after* our last home game on December 17," Modell said, looking each man in the eye. Everyone agreed without hesitation. It was in nobody's best interest to leak news of this before the right time.

67

# DIRECT APPEAL TO NFL TEAM OWNERS TO OVERRULE THE MOVE

TUESDAY, NOVEMBER 7, 1995

*NFL owners had descended on Dallas for a scheduled meeting. Art* Modell arrived aboard Al Lerner's jet. Yesterday, during his Baltimore press conference, Cleveland mayor Michael White vowed to fight to keep the Browns. He wasn't wasting any time. He jetted to Dallas (coach class) to attend the owners meeting himself. The owners were not scheduled to vote on allowing Modell to move until their postseason meeting in January. But this would be an ideal setting in which to lobby the owners to your side. Modell would be arguing why the other owners should let him go; White would be arguing why they should vote no.

During a break in the action, White came outside to greet the two to three dozen Browns Backers who'd shown up with picket signs to protest the move.

"Gentlemen, I can't thank you enough, the people of Cleveland can't thank you enough, for coming out here to show your support for our cause! I am gonna fight this thing. I am gonna fight it hard! I can't promise I'll be successful, but this is wrong, and I am gonna give it everything I've got."

"Give 'em hell, mayor!" someone shouted, and the small group cheered. Though White won over the crowd outside, Modell won over the fellow owners, swaying a few of the holdouts to his side.

While White was applying direct pressure to the NFL owners in Texas, U.S. Senator John Glenn of Ohio (who was also the first man to orbit the Earth) announced he was preparing to apply pressure on the NFL from Washington. He would be sponsoring the "Fan Rights Act" bill later in the week. It would require NFL team owners to announce their intent to leave their home city a full 120 days prior to committing to do so, so the incumbent city would have proper time to prepare a counteroffer. The law, once ratified, would be retroactive. Its immediate purpose was to keep the Browns in Cleveland.

Those fans in Texas used their presence, their placards, and their protest pleas in a vain effort to prevent the Browns from moving. (If ever there was a time for a prevent defense, this was it.) Meanwhile, back in Cleveland, the hometown fans sent a message to Modell through the ballot box (which was ultimately just as ineffective). The sin tax extension was overwhelmingly approved, thus securing $175 million in funding for a complete remodeling of the stadium.

The improved stadium would include a new restaurant, lounge, club seats, more loges, bathrooms that would actually be an improvement over pissing in the street and would pull the old derelict stadium out of the gutter into some semblance of respectability. Best of all it would triple the amount the city figured had been Modell's revenues to about $19 million a year—decidedly shy of his proposed haul in Baltimore, but not too shabby for a man who said he wasn't in it for the money, that he just didn't want to go broke.

In what must be one of history's top ten cosmic slaps in the face, on November 7, the very day the citizen/fans of Cleveland approved the ballot measure, proving their support of and loyalty to the Browns, season ticket holders received a mailing from the Cleveland Browns. Obviously prepared months prior and mailed "a long time ago" (according to Browns spokesman Kevin Byrne), the mailing consisted of a glossy magazine and a letter from Arthur Modell.

In the letter, Modell stated:

> As I've said many times before, our loyal fans are the envy of many National Football League clubs. As a season-ticket buyer, your support, loyalty, and interest in the Cleveland Browns is paramount in our efforts to continue the strong and enduring tradition of our team.

Ouch.

To that injury, Chris Widmaier, director of corporate communications at NFL Properties, added this insult:

> In 1982, the clubs agreed to also have us do their licensing, and we have the right to use the trademarks and logos of all 30 teams. The Cleveland Browns are a trademark name, and they will retain that name in Baltimore. Any illegal or unauthorized use of a trademark name is aggressively pursued by us.

In other words, if Art moves his team to Baltimore, the "Browns" name and the colors go with him. The history, the legacy, the loyalty of the Cleveland fans means nothing.

Double ouch.

Speaking with *Baltimore Sun* reporters on November 7, Modell said: "I will say right now, I'm certain Bill Belichick will coach this team next year. I'm a great believer in continuity. I think he's done a good job."

One must wonder: Would the legend Bill Belichick have ever been born had Modell dragged Coach MyWay with him to Baltimore?

Sneaking into Browns headquarters the day after flying in from the Dallas owners meetings, Modell tried to turn the focus to football. He addressed the players for fifteen minutes or so while in Berea, urging them to close out the season like winners, despite the distractions. He also told them:

> I will be generous to all of you in our move to Baltimore. We will work with each of you individually, and we will treat you with generosity and compassion. We will make this move as smooth as we can for you. We will review every player's needs and problems. We will have a facility that will match and, if possible, be better than this one. We will do everything possible to give you an environment that helps winning.

He then urged the players to try to salvage the season:

> I challenge you and appeal to your pride to play your rear ends off in the next seven games. We can still win the division. I'm not asking you to win for me or anything like that. I'm asking you to win for yourselves. We want to go to Baltimore as winners. From the bottom of my heart, I ask you to play for yourselves, to play with passion, to play to win.
>
> I appeal to the veterans on this team. You know what it takes to win late in the season. Teach that to our younger players. We can make a statement to the whole country Monday night in Pittsburgh. Do that for yourselves.

Most players were shocked to see the team owner in the building. Generally, they had favorable impressions of his impassioned speech. Several players, however, divulged to reporters that "a storm has been brewing" on the team that predated the news of the move, that if "not corrected, could tear the team apart."

## 68

# IN SOLIDARITY WITH THE ENEMY
# OR
# THE FUNERAL CARAVAN

NOVEMBER 13, 1995

*A caravan of thirteen buses, led and tailed by motorcycle cops, departed* Cleveland for Pittsburgh around 4 p.m. on Monday. Plenty of passenger cars joined the parade. Organizer Duane Salls, chairman of the Save Our Browns Committee, warned the somber guests ahead of time: "We're asking everyone to be ladies and gentlemen. If that doesn't happen, we'll blow our case. If you're coming to have a drunken party, you're not invited."

Through history, most every caravan to an NFL game has been a joyful procession, akin to a wedding celebration. This trip felt more like a funeral. The fans had serious work to do. They would hold a protest outside the Steelers' Three Rivers Stadium prior to the ABC telecast of *Monday Night Football,* in yet another bid to convince the NFL team owners to vote no on the proposed move during their January 1996 meeting.

This was the game that both teams had circled before the season started. Cleveland saw Pittsburgh, who had knocked the Browns out of the playoffs last year and had beaten them two more times in the previous regular season, as the last hurdle for the Browns. If they could beat Pittsburgh, they could potentially go all the way. Pittsburgh, like everyone, saw the Browns' growth in 1994 and expected them to challenge for the Central and, if they could get past Pittsburgh, the NFL title. Plus, there was a lifetime of rivalry. Each team was the one the other loved to hate.

On this strange day, cats and dogs got along, the lion laid down with the lamb, Drew Carey and nemesis Mimi became fast friends—and none of it was as weird as the scene at Three Rivers Stadium. As Cleveland Mayor Mike White was boosted by fans onto a concrete platform in the Three Rivers parking lot to address the band of travelers, he was struck by the sight of Steelers fans standing in harmony with their rivals. Many Pittsburghers wore orange arm bands in solidarity. As Clevelanders shouted "Save Our Browns," and "No Team, No Peace," some of them crying, more than a handful of the Steelers' faithful used their Terrible Towels to dry their own tears.

Inside the stadium, it was a different story. Primal passion won out in the stands, and the Western Pennsylvanians wished nothing but misery upon their kindred fans from Northeast Ohio. The hometown fans, though, were downright hospitable to the few visiting Clevelanders compared to the merciless 20-3 beatdown the Steelers players inflicted upon their rivals.

Bill Belichick was now 0-5 at Three Rivers, and his team had now lost five straight regular season contests to the measuring stick in their division. Coach MyWay's Hail Mary of sacking Vinny Testaverde in favor of rookie Eric Zeier was now exposed as idiocy, as the young quarterback completed only seven passes for 67 yards for the game. It looked like a storm was indeed brewing on this Browns team.

Back in Berea during the week after the Steelers game, Art Modell was miserable:

"I could be ruined, I could be ruined, ah hell, what have I done? I thought I had financial problems before! I should have worked with these bastards. Why couldn't they just treat me with the consideration I deserved? Now everybody in Cleveland is suing me!"

He was ranting. He was raving. The mounting losses were wearing on him. The prime-time flops were making matters worse. But that was just his football team. They'd had bad seasons before. What really clamped Modell in a tightening vice was the ever-growing docket of lawsuits. "It's miserable to lose to the Steelers—for the sixth time in a row—by a lopsided score on *Monday Night Football.* It's quite another to have a $1.9 billion lawsuit brought against you! And that was the *ninth* move-related lawsuit. *So far!*"

Al Lerner was the yin to Modell's yang. "Calm down, Art, we'll negotiate out of this some way. Look at Georgia Frontiere. For Pete's sake, look at Al Davis! Nobody held them back. It's still a free country, and we'll find an acceptable way to get outta this, I promise you."

Modell was mostly emotion, Lerner strictly bottom line.

"Art, this has all been mapped out," he said. "Stay the course."

## 69

# BALTIMORE LOSES A WINNER

NOVEMBER 19, 1995

***On the very same day the professional football team from Baltimore*** won the league championship in front of a stadium filled with 52,000 fans, with millions more tuning in on TV from across the continent, the Browns played their first home game since news of the move had hit like a bomb.

Oh, the irony! That the Baltimore Stallions, freshly minted Grey Cup Champions of the Canadian Football League (CFL), would soon be displaced by this dysfunctional team from Cleveland. For the fans in Baltimore, was losing the CFL champions to get *this* NFL franchise really an upgrade? So, not only were Cleveland Browns fans having their beloved team torn from their city, so were the Baltimore Stallions fans!

The Browns were apparently trying to make their departure from Cleveland easier for their Ohio fan base. Brett Favre and the Packers pounded the Browns 31-20. Coach MyWay's answer at quarterback floundered again, and Bill Belichick reluctantly replaced Eric Zeier with the 3-1 Vinny Testaverde.

With every bad play, the stands would erupt with the taunt, "Muck Fodell" (or something like that). The heckling would have been worse, but over 15,000 tickets went unused, and half the crowd that *did* show up was swaddled in the green and yellow garb and wedge-shaped headwear of the visitors.

The proud Jim Brown, who had quit football rather than bow to the demands of a young Art Modell, now supported him. When he jogged off the field after the game, a fan shouted, "You're leaving this city behind, Jim!"

He retorted "I ain't leaving nothin!"

The Browns, the early season Super Bowl favorite, were in free fall. They'd lost six of the previous seven games and would lose four out of the next five, finishing the season at 5-11, the worst record of the underwhelming Belichick era. The lone bright spot would be the final game ever played at Cleveland Stadium, against Cincinnati, one week before Christmas Eve.

Modell had opened the Browns' new office in Baltimore on December 8, 1995. However, with preliminary court injunctions in place designed to prevent the move, with lawsuits pending, and with NFL Commissioner Paul Tagliabue declaring that Modell's deal with Baltimore "may not be that ironclad," nobody knew for sure that this would be the last time the Browns played in Cleveland. Just the same, an ominous shroud of finality hung over the field like a thick dark cloud.

70

# CLEVELAND BROWNS' FINAL HOME GAME

December 17, 1995—Cleveland Municipal Stadium

*All the advertisers had pulled out. There were no signs pitching beer,* cigarettes, hot dogs, or auto insurance. Some of the lighted signs had their translucent glass or plexiglass fronts slid out from their fixtures, reversed, and slid back into place. The result was a faded and backward representation of the advertisers' logos . . . how fitting for this team. Other signs were painted over with black spray paint. This was not due to petty, mindless vandalism. Advertisers had stopped paying, not wanting to be associated with this act of betrayal.

National media descended on the stadium as though this were a playoff or championship game. Three New York newspapers sent reporters, as did the *Tampa Tribune*. CNN and ESPN were on hand. *Sports Illustrated*, who'd picked this team for the Super Bowl just four months prior, and who'd placed a cartoon of Art Modell punching a fan in the stomach on its cover just a few issues earlier, sent a cadre to record the historic occasion.

Former Browns players quarterback Brian Sipe and defensive lineman Jerry Sherk of the Kardiac Kids era fifteen years earlier drove cross-country from San Diego on an odyssey that culminated at the stadium on this day of infamy. They videorecorded interviews with fans and former players throughout their travels, unleashing an outpouring of emotion all across the country.

"Man, this place *is* a dump," Sipe said to Sherk when they arrived.

"Yeah, but it's *our* dump," Sherk said.

"Man, I loved playing here!" Sipe said. "As bad as the field was . . . the baseball infield, and the damp locker rooms—"

"The fans were the best," Sherk said. "The Dawg Pound!"

"How about running out of that tunnel?" the old quarterback queried, his eyes fixed in the thousand-yard stare of recollection.

"Yeah, like running into the Roman Coliseum—the roar! Man, that gives me goosebumps just thinking about it!"

They fell silent for a moment.

"That's what makes this whole thing so unbelievable," Sherk said. "The fans are really getting the shaft."

"What if we could pull off a last-second comeback, like the Kardiac Kids? What if somehow the NFL, or the courts, or even old Modell himself reversed this whole thing?" Sipe was almost starting to believe it could happen.

"Brian, I like where you are going with this, but you gotta remember, the Kardiac Kids lost some last-second games too."

In some ways, today's opponent, the visiting Cincinnati Bengals, had reason for contemplation and mourning in nearly equal measure with the Browns and their fans. The visiting team's owner, Mike Brown, and head coach, Dave Shula (each the son of one of the top three coaches in the history of professional football) both had sanguine memories ingrained in them as boys that involved the Browns and Cleveland Stadium.

Bengals owner Mike Brown was the son of Paul Brown, the founder and namesake of the team that his current team would be playing today. He remembered attending the very first Browns training camp at Bowling Green University. He was around the team through its historic success under his father's watch, all the way up until 1962 when the Browns' current owner, who was now ripping the team away from the city that loved it, fired his father, the coach the city loved.

The very first NFL game that current Bengals head coach Dave Shula attended was the 1964 Colts/Browns NFL Championship Game. His dad, Don Shula, coached the heavily favored Baltimore squad. When five-year-old David accompanied his father into the post-game Colts locker room, it was the first time he saw grown men cry. It was one of his first memories and it was burned into his consciousness.

The December air was charged with a dangerous electricity. Over 55,000 grieving, helpless, angry and increasingly intoxicated fans could overwhelm any attempts at crowd control, even though security had been reinforced for this contest. There was an impending feeling not just of melancholic loss but of doom. The Rolling Stones concert at Altamont. The Who concert in Cincinnati. Fans had died at those events. It felt like something was going to go wrong. Very wrong.

Instead, it was a rare Cleveland victory! After a scoreless first quarter, the Browns took control, and the game's outcome was never really in doubt from the middle of the second quarter. Had the action been reversed, there's no telling what carnage may have ensued. Still, danger abounded. Fans, equipped with wrenches, were tearing out sections of seating. Each bench was a heavy row of maybe eight ancient wooden seats with metal legs and armrests. These were being passed overhead from the back rows, down, row by row, and eventually were tossed onto the field. (Talk about rearranging the deck chairs on the *Titanic*!)

Pay too much attention watching the action on the field and you could end up crushed under the weight of history—and about 300 pounds of wooden slats, metal castings, and sixty coats of paint. Fans also ravaged the bathrooms; each one of them was nearly completely destroyed, resulting in close to $8.00 in damage. Okay, maybe $8.00 is a slight exaggeration. If you remember the condition of those restrooms, with their rusty metal troughs, the damage might have been closer to $4.50.

When the game was over, the Browns had prevailed 26-10. In no way did the Bengals "throw the game"; they were there to win. But their primary aim that afternoon had to have been to simply get out of Cleveland Stadium alive.

Bengals owner Mike Brown put it best: "In a way, the event outweighed the game. We were not trying to please the fans . . . we were trying to win the game. When it was over, I was angry until I thought maybe this is the best way. They go out on a high note. The crowd loves them, hugs the players if you will, and it's over."

In the waning daylight shortly after the game was over, fans stayed in their seats (if their seat hadn't been heaved overboard). Most players seemed to want to linger just as much as the fans did. Earnest Byner, whose fumble in the 1987 AFC Championship Game had been one of the most heartrending events in the team's history, had had a great game—his first 100-yard game in three years. He seemed to be the most grateful of any of the players. He headed to the left side of the

Dawg Pound and made his way, around its arc, all the way to the right side.

Along the way, he connected with fans. They'd been just as much a part of his trials and triumphs as he had. They had felt his anguish as he had. They had learned to forgive him as he had learned to forgive himself (although it took him longer). "We love you, Earnest!" And when they said it, they said it in earnest. He noticed tears running down fans' faces. Holy tears of absolution, of communion.

Left tackle Tony Jones, all 290 pounds of him, navigated to the Dawg Pound. He tossed a football to a particular fan: *The Fan*. You could accurately call him the Browns' *biggest* fan: "Big Dawg" John Thompson outweighed the hulking offensive lineman who'd tossed him the pigskin by an easy 100 pounds. Big Dawg took off his trademark dog mask, confirming what could easily be gleaned by watching his massive shoulders shudder, his chest heave. He was bawling his eyes out.

In this business of sports, especially with the owner pulling the rug out from under the whole big party, it was easy to forget the heart, the love, the appreciation, and the respect that continued to make the game vital. In this moment, all the corruption wrought by big money, all the cynicism borne from self-serving agendas, all the frustration of never having made the Super Bowl . . . it all faded away. It was like a funeral: What really matters but is so rarely acknowledged in day-to-day life—matters of heart and soul—come sharply into focus.

A week later, the Browns closed the season, and an era, on the road—in expansion city Jacksonville. The Jaguars had lost seven in a row, most recently by 44 points to Detroit. The last time the Jags had won was against the Browns, way back in October. Win or lose, Jacksonville was assured the worst record in the AFC Central. Yet as this final game of this final season of the original Cleveland Browns wound down, the Jags were positioned to go for a rare season win. The fourth win in their short history.

With scant seconds left in the game, and with the score tied at 21, the Jags' field goal attempt clanged off the upright and fell away. But wait! The Browns were offsides. For good measure, *two* Browns players were offsides. From closer range, with no time remaining, the field goal sailed through. The Browns had lost. The Browns had lost to this expansion team, the team with the worst record in the NFL, twice in the same season. The Super Bowl favorite just months before finished the season at 5-11. The team that had been as synonymous with its hometown as any in sports was about to be no more.

And that was it. It was over. Fans and Cleveland politicians held out a faint ray of hope that the courts or NFL owners would block the move. But they rightly sensed it couldn't be stopped now.

# SOMEWHERE THERE'S A FAT LADY SINGING

## After Fifty Years, It's All Over

***The fire was out. A few embers of hope and unfinished business pulsed*** on occasion, while glowing ever duller orange. The NFL owners had their meeting and approved the Browns' move. Mayor White blew some hot air over the coals, trying in vain to keep the Browns' home fires burning in Cleveland. John "Big Dawg" Thompson testified before Congress in Washington in support of two bills that Ohio lawmakers had introduced, designed to keep the Browns in Cleveland or at least salvage some kind of compensation.

In early February, the last ember of hope that the Browns would stay in Cleveland died, but not before kicking off an orange spark that would be carried aloft, destined to eventually glow again by the lakeside. That spark was the three-way deal made between Art Modell, the City of Cleveland, and the NFL.

The negotiated settlement would avoid the looming lawsuits and allow Modell to move his team to Baltimore—thus the ember had burned out; there was no way this team was staying in Cleveland. But the living spark was that he would agree to leave the "Cleveland Browns" name behind, along with the team colors and all its rich history. The NFL would benefit by being protected from anti-trust and other lawsuits.

"The new team, whether expansion or existing, will bear the name of the Cleveland Browns," Mayor Michael White said. "They will wear the colors of the Cleveland Browns. They will be the Cleveland Browns."

So, now, it was truly over. The team formerly known as the Cleveland Browns was gone forever. Yet there was a spark of hope. A promise. A seed that would land sometime in the next three years by the lakeside. The new Cleveland Browns, clad in orange, white, and brown, and harkening back to their glory days, would one day be born anew.

72

# AFTER IT WAS OVER, BUT BEFORE IT BEGAN

FEBRUARY 12, 1996, BALTIMORE'S NEW HEADQUARTERS

*Art Modell hadn't slept well since the November announcement, and,* truthfully, for weeks leading up to it. Even if he hadn't convinced anyone in Cleveland that he was forced to make the move, that he had no alternative, now, as a matter of sanity, as a matter of survival, he had convinced himself that he was a victim in the whole ordeal. The *victim*. This allowed him some measure of satisfaction with his new situation. A satisfaction that had been lacking for months despite the financial windfall that lay like an open chest of gold beside Baltimore's Inner Harbor.

The moving vans from Cleveland had relocated everything from Berea to the new headquarters in Charm City. Some of it had even been put away. As Modell sat down this morning in the new Baltimore HQ, he *really* wanted to find that contract from 1964. However, that could wait. He had one objective for this day. He'd have to break his word, an assurance that he'd given only several weeks ago. But then again, just like with his (broken) promise to never move the Browns from Cleveland, he had to absolve himself. He was not culpable of breaking his promise; circumstances had changed.

He pulled out an accordion folder labeled "Coaching Search 1991" from one of the filing cabinets. Modell had decided: He was going to fire Bill Belichick. He knew that doing so would break his pledge not to fire his head coach and would oblige him to pay off the rest of Belichick's contract—one that ironically was originally set to expire at the end of the 1995 season, but which Modell had voluntarily extended by two years. Modell wanted to see the fine print. Would he owe him $1.8 million exactly? $1.75 million? $1.85 million?

Modell unwound the little string that held the bulging folder closed. The first paper he pulled out was the cryptic fax from the final frantic moments of the search back in '91. Modell's mind harkened back to that frenzied time. The fax was a copy of part of the old "contract" from 1964; the contract that supposedly won the championship for the Browns but seemed to be exacting a heavy price ever since. Modell saw the reference to Blanton Collier, to winning the 1964 championship, and the prediction that Collier would never win the big one again. All of which had come true.

Then he saw something that shocked him! Something that would make perfect sense in a few minutes but was enigmatic and seemingly meaningless when he'd read it in 1991. He saw the warning against Mike White: "If you make a move on Mike White, he will fight you tooth and nail." Modell remembered Mike White, quarterback coach with the Raiders in 1991, was a head coaching finalist they had been strongly considering instead of Belichick. The next sentence seemed redundant: "Don't make a big move you will forever regret because of Michael R. White."

Art read the name aloud, "Michael R. White. Michael *R.* White? Michael R. White is the *mayor*!"

He yelled down the hall to his son.

"David, find out the middle name of Mike White—the Mike White we almost hired as head coach instead of Belichick."

"What? What on earth do you need that for?"

"The Mike White that was with Bill Walsh in San Francisco back in the late seventies. I just think it's funny there is a Mike White coach and a Mike White mayor in Cleveland. Just find out, alright!"

The younger Modell, outside of the old man's earshot, rolled his eyes, thinking, *Oh, this is important stuff! Watch out NFL. This new Baltimore team is really doing some important research to get the year started.*

Art continued reading the contract. He wondered if the splotches of ink all over it were a result of aging, or if they had been there all along. In this moment, he didn't remember them being there initially. His interpolation of the obscured passages revealed a glowing recommendation of Bill Belichick. It talked about him winning 70 percent of his games in Cleveland. Only the "land" was visible, the "Cleve" was covered with a blot of ink, but Art could piece it together.

"What a crock!" Belichick had amassed the second-worst record of any Browns coach (excluding several future coaches of the New Browns). "He had only one winning season out of five for crying out loud!"

"'He will rule his era,'" Art read. "'He will make people forget all about Paul Brown'—what a laugh!" Only Art was not laughing. He was furious.

"This contract is a crock of $hit! It's full of lies!" Art remembered this fax clearly now. He even remembered that it was littered with splotches when he first saw it. This section of the contract outlined all the promises that had swung him to hire Belichick. Now he saw all these promises were too good to have been true. He was seething. He couldn't wait to call Belichick to tell him he was fired. He didn't care now if he owed him $1.8 million or $1.85 million or $185 million! He wanted him gone!

"'Rule his era,' my ass! He'll never be a head coach in this league again!"

"Dad. Dad. Hello?" Consumed in his anger, Art hadn't heard David calling to him from the door to his office.

"Uh, yes, what is it?"

"Kavanaugh."

"Kavanaugh? Who the hell is Kavanaugh?"

"Mike White's middle name is Kavanaugh. Michael K. White."

"Oh. Oh yeah, Mike White, the other Mike White, from Oakland. . . . Uh, thanks, David."

David walked away thinking the move had finally driven his old man completely insane. He shook his head as he mused, *What the hell does he care about this Michael K. White guy?*

Art sank in his chair. His anger rapidly gave way to dread. So, the Mike White referenced in the fax was Mike White the mayor, Michael *R.* White. Art studied the fax: "If you make a move on Mike White, he'll fight you tooth and nail." Art reread the sentence.

Images from November 1995 through February 1996 flashed in his head. Michael R. White vowing to oppose Art's move from behind a makeshift podium at the Baltimore Marriott. Michael R. White in Dallas, rallying protesting Browns fans at the owners meeting. Michael

R. White on TV. Michael R. White in Washington, DC, testifying before Congress. Fighting. Fighting against Modell. Fighting Modell's move. Fighting tooth and nail.

Art's brow dripped with sweat. His mind raced. A moment ago, the sender of this fax, the author of this contract, had seemed a rank liar or an extremely poor prognosticator. Its author had been way off the mark on Belichick, but he was dead on regarding the fight in Michael R. White. And that word "*move.*" "Don't make a big *move* you will regret because of Michael R. White." The move had been *because of* Michael R. White—well, him and the rest of the Cleveland City Fathers' neglect and disrespect toward Art. Had Art remained the toast of the town, he would have worked through the finances to stay in Cleveland.

Art thought back to the original impetus behind talking with Al Lerner about reaching out to the Baltimore Stadium Authority. It had been this same inscrutable character who had authored the faxed contract that Art now reviewed. Why was it that every time Art dealt with this guy, he felt delusional?

Art—who had just turned the corner and had convinced himself that he had made the right choice in moving—now was terrified he may have made the wrong choice. He called Al Lerner for assurance that he'd made the right decision in leaving Cleveland for Baltimore. Lerner didn't answer. Art, elbows on the desk, stared blankly downward, holding his head in his hands, when his office phone rang.

"Mr. Modell, how are you finding your new offices?" Art recognized the haunting voice at once.

"They're fine. My office in Berea was tough to leave. That was a nice facility."

"Arthur, your voice. You seem troubled. I should think you'd be delighted. That was quite a deal you got to move to Baltimore."

"Well, you wouldn't know what I've gone through."

"I suppose I wouldn't. I do have some very good news for your though."

"What is it? I could use some."

"Well, let's just say the scales are balanced."

"What? What do you mean? What is the meaning of 'the scales are balanced'?"

"By rights, you should have lost to Baltimore in 1964. But we made a deal, and you and your team were able to win your first championship.

That was great. For you, for your team. For Cleveland. But not so good for the Colts or for Baltimore. I should say that Baltimore has gotten its revenge now, wouldn't you, Mr. Modell?"

"Well, I don't know if I'd look at it that way—"

"Well, of course you should. It's the ultimate revenge, with compound interest. Your team beat theirs, but then their city steals your fans' entire team. It's poetic! And best of all you were instrumental in making it happen. And now you are very rich for your part in all this."

"I was forced into this by my finances!"

"Relax, Art. I want you to know that whatever debt you owed has been paid, you are free of any, shall I say, 'outside' influence on your team's fortunes."

"I am not sure I follow you."

"It's alright, Arthur. Just know that your new team will win or lose or draw on its own merits. And for you personally, I will have no further hand in your fate. Your own decisions will dictate your personal circumstances."

Art just sighed heavily. He'd resolved to fire Belichick this very day when he'd come in this morning. Now he was exhausted. Tomorrow he'd fly back to his safe haven in West Palm Beach. Now, mentally and spiritually depleted, he knew he'd need to defer the inevitable until he got there.

73

# MYWAY, MEET HIGHWAY

VALENTINE'S DAY 1996

***Bernie Kosar had been like a son to Art Modell throughout the second*** half of the eighties and the early nineties. But that paternalistic love was superseded by Modell's rapturous infatuation with Bill Belichick, the coach that Modell hired to a five-year contract in 1991, then preemptively extended for an additional two years before its expiration. When Coach MyWay heaved Kosar over the side of the USS *Cleveland Browns*, Modell didn't so much as throw Bernie a life preserver. Instead, he feted Captain MyWay, convinced he would navigate his team over the horizon to the elusive Promised Land.

With two years left on Belichick's contract and with an earlier pledge by the owner that Belichick would be his coach after the move to Baltimore, it seemed Coach MyWay would soon be coaching just thirty miles north of where his earliest memories were formed as his father, Steve, coached the U.S. Naval Academy. Bill Belichick had lived in Annapolis from the age of four, right through his graduation from Annapolis High.

Modell, in his West Palm Beach home, was pacing. It was 6 a.m. Pat was still fast asleep. She didn't realize it was Valentine's Day because she was still slumbering; her husband didn't realize because he was preoccupied.

"How much later do I need to wait before I call him?" Art wondered aloud, to nobody but himself. "He never sleeps during the season."

More pacing, then finally he decided that the time was right, even if it wasn't.

He pressed the numbers. He heard the electronic tones indicating the phone was ringing in the Belichick residence. Four full rings. Art was ready for the answering machine to kick on. He wasn't going to leave a message. That would be too low. As Art prepared to hang up, resolved to call back in fifteen minutes, lo and behold, the man he was seeking answered.

"Hello," the gruff coach answered, groggily.

"Bill!" Modell instinctively let out a glib salutation. Then he found himself shifting down several gears to a more appropriate, somber tone.

"Bill, this is Art Modell." As if he needed to identify himself with his full name. Nerves were getting to him.

"Yeah, hi, Art. It's kinda early, isn't it?"

"Bill, I called to say how much I've appreciated all you've done for me. For the Cleveland Browns these last five years. Especially this last one. It's really been a crazy ride. . . ."

Belichick, his grogginess wearing off, was trying to size up what was going on. Something told him that the man who'd hired him wouldn't call and wake him up just to give him words of praise. Belichick's forehead furrowed. Suddenly, he feared the worst.

"Art, are you calling to wish me a Happy Valentine's Day?"

This knocked Modell off script. "What? *Valentine's Day*?"

"You're calling to *fire me*! Is that what this is?"

"Bill, I believe we need to make a fresh start. With this move to Baltimore, now is the right time to make the change."

"Art, every coach knows this can happen, but this doesn't make sense. No coach could've won last year with the move hangin' over everyone's head. With that settled, and with the players we have now, I know we can win big next year."

"Bill, this is very hard for me. I really believed in you. And I still do. I think you will be a great coach in this league someday. But we just need to go in a different direction next year."

"This sucks! This really sucks! You know there isn't a coach out there that could have done anything under those circumstances. Not even Vince Lombardi. Or Paul Brown. Or Don Shula!"

"Bill, look, I didn't want to get into this. But we were favored to go to the Super Bowl last year when the season started. And I know the move upset the apple cart. But we were only 4-4 before word got out. And we'd already lost to the expansion team from Jacksonville, for crying out loud! Bill, I don't want this to get personal. But my decision is final."

Belichick's mind was racing. You don't get to be an NFL coach if you are not a fierce competitor, and every instinct in him urged him to fight. But instead of going for the jugular, he went for the heartstrings: "Art, you just extended me. When my contract wasn't even up, and you extended it out two more years. That's the faith you had in me. You know I will be successful, and soon, now that the move is all settled."

Art had to end this discussion fast. He didn't want to be talked out of what he'd resolved to do. He genuinely believed Coach MyWay would be an exceptional coach one day. He also knew that he wanted *his* coach to be a better part of the community. To not only win but to be collegial with the reporters. Since news of the move broke, Modell had been cast in the role of the villain, a role to which he was not accustomed and didn't like. He didn't want any part of his organization to play that role.

"Bill, I'm sorry. I really am. But my decision is final. I wish you the best of luck."

Belichick considered laying into his (former?) boss with all he had in him. After making a few facial contortions, and trying to decide exactly what to say, he instead just slammed down the receiver.

"He'll be sorry!" Belichick said. "I will coach somebody to the Super Bowl before he ever gets there!"

If he meant as a head coach, he was wrong about that.

# THE BALTIMORE . . . RAVENS

MARCH 29, 1996

*On the twelve-year anniversary of that day that shall live in infamy in* Baltimore history—the night that the caravan of moving vans, bound for Indianapolis, ripped the Colts from their fans—a group of team officials accompanied Art Modell for the announcement. A few hundred expectant fans hid from the drizzle under umbrellas beside Baltimore's Inner Harbor. They and 33,000 of their fandom flock had voted on the name for Baltimore's new NFL team. The winning entry garnered around two-thirds of the phone-in vote.

From behind the lectern that held a half-dozen microphones, the smiling owner held up a sign that measured no more than 12 inches wide by 6 inches high. At the top, centered on the page, was the NFL shield logo. And beneath it, tap, tap, tapping into the city's literary past was the team's name: *Ravens*. Edgar Allen Poe's famous poem had haunted readers for over 150 years to this point. Fans of the Cleveland Browns hoped Art Modell's new franchise would not be haunting their lives forevermore.

75

# RAVENS' FIRST DRAFT IS ONE FOR THE AGES

April 20, 1996

*The City of Cleveland had (unwillingly) gifted the City of Baltimore* with a football team. The gifting didn't end when moving vans arrived in Baltimore. This was the gift that kept on giving. By virtue of Cleveland's terrible 1995 record—which would not have been nearly as bad if the football team hadn't been extracted from Cleveland like a rotting molar—the team formerly known as the Browns had earned the number four selection in the 1996 draft. The Baltimore Ravens would be the beneficiaries of the Browns' pathetic performance.

The Cleveland Browns hadn't drafted a Hall of Fame player since selecting tight end Ozzie Newsome in 1978. Now Baltimore's director of football operations was none other than Ozzie Newsome. In this capacity, "the Wizard" would be responsible for conducting his team's inaugural draft. With the Baltimore Ravens' first-ever draft pick, he selected a Hall of Famer, offensive tackle Jonathan Ogden.

Newsome then spent the Ravens' second first-round pick (acquired when Bill Belichick and the Browns panicked last year and were fleeced by the 49ers) on one of the most dominant linebackers of all time: Ray Lewis. It was still early going on this first day of the draft, and the Ravens had made two draft picks in their history. The Wizard was two for two; both selections were destined to be enshrined in the Pro Football Hall of Fame! A few years later, he would pick another Hall of Famer, Ed Reed, before the New Browns would finally nab one in Joe Thomas, despite Cleveland having much higher draft picks each year.

76

# TRAINING CAMP MINUS THE TRAINING

## Echo of a Glorious Past

*The first hint that fall awaits comes in the middle of July every year.* Just as February's MLB spring training presages summer swelter, the annual NFL training camp rite reminds nervous kids that school is just around the corner. Every adult cringes with the realization that they'll be raking leaves before they know it. Each year, in every NFL city, mid-July is filled with hope. Eighty or so players scrimmage and toil, eventually to be cut down to the final fifty-three who make the final roster just before the season starts.

On July 14, 1996, eighty or so players descended on Hiram College, which was the site of the Browns' training camp from 1952 to 1974. You could say not even one of them was a rookie. Just like any other team's training camp, plenty of fans came to gather autographs. This humble Division III collegiate football field was the same setting where a nine-year-old Bill Belichick had watched Jim Brown practice during the 1961 training camp. This same Jim Brown, now thirty-five years older, had altered his busy schedule to be here today, along with about eighty other proud Cleveland Browns.

The difference between this gathering and all the other NFL training camps: These players were all retired, many of them for decades. A few, like Jim Brown, Dante Lavelli, and Lou Groza, were legends. Many others had barely been backups when they played and were remembered only by a handful of the gathered fans. Instead of scrimmaging and running drills, there would be picnicking and reminiscing.

Each former player traveled on his own dime, and all the autographs would be signed for free.

This was no corporate money-grubbing scheme. The once mighty and glorious team of which these former players had been vital parts had died. After a fifty-year run, which was supposed to last forever, their team had ceased to exist. Having moped impotently through nine months of mourning, today was a celebration of life. A time to reflect on all the past glory, all the achievements, all the memories.

When Art Modell moved the team, the men who had played here in Northeast Ohio felt the need to right a wrong as best they could. They felt called to assure themselves and the fans that the recent move—as painful as it was—didn't negate the past, didn't diminish them, didn't invalidate the fans' memories. The reunion was cherished by fans and clearly meant the world to the retired players.

Ed Modzelewski, backup fullback from forty years prior, told the *Plain Dealer*'s Tony Grossi: "I am so overwhelmed by this. I'm getting a bigger thrill out of this than the people. This feeling is hard to describe. I remember feeling like this only two other times—being introduced in the stadium the first time and playing in the 1955 NFL championship."

The next day, NFL training camp fields in all NFL cities were sweaty, smelly, noisy beehives of activity. Hiram College's field was again empty, silent.

A few weeks later, on August 10, Roy Firestone interviewed Art Modell on his ESPN show.

A defiant Modell explained his rationale for move—that he was taken for granted by the city when it was taking care of the Indians and Cavaliers. The one regret that Modell expressed was that he'd never make it to the Pro Football Hall of Fame because of the move. "I know it will never happen now," he said. "I can't even go to Canton if I wanted to. I can't step foot in Ohio. I know because of this deal that I'll never get to the Hall of Fame, and I thought about it when I made this deal, and it was the hardest position of all to come to grips with. And I feel very sad about that."

77

# THE FIRST SIGN OF A NEW STADIUM

October 15, 1996

*Ten months after he was seen bawling in the Dawg Pound, in the after-*math of the last game ever played at Cleveland Municipal Stadium, Big Dawg John Thompson bought a private seat license for the yet-to-be-built new Browns stadium. The PSL was a new scheme for charging people for the right to buy a season ticket. Big Dawg bought his for $250—the cheapest one—"only one I can afford," he said. He was dubious of the NFL consultant's comments that "PSL owners felt more significantly bonded with their team." "B.S.! They should have just said they need them to build the new stadium," Thompson said. "At least it's taxing the people who will use it, and not the whole city." The Browns' "biggest fan," who since that tear-filled day last December had testified in front of the U.S. Congress in a vain effort to keep the Browns in Cleveland, was accused by some of being a turncoat. Some whined that he was like a beaten dog who nonetheless would wag its tail while running back to its abusive owner to lick his face.

"No way I sold out! When they moved it hurt like hell. But what can we do? We have to move on."

78

# SHUFFLIN' OFF TO BUFFALO

NOVEMBER 17, 1996

*"Big Dawg" John Thompson was not waiting for a new stadium to be* built in Cleveland, nor for a new Browns team to begin play. He was ready for some football! Fortunately for Big Dawg, Buffalo Bills owner Ralph Wilson, the only owner other than Pittsburgh's Dan Rooney to vote against Modell moving the Browns to Baltimore, had declared today's Bills matchup versus the Bengals as "Browns Day."

Wilson may have gotten the idea for this gracious act last December when the Big Dawg had attended the Miami vs. Buffalo game and had handed out about 2,000 "Save our Browns" yard signs. Buffalo's fans had enthusiastically waved the signs and chanted with Big Dawg during timeouts. Wilson made about 5,000 tickets available to Browns fans for today's game, and about half were snapped up.

One year and four days prior (though it seemed an eternity), a sad caravan of buses had convoyed to Pittsburgh to protest the Browns' impending move to Baltimore. Today, a convergence of chartered buses and vans from Cleveland and various Ohio cities and towns motored to Interstate 90 and rambled happily east toward Rich Stadium in Orchard Park. Big Dawg was one of the fans clad in brown and orange shuffling off to Buffalo to accept this unique invitation.

When he and the 2,500 or so Browns Backers got to the game, they were welcomed like kings. Buffalo, another Rust Belt city on the Great Lakes, had a fan base that could identify with the fans of Cleveland. It wasn't just the Buffalo fans that made the Clevelanders feel at home.

Wilson and his staff rolled out the red carpet and made the Cleveland contingent feel right at home.

"The Bills brought in the Massillon Washington High School marching band and had Andrew Butts perform the national anthem as he used to do in Cleveland. Fairview Park American Legion Post 738 presented the colors. Former Browns Tony Adamle, Bubba Baker, Herman Fontenot, Bryan Wagner, Felix Wright, and Dante Lavelli were introduced before the game, Lavelli handling the coin toss. John 'Big Dawg' Thompson got a nice response when he fired up his followers."

Just about every Browns fan rooted for Buffalo. If, for some reason, someone wasn't when they got there, they were by the time they left for home. The Bills prevailed 31-17, claiming sole possession of first place in the AFC East in the process. The *Plain Dealer*'s Tony Grossi reported that jubilant Bills players, led by their star quarterback, Jim Kelley, "trotted to the 'relocated' Dawg Pound at one end zone and saluted the Clevelanders who accepted owner Ralph Wilson's invitation to the game":

> "We just wanted to show our appreciation [to the Clevelanders] for coming," said running back Thurman Thomas. "We know they're upset with losing their team. We wanted to make them feel at home."
>
> "Everybody's thanking me," Wilson said of the Cleveland faithful, "but I'm thanking them. "Tell the people of Cleveland we appreciate them."

## 79

# DEMOLITION

### In Memory of Cleveland Municipal Stadium

***What had transpired at Rich Stadium was uplifting, heartwarming,*** affirming, and restored one's hope that NFL was about football and fellowship, not profit, and that all was right in the world. In short, the exact opposite of what Browns fans had been through the last thirteen months. Browns Day, with its cordial embrace of these fans without a team, was the perfect way to start a cheerful holiday season. It was set up perfectly: Buffalo's Browns Day, Thanksgiving, and the buildup to Christmas.

Within days of when the merry band of travelers had returned from Orchard Park, a grim reminder of their plight spoiled their holiday cheer. The hulking steel, aluminum, and concrete structure that had hosted the Browns for half a century was being demolished. There was no satisfying detonation of explosives and a quick cleanup. It was a slow, methodical deconstruction. Like a Cleveland winter, it was lifeless, depressing, and dragged on 'til spring.

Cleveland's Osbourn Engineering Company oversaw the project. Sixty-five years earlier, this same company helped build what was then the stadium with the world's largest outdoor seating capacity. On July 3, 1931, in the middle of the Great Depression, German heavyweight boxing world champion Max Schmeling defeated Young Stribling in the huge venue's first event. The Indians debuted a year later, on July 31, 1932.

Two World Series would be played at Cleveland Municipal Stadium—in 1948 and 1954. The Browns won three of their four AAFC Championships here. When the Browns moved to the NFL in 1950, they played five more championship games in these confines. A month before they moved to Los Angeles, the Cleveland Rams won the 1945 NFL Championship here.

The Beatles, the Stones, The Who, Pink Floyd, U2, Bruce Springsteen, and dozens more of the biggest rock bands of all time all played at Cleveland Municipal Stadium. Billy Graham held crusades there. The Roman Catholic Church's Seventh Eucharistic Congress drew 75,000 people to its midnight Mass in 1935.

And who could ever forget 1974's 10-Cent Beer Night? The fans got so rowdy the Indians were forced to forfeit the game. Yes, the old stadium had seen a lot of history.

And now it *was* history. Its ruins were temporarily headed for the scrap heap. Suitable rubble was destined to eventually form several artificial reefs in Lake Erie.

# 80

# RIP ROZELLE

DECEMBER 6, 1996

*Pete Rozelle began his reign as NFL commissioner in 1960, just two* years before Art Modell became owner of the Cleveland Browns. Both in their mid-thirties, these two men took their places at the top of a professional sports league that would supplant every other football league and even displace the once-dominant Major League as America's Game by the time they were finished. In the early days of Rozelle's tenure, teams often played in half-empty stadiums and few teams had TV contracts. Under his stewardship—with influence and guidance from his friend Art Modell—that would soon change.

Modell had a background in advertising and television, and Rozelle was keen to follow the rival AFL in selling his content—NFL games—to television networks. Within a few years, Rozelle had worked out team revenue sharing and had secured contracts for all NFL games to be televised.

By 1966, Rozelle was testifying before Congress to push for a merger of the AFL and NFL—which would soon be agreed to and ultimately take place in 1970. Rozelle was instrumental in establishing the AFL-NFL Championship Game—which immediately became known as the Super Bowl—as soon as the leagues agreed to merge in 1966.

Rozelle sold ABC President Roone Arledge on *Monday Night Football.* The first *Monday Night Football* game featured the New York Jets playing against Modell's Browns at Cleveland Municipal Stadium.

This was another stroke of genius for the young commissioner, as *Monday Night Football* would immediately command massive ratings that would never abate for over fifty years. For Modell, this was the joyous synthesis of his first career in television and his current vocation in football.

"It was a long, enduring friendship," Modell told the Associated Press after Rozelle died of brain cancer on December 6, 1996. "We had great fun together over the years."

After giving that interview by phone from his Baltimore office, Modell became quiet in his grief. A good friend had died. But it was more than that. Rozelle was his contemporary. They had both been young men, shaking up the league back in the 1960s. They had been indomitable.

Now, his friend was dead at just seventy years of age. Pete Rozelle had made his way into the NFL Hall of Fame before he even had retired, in 1989. Pete and his wife Carrie had stayed at Art and Pat's house the weekend Rozelle was inducted, just down the road in Canton. "Art, in a few short years, you'll be joining me in this hallowed hall," Pete had said.

But now, after the move from Cleveland, Art knew he'd never make it. His friend's bust would be forever on display to remind future generations, like a modern-day King Tut preserved for eternity. Art Modell felt his own legacy might as well have been written in the wind-blown desert sand.

His mood wasn't helped by his team's performance on the field, either. The 1996 season was drawing to a close. The Ravens would finish 4-12, last in the division and worse than in any years that Bill Belichick coached for him. Meanwhile, Belichick made it to the Super Bowl less than a year after Modell had fired him. Modell took some solace in the fact that Belichick wasn't the head coach of the Patriots but only the defensive coordinator, paired back up with his former head coach Bill Parcells. When Green Bay beat New England in the big game, it was almost enough to make Modell smile. Almost.

81

# NEWS OF THE WEIRD

## Tuna Helper Edition

*Since the Browns were out of the league . . . and weird stuff still must* happen, it followed Bill Belichick.

Patriots owner Robert Kraft and head coach Bill "Big Tuna" Parcells had been feuding during the 1996 season. Big Tuna wanted out of New England and had found a suitor in the New York Jets. Contractually, Parcells was forbidden from leaving the Patriots to work in a similar capacity until after the 1997 season. If it ended up happening, the team employing him would owe the Patriots draft picks and possibly other compensation.

In early February, the Jets hired Parcells as a "consultant," arguing that they were within their rights and not violating Big Tuna's contract with AFC East rival and reigning AFC Champion New England. Thus, they argued, they could keep their draft picks. The Jets then hired Belichick as head coach to keep the seat warm for a year until Parcells could take the mantle.

Belichick, just a year after being fired following an unimpressive five-year head coaching stint with the Browns, was back in charge as a head coach in the NFL. He had gone from "Tuna helper" in New England to "Tuna sub" in New York. (New York sportswriters got creative with the nicknames.)

Upon notice of Belichick's hiring as the Jets' head coach, the Cleveland media and much of the civilized world saw it like *Plain Dealer* sports columnist Bill Livingston, who wrote, "I don't think Belichick is evil. . . . He just isn't cut out to be a head coach. New York will find that out. It won't take five years and a franchise shift, either."

The Jets didn't find out anything about Belichick's coaching prowess.

NFL Commissioner Paul Tagliabue mediated a resolution to the dispute between the Patriots and the Jets about whether New York could reel in the Big Tuna. Tagliabue awarded the Patriots the Jets' third- and fourth-round choices in the 1997 draft, their second-round choice in 1998, and a first rounder in 1999. Thus, the path was clear for the Jets to drop the charade and for Parcells to step immediately into the head coaching position. Instead of one year, Belichick kept the Jets' head coaching seat warm for Big Tuna for one week. "Tuna sub" was back to being "Tuna helper."

Coach MyWay's tenure as head coach of the New York Jets lasted less than a week. As crazy as this is, it pales in comparison with another soap opera that would occur nearly three years later and would involve all the same characters.

82

# CLEVELAND: INDIANS TOWN

## Indians' Success Makes a Bitter Pill Easier to Swallow

*While the Cleveland Browns National Football League franchise was* officially in hibernation, the Cleveland Indians became the main show in town. They rose to the occasion. The Indians were so good and so much fun that a special marker hangs in the upper deck of right field. There, along with the other nine blue circular markers with red outlines, each containing the white numeral indicating the jersey number of a retired Indians great (and Jackie Robinson's 42, which is retired throughout the Major Leagues) there is the number: 455. Each of the jersey numbers is accompanied by the name of its corresponding player. Accompanying the only three-digit numeral to appear in any Major League park is the word "Fans." The number refers to the length of the then-record consecutive regular season Major League sellout streak.

The sellout streak stretched from before the original Browns started their final season until after the New Browns had concluded their second season. In the seven seasons that the streak was active, the Indians won the American League Central six times and finished second once. They made the playoffs in six of the seven years. In 1995 they made the World Series, after a forty-year playoff drought. Fans generally were giddy, despite the loss to a talented Atlanta team featuring three Hall of Fame pitchers. The Indians couldn't make it past Baltimore in the 1996 American League Division Series (ALDS) despite having amassed the best record in the Majors that year. Then came 1997.

The Tribe's record, 86-75, was hardly superlative but good enough to win the weak American League Central. Fans had immediate hope when the Indians took out the mighty Yankees in the ALDS. The high hopes were accompanied by high expectations. When the Tribe knocked off the American League East–winning Orioles, optimism ran high in Cleveland. True, they'd now be facing the team that had just beaten the Atlanta Braves in the NLCS to reach the World Series, but the Florida Marlins were a five-year-old franchise. The Indians hadn't won a World Series in forty-three years. The Marlins could wait.

**Florida Marlins Season Records (Team founded in 1993)**

| Year | Record | Place in Division |
|---|---|---|
| 1993 | 64-98 | 6th |
| 1994 | 51-64 | 5th (strike shortened) |
| 1995 | 67-76 | 4th (strike delayed) |
| 1996 | 80-82 | 3rd |
| 1997 | 92-70 | 2nd (World Series season versus Indians) |
| 1998 | 54-108 | 5th (last place) |

It was Monday, October 26. The Florida Marlins and Cleveland Indians were in Miami, about to start game 7 of the 1997 World Series. A family of three were crammed by the TV in the living room of their first-floor apartment in a double in Cleveland's Clark-Fulton neighborhood.

"Please God, if there is any justice, let the Indians win the Series!"

Manny had barely gotten the words out when his wife Marta told him Sammy needed to get to bed, then added: "It's a school night!"

"Awww, Mommy, let me stay up, I love the Indians!"

Manny pleaded his daughter's case: "Yeah, honey, I know the Indians were just in the World Series two years ago, but they might not get there again for a long time. It might take forty more years. Sammy could be a gramma by then!"

Sammy laughed out loud, exposing a mouth that seemed to be equal parts baby teeth, adult teeth, and missing teeth.

"She'll be too tired for school tomorrow." Marta said, her resolve weakening.

"I'll help her study for a week if she misses anything," Manny said, looking earnest.

The series had seesawed to this deciding seventh game. The Marlins would go up by a game, and the Indians would even the series. That had happened three times so far. The Indians would have to break the pattern tonight. Allowing the Marlins to go up one game was no longer an option.

Sammy was a daddy's girl and had watched games on TV by Manny's side since she could sit up. What had really cemented her love for the Tribe was going to the game the past Friday night. That was game 5, one that the Indians would lose—although they didn't stick around to see the defeat. In fact, they never were inside Jacobs Field at all.

Manny double-parked the family Caravan on Ontario and sprinted up Eagle Avenue, Sammy clinging to his hand, right up to the left-field gate. Even from her perch atop Manny's shoulders, the view wasn't great. But that didn't matter. She could see the lights, hear the cheers, smell the hot dogs, and feel the electric energy. She was hooked for life.

And that was before Sandy Alomar hit the three-run homer to left field in the third inning, putting the Tribe on top 3-2! (Sammy would call herself "Sammy Alomar" until she was eleven.) They left shortly thereafter, Manny carrying Sammy on his shoulders, hustling back to the car before it got towed!

Manny felt like maybe this was the Indians' year after Tony Fernandez put the Tribe ahead 2-0 in the third inning of this decisive game 7 with a line drive to center field. Fernandez had homered in the ALCS's game 6 against Baltimore to put the Tribe into the World Series. Maybe he'd be the hero again in the World Series. Jaret Wright was pitching well and entered the seventh tossing a shutout. Florida's Bobby Bonilla changed that with a solo shot to right field.

"Ah, Jaret, come on, man!" Manny yelled. "Come on, we need to beat these guys. This is the first year they ever had a winning record! They don't deserve to win a World Series! They've only been a team for five years!" And then he drifted off into his native tongue, a tell that he was getting heated: "Hijo de la—!"

Marta shot him a dirty look before he could finish the phrase.

The Indians were ahead 2-1 entering the ninth inning. "Okay Sammy, this is the last inning. If the Indians are still winning at the end of this inning, they will be the *World Series Champions*!" With the last three words, he raised his hands and his voice. Sammy immediately parroted her father, standing on the couch and jumping off as she yelled "Champions!"

*Hopefully the Indians can score an insurance run or two,* Manny thought to himself.

Matt Williams was up to bat to start the Indians' half of the ninth inning. With three balls and a strike on Williams, announcer Bob Costas *had* to bring it up: "You know, we mentioned the Curse of Rocky Colavito, but even in recent years, in a sense, this has been a star-crossed franchise."

Manny made the sign of the cross as he chided the announcer. "Oh no, Costas, don't bring up the Curse!"

But Costas did it anyway. "In 1993, one of the most tragic events in baseball history occurred to the Cleveland Indians when pitchers Steve Olin and Tim Cruz were killed in a boating accident in Florida during spring training. And another pitcher, Bob Ojeda, was very seriously injured." Ball four to Williams, and he's aboard to start the ninth.

Costas continued: "Keith Olbermann asked Mike Hargrove how often he thinks of Steve Olin and Tim Cruz now, four years later. He says, 'Every day. Not a day goes by.' In 1994 they finally had a contending team, and a strike washed out the season. In '95 they had one of the best single-season teams in recent history. One hundred victories, forty-four losses, lost in six in the World Series. Last year they had the highest victory total in the American League: ninety-nine—"

"Daddy, Sandy Alomar!" Sammy was right; her favorite player was up to bat. He had been the All-Star Game MVP that year (played in Cleveland), why not become a World Series hero right now? "Hit a home run, Sandy!" Sammy yelled at the TV.

Costas announced: "Bouncing ball to short! [Edgar] Renteria charges! Has trouble getting it out of his glove and so they'll get only one as Williams takes care of [Craig] Counsell on the pivot. It could have been a double play."

"Oh, Sandy, Sandy." Manny patted his heart repeatedly.

With one out, Jim Thome ripped a pitch to right field for a single. Alomar sprinted all the way to third.

"Nice job Thome!" Manny said. "Great job, Sandy!"

"Daddy, did Sandy make a home run?"

"No, no . . . he's on third base. But he did a good job. He ran really fast all the way from first base when Thome hit the ball."

"Great job, Sandy!" Sammy repeated her father.

As the Marlins' manager Jim Leyland walked to the mound, fidgeting with his glasses like he always did, giving him the appearance of a nervous librarian, Manny told Sammy, "It's getting late, Sammy Alomar. You need to get to bed soon. You have school in the morning, and your mommy's getting mad at me."

"Can't I stay up to watch the end? I'm not tired!"

"I'll let you stay up until the end of the ninth inning. Hopefully, the Indians will win it by then. But whatever the Indians do here, the Marlins will still get a chance to bat this inning. That's why I hope we can score some more runs right now."

But the Indians didn't. Alomar was thrown out at home on a chopper that shortstop Edgar Renteria charged. Then Brian Giles flew out to Moises Alou in left field. Marlins closer Robb Nen had done his job. Now it was time for the Indians' closer to do his.

"C'mon Jose, we need you now!" Manny said. "Just three outs! Get three outs with no runs!" He was reciting these lines like an incantation. Sammy, watching her father, repeated after him, wide-eyed.

Jose Mesa was sent out to try to earn the save and bring Cleveland its first World Championship since 1948. Two years prior Mesa came in second in Cy Young voting—as a reliever! He had finished the '95 season with forty-six saves, the most in the Majors, and even finished fourth in the American League Most Valuable Player race! In 1997, he was no slouch, but decidedly not the dominant "Señor Smoke" of 1995. He had saved game 6 last night.

He gave up a soft single to the first batter, Moises Alou. Bobby Bonilla, who'd homered in his previous at bat, got behind 0-2, but worked the count full before Señor Smoke finally struck him out.

"Just two more outs, Sammy! If we can just get two more outs, we'll be the World Champions!"

On a 1-2 pitch, catcher Charles Johnson lashed a single to right field. Alou sprinted all the way to third. "Oh no, no!" Manny cupped his head in his hands, his heart beating hard.

Sammy was wide-eyed. "Did we lose, Daddy?"

"No, but it's not looking so good right now."

Craig Counsell came to the plate and smashed a fly ball to near the warning track. Alou tagged and easily scored from third on the fielder's choice.

"*Hijo de la ching—*"

"It's time for Sammy to go to bed," Marta said, giving Manny a dirty look.

"I can't believe that baby face punk just tied the game!" Manny said. "Oh, Sammy, the Indians can't win in nine innings now; you might as well go to bed. If the Indians win, I will wake you up!"

"We'll see about that," Marta said.

Mesa was able to retire Jim Eisenreich to end the inning, but the save had been blown. If the Indians were going to win, they'd have to do it in extra innings.

Omar Vizquel struck out swinging to start the top of the tenth. Tony Fernandez, who would have had the game-winning hit of the 1997 World Series if not for Craig Counsell's ninth-inning sac fly, came up to bat next. Fernandez hit a single between short and third to set the table with "Baby Bull" Manny Ramirez coming to the plate. Manny fouled off the first two pitches and was quickly down 0-2.

"Hit a homer, Manny! Hit one out!"

Instead, Ramirez swung under a high fastball for Cleveland's second out of the tenth. David Justice came up next for the Indians. He had helped defeat the Indians in the 1995 World Series with a home run for Atlanta in that year's decisive game 6. Would divine justice be served here tonight? Would the man who taketh away now giveth Cleveland a long elusive championship?

"C'mon, Justice, get a homer here!" Manny prayed. "Or at least a hit. Keep it going!"

But Justice was swinging and missing at Robb Nen's pitches and became the third strikeout victim of the inning.

"All right, Jose, you got us into this mess, you gotta hold 'em here."

On a 2-2 pitch Devon White smashed a ball right up the middle. It hit Mesa's leg and caromed to shortstop Omar Vizquel, who threw the runner out at first.

"Yes!" Manny yelled. If Sammy had dozed off, she must have been awakened by her father's outburst.

Mesa then gave up a single to Renteria. The winning run was on, with just one out. Gary Sheffield came up. On a 1-1 pitch Mesa threw what would have been a wild pitch if not for an incredible hockey goalie–like save by Sandy Alomar.

"Mesa, what are you doing!?" Manny was sweating now.

On 2-2 Mesa threw another ugly pitch that Alomar had to make a great stop on. Renteria was sent running. Sheffield made contact and dribbled it to Vizquel at short. Had it been hit harder it would have been a tailor-made double play. Instead, Vizquel just ate the ball. One out with runners on first and second. Manny made the sign of the cross, mumbling under his breath. Mesa and the hitter John Cangelosi were locked in battle and the count stood at 3-2. Mesa threw a curve. Cangelosi took it, and started running to first, but the umpire called a strike. Two down.

Tribe manager Mike Hargrove pulled Mesa and put in Charlie Nagy—who'd been passed over in favor of Jaret Wright to start tonight's game—to try to finish off the Marlins with no damage in the tenth. He'd be facing Moises Alou, who started the ninth with a hit and had scored the tying run. Nagy got Alou to pop up to shallow right.

"Phew!" Manny exclaimed.

But Manny Ramirez—a notoriously uneven outfielder—and second baseman Tony Fernandez began converging on the ball.

"Oh no, no!"

It was shaping up awkwardly on the field. But Fernandez pulled away and Ramirez made the catch for the third out. This game would go to at least the eleventh! Manny looked around and noticed Marta had left the room and probably had gone to bed.

Jay Powell relieved Robb Nen to start the eleventh. Matt Williams led off for Cleveland. Powell got behind 0-3 to the power-hitting third baseman, then tightened the count before walking him. Sandy Alomar came up. He laid down a bunt to try to advance Williams into scoring position. But the bunt went straight toward the pitcher who was able to throw Williams out at second. Big Jim Thome came to the plate. The strapping lefty quickly went down 0-2. Thome then hit into an inning-ending double play.

Manny was silent. He had a sinking feeling. It would have to go at least twelve innings now if the Indians were to win. But the Marlins could win it right here.

Nagy quickly got ahead of Bonilla 0-2. But Bonilla drove a grounder up the middle for a leadoff hit on the next pitch. Gregg Zaun missed on two bunt attempts to go down 0-2. He attempted to bunt a third time and elevated it to Nagy, who caught it, hesitated, then threw to first to try to double up Bobby Bonilla. But the runner got back in time. One out in the bottom of the eleventh.

Craig Counsell fell behind Nagy 0-2.

"Come on. Double play! Double play, please . . . please."

After fouling off a couple and taking a ball, Counsell hit a weak grounder to second baseman Tony Fernandez, who was ranging to his right.

Manny stood up, ready to celebrate a double play and the end of the inning.

But Fernandez booted it.

"No!" Manny reflexively jumped, coming down with a BOOM that shook the house.

Bonilla was able to scoot all the way to third. Counsell was safe at first. Still just one out.

Nagy intentionally walked Jim Eisenreich to load the bases and set up a force-out at home. On the first pitch to Devon White, the batter hit it to Fernandez on a hop. Fernandez threw home and got the force-out there. Two down. Men on second and third.

Renteria came up to bat. He took the first pitch for a strike. The next pitch he hit up the middle, toward Nagy, one of the best-fielding pitchers in baseball. Nagy reached straight up and the ball grazed his glove, but kept on going, landing in shallow center field as Craig Counsell sprinted home for the win.

Manny sat in shock. The game was suddenly over. For the Indians, and for their fans, it was sudden death. For the second time in a three-year span, the Indians had lost the World Series. Manny's heart hurt. His head hurt.

The loss to the Braves in 1995 obviously wasn't as good as winning would have been, but somehow it didn't sting like this. Manny felt out of sorts. He had wished he could have provoked Marta's wrath by waking up Sammy, now, just after midnight, to tell her the Indians had won the World Series. He would let her watch the players spray each other with champagne. They would keep a special eye out for Sandy Alomar, her favorite!

But now this magic moment had been stolen away from him. From them. Stolen by a stupid Florida Marlins team that still had founding members on it. Because the franchise was only *five years old!* If the Indians still had founding players playing in this World Series, they'd be about 120 years old!

Manny's confusion gave way to frustration. His face flushed. He paced the family room, catching a glimpse of photos of his sweet Sammy. *This would have been such a good memory for her,* he thought. Finally, he paced out to the front porch and let it out: "*Hijo de la chingada!*"

## 83

# SLEEPING WITH THE FISHES

LAKE ERIE

***In November, as the sting of the World Series loss began to fade, the City*** of Cleveland floated the barges to the appointed areas and sank the concrete rubble, thus creating two artificial reefs, each about a mile offshore. One was just west of the former site of Cleveland Municipal Stadium, the other a few miles east.

The idea was originally hatched by David Taylor, proprietor of Cleveland's Ketchmor Rod and Tackle. Envisioning improved fishing in the waters near his shop, he'd started dreaming of the reefs in 1993, when there was still a possibility the Browns would abandon Cleveland Municipal Stadium for the Gateway district. That never materialized. When Art Modell moved the team in 1995, Taylor was ready to act.

He found an advocate in Cleveland City Councilman Timothy Melena, and together they overcame initial snickers and convinced the city council to secure the necessary permits from the Army Corps of Engineers and to spend the $150,000 for the project.

"Once we put this stuff in the lake, we never have to spend another dime on it," Melena said. "This is the way government ought to spend money—a moderate investment reaping continuous rewards for the community.'"

Studies suggested that the city would recoup its revenues three times over in the first year alone through increased tax revenues connected with fishing, boating, and recreation. And every year after that it was just more gravy for the city.

How ironic: The city was losing money on the massive stadium in 1972 and offloaded it to Art Modell's Stadium Corporation. Modell eventually lost his tenant, the Indians, and had burdened himself with high interest loans trying to rehabilitate the stadium into the early to mid-1990s. Now the city was poised to benefit from a perpetual annuity because the stadium had been dismantled and arranged in piles at the bottom of Lake Erie.

Six months later, D'arcy Egan of the *Plain Dealer* quoted a Mayfield Heights man who took his son fishing in the rubble reef and caught a few two- to three-pound smallmouth bass and a twenty-seven-inch walleye.

"We thought it would take a year, or two, for the new artificial reef to be a good spot for smallmouth bass," said Bill Jevnikar. "It's already happening. Thanks a lot, Art Modell, for leaving town!"

84

# YEARS BETWEEN THE BROWNS

## TRIBE TRIES, COMES UP JUST SHORT

*The Indians again won the American League Central Division in 1998* and returned to the playoffs for the fourth straight year. They were crushed in Jacobs Field in the first game of the ALDS by Boston; 11-3. But the Indians would take the next three games and advance, for the third time in four years, to the American League Championship Series.

Their opponent would be a New York Yankees team that had won more regular season games than any other in the glorious history of baseball's most storied team: 114. After losing game 1, Cleveland would beat the Yankees in twelve innings in game 2. The Tribe would take the series lead, 2-1, after winning game 3. But the Yankees were too much. The Bronx Bombers reeled off three straight wins to vanquish the Indians and advance to the World Series.

The National League's San Diego Padres were swept by the steamrolling New Yorkers, just as the Texas Rangers had been during the Yankee's ALDS matchup.

There are no consolation awards for being the only team to win any postseason games against one of history's greatest teams. It was the Yankee's twenty-fourth World Championship. They'd win their twenty-fifth the next season and ring in the new millennium with their twenty-sixth the year after that. What could have been a World Series–winning Cleveland team was a victim of historically bad timing.

As for the Cavaliers during the three Browns-less years in the Cleveland sports-scape, they were decent, posting winning records in

1995-96, 1996-97, 1997-98 and reaching the playoffs twice. They lost in the first round both times, winning a grand total of one playoff game over that stretch.

Cleveland, like every NBA city, was without professional basketball for much of the 1998-99 season, as owners locked out the players due to labor strife. It was just as well, as the Cavs were embarking on a prolonged stretch of ineptitude that wouldn't be cured until the second year of The King's (LeBron James) reign in 2004.

As for the team formerly known as the Browns and that formerly played in Cleveland: Fortunately for the people of Northeast Ohio, Art Modell's team didn't rocket straight to the Super Bowl. While Cleveland waited for its new team, the Ravens posted the following records:

| Season | Wins | Losses | Ties | Divisional Standing |
|---|---|---|---|---|
| 1996 | 4 | 12 | | 5th of 5 |
| 1997 | 6 | 9 | 1 | 5th of 5 |
| 1998 | 6 | 10 | | 4th of 5 |

Surely the fans in Maryland had expected more. Maybe crime didn't pay, after all. The people of Cleveland were not about to give a refund to their friends in Charm City. Baltimore had stolen them, and they were stuck with them. (But, in just two years, they'd be glad they were.)

# THE REAL AMERICA'S TEAM

## Reflecting National Trial and Triumph

***The Cleveland Browns were the original baby boomers. Born when the*** GIs came home triumphant from World War II and America was the toast of the world, the Browns, ever victorious, became the toast of the All-America Football Conference. To the exclusion of every country on Earth, America stood alone on a pedestal throughout the second half of the 1940s. And the Cleveland Browns mirrored that stature.

**All-America Football Conference Franchise List and results**

| Franchise | Years Active | League Championships |
|---|---|---|
| Baltimore Colts | 1947-1949 | None |
| Brooklyn Dodgers | 1946-1948 | None |
| Brooklyn-New York Yankees | 1949 | None |
| Buffalo Bills | 1947-1949 | None |
| Buffalo Bisons | 1946 | None |
| Chicago Hornets | 1949 | None |
| Chicago Rockets | 1946-1948 | None |
| **Cleveland Browns** | **1946-1949** | **1946, 1947, 1948, 1949** |
| Los Angeles Dons | 1946-1949 | None |
| Miami Seahawks | 1946 | None |
| New York Yankees | 1946-1948 | None |
| San Francisco 49ers | 1946-1949 | None |

As America entered the 1950s and enjoyed unprecedented prosperity, the Browns entered the NFL and prospered right from the start. America emerged as the strongest nation in the world, maybe the strongest nation the world had ever known. The Browns dominated the decade in much the same way.

The fifties ushered in the dawning of rock 'n' roll. The biggest star in the new pop-culture world was Elvis Presley, whose favorite team was the Cleveland Browns. The U.S. economy soared. Cities expanded, suburbs and highways were built. Cars sprouted fins, and big cars grew into land yachts. Prosperity flourished like never before. And the Browns won. And won. And won some more. They reached the NFL Championship Game seven times in the decade, winning it thrice.

In the great tumult of the 1960s, the Browns' founding coach and namesake was overthrown as brash young owner Arthur Modell upended the establishment. Only one championship was gained, and the best player in the history of the team (Jim Brown, of course) was lost to early retirement in a dispute with the owner.

Likewise, the USA lost star leaders far too early. First taken, in 1963, was President John F. Kennedy. His brother, Senator Robert F. Kennedy, lamented the April 4, 1968, assassination of Martin Luther King Jr., the day after King was slain in a speech given to the Cleveland City Club and broadcast to the world. Just two months later, Robert F. Kennedy would be assassinated too. Malcolm X had been killed in 1965.

Jim Brown's foray into civil rights was a reaction to and a propellant for American society's nascent reckoning with its history. Jim Brown was a proud, multifaceted Black man who would not be defined by others' expectations. His convictions led him to quit football while still in his prime.

In June 1967 he convened "The Cleveland Summit," bringing a who's who of eminent Black athletes together in a workaday Cleveland office building to tackle racial and other issues. Besides Jim Brown and Muhamed Ali, the group included Bill Russell, Lew Alcindor (Kareem Abdul-Jabbar), and other prominent athletes, as well as Carl Stokes, one of the first Black mayors of a major American city. The most pressing issue at the time was supporting Muhammed Ali in his conscientious objection to being drafted and serving in the Vietnam war.

Long-suppressed fissures were rupturing. A counterculture developed to challenge the norms that had been established and followed a generation earlier. The team and the country would finish out the decade on uncertain footing.

In the 1970s, the Vietnam war dragged on and Nixon resigned, disgraced in the Watergate debacle. Likewise, the Browns seemed rudderless. Cleveland was better known for bombings and bankruptcy than for its NFL team. The Browns were barely .500 for the decade and lost the only two playoff games they saw. The most famous Browns fan, Elvis, died, his life and career having become a vague, bloated shadow of what they had been.

The jubilation of the late 1940s, the prosperity of the fifties, and the idealism of the sixties, all gave way to a malaise. The traditionally dominant Browns saw division rival Pittsburgh wrest control of the AFC Central and win four Super Bowls. Similarly, Hondas, Datsuns, and Toyotas began to crowd Fords, Chevies, and Plymouths off the roads. The "unassailable" U.S. auto industry faltered as rival Japan's auto industry and economy soared. The United States, it seemed, could not keep up. So it was for the Browns.

In the 1980s, America's economy saw a resurgence, its global prestige partially restored to its former glory. And so, again, it was with the Browns. Starting off with the Kardiac Kids, and getting another boost from Bernie Kosar, the Browns were perennial contenders (if also perennial bridesmaids) for most of the eighties. The magnetic, affable Ronald Reagan led the country and was relieved by no-nonsense George H.W. Bush. Likewise, the Browns were led by the quotable, colorful Sam Rutigliano followed by the dependable but boring Marty Schottenheimer.

Let's all be glad that the parallels between the Cleveland Browns and the United States of America petered out by the 1990s. Had that not been the case, America would have lost to Saddam Hussein in the Gulf War. Uncle Sam would have gone into hiding for three years, then reemerged to find itself one of the weakest countries on Earth for the next two decades.

Maybe the Browns hadn't trademarked the term "America's Team." But with fifty-three years of near-sellout attendance at home games, top local TV ratings among NFL franchises, the Browns Backers fan club with a chapter in every major city in the United States, and a membership of over 300,000 spanning the globe, they had earned that distinction.

It was truly uncanny the way the Cleveland Browns had cleaved so closely to the tenor of the times in America. The Cleveland Browns truly had been America's Team. And now they were no more.

86

# UNFINISHED BUSINESS

## No Rest for the Wicked

*A black luxury sedan was idling in the parking lot of the Great Lakes* Science Center. A man in an immaculately tailored cashmere coat sat in the passenger seat. He no longer worked alone. He was accompanied by three underlings. Instead of the classical music he favored, they listened to a rock station. The Stones' "Sympathy for the Devil" faded, and Don McLean's famous song came on.

Having watched construction crews work on the new Cleveland Browns Stadium for the past half hour, the acolytes congratulated their boss on all that had transpired on this site over the last three decades.

The boss sat silently, looking preoccupied. The music softly played . . .

*The players tried for a forward pass*
*With the jester on the sidelines in a cast*

A lackey in the back seat, who was up from New Orleans and went by Absinthe, inquired: "So the stadium that used to be here is in the lake now?"

The man in cashmere just stared at the construction site.

"That's how effective the boss was," another lackey responded. "The old stadium was like a temple to these people. And now it's keeping company with bottom-feeders. Classic!"

Absinthe chuckled.

The man in the cashmere coat chided them, "Can you not see they've rebuilt the 'temple'?" He made air quotes as he said this. "We'll have our work cut out here again, soon enough."

There was silence in the car save for the music softly playing on the radio.

*Jack Flash sat on a candlestick*
*'Cause fire is the Devil's only friend*

From the passenger seat, the boss told the driver, "Let's roll." He allowed himself a moment's reflection and a rare smile to crack his face. He cranked up the volume.

*No angel born in Hell*
*Could break that Satan spell*
*And as the flames climbed high into the night*
*To light the sacrificial rite*
*I saw Satan laughing with delight*
*The day the music died*

# SOURCES

**Books**

Coughlan, Dan. *Crazy with the Papers to Prove It: Stories About the Most Unusual, Eccentric & Outlandish People I've Known in 45 Years as a Sports Journalist*. Gray & Company, 2010.

Holli, Melvin G. *The American Mayor: The Best & The Worst Big-City Leaders*. Penn State University Press, 1999.

Knight, Jonathan. *Opening Day: Cleveland, the Indians, and a New Beginning*. Kent State University Press, 2004.

Morgan, Jon. *Glory for Sale: Fans, Dollars, and the New NFL*. Bancroft Press, 1997

Pluto, Terry. *Browns Town 1964 – The Cleveland Browns and the 1964 Championship*. Gray & Company, 1997

Rose, William Ganson. *Cleveland: Making of a City*. Kent State University Press, 1990.

**Articles**

Associated Press. "Basketball star Bias, 22, is dead." June 19, 1986.

Associated Press. "Rozelle hailed as a visionary." *Plain Dealer*, December 8, 1996, 12C.

Grossi, Tony. "51-0! Carson's debut a smashing success." *Plain Dealer*, September 11, 1989.

Bembry, Jerry. "A Life Too Short." *Andscape*, June 27, 2016.

Cabot, Mary Kay. "Modell Interviews Belichick." *Plain Dealer*, February 1, 1991.

Cabot, Mary Kay. "Who's who in Browns' search for next coach." *Plain Dealer*, January 6, 1991.

Cabot, Mary Kay. "Modell sees 'great coach' in making." *Plain Dealer*, November 19, 1991.

Cabot, Mary Kay. "Man for all reasons Belichick stamping Browns in his own image." *Plain Dealer*, September 4, 1992.

Cabot, Mary Kay. ".Sacked Browns bounce Bernie. He's lost it." *Plain Dealer*, November 9, 1993.

Cabot, Mary Kay. "Modell unworried about Tribe run." *Plain Dealer*, July 17, 1994, 9D.

Cabot, Mary Kay. "New season, new talent, old goals: Belichick starts fourth season full of confidence," *Plain Dealer*, July 17, 1994, 1D.
Cabot, Mary Kay and Amy Rosewater. "Fans win a game ball from coach." *Plain Dealer*, January 2, 1995.
Cabot, Mary Kay and Amy Rosewater. "Modell says Super Bowl was obsession in the '80s." *Plain Dealer*, January 7, 1995.
Cabot, Mary Kay. "Metcalf traded to Atlanta." *Plain Dealer*, March 26, 1995.
Cabot, Mary Kay. "Browns hope draft pick rates a 10." *Plain Dealer*, April 16, 1995.
Cabot, Mary Kay. "Browns toast Tribe pennant," *Plain Dealer*, October 19, 1995.
Cabot, Mary Kay. "No vote of confidence for Belichick." *Plain Dealer*, October 24, 1995, 10D.
Cabot, Mary Kay. "Testaverde says benching stinks QB says he is in." *Plain Dealer*, October 26, 1995, 1D.
Cabot, Mary Kay. ".Browns win long, wild one Zeier leads team past Bengals" *Plain Dealer*, October 30, 1995, 1C.
Cabot, Mary Kay. "Kosar would like to bring a team here" *Plain Dealer*, November 6, 1995, 13C
Cabot, Mary Kay. "Modell: Belichick next year's coach" *Plain Dealer*, November 8, 1995, 8D
Egan, D'arcy. ".New reefs already luring bass, walleye." *Plain Dealer*, May 29, 1998, 11D.
Graeff, Burt. "Steelers dominate Browns' defense." *Plain Dealer*, January 8, 1995, 13D.
Grossi, Tony and Cabot, Mary Kay. "Report: Jackson criticizes Belichick." *Plain Dealer*, October 15, 1993, page 1D.
Grossi, Tony. "Parcells says Belichick ready." *Plain Dealer*, January 24, 1991.
Grossi, Tony. "Langhorne: 'Worst year of my life.'" *Plain Dealer*, March 31, 1992.
Grossi, Tony. "Kosar has nowhere to run or hide." *Plain Dealer*, May 1, 1992, page 2E.
Grossi, Tony. "Modell's jokes fail to hide sadness as chances slip away." *Plain Dealer*, December 31, 1992, page IC.
Grossi, Tony. "Belichick, Kosar aren't in sync." *Plain Dealer*, October 11, 1993, 10D.

Grossi, Tony. "Modell dismisses permanent seat licenses." *Plain Dealer*, July 23, 1995, 13D.

Grossi, Tony. "Modell takes off as Tribe heats up." *Plain Dealer*, October 16, 1995, *1C*.

Grossi, Tony. "Modell to blast Cleveland on TV." *Plain Dealer*, August 9, 1996, 1D.

Grossi, Tony. "The dawgs get a chance to go outside and bark." *Plain Dealer*, November 18, 1996, 1C.

Heaton, Chuck. "Browns' title bid ends 34-0." *Plain Dealer*, December 28, 1964.

Heaton, Chuck. "Modell says he's proud of job done by Carson." *Plain Dealer*, January 15, 1990, page 3D.

Heaton, Chuck. "Modell to 'reflect' on Carson's status" *Plain Dealer*, November 5, 1990, page 6E.

Heaton, Chuck. "Modell says offense is off-season priority." *Plain Dealer*, December 28, 1992, page 7D.

Koff, Stephen, Timothy Heider and Tony Grossi. "Cleveland, NFL strike deal to bring new team here." *Plain Dealer*, February 9, 1996, IA.

Livingston, Bill. "Belichick benches the media." *Plain Dealer*, September 4, 1991, IE.

Livingston, Bill. "Nothing personal: Just risky business." *Plain Dealer*, November 10, 1993, 1E.

Livingston, Bill. "Belichick's hiring an interim sham." *Plain Dealer*, February 5, 1997, 1D.

Maxse, Joe. ".Stray dawgs about 2,000 barking Browns fans find a temporary 'pound' in Buffalo" *Plain Dealer*, November 18, 1996, 1A.

"Sizzling Browns fans scorch phone lines." *Plain Dealer*, January 27, 1970.

Schneider, Russell. "Comeback by Browns ends Steelers' spell." *Plain Dealer*, October 27, 1980, front page.

Vickers, Robert J. ".Old stadium parts set to go underwater" *Plain Dealer*, October 16, 1997, 1B.

"What others had to say." *Plain Dealer*, April 5, 1994, 10D.

Heiss, Timothy, Diemer, Tom, Theiss, Evelyn. "Browns bolt: Modell warned mayor, governor for month." *Plain Dealer*, November 7, 1995, front page.

**Websites:**
Pro-football-reference.com
Funwhileitlasted.net
Footballdb.com
Wikipedia
YouTube - @comradedobler3407
NFL.com
Cleveland.com

# ABOUT THE AUTHOR

I was one of the weird ones at engineering school who got a lot out of the lone pair of required liberal arts classes: Great Ideas in Western Culture I & II (GFI, for short). One professor, Lewis P. Hinchman, even nominated me to study at a summer writing program where tuition would be covered, and I'd receive a stipend for expenses. Foolishly, I turned down this chance of a lifetime down.

Decades later, I couldn't stand the futility of the Browns of the mid-2010s. This restlessness compelled me to start writing this, my debut book. Had I known it would take nine years, I may not have set figurative pen to paper. But, once I did, I had a way to channel this overwhelming frustration—and let people know of this curse so that it might finally be broken.

I grew up in Upstate New York, where my dad and I were the only Browns fans for hundreds of miles. In 1993, I moved to Cleveland for a technical sales job and to be closer to my fiancé, whom I'd met in enemy territory in Pittsburgh. The Browns moved to Baltimore two years later, and Dad's affiliation switched to the Ravens. Dad has cheered on a consistently good team that has won two Super Bowls, while I've been stuck with an undying passion—that he instilled in me—for the Cleveland Browns. At least writing is cheaper than therapy.

www.ingramcontent.com/pod-product-compliance
Lightning Source LLC
Chambersburg PA
CBHW030351310726
48979CB00001B/259

* 9 7 8 1 9 6 6 9 8 1 0 7 7 *